The
Sea Gate

JANE JOHNSON is a British novelist
and publisher. She is the UK editor for
George R.R. Martin, Robin Hobb and Dean
Koontz and was for many years publisher
of the works of J.R.R. Tolkien. Married to
a Berber chef she met while researching
The Tenth Gift, she lives in Cornwall
and Morocco.

ALSO BY JANE JOHNSON

The Tenth Gift
The Salt Road
The Sultan's Wife
Pillars of Light
Court of Lions

Jane Johnson

The
Sea Gate

HEAD
ZEUS

First published in the UK in 2020 by Head of Zeus Ltd

9 7 5 3 1 2 4 6 8

A catalogue record for this book is available from
the British Library.

ISBN (HB): 9781789545166
ISBN (XTPB): 9781789545173
ISBN (E): 9781789545142

Typeset by Silicon Chips

MIX
Paper from
responsible sources
FSC
www.fsc.org
FSC® C020471

Printed and bound in Great Britain by
CPI Group (UK) Ltd, Croydon CR0 4YY

Head of Zeus Ltd
5–8 Hardwick Street
London EC1R 4RG

WWW.HEADOFZEUS.COM

Love deep as the sea as a rose must wither,
As the rose-red seaweed that mocks the rose.
Shall the dead take thought for the dead to love them?
What love was ever as deep as a grave?
They are loveless now as the grass above them
Or the wave.

All are at one now, roses and lovers,
Not known of the cliffs and the fields and the sea.
Not a breath of the time that has been hovers
In the air now soft with a summer to be.

From 'A Forsaken Garden'
by Algernon Charles Swinburne

1

Becky

I TAKE THE PHONE AWAY FROM MY EAR, END THE CALL and stand looking at the impression of oil and powder left on its blank screen, traces of make-up I so rarely wear. I wipe the mark away with my thumb and transfer the phone to my jacket pocket. It is hard to take in the words that have just oozed into my ear.

There was something on the scan...

Across the street two women are still engaged in the noisy altercation that started just as my phone rang. The woman in the red car drove into a parking space that the woman in the muddy SUV was preparing to reverse into. The traffic is halted on either side of them: people have stopped on the pavement to watch the argument. Some are taking sides. Heated words are exchanged, photos taken. A moment ago I had been diverted by this intense little drama; now, it seems absurd and I experience the urge to run across the road and tell them that life is too short to get angry over something so trivial. But I don't. I am feeling dislocated from the world. Words from the phone call buzz in my brain like angry bees, then spiral away again, trailing bitterness and regret, tinged with fear.

It may not be anything, but we should scan you again, just to be sure.

I find myself thinking, 'I must tell Mum,' and then remember why I am here. I cannot tell Mum anything ever again, not in this life.

A commuter sounds two angry blasts of their horn, summoning me back, and I watch the muddy-SUV woman concede defeat and drive off with a screech of tyres. The tide of humanity resumes, flowing around me as I stand on the corner, a still point, a pebble in a stream. Then the horn sounds again and someone calls my name.

'Becky? Come on, we're going to be late. Honestly, women drivers, shouldn't be on the road. I've been sitting in this sodding traffic for ten minutes!'

It is my brother, James, in his shiny Lexus, and beside him in the passenger seat his wife, Evie. My heart sinks. At the best of times Evie makes me feel like a bag lady, with her exquisitely put-together look and superior manner. Feeling self-conscious in my ill-fitting black skirt, which I have not worn in years, I scramble into the back seat and give them a tight smile, keeping my terrors behind my teeth. My brother and his wife feel like members of a different species to me.

Funerals are uncomfortable occasions, no matter what your connection to the deceased. In unfamiliar surroundings, in unfamiliar clothes, you bid farewell to someone who can no longer see or hear you, and are not sure whether to sit or stand, almost more stressed by the rituals than by the loss itself. There is always something to knock you out of the moment, something out of place: the brisk compassion of a celebrant who never even met your loved one; a child's cry erupting suddenly into silent contemplation; a bum note sung during the parting hymn. And when this happens you stand alone in your own head, your connection to the departed suddenly stretched so thin it is like a span of spider silk trembling in the air, and you don't know who you are. And then, just as abruptly, grief at the transience of life almost bowls you over and you find your hands are trembling so much that the words on the hymn sheet have become unreadable. And then you catch yourself wondering if you are honestly grieving for your mother, or whether a selfish grain or two of self-pity may not have crept in and salted the occasion with terror about your own mortality.

At the end of the service I look around. Apart from James and Evie, I recognize only a couple of Mum's friends from the Ramblers' Association – one chap accompanied by a grey-haired woman in a dark red hat with a net veil that has probably not been out of its box since a wedding decades ago – and a family of four: Rosa, a blonde Lithuanian woman who used to come in to help Mum with the housework, her husband and their two children. Rosa and I hug briefly afterwards outside the crematorium in the bright daylight.

'I'm so sorry about your mother. The news came as a terrible surprise.' She considers me. 'You look so pale! How are you, Becky?' she asks, and I give the usual reply. She peers over my shoulder. 'And where's your handsome man?'

That's a good question. I experience a physical yearning

for Eddie that rushes through me like fire. I mumble something about unfortunate timing and quickly change the subject, brightening my tone. 'How about you and Lukas, are you well? You look well! And your girls have grown so much!'

'Anna is just finishing Key Stage 2. It's a good time for us to move.'

'You're moving? Where are you going?'

She looks surprised, as if the answer is obvious. 'Back to Lithuania. To be honest, we don't really feel welcome here any more. Besides, Lukas says there are good jobs to be had with the energy company, so it makes sense for us to go.' She puts her hand on my arm. 'You know, I would have come in and helped Jenny more if I'd known she was ill. Not for money, you understand,' she adds quickly. 'But she didn't tell me she was sick.'

'She didn't tell any of us,' I say. Her death feels unreal. Why hadn't I paid more attention during our twice-weekly calls? I must have missed so many little clues. Had there been some small hesitation when I asked how she was? The answer was always, 'Fine, dear. But more importantly, how are you?' and I hadn't recognized this as deflection. Mum had been putting others before herself all her life. I didn't even know she was in hospital when we last spoke: my mother used the same mobile phone no matter where she was.

'Why didn't she tell us she was so ill?' I had asked my brother when he called to break the terrible news.

An uncomfortable pause. 'She told me,' he said. 'But only recently. She said there was nothing that could be done, and you already had enough on your plate. She knew I wouldn't fuss and would just get on with doing what she wanted.'

The word 'fuss' cut deep. I had always unloaded my problems on Mum, because if you can't tell your mother your deepest fears and your daily disasters, then who can you tell? Every time something awful happened I would think, *Well, at least it'll give me something to talk about with Mum*, and would gather amusing or gruesome details with which to embroider the telling.

The realization was a sort of second bereavement, a mourning for the relationship we shared, as well as for the mother I lost. It is confirmation of how weak Mum must have thought me, and now I will never have the opportunity to change her perception.

The next day James, Evie and I make our way to Mum's flat, which lies at the top of an unprepossessing building on the edge of Warwick. James turns the spare key in the lock and pushes the door, but it won't budge more than a few inches. I drop to my knees on the dusty doorstep and reach around the frame to find that the obstruction is a pile of unopened post. I claw it away till the door opens a bit wider and James steps inside. I am about to get up to follow him, but Evie presses a hand down on my shoulder and steps over me, placing the spiked heels of her crocodile-skin boots carefully into the islands of floorboard revealed between the ocean of envelopes and flyers. 'Good grief,' she says as she passes. 'Anyone would think she'd been dead for years.'

I stare at her retreating back in disbelief.

She stalks down the hallway and stares in passing at the

framed pictures on the wall, dismissing them as worthless. Yes, Evie, they're barely worth the cost of the canvas they're daubed on: I painted them.

I gather the post into a pile, imagining Mum lying in her hospital bed with the stupid, oppressive reminders of ordinary life spilling through the letter box day after day. Sixty-four years old, gone without warning; of course the bills and letters and junk mail have kept on coming – no one expected this sudden departure. Again, the enormity of her passing hits me. I will never be able to call her on a whim, to ask if she's seen the size of the moon tonight, or to check on her recipe for scones; never share another Christmas lunch with her, never have to sneakily return ill-fitting birthday presents to Marks & Spencer. Never be able to hear her say, *Don't worry, darling, I'm sure it's nothing.* I sniff back tears.

James reappears with a roll of black bin bags, a long length of which he tears off and passes to me. 'Here you go. Evie, bless her, is going through Mum's clothes.'

I feel suddenly hot with outrage. 'Don't you think you should have asked me to do that?'

'Calm down! We thought it'd be too much for you, so Evie volunteered. You should be grateful: you know what a good eye she has. She'll be able to tell at a glance if there's anything worth selling on, though she said right away she thinks most of it will have to go into recycling or to charity shops—'

'It's not Mum's fault she didn't dress the way Evie thinks she should. Dad left with all the money and then fucked off and died after spending the lot on his mistress!'

James shuffles his feet. 'No need to swear, not very ladylike.'

Not very ladylike, I mouth at his back. When did my brother become such a prig? Probably ever since Evie started campaigning.

Gathering the post into my arms, I take it into the lounge and dump it on the coffee table, knocking a framed photograph to the floor in the process. James picks it up and stares at it, hands it to me. The photo is faded into the ochre and pale blue of old Kodak stock. It shows the four of us, Mum and Dad with James and me, standing in front of a hedge and old gate, and beyond us a shining expanse of sea stretching into flared-out infinity. James and I look about eight or so. You'd never know we were twins. We don't look alike, have never even had much in common. As soon as we'd developed our own little personalities the family had fractured along gender lines: me and Mum, with our fine, fair hair and introversion, our love of books and plants; James and Dad, dark and confident and loud, disappearing to take part in manly pursuits. It's a window into a lost age.

'I wonder who took it?' I muse. 'It obviously meant a lot to her but I can't remember where or when it was taken.'

James shrugs, uninterested. 'May as well chuck it. The frame's just plastic.'

'I'm going to keep it.' I pick at the black metal clips on the back so that I can remove the precious print, but James has already moved on and is opening cupboards and exclaiming at the crammed contents.

Mum moved into this flat when she and Dad divorced, declaring that she loved that it was bijou – like a jewel – and so

7

much easier to look after than their big old four-bedroomed house. Which I took at face value, never looking past the fresh paint, the bright curtains and rugs, to see that the underlying carpets were worn, that mould was encroaching in the bathroom and beneath the bedroom window, that its peeling, unloved state mirrored her own. Looking past James, I see damp has brought down a sizable chunk of cornicing. It must have fallen recently, since it has not been cleared away, as if it was holding on all this time and as soon as Mum was gone, simply let go.

'If you go through the post I'll check her bureau for the documents we need for probate. Just chuck all the crap and keep the official stuff and bills.' And off he goes to the spare room. Beyond, I can hear the clack of clothes hangers and the efficient rustle of discarded garments being thrust into bin bags.

Boy jobs and girl jobs.

I turn my attention to the pile of post. Bills. Bank statements. Credit card demands. More bills. Catalogues, flyers for local reading groups, adverts for mobility scooters, circulation improvers, novelty garden ornaments, solar panels. I sigh. It's tragic how little a life can be reduced to, how much of it is transient and disposable.

Evie appears carrying a bulging bin bag in each rubber-gloved hand. Did she bring the Marigolds with her? I wonder. Does she have a full hazmat suit tucked away in her Prada handbag? 'Sooo much to go through!' she trills. 'It's like the aftermath of a jumble sale in there.' She manoeuvres the stuffed bags through the doorway and out into the hall, reappears empty-handed. 'We should have hired a skip!'

My throat feels hard and swollen, as if bulky words are trying to choke me. I watch her peel off the gloves finger by finger, snapping them back into shape with brisk efficiency as if performing a medical procedure. Her nail varnish is a shade of dark plum, like old blood.

'Poor Becky.' She knows I don't like her calling me that: it's too intimate. 'It's so awful to lose your mother after all you've been through.' She pauses. 'Such a shame Eddie couldn't be here to support you.'

Is there any real concern here, or is she just point-scoring?

'I mean, it's a bit much, not coming to your mother's funeral. And with you so fragile.'

I hate that she knows so much about the sinkholes in my life. But the worst part is she's completely right. Tears sting the back of my eyes, but I cannot cry in front of Evie. I thrust myself to my feet. 'Need a cigarette,' I mutter, and flee.

I don't smoke, actually – never have. Out on the concrete steps I sit and fiddle with my phone, selecting my home number with trembling fingers. I need to hear Eddie's voice: it will calm me down.

When I told him tearfully about the awful readings James had chosen, and the soulless venue for the funeral, he had held me close and let me weep into his chest. But as soon as I mentioned getting his suit dry-cleaned, he'd gazed at me as if I'd mortally wounded him.

'Becks, you *know* I don't do suits and funerals – I'm an *artist*.' He ran a hand through his wild, dark hair, exasperated by my failure to understand something so fundamental to his being. 'Look, you know how fond I was of your mum. I'd love to help you give her a proper send-off. But I just can't afford to lose the time, not now, for God's sake, Rebecca, my *exhibition*! I can't lose an hour, let alone days! Besides, what does it matter? Jenny's gone, and anyway she'd hate all the ritual and empty show. She'd say, "Eddie, for goodness' sake, you've got to make your exhibition a success. It's so important."'

My mother would have said exactly this. At once I had felt mean and unworthy. But that was before yesterday's world-altering phone call, which has ricocheted around my skull all through the night, nicking little edges of sentient matter here and there, leaving me thick and dull after barely two hours of sleep. I want to share the content of that call with Eddie. But I can't: that really would be selfish. He's already been through so much with me. I'll tell him after the exhibition, but for now all I want is to hear his voice, to receive a virtual hug from the man I've lived with for ten years.

We never actually got married, because Eddie said marriage was a bourgeois social construct designed to control people's individuality. 'All that parading around in fancy clothes, while a load of people you don't really like, who've bought you gifts you don't really want, stuff their faces with food and booze you've paid for with money you don't have!' I had sort of agreed with him: we didn't need a piece of paper to prove how much we loved one another, and neither of us was religious. Besides, we were broke.

But if we had been married and if he had come with me to Mum's funeral, I would have felt more armoured against the world, including Evie's sniping, which in the bigger picture is such a small thing.

The bigger picture looms at me again, and I push it to the back of my mind, and tap our home number in the Contacts list. The ringback tone goes on and on. I can imagine the phone sounding out in the lounge of our London maisonette, echoing off the walls, the mismatched furniture, the blank TV screen, the half-drawn curtains. I let it ring on in case Eddie's in another room, but I know he's not there. I cut the call and try his mobile and for a moment my heart rises as I hear his hello, then falls as I realize it's just his voicemail message. He must be in the studio, cracking on with the last pieces for the exhibition. It's an exciting opportunity for him, and he really deserves a break, that crucial bit of luck all artists need.

When I go back in I am relieved to find no one in the lounge, though the furniture appears to have acquired coloured stickers: white ones on the sofa, the armchair, the coffee table, the bookcase; a red one on the television and the Georgian mirror that was Granny Jo's. I frown. Somewhere overhead the joists creak: James up in the attic, rummaging for anything saleable amongst the detritus of our mother's stored hopes and faded dreams.

Forcing myself to my task, I discard the catalogues and junk mail into a bin bag and stack up the official-looking letters. I have got through over half of the pile before I come upon a pale blue envelope addressed in an emphatic hand to *Mrs Geneviève Young*.

I slit it open. Inside are two folded sheets of Basildon Bond, covered in erratic handwriting.

Dearest Jenny

Someone who knows Mum well, then, to use that rare, affectionate shortening.

I must ask you to come down RIGHT AWAY.

This is so savagely underlined that the pen's nib has gone right through the paper.

They are talking about putting me away, the devils, in one of those establishments so erroneously referred to as 'care homes'. But I DO NOT want to go. I may be ninety-odd, and I dare say there are some who would place the emphasis on 'odd', but I am not losing my marbles! Chynalls is my home. My BELOVED home. I was born in this house and I am determined to die in it! THEY WILL HAVE TO CARRY ME OUT OF HERE FEET FIRST!

It is a frightful nuisance not to be able to get up the stairs. The deterioration of the flesh is a grim business. Trips to the privy are getting to be as bad as Polar treks. I always hated the cold. Hot countries hold far greater appeal. I walked in the Sahara Desert once...

Who is this person? I turn to the last page to find a florid signature beneath the words *Your cousin, Olivia Kitto*, the K looping as madly as an inky Elizabethan capital. The name jolts a distant memory – a long-ago family holiday redolent of seaweed and saltwater. Rock pools and shrimping nets, the rub of a sandy towel on my thighs. The letterhead reads: Chynalls, Porth Enys,

Cornwall. No postcode, as if the house is in Narnia, not part of the modern world at all.

Batty old biddy. I can hear Dad's voice. *Queer old bird.*

Did we visit her? Yes, I remember it now, that long-ago Cornish visit. A hazy image of an enormous house, a smell that stings the nose, a strange sense of apprehension...

I need your help in getting Chynalls in order so that I can stay in my own house. Social Services say I must have a proper bathroom. Proper bathroom!! Who are they to determine what is proper and what is not? Ridiculous RED TAPE! I'm perfectly fine with a lick and a spit. I lived through a war, I told them. We didn't have hot baths and power showers then. A fig for all their HEALTH & SAFETY! And they had the gall to complain about Gabriel, too! My only companion for all these years! Dirty and unhygienic, they called him.

Chynalls was beautiful once, and I suppose I was too. Both of us are rather decrepit now. There's not much you can do to get me lickity spit but, Jenny dear, I need your help to get the house shipshape. Humilitas occidit superbiam and all that, but I am forced to throw myself on your mercy, since you are my only living relatives, you and your little girl, charming manners, name escapes me. I CAN TRUST NO ONE ELSE! They circle like vultures. If you come down we shall see them off! We must keep them AT BAY. When you arrive I will tell you all. You can stay in the upstairs rooms: they are COMPLETELY PRISTINE!

The capital letters, underlinings and incomprehensible Latin are alarming, but I begin to feel sorry for her: an elderly woman, beset by illness and infirmity and the complex manoeuvrings of social services. It must have been hard for her to overcome her pride enough to cry out for help.

'What's that?'

James appears, burdened by a large cardboard box. I fold the letter away. 'Oh, nothing, a note from some old biddy.' Daddy's word.

I watch him put the box down and his shirt rides up out of his trousers. Red chinos: who wears red canvas trousers in their thirties? Husbands of Tory councillors, I suppose.

'What have you found?' I ask.

'Usual rubbish. Did you know she even kept those hideous old dining room curtains from the old house, the ones with the giant poppies on them?'

I do know. Mum was constantly promising them to me, *when you and Eddie buy a place of your own.* Another lump forms in my throat. 'Nothing else?'

'Some personal papers. I suppose we ought to go through them to make sure there's nothing important before the house clearance people come in.'

'House clearance? But we haven't even discussed...'

My brother shrugs. 'It's the only practical solution, Becks. I mean, we have our lives elsewhere: us down in Surrey and you in London. We can't keep running up and down to Warwick, and life moves on, you know. There will be a ton of admin to do, and you know that's not your forte... That's exactly why Mum asked me and Evie to deal with everything.'

So Mum had specifically invited Evie to come here, into

her inner sanctum. My sinuses burn and I blink and blink. Tears slide out of the corners of my eyes and spill, scalding.

'Oh God, you see? Mum knew you wouldn't cope with it. "Let Rebecca choose any of the jewellery or paintings she wants to keep," she said. "And then get rid of the rest. I know there's nothing worth keeping."'

Nothing worth keeping. So Mum knew all along she was living a half-life among the decaying fragments of our broken family life. All that pain and betrayal, cruelty and sadness. I feel my heart may crack open.

James is still talking, individual words leaping out of a blur of sound.

'...counterpart lease... grant of representation... insurance documents...'

I brush my hand across my cheeks, wiping the tears away, and make an effort to concentrate.

'... make a stab at the probate value of the estate and get all the forms filled in. Just check through this lot and see if there's anything we need to keep.'

And he's off again, to check on Evie and her progress through the bedrooms.

I go back to Olivia Kitto's letter. Such a lovely name. I didn't know we had Kittos in the family: a proper Cornish cousin. Poor old woman, beset by officious nitpickers in her hour of need, reaching out to my mother – too late. I scan the first page but there's no date on it, and the postmark on the envelope is smudged. I wonder how long it's been sitting here. Weeks, maybe? Perhaps she's already in a home, or worse, passed away. But what if she's not? What if she's trapped in hospital waiting for her last living relative to rescue her?

A mad thought strikes me. Perhaps *I* could step into Mum's shoes and prove I am not completely useless. I could nip down to Cornwall to find out what needs to be done, see if I can help in any way. And let Olivia know that Mum is dead, poor old dear. I need something positive to focus on, and the universe has provided. It's a gift, isn't it? A gift to both Olivia and to me, both of us beset and bereaved.

Filled with new energy, I burn through the rest of the mountain of post, filling a bag with rubbish, and placing the remaining official letters into a neat pile. In a heap of correspondence beside Mum's armchair I find more letters from our Cornish cousin. I am just sifting through these when James and Evie reappear, James with more full bin bags, Evie with a cardboard box. James deposits the bags in the hall, then comes back in, rubbing his hands on his trousers. 'We'd better get cracking,' he says.

'The town planner and her husband are coming for dinner tonight,' Evie says brightly over the top of the box. 'I was going to put them off, but sometimes it's good to have practical things to focus on, don't you think?'

I am so gobsmacked I can't find any words. I just look at my twin in disbelief. To give him some credit, he looks abashed. 'Sorry, Becks. Life goes on, eh?'

I swallow, and nod. Getting to my feet, I add the pile of official correspondence to the cardboard box.

'Can I give you a lift to the station?' James asks.

I shake my head. 'I'll hang on here for a bit.'

Evie leans forward to give me an air kiss and I can smell her perfume – something musky and expensive, tainted by the lingering trace of rubber gloves. 'I left your mother's jewellery box on the bed,' she says, nodding back towards the bedroom. 'It's all cheap costume stuff but you may want to keep something out of sentimental value. Oh and,' she hands the box to James then reaches into her handbag and gives me the roll of red stickers. 'You may want to put these on the paintings you don't want the clearance chaps to take.' She pulls away. 'And you know, dear, you shouldn't smoke…' A meaningful pause.

I stare hotly at the sticky labels, then at James.

'Take care of yourself, sis,' he says, then shoulders his way out of the narrow door, and just like that they are gone. I can almost feel the apartment sigh in relief, its violations at an end.

I go into Mum's room. It shows little trace of Evie's depredations, but when I open the wardrobe doors, there is nothing left inside but the smell of camphor and a couple of dozen empty hangers. The jewellery box lies on the floral duvet covering the bed where Mum has not lain for two months. There is nothing left of her, nothing left but absence itself. Disconsolately, I open the box and gaze at the meagre contents: strands of coloured beads, a coral necklace with a broken clasp, an old cameo brooch, some rings. I remember Mum wearing this one: a dress ring with a long green stone set in silver. When I pick it up I am suddenly assailed by her perfume. *Je Reviens* by Worth. *I will return.* Except she won't, not ever. I remember her wearing this ring so clearly, holding her hand out to admire it. 'Who cares if it's not valuable?' she said. 'It could have come out of a cracker and I'd still love it. You should never wear jewellery you don't love.'

Oh, Mum. I put it away: a keepsake.

Going to her bedroom window, I press my hand against

the pane, my breath making a bloom on the glass, just in time to see James's Lexus disappear at the junction. My splayed fingers look like a plea for help and the little winking stone in my 'engagement' ring seems to mock me.

I call Eddie's number one more time, and one more time I get his voicemail. 'Hi there, it's me, Becks,' I tell the message recorder. 'Look, it's a bit complicated, and I'll explain properly when we speak, but I'm going to Cornwall for a few days. It's a family thing. It'll give you time to finish the final preparations for the show.' I pause. 'Eddie? I wish you'd been able to come with me.' I tap the red phone icon and stare at the screen. I wish I hadn't said the last bit. It sounds whiny, needy; weak.

Am I making a foolish, even dangerous, mistake? Or is this the chance to do something for someone worse off than me? Though perhaps she isn't worse off than me. After all, this cousin, this Olivia Kitto, is ancient and I've barely lived at all.

No self-pity, you're stronger than you think, darling.

Sometimes it's as if Mum's voice is right there inside my head.

You know, my engagement ring really is hideous. I've never even liked it, let alone loved it. I lick my finger, tug and twist, and force it over swollen, reddening flesh until at last it comes off. It lies in my palm, two curlicues of cheap nine-carat gold joined by a single zircon. Thirty quid, from a cheap jewellery chain that no longer exists, bought because... I can't even remember exactly why. The only way Eddie and I could book a hotel room? An empty gesture? A joke? Certainly, it wasn't meant to be a proper engagement ring, binding two hearts together for all time, though I so wanted it to be, so there it has been all this time, a small and tawdry lie.

Without it, my hand looks naked, the skin pale.

But I feel unshackled.

2

'ARE YOU SURE THIS IS THE PLACE?' I LOOK UP AT THE house, indistinct against a wooded hill. Grey granite, grey trees merging into a grey, grey sky.

The taxi driver mutters something. I am too strung out after the journey, which has taken the best part of eight hours, including two changes and a lot of running up and down station stairs with my luggage, on the fraying edge of missing every train, to ask him to repeat himself. I have spent much of the journey trying to convince myself that my decision is a good one, but it seemed increasingly unlikely as the train crawled through the longest county in the country, making every mile count.

'Fifteen seventy-five,' the driver says, possibly again, and not even with a 'please'. Unbelievable! We have come only three miles.

I hand over a precious twenty-pound note and defiantly take all the change. The driver huffs out of the car, pops the boot, and wrestles my case out onto the side of the road where it promptly falls over. Without setting it upright, or offering a word of farewell, he gets back into the car, slams the door, performs an angry five-point turn and drives off down the unmade road, leaving a swirling cloud of dust in his wake.

The gate below the house bears no name: I don't even know if this is the right place. The house regards me from brooding blank windows.

I get my phone out to let Eddie know I've arrived. There is, of course, no signal. The sense that I am making a monumental mistake begins to mount up. What do I know about helping an elderly lady? I've made such a mess of my own life, it is sheer hubris to think I can take on someone else's problems. But it seems there is no immediate choice than to go up to the house and say hello, tell her the sad news. And maybe then I can call for a taxi and flee.

Tugging my case, I step through the gate and forge a path through the vegetation. Clusters of bright orange flowers flame above shanks of pale, bladed leaves; brambles snake out to snag my coat. Somewhere in the midst of all this I can smell lavender.

At last, huffing from the effort, I reach a shanty of a porch whose indeterminate shade of paint has flaked back to silvered wood. The corpses of long-dead insects twist in thick corner webs. Dusty shelves sit to either side of the structure, stacked with bric-a-brac. Panels of stained glass flank an old-fashioned doorbell which, nervously, I ring. The bell makes a tired ratcheting noise as if I have set off some dysfunctional mechanical on the other side. The sound is met only by a watchful silence as if the house is holding its breath, waiting for me to give up and go away. Then a harsh voice shrieks, 'Bugger off, arsehole!'

Shocked, I take a step backwards, and trip over my

suitcase. I lunge for the porch frame to steady myself, but fall backwards anyway. A loud splintering sound is followed by a long moment of imminence, as if some key part of the world hangs in the balance, then the whole rickety structure comes down with a groan, showering me in shards of rotten wood and glass. Rolling sideways, I manage to get out of the way just before the porch's pitched roof lands like a miniature pyramid amid the carnage.

Sitting up, I register that I have a sore tailbone and a grazed palm. My right ankle throbs. I test it, circling my foot. Not broken. I stare up at the house, at the naked patch of granite that has been sheltered by the porch for, no doubt, centuries, through the rise and fall of kings and queens and two world wars, and feel sick.

Despite the noise, the door remains closed and no face appears at the dark windows, and after a time it becomes clear no one is coming out.

My belongings have sprung out of my suitcase and strewn themselves down the steps: a spill of knickers, make-up and spare clothes mingling with escaped letters and notebooks. And then the sky turns black, and rain comes pelting down, soaking everything in an instant.

I stumble down the steps, half blinded by weather, swearing in frustration, and quickly gather the letters before they can be ruined or fly off into the storm. So intent am I, that I do not hear footsteps until a pair of feet comes into view, clad in a pair of huge, scuffed brogues tied with mismatched laces.

Pushing wet hair out of my eyes, I stare up into a face as wrinkled as an old russet apple, haloed by a misshapen golf umbrella with two or three broken struts hanging down.

'Mind the stingers, bird,' this person says and holds out something black and green.

My most fancy knickers, a strand of stinging nettle tangled in the leg opening. Grasping the nettle is something I have consistently failed to do in my life and now is no exception. I burst into tears.

'Ah, don't take on.' The umbrella-holder stuffs the underwear into a pocket and extends a large hand. 'The Lord sends such travails to try our faith.'

I force a grin. 'I'm fine, really.'

'That's splann. Upsadaisy.'

A hand snakes under my armpit. Shocked by this unwanted intimacy, I shoot to my feet, cradling the broken suitcase, clothes lolling out of it like intestines from a slit belly. 'I'm sorry about the porch,' I say.

The person stoops to pick up the basket. 'It were only held together by spider-thread and memories.'

Is this Olivia Kitto? She, or he, certainly looks old enough. But if it is Cousin Olivia, then who shouted the obscenity?

It's as if the embrogued person has read my thoughts. 'I'm Jeremiah Sparrow. Folk call me Jem,' he says, covering me with the broken umbrella, though it is far too late for this courtly gesture. 'And who are you? She never been one for welcoming strangers.'

'I'm Rebecca Young. I've come instead of my mum, who's...' I can't bring myself to say the word.

Jem's expression becomes guarded. 'Oh ah? She never mentioned you. Why you here?'

'Cousin Olivia wrote to Mum to ask if she'd come down to help her.'

Jeremiah stills. Then he turns his head up to the house, scrutinizing it through half-closed eyes. 'Did she now?' he says softly. 'Never mentioned it to me or the missus.' He looks back at me. 'Well, I'm here to see to Gabriel.'

Gabriel. I remember now that in Mum's letter, Olivia had referred to her companion. Her unhygienic companion. Feeling some trepidation, I follow Jem to the door, which he opens up, and we enter a gloomy hallway.

Inside, the house seems huge, much bigger than it appears from outside. A long corridor between panelled walls disappears into distant murk. A staircase ascends into darkness. The place smells of mildew, and something worse. I set my suitcase down on the tiles, ready to greet my elderly relative. Jem does not announce himself but just crosses the hall and flicks the light switch. Nothing happens. 'Agh, bleddy thing. I swear this house is haunted by spriggans.' He goes down the hall and drags an aluminium half-ladder out from a cupboard, sets it beneath the junction box and climbs awkwardly to the top step.

'Where is Miss Kitto?' I ask. Jem is muttering over the thick tangle of wires and with a sinking feeling I am sure I know the answer. There was no date on the letter. How long did it sit unopened at Mum's flat? Weeks, or months? With some cruel symmetry have they passed away within days of one another?

Jem's voice cuts in. 'If you could go and open up the drawing room shutters I could see what I'm doing.'

I guess at the first door on the left. The brass doorknob fills my hand, and the catch yields with a creak. As I walk into semi-darkness, a stench stings the back of my nose as sharply as mustard. And then I feel eyes on me, a distinctly primeval sensation. Is Cousin Olivia sitting in the darkness, watching me? Or does her shade occupy one of the hulking easy chairs, a malevolent ghost bent on scaring the shit out of anyone who dares to cross the threshold? The thought is so eerie I run towards the window.

As soon as I set my hand on the shutter-bar the air in the room stirs and an unseen entity whooshes past my head.

'Bl—ack! Blackkk!'

Something brushes my face and I yelp. Hauling the shutters open to flood the room with light, I turn to face the demon... which is regarding me balefully out of a cold, white-ringed eye from the top of the standard lamp.

It is a parrot. A grey parrot with a hooked beak and a neat fan of crimson tail-feathers and I am cast back to that long-ago Cornish holiday – a big, sunny sitting room where Mum and I sat side by side on a lumpy chintz sofa eating spicy yellow bread studded with dried fruit and spread thick with butter while from the top of a bookcase a large grey bird scrutinized our every move. I had looked away, unnerved, and in that moment it had descended on outstretched wings, dug its scaly grey claws into my saffron cake, and with a loud clatter of feathers retreated to the shelves to consume its booty. Surely it can't be the same bird? How long do parrots live?

'That will teach you to pay attention!' Olivia had laughed. 'What Gabriel wants Gabriel takes.' Turning to him she said, 'What will our guests think? I don't know why we named you for an angel: you are the very devil!'

'Shut the fuck up!' the creature retorted.

Mum had gasped and I had clapped my hands to my mouth as if it had been me, not the bird, who had uttered these forbidden words. But the old woman was laughing, and the parrot hopped from foot to foot, hugely pleased with itself, and I suddenly burst out in such giggles that even Mum had smiled.

How could I have forgotten such a bizarre incident?

The room looks smaller now, and infinitely shabbier. The chintz roses are faded to ambiguity and all the surfaces are covered in dust and guano.

Jem shows his face at the door. 'I see you found Gabriel,' he says and at the sight of him Gabriel lets out a banshee caw followed by, 'Messy moose key.' Jem grimaces. 'You'd think it were human sometimes.' He wags his finger at the bird. 'Picked the lock again, did you, you old bugger? Bleddy thing ought to have its neck wrung.' He looks at me sharply. 'Pardon my French. Don't suppose you'll want to stay: lots of diseases you can get from parrots, they say.'

'Oh yes, psittacosis,' I say, the word popping into my mouth. 'But I'm sure it can be cleaned up.' I look around. 'This must be such a lovely room in summer, all these windows, and the views over the garden.' And the rubble of the porch. 'But it doesn't look as if Cousin Olivia has used it in ages. Where is she?' I dread the answer.

Jem offers an unfamiliar word, then adds, 'Hospital. Took a tumble and broke her leg.'

I feel an inner pang at the very word 'hospital'. How I hate them. 'Oh no. How is she doing?'

He gives me a humourless smile. 'If you knew her you'd be more concerned about the nurses.'

'Bit of a termagant, is she?'

'She'm some heller.'

He makes a move towards the bird, which allows him

to approach before lofting into the air and skimming past his head to the bookcase, where it sits making a noise like a cane hitting flesh. *Clack, clack, clack.* It sounds taunting, triumphant.

'I'll wring your neck one day, boy. Killed plenty chickens in my time.' Jem turns back to me. 'My missus keeps house for Miss Olivia but she won't set foot in this room.'

Is he trying to change the subject? 'Is the hospital far? I must go and see Olivia.'

Grasping the nettle, darling: well done.

'Truro,' he replies.

I remember passing Truro on the train – an attractive little city gathered around a cathedral in a dip between low hills. But it seemed to take ages from Truro to Penzance and the idea of making my way back to the station, then to the hospital in Truro and back again tonight is daunting.

Jem notes my despair. 'There be a pub with rooms in the village, you can stay there overnight. Missus can take you into Truro to see Miss Olivia tomorrow.'

I think about this for a moment. I haven't been able to work much these past months and there isn't much in the bank. 'If it's OK I'll stay here. Olivia said in her letter that the upstairs was pristine. Would that be all right?'

Jem makes a face. 'Suit yourself, bird. If you'm staying, you can feed Gabriel. There's food for un in the scullery.'

And with that he is off, leaving me alone. With the parrot.

Gabriel fixes me with a black regard.

'What on earth am I going to do with you?' I ask.

'Fuck off,' he says, so quietly it is almost an endearment.

'You are very rude.'

I pick my way across the room between the splats of

guano, but as I take hold of the door handle there is a titanic thud on my shoulder as Gabriel lands on me, his claws digging through my coat. When I scream the bird echoes my cry with perfect pitch, making my eardrums ring. Then he takes off again to land on top of his cage, where he sits and preens, as if this is a fine old game.

Now that Jem has restored the electrics, the hall is lit by an unshaded electric light, its illumination unforgiving. The mud of years has been ground into the tiles and runners; the floral wallpaper has faded to an unalluring palette of browns, like the husks of dead wildflowers. In the hall behind the staircase a silent longcase clock stands casting the shadow of a huge sentinel. I hear neither tick nor tock from it and the window into its innards shows a pendulum hanging motionless. It's a handsome antique, but I am rather relieved it's not working – is there anything eerier than late-night chimes echoing through an empty house?

Beyond the clock lies a series of closed doors. I open the first one and find a dining room full of big dark furniture, chinaware laid as if for dinner, like something off the *Marie Celeste*.

Opposite are two narrow doors. The first opens in a slant beneath the stairs and contains brooms and buckets and the half-ladder Jem used. When I try the neighbouring door I find it locked, the iron handle freezing, and chilly air seeps out around my wet feet.

At the end of the hall is a door held on a latch. I depress the catch, flick on the light switch – an old-fashioned brass one with a bobble on the end – and find a damp-smelling room containing an ancient range and a pair of stained, shallow copper sinks beneath a window. On the floor sits a metal tub of what appears to be verdigris-stained copper; pushed against the far wall is a strange contraption with a wooden handle, and beside it a tiled worktop upon which sits a dish of apples and a sack labelled 'Pretty Boy Parrot Food'.

A channel cut into the floor leads to a door to the outside. To let water out? Or worse, blood? I shiver. The room is as cold as if it has absorbed a hundred winters. It is like stepping back into another century. But I am the one who feels like a ghost.

I go back into the hallway to explore further. The next door offers a kitchen of sorts, comprising a ramshackle collection of wooden cupboards, an old range, a butler's sink and an armpit-high fridge bearing an Electrolux banner in a typeface no one has used in fifty years. The pale-blue interior contains complex mouldings inhabited by a milk bottle, something in a brown paper bag that turns out to be half a loaf of bread, a dish of butter, half a packet of chocolate digestives and some eggs. I lift the bottle and sniff it cautiously. How long did Jem say Olivia had been in hospital? Weeks? But there's no mould, and it doesn't smell sour. Someone has been using the kitchen, maybe Jem's wife when she comes to clean the house. I am somewhat comforted: at least supper is sorted. The central door of the range is still warm to the touch and when I look inside I can see the glow of embers, as if someone has just been here, stoking it.

Once more I have the feeling of eyes upon me, and when I spin around I see above the wooden table a portrait of a young woman with a piercing black gaze. Her sleeves are rolled up and there's some muscle on her forearms, which are folded: guarded and defiant. She's wearing what appear to be men's clothes and her face has an emphatic bone structure. I forget the eerie sensation, captivated by the skill of the artist. There's a lot more texture in the painting than you'd expect, as if the oils have been laid on with a palette knife rather than a brush. The style is loose and daring, the application of light done in bold blocks of cadmium.

Continuing my explorations, I discover two further rooms, one entirely panelled with books, with a leather armchair pulled up beside an inglenooked woodburner; the other containing a camp bed covered in blankets and a candle-lantern on a makeshift table beside it. A pile of clothes in the corner are in need of a wash, and behind a hand-painted screen depicting Adam and Eve in the Garden of Eden there is an exceptionally large, but thankfully empty, Victorian Flow Blue chamber pot. My grin is short-lived as I remember the bit in the letter about the polar trek to the 'privy'. Oh, dear God. I am overtaken by an urgent need to pee.

I run upstairs and open door after door. Bedroom. Bedroom. Box room. Bedroom. Linens cupboard.

No bathroom.

'I am not,' I say out loud, running back down the stairs, 'using that bloody pot. I would rather *die*!' My voice disappears into the empty spaces of the house.

From the front sitting room comes a sardonic cackle.

The scullery door gives out onto an unevenly paved area, the stone underfoot rosetted with lichen. In the falling gloom, through the still-falling rain, I spy a brick shed. I make a run for it and push the door open. Lurking within is a toilet of cracked porcelain. Spider webs drape the dark spaces between the high cistern and ceiling, map out territory between the bricks, festoon the toilet roll holder with its roll of shiny Izal. I shudder. Perhaps the pot after all? No: I simply can't.

I feel for a light switch. There is no light switch. I feel the walls of my self-control begin to crumble.

Pull yourself together, Becky, the voice of my mother chides me gently.

Sitting in the dark on the cold Bakelite seat, watched by myriad arachnid eyes, I curse my impulsiveness. It appears I have travelled not just three hundred miles, but three hundred years back in time.

3

THE NEXT MORNING I ROLL OFF THE BED IN THE LEAST
mildewy of the upstairs rooms, pad to the window and
pull back the heavy curtains, expecting to look out into a
grey landscape and lashing rain. Instead, I feel the sun on
my face, like a benediction. Sea and sky fuse at the distant
horizon. Spangles of light glitter like spilled treasure,
undulating with the rolling of the waves. Far out, a single
crabber ploughs across the bay, as squat as a child's toy.
To the east, St Michael's Mount, misty as legend, a barely
sketched Disney castle rising out of the sea.

This is the Cornwall I have always imagined. The sense
of wildness and isolation, of fairy tale and possibility. There
is a luminous quality to the air as if everything has been
renewed overnight. No smell of diesel fumes or frying onions
from the kebab shop, no rumble of buses or aeroplanes.
No shouting neighbours or wailing children, no booming
bass from the flat upstairs. Nothing but the cry of a solitary
seagull perched on the hedge in the lane below.

When it lifts off into the blue air I see what appears to

be the top of a gate, an indentation in the hedge below the house. I wonder what it opens onto?

Filled with sudden energy, I pull on jeans and trainers to go with the T-shirt I have slept in and run downstairs. Even the outhouse holds no horrors for me. I leave the door ajar and sit there with sunlight angling across my thighs, looking out at tumbles of red and orange nasturtiums, their peppery smell scenting the air. I wash my hands in the scullery, wiping my hands dry on a tea towel, and dash out of the front door, through the debris of the collapsed porch and down the steps, and across the narrow track where the taxi dropped me the previous day – and yes, there it is! Strangled by weeds and brambles, but tantalizingly present, a little wooden gate, its paint flaking charmingly.

The latch is rusty but lifts cleanly from the keeper. Great whorls of convolvulus and goosegrass wind in and out of the strakes. I pull them away by the handful and run my hand over the carved top bar wonderingly. Beyond it, steep earth steps, just visible between overgrown vegetation, lead down to the sea.

I slip through the gate and turn to click it shut, and as I do my eye is caught by a series of oblique squares – diamonds one inside another, like a string of eyes – that have been cut all the way down the open side, giving the plain back a rich artisan touch. The house has no indoor bathroom, indeed no luxuries at all, yet someone has lavished attention on a little rustic sea gate! It is a delightful incongruity.

The pitch of the path is fearsome, but I odge down on my haunches, brushing nettles aside with my feet as I go, steadying myself by catching hold of exposed twists of hawthorn roots, and finding them polished as if from long use as handles. I think about the people who have used this path and these roots before me – Olivia as a child, her parents, their parents. And my mother. For among the other papers I found near Mum's armchair were other letters from her cousin, reminiscing about Mum's childhood holidays in Cornwall, how she had stayed here at Chynalls with Olivia and my grandparents. How Mum's father was related to Olivia's mother in some way: a branch of the family that lost contact, if Mum and I are the only ones left to whom the old lady can turn. I can imagine women bundling up their skirts, crabbing down just as I am, picnic baskets balanced in their laps, while their children scramble towards the sea, as nimble as monkeys. As I touch the rocks and roots, I imagine my mother touching them as she must have as a child, and a lovely arc of connection runs through me like electricity.

At last the vegetation gives way to bare cliff and I can see a tiny cove embraced by two arms of rock beyond which the surf boils and bashes. A moment later I am down on the pebbles, looking out to where white-gold sand is buffered by wave-smoothed boulders littered with strands of bladderwrack and kelp. I breathe in the sharp, clean air, gaze out at the sparkling sea. It is as if the world is saying: *time for a new start.*

Taking off my trainers, I walk to the lace-edged water and am briefly shocked by the cold, then enjoy the sensation of the waves as they withdraw, sucking the sand from between my toes. A boat heads eastwards beyond the necklace of rocks, trailing a cloud of white gulls. It could be any time, and no time. I am in the moment, and life is good.

I walk up the beach to poke between the pebbles and

seaweed, picking up a pretty stone or a piece of cloudy green seaglass, finding conical spiral shells of purple and pearly white; little round winkles as bold as brass and gold as gorse; blue-black mussel shells paired like dark angels' wings, and once a tiny white cowrie, no bigger than the nail of my little finger, the curve of its delicately corrugated lips leading into rosy depths, like a secret smile.

In the rock pools translucent shrimps dart out of fissures towards curtains of green weed, chased by little blennies. Anemones as round and shiny as jellies cluster below the waterline; colonies of barnacles encrust the sides. I take a lone limpet by surprise, moving it a couple of millimetres before its great yellow foot clamps down to anchor it fast. It occurs to me that the last time I played like this – happily, purposelessly absorbed – I was a child.

At last, my stomach growls, desperate for coffee and toast. I decide to walk down into the village to buy provisions, and see if Eddie has called me back. The thought brings with it a dull pain. He has not answered my many calls, maybe has not even listened to my message, though I checked my phone all the way down on the train. I know he must be busy, finishing his pots, head down in the studio. When he works it is with total focus. I love to watch Eddie work: his skill and artistry make my heart swell with pride. And when his hands caress the clay as the wheel turns I remember the way those hands have touched my body, though not always with such care. Is it possible to feel jealous of clay?

I brush the sand off my bare feet, put on my trainers and walk back towards the earth steps. And that's when I see it: another gate made of iron bars set into the cliff at the back of the bay. I crunch up the shingle and see that behind the gate is a cave. I press my face to the rusty bars, but the darkness beyond is forbidding. It must go right under the road. Maybe even under the house. Perhaps there's a secret entrance from the cellar? All manner of fantasies fill the darkness beyond: smugglers and pirates, excise men and revolutionaries. Echoes of *Moonfleet*, *Jamaica Inn* and *Poldark*.

I expect the gate's latch to be fused by rust but it rises smoothly and I step into the cave. As my eyes adjust to the darkness, I make out rock walls a metre or so apart, a sandy floor. Using my hands to guide me, I move inside. The chill strikes through to my bones.

Further in there is a pinch point, then the cave widens again. It's dark this far in, but I can feel barnacles to waist height so the sea must come in this far. I will just go a little further, I tell myself, see if the cave comes to a natural end. The cave begins to slant uphill. I pass my hands up and down the rock walls as I go and soon come to a point where I find no barnacles. *Well, at least I won't drown*, I think, only half amused. I shuffle carefully, but rock strikes my shin. Reaching down, I find a void above it, then more rock. Steps? I stand up on the first step, find the level of the second with my hand and the riser of the third. Reaching overhead to make sure the roof of the cave won't brain me, I move up again, and again. The steps seem to go up for ever. I think about turning back.

Come on, Becks, you wanted an adventure!

Do I, though? Life has not been very encouraging lately, and it is so dark. Anxiety bites but I am curious to find out where this tunnel ends. On I go. At last, the ground levels out and I reach an obstacle. Flattening my hands against it, I find a substance warmer than the surrounding rock. Wood? A door? I pass my hands carefully from top to bottom, feeling indentations, regular and sharp, but no handle. This is frustrating. I will have to come back with a torch.

I retreat slowly, hands braced against the cold, rough rock walls: better not slip and knock myself out here where no one will find me. No one knows I am here, except the old man – Jem – who will probably just think I've abandoned my ruined clothes and gone home.

Suddenly, dark thoughts threaten. *Might it not be for the best?* they whisper. *Remember the phone call. Just think what's awaiting you in London. Maybe the best way out would be simply to let the sea take you. Then it will be your choice and you won't have to go through it all again: the tests, the hospital, the tubes and the poison; and Eddie's disappointed face:* 'Not again, Becks, not again...'

My legs start to tremble and for an instant I feel as weak as I was after surgery, when I hobbled up the high street for the first time, overtaken constantly by octogenarians, convinced I was going to black out at any moment.

Stop it, darling. My mother's voice is so strong it almost echoes. *Concentrate on this moment, right now. It's all we ever truly have.*

Forcing the dark thoughts away, I retrace my path back along the tunnel to the pinch point – where I hear lapping water. The tide has crept in!

Abruptly I feel oppressed by the weight of rock above and around me. It feels like the grave. Splashing through the water, not caring that I am soaking my jeans and my trainers, I blast out of the cave and at last stand with the sea swirling around my knees, sucking in the cold, salty air, feeling the sun's welcome warmth on my face. It is shockingly, beautifully bright.

That's my girl. One battle at a time.

From the earth steps that lead up to the sea gate and then the house, I look back at the cove. It seemed so serene, a gift offered only to me, but maybe it is a place of guile and secrets, of gifts extended with one hand, then taken away with another.

Closing the front door of the house behind me, I hear noises. And a smell too – unmistakable. I make my way down the light-dappled corridor to the kitchen, where I find a figure prodding a pan on the stove: a dumpy woman in an outdoor coat and a hat jammed down over her hair, like an elderly Paddington Bear. I clear my throat, and she turns, her front view hardly dispelling the image. 'Brought a bit of breakfast for you.'

Bacon sizzles in the pan and my mouth runs with saliva. 'Thank you so much. You must be Jem's wife?'

'Yes. Call me Rosie.'

She tucks her frizzy ginger hair behind her ears. Her face is pale and nondescript: it's hard to judge her age. When she smiles I am shocked by the brilliant evenness of her teeth. These are not the stained and gappy teeth of an elderly woman, but of a Hollywood starlet. Veneers? But that would have cost a fortune. I think of Jem and his scuffed brogues and broken umbrella: must be dentures, then.

I get two teacups down and place them beside the teapot that is warming. Rosie picks one of them up – printed with fading forget-me-nots – and puts it to one side. 'Don't use that one. That's Miss Olivia's!' she tells me sharply. She fiddles around in the cupboard and extracts another, decorated with buttercups.

We sit at the table under the disapproving eyes of the portrait, eating bacon and eggs. 'I shouldn't really,' says Rosie, patting her stomach. 'I already ate with Jem.'

'I couldn't eat all this on my own.'

'You're no more than a stick.' She gets up to clear away the plates, says over her shoulder, 'Jem said you come down to see Miss Olivia about a letter?'

'Yes, she wrote to ask for my mother's help.'

'Oh? What were that about, then?'

'I'm not sure. I was hoping to go and see her at the hospital to get a better idea of what she had in mind.'

'Don't know what help she needs, old besom. Jem and I do everything for her, always have,' she grumbles.

'I'm sure you do, and I'm sure she's grateful.'

Rosie barks out a laugh. 'Grateful? Not that one. Well, if you want to see her I'll drive you in. Got to go visit Jem's dad anyway.'

'Oh, is he in the same hospital?'

She gives a noncommittal grunt. 'Them poor nurses... I said to Jem if I ever get that way you just put a pillow over my face.'

'Oh dear. Is he a bit of a monster then?'

'I meant Miss Olivia.' Rosie puts the plates in the sink and pours hot water from the kettle on top of them. 'Dementia, poor old soul. Better pack your things and bring them with you – once you seen her you'll be wanting dropping at the station so you can get the train back home.'

*

The hospital is an hour's drive away, a rambling sprawl of low-rise utilitarian glass and concrete fronted by a crammed car park. Rosie drives her enormous boat of a Mercedes round and round, making me wince as she misses wing mirrors and bumpers by millimetres. There has already been a bit of a misunderstanding at the Chiverton roundabout which provoked a symphony of horns, and now there is a standoff with a disgruntled driver whose space Rosie just shot into, grazing the passenger side door. 'Ah, bugger it!' she groans. 'They make these spaces too darn narrow.' She opens her own door wide and grumps her way out, oblivious to the furious gesticulations of the other driver.

I crawl over the gearstick and follow Rosie out of the driver's side, dragging a carrier bag of grapes, chocolate and magazines with me.

'She won't thank you for any of that nonsense.' Rosie reaches into a bag behind the driver's seat and takes out a small Thermos. 'But she'll thank me for this.'

'What is it?'

'Her special tea, just the way she likes it. She complains something awful about the weak stuff they give you in this place.'

'That's kind of you.'

Rosie stands there for a moment as if remembering something, then tucks her necklace inside her blouse. 'Hands,' she says, cryptically. 'Come along, then.'

*

'Wake up, Miss Olivia. You got a visitor.' Rosie plonks herself on the bed at the end of the geriatric ward. I look down at the woman in the chair beside the bed, shoulders rounded, head hanging down, pink scalp showing beneath the strands of white hair. Slack skin falls in a slump of folds and wrinkles that so engulf her features that she resembles a half-melted waxwork. She looks so frail, nothing like the owner of the blustering voice that bellowed out of the letters, and my heart sinks. Surely Jem was right: she won't be strong enough to go home.

'Cousin Olivia?' I say timidly.

The old lady does not stir.

This is the moment I could just walk away. I am shocked by the thought, but before I can act upon it her head comes up, the black eyes open and she fixes me with a merciless stare and I am pinned, like a trapped butterfly, to my fate.

'Who are you?' She looks me up and down. 'No uniform? Not a nurse?'

I shake my head.

'God-botherer? Can't stand God-botherers. If you're one of those you can just bugger off. Try to get a nap and bloody God-botherers come and disturb you just as you're drifting off. Blasted nuisance.'

'I'm not a God-botherer. I brought you these,' I say, offering gifts as if appeasing a volatile minor deity.

Olivia peers into the carrier bag. 'Fruit is for birds and magazines are for idiots. You can leave the chocolate on the side.'

Rosie rolls her pale eyes. 'You see?' she says to me. To Cousin Olivia she says, 'Now you be civil to this girl. She's come a long way to see you. Says you wrote to her ma in a state of panic. What did you go and do that for? Don't we look after you, me and Jem?'

The old woman narrows her gaze. 'I know exactly what you do for me, Rosie Sparrow. Now why don't you just bugger off?' The black regard, as beady as Gabriel's, is malicious and I am reminded of the portrait in the kitchen, the eyes that follow your every movement.

Rosie pushes herself to her feet. 'Be like that, then.' To me she says quietly, 'Don't believe a word she says.' She taps her temple. 'I'll see you back in the car park in an hour. Don't be late or I'll go without you.'

She trundles off through the ward, stopping to pass the flask to a woman wheeling a tea trolley.

Olivia tugs my sleeve. 'We must be quick.'

'Sorry?'

'I'll need a coat. Yours will do. There's twenty pounds in my handbag. We'll get a taxi.' She shuffles her saggy old body into a more upright position, takes hold of her bound and plastered leg, resting on the footstool, and lifts it till the heel of the foot is on the ground. She wriggles her toes and gives a satisfied nod. 'Right, you cause a disturbance and I'll nip past you when they're not looking. I'll meet you by the lift. Now, where's my stick?'

'I, ah…' I look around, alarmed, and at that moment one of the nurses comes past.

'Planning your escape again, are you, Mrs Kitto?'

'Miss Kitto,' Olivia growls.

The nurse grins at me. 'Don't let her lure you into her schemes! We've already caught her sweet-talking the volunteer reader and trying to sneak out past the night staff. Luckily the lift was out of order, wasn't it, Mrs Kitto?'

Olivia gives her a death-stare, which just makes the nurse's smile wider. 'Oh, she's a character.'

'Fuck off.'

The nurse sighs. 'Luckily I do have some nice, polite patients to see to.' She wags a finger at Olivia. 'Now, you behave yourself.'

Olivia watches her go on her way, then swings her gaze back to me. 'Interfering creature. Now, who are you and what are you doing here?'

I gather myself. 'I'm Rebecca, Geneviève's daughter. You wrote to her – do you remember? Asking for her help?'

Olivia frowns. 'Her daughter, you say? That letter was a jolly long time ago. So rude not to reply at once, but I suppose it's better late than never. Where is she, your mother?'

'She's—she's…' Still so hard to say it. 'She died a couple of weeks ago. I found your letter at her flat and came down to offer you my help in her place.'

Olivia cocks her head. 'Well, that's extremely inconvenient. I always thought our family had a bit more gumption.'

Gumption? I feel my cheeks flush. 'She had cancer.' The vile word slips out, leaving my mouth dry and bitter.

The old woman subsides as if air has been let out of her. 'I can't believe it. Not Jenny.'

Only those who knew Mum well called her Jenny. It was always the full Geneviève, though Dad sometimes called her Vivi or Vivien.

'But she's far too young. Are you quite sure?'

How could I be unsure if my mother were alive or dead? I nod miserably.

There follows a long pause, then Olivia says, so quietly

that I almost miss it, 'I loved her so. How much more must I lose?' Her gaze becomes rheumy, and she turns her head sharply away and rubs her face as if to erase the pain. She blinks several times then turns back and grasps my arm. 'How is Gabriel? Is he well? Is he eating? I miss him terribly: he's all I have left in the world.'

'He's fine,' I reassure her. I do not mention the ruined carpet, the shit-stained furniture, the stench. 'He had a good peck at the apple I gave him earlier and was very well behaved about it.'

Gabriel had flown to the lamp to get a good vantage on the offerings I brought, then had alighted on my forearm, making charming little cooing noises designed to assure me of his peaceable intentions. I had stood mesmerized, but also touched by the bird's trust, watching him peck greedily at the apple, feeling his weight on my arm. Occasionally, he would cock his head and give me a disconcertingly intelligent look: *You see? We can get along famously. But if you try anything underhand…* The nictitating membrane had come down over the beady eye like a wink.

Olivia grins, showing dark yellow teeth. 'Gabriel is an excellent judge of character. If he likes you, you must be trustworthy. Sit here on the bed and let me have a look at you.'

I sit down.

'You don't look much like Jenny,' she says after a moment. 'Put your hair up. Such a mess like that anyway. Let me see your face properly.'

So rude! Still, I catch my hair up with one hand and gather it into a ponytail with the elasticated hairband from my coat pocket. It does feel rough: sticky from saltwater. I will have to find a way to wash it.

'Better. Lean towards me – my eyesight is wretched these days.'

Olivia takes hold of my chin, tilts my head this way and that. 'Hmmm. Good bones. I can see your mother in you now. Your face has character, young lady.'

The nurse is back, wheeling a machine. 'Time to check your blood pressure, Mrs Kitto.'

Olivia ignores her, but lets go of my chin. 'I think it's time to leave, dear. Where are my shoes?' She gazes at the plaster on her leg as if it has appeared overnight by magic. 'What's this wretched thing doing here? Well, that's a blasted nuisance. Still, I'm sure we shall overcome.' She turns to the nurse. 'If you've got some scissors on you we can cut one leg of my trousers and I can get dressed. Come on, girl, be useful. Then my young relative here can drive me home. You've brought a car, haven't you, dear? Or do you have a driver?'

Oh dear, I'm beginning to see what Rosie meant.

The nurse grins at me. 'Very inventive.' She raises her voice. 'You're very inventive, aren't you, Mrs Kitto?'

'*Miss* Kitto,' Olivia rumbles back softly but the confidence has gone out of her. She lets the young woman cuff her arm and take her blood pressure. When the nurse wheels away the machine, she says to me, 'They can't imagine how anyone my age never married, these young chits. Things were different in my time. I survived a war, you know!'

'You must tell me all your stories. I'd love to hear them.'

She swings her head around to gaze at me suspiciously. 'Why? What have you heard?'

'Nothing,' I assure her. 'I don't know anything at all.'

'Well, that's quite clear. Now then… if you're not going

to help me out of here at least you can be useful. I'll dictate – do you have a pen?'

Half an hour later I am back in the car park, my head spinning, glad to have escaped the confines of the hospital with all those familiar hospital smells of disinfectant, urine and grief. There is a list of instructions folded in my coat pocket: Cousin Olivia has been exigent in her demands. In my handbag is her cheque book, with the first three cheques blank but signed and dated and the fourth one made out to me for a thousand pounds. 'For your expenses,' Olivia had said, as if I were her employee. Do cheques even work any more? Apparently, social services have decreed that she'll need a fully equipped indoor bathroom complete with grab rails – 'Grab rails, I ask you! Namby-pamby nonsense.' – wheelchair access to her downstairs rooms and a proper bed before she can be released to her own home. That, or she'll have to go into care. I can see that all this makes sense, given the state of Chynalls, and is in her best interest, but it does seem rather intrusive, and entirely overwhelming.

Rosie is sitting in the front seat of the Mercedes, finishing the nub end of a pasty. She makes no move to open the passenger door for me and hardly seems to notice the trouble I have getting in. 'See what I mean?' she says indistinctly with her mouth full.

'She is certainly quite a character.'

Completing her meal, she opens her window and throws the paper bag out. I open my mouth, but she presses the car's ignition button so that the engine roars to life and drowns my protest.

'And how is Jem's father?' I ask when we are out on the main road.

By way of an answer Rosie forces the car into an unwise overtaking manoeuvre that causes me to shut my eyes.

I force myself to think. The list Olivia has given me would take weeks – months – to carry out. How can I stay here all that time? And do I even want to? But duty presses upon me: I am her last surviving relative, daughter of her beloved 'Jenny'. If I run away I will feel I am letting down not only this batty old relative, but also Mum. But what will Eddie say? And what about my own life? Shouldn't I go back and submit myself to the consultants? What they have seen on the scan may be nothing, after all. But if it isn't nothing, then it is everything, the end of everything...

My mind shies away from this. There are times when considering the renovation of someone else's decrepit old house is more attractive than dealing with your own reality. But I've hardly made a single decision in two years: Eddie's had to take charge of everything. Suddenly I miss him so badly I could cry.

Eddie and I met at an art fair. I was setting up my stall and having problems with the lighting. He had the adjoining stall and, it turned out, had overloaded the electrical point with his own rig. 'There was a spark between us,' he always says with a laugh. Eddie made pots – beautiful pots, round-bellied and solid, with beautiful turquoise raku glazing. I sold my paintings. I made hardly anything out of it, but I didn't mind. It was Eddie who encouraged me to 'monetize the product': apart from pots, Eddie produced greetings cards and prints and had a website and pages on Etsy and Instagram. 'People can't afford to buy original pieces when times are hard,' he explained. 'But they feel guilty coming away from your stall empty-handed, so you might at least get a couple of quid out of them.' He did well, but never well enough. It was Eddie who – without my knowledge – managed to wangle enough out of Mum to buy a garage at the back of our building and turn it into a studio so he could 'expand the business'. I was furious when I found out but Mum had been adamant she didn't want the money back. 'You have to follow your dreams, darling. I never followed mine and I've regretted it. You're a lovely artist and I want to see you happy.' So he had obviously told her that the studio was for me, not him. I could imagine him doing it: Eddie was always so good with Mum, flirting with her, heaping extravagant flattery upon her. They laughed together a lot – it's one of the things I shall miss so much now that she's gone. I could call him now – I've got signal, and it looks as if I have some missed calls. But the conversation isn't one I want to share with anyone else, let alone a stranger driving like a maniac. Even as I think this Rosie brakes to avoid rear-ending a car turning off through the roadworks at St Erth.

'Bleddy terrible driver,' she rails, giving them the V-sign as they turn off.

'Can you recommend any good builders, Rosie?' I say into the charged silence that follows.

'What she want done, then? Jem and the boys have always done Olivia's little jobs.'

'It's more than a little job. Social services say she needs to have a bathroom put in for when she comes home. A proper bathroom, downstairs, adjoining her bedroom with an indoor loo and walk-in bath/shower with rails and safety handles and all that sort of thing.'

Rosie grunts. 'She's managed very well all this time. Besides, poor old bird won't be coming home. You've seen the state of her.'

I bite my lip, thinking of the old lady I have just met. There's still so much fire in her, so much character, a sort of fierce, frail heroism. I wish I'd known Olivia when she was younger.

4

Olivia

April 1943

THROUGH THE CRACK BETWEEN THE SITTING ROOM DOOR
and its wooden jamb, Olivia watched as her parents
embraced. Their argument that morning had been so severe
that her mother had stormed out into the garden; from
her eyrie upstairs, Olivia had heard the shouting and felt
the front door slam so hard that she could not imagine
how the stained glass would survive. She had watched her
mother running towards the orchard, her red tea-dress a
danger flag amongst the tall grass and straggling flowers,
her father in pursuit, limping just a little, remonstrating but
being ignored.

Her parents had what her mother called 'a relationship
full of passion. He is chalk and I am cheese, a fine Brie de
Meaux!' It sounded very exotic in Mummy's French accent.
Olivia had come to accept these eruptions as a normal part
of the pattern of their lives: they laughed and caroused and
lived life noisily when they were afforded the luxury of time

together, but every so often something would slip out of kilter in the smooth machinery of their marriage and a row would come racketing out.

Her mother, almost as tall as her father in her heels, was holding him so tight now that her knuckles were white and her varnished nails were almost completely buried in the serge of his jacket. Olivia could tell from the way her shoulders trembled that she was crying, which her mother never did. She shouted, and screamed and swore, but she never cried. Her father, handsome in the uniform he had put on again after weeks in slacks and checked shirts, cradled his wife's dark head but he was gazing past her with a faraway look in his pale blue eyes, as if he were already back in North Africa with his comrades. 'Hush, Estelle,' he whispered. 'It's not the end of the world.'

Olivia bent her ears towards his words. What could he mean? That he was returning to his regiment? But they had known this day was coming for the whole time he'd been back here on recuperation, so why was Mummy crying now? Was it something she, Olivia, had done? Guiltily, she recollected her recent misdemeanours: tea spilled on the best rug, the badly done chores, the fight with Nipper up at the farm, being brought home red and furious. It hadn't been her fault: she'd only been trying to save Mamie from the boys teasing her, flipping up her skirt to find out the colour of her knickers. Mamie was the farmer's youngest, at nearly thirteen, and was what local folk called simple, with a flattened face, a sweet expression and small black eyes. Olivia felt very protective towards her, which was why she had got into the fight, even though Mummy was always telling her she was a young lady now and that she should behave like one. '*Tu es un garçon manqué*, Olivia,' she would scold. 'A tomboy, a hoyden.' Olivia's cheeks flamed at the memory of how Nipper had tried to grope her breasts, a recent addition to her changing body, and one she hated. She'd been caught by Jago, the farm manager, kicking his nephew in the privates, and he had hauled her off and delivered her home, though he hadn't told her parents the half of it, for which she was grateful.

But that had taken place three days ago and surely would not have arisen again today of all days, when her father was leaving them to return to active service?

'Come along,' Tony Kitto said soothingly now. 'Let's not waste the time we have left in recriminations.'

Olivia frowned. Recriminations meant someone had done something wrong, but for once it didn't sound as if that someone was her.

Her father started towards the door, pulling Estelle with him. 'Let's go upstairs and say our farewells properly.'

Olivia fled, socked feet gliding noiselessly over the beeswaxed tiles. She managed to get as far as the dining room before her parents emerged and started up the stairs. Just another of their rows, then, nothing world-shattering. But the words 'the time we have left' skittered through her uneasy mind.

She let herself into the kitchen where the sun poured in through the window to cast a rhombus of light across the newly baked bread. Outside, the gold and orange trumpets of nasturtiums tumbled down the wall in a shocking burst of colour. When Daddy was here everything seemed brighter and better; every room in the house felt put to good use, full of light and life and energy. He lit fires on dull days and strewed his belongings through the rooms – his pipe and tobacco pouch alongside a book left split-spined and upside-down on the lightstand in the snug; a sketchbook and sticks of charcoal on the hall console; the draughts board and its scattered pieces on the table in the dining room, where the radiogram played swing band music. When he wasn't home she and Mummy only used the parlour and the kitchen, and Olivia found herself creeping quietly like a trespasser around the rest of Chynalls.

She helped herself to the crust off the new bread and spread it with too much butter and honey and chewed ruminatively.

Half an hour later her parents were back downstairs and Daddy was carrying his kitbag. Mummy's eyes were overly bright, but she had reapplied her make-up and looked like a film star. Mrs Kitto caught sight of her daughter. 'Fetch your bathers, *chérie*, we'll go for a swim on the way back!'

This was an unexpected gift. Olivia thudded upstairs to her room, grabbed her knitted navy swimming costume and a towel and was back in the hall in seconds flat. 'There's my girl!' Daddy tousled her hair. When Estelle bent to pack Olivia's things into her basket, he reached into his pocket and drew out a ten shilling note – a small fortune! – which he passed surreptitiously to his daughter, putting a finger to his lips. Olivia grinned and tucked it away in her shorts pocket, already planning how she might spend it. Then they walked up the steep path through the wood behind the house to the old barn where the car was kept.

*

Olivia loved to be taken out in the Standard Flying 8. It was a majestic car, with its long running boards and sweeping mudguards, and though it was a bit cramped in the back she felt like Princess Elizabeth being chauffeured around, sometimes practising a regal wave to the villagers and farmhands they passed. Her father drove carefully, letting the road spool out in graceful spans and parabolas, taking the bends gently so that Olivia didn't shoot sideways across the hard leather seat. She hugged his kitbag to her, breathing in the smell that defined him: tobacco, ironed cotton, leather polish, things he would take back with him all the way to North Africa. When he'd come home he had had to show her where it was in the atlas. Olivia loved his old atlas: her father hadn't been much younger than she was now when he'd won it. In pencil on the title page was inscribed the rubric: 'First prize for Geography to Antony John Kitto, Bolitho School, Penzance, 5th June 1917'. Imagine: they had both been teenagers during a war! She remembered how he had tracked his finger across the Channel, through France and across the Mediterranean to Tunisia and Algeria, so far away. 'I can't tell you exactly where I was or what I was doing there: walls have ears,' he'd said with a grin. Impossible to imagine that a war was going on in the world, a world in which her father had taken a bullet, when Cornwall was so peaceful.

She tuned back into her parents' quiet conversation. 'I could be very useful,' her mother was saying. She shot a look in the rear-view mirror and started to speak rapid French. Even concentrating hard, Olivia could catch only one word in ten – something about translating and connections; her father listening but evidently disagreeing. He spoke more slowly so that Olivia caught the words *péril* and *les lignes ennemies*, then her mother rattled away once more, and at last said to her husband in crisp English, 'Even after all this time, Tony, your accent is quite execrable!'

'Other things to do than polish up my language skills, darling.'

They exchanged a freighted glance, then Estelle laid a hand on her husband's arm. 'You won't do anything heroic, will you? You won't take unnecessary risks?'

He turned his head. 'Don't you want us to win the war? Perhaps your heart lies with the Vichy regime after all?'

'*Espèce d'idiot!*'

Then they were laughing and the tension seemed to pass.

All too soon they were pulling up to the station, where passengers were milling about, some in uniform, most in civvies. Olivia watched a gaggle of children emerging in Indian file, wearing belted macs and satchels slung across their chests, being marshalled by a pair of bespectacled women.

'Evacuees,' her father said quietly.

Estelle firmed her lips but did not reply.

Tony Kitto drew the Flying 8 up outside the station, shut off the engine and got out, then opened the back door and Olivia passed him his greatcoat and cap and shoved the kitbag along the leather seat, then slid across and jumped out beside him.

'Haven't you grown?' he observed, as if he hadn't really noticed her in these past weeks. His pale eyes were slitted against the sun, the skin crinkled at the corners. A breeze blew his sandy hair across his face and he swept it back with an impatient hand then jammed his cap down over it, in an instant becoming a man in uniform, a soldier, and not Daddy any more.

Olivia felt abruptly bereft. 'I'll be sixteen soon,' she said in an attempt to re-establish their connection.

He regarded her solemnly. 'So you will.' Dropping to one knee, he rummaged in his kitbag, coming back up with a sturdy leather pouch in his hand. He held it out to Olivia and she took it tentatively and nearly dropped it, taken aback by its weight. Turning it over, she saw the word 'Leica' stamped into the leather.

'Your camera,' she said in awe.

'By the time I come back I expect you to have mastered the art of taking and printing a good picture,' he told her. 'You'll find everything you need – the manuals and books, the printing paper and the chemicals – in the back bedroom.'

Estelle made a face. 'Don't you think she's too young for such an expensive camera, *chéri*?'

'Never too young, and why start with something sub-standard? Besides, she's inherited my artistic eye and should be encouraged, eh, Livy?'

Olivia hugged the camera case possessively: she wasn't giving it back now. It felt heavy and significant beyond its physical being, symbolic, somehow, of her passage from childhood into a more grown-up world. 'I'll treasure it,' she promised.

Estelle wavered. 'Are you sure you won't you need it?'

Tony shrugged. 'I'll pick up another one in London on my way through,' he said insouciantly, as if Leicas were two a penny, rather than the best German technology you could buy. He touched his wife's cheek. 'Now, remember the instructions from the Ministry? Keep the car locked in the garage and the fuel canisters in the stonehouse, and take the starting handle into the house with you, and if you're not going to use the car at all, put it out of action. Jago will help – and he knows how to drive it if you need him to.'

'I can too!' Olivia piped up and her father grinned.

'Best not, Livy, not without me.'

'I should think not,' her mother declared.

'And if the Germans come, destroy all the maps and get yourselves down into the cellar, yes? The key's over the lintel; lock the door behind you. Everything you need is down there – the camping stove, emergency rations, blankets, candles, matches. Keep the water canisters refreshed, just in case; and if worse comes to worst you can go down the tunnel to the cove and swim out.'

Estelle stared at him. 'Surely the Germans won't invade Cornwall now. I thought you said the tide was turning?'

'Who can read the future?' He put a finger to her lips then kissed her, smearing her lipstick.

Olivia looked away, embarrassed. When she looked back he was striding towards the waiting train, then the clouds of steam swallowed him up.

Her mother drove them back out along the main road, where all the signposts had been taken down to confuse any enemy that landed. The lanes of West Penwith were a maze at the best of times – it was easy to lose your bearings when taking shortcuts – but when they suddenly turned off St Buryan Hill, Olivia knew exactly where they were headed. The car lurched over the uneven stones of the lane towards Treen Farm but as they reached the Logan Rock Inn a uniformed soldier stepped into the road and waved for them to stop.

'Where are you going?'

Estelle put the handbrake on but didn't turn off the engine. She rolled down the window and bestowed a dazzling smile upon the young corporal. 'We've just dropped my husband, Captain Antony Kitto, at the station so he can return to his regiment. It's made our daughter terribly, terribly upset – hasn't it, darling?' She turned to Olivia and gave a barely perceptible wink, and Olivia, who till now had been successfully holding back tears at the thought of Daddy going back to the war, gave a snuffle and nodded. How curious, she thought, to hear her mother putting on such a very English voice. She sounded like an actress and Olivia felt a sudden gulf open between them. 'So I promised her that we could go for a quick dip to take her mind off losing her father.'

The corporal looked embarrassed. 'I'm afraid all the beaches are closed off around here, ma'am. It's a prohibited zone.'

'Well, I know we have to protect the Atlantic Cable Station for reasons of national security,' Estelle continued crisply, which made the young man look even more uncomfortable, 'but we're not heading to Porthcurnow, only to one of the little coves before there.'

'It's not safe, ma'am. I've been instructed to turn everyone back, unless you've got a pass?'

Estelle frowned. 'But really—'

'I'm sorry, ma'am: everyone. And if you haven't a pass I have to charge you a five-pound fine.'

Five pounds! 'It's all right, Mummy,' Olivia said quietly, 'we can go down through the sea gate and swim in our own cove. I don't mind.'

Her mother rounded on her. 'Don't interrupt when adults are speaking!' She returned her attention to the soldier, leaving Olivia feeling stung. 'Are you under Major Ellery's command?'

'Yes, ma'am.'

'Well then, just tell him Mrs Estelle Kitto sends her regards and looks forward to beating him at bridge next week. Five pounds, indeed!'

The young man shuffled his feet. Despite his rank and uniform, he was probably only a couple of years older than her, Olivia thought, and did her best to pull herself together so that he did not think her a cry-baby. Which she most definitely was not.

'I'll do that, ma'am.' He hesitated. 'But I still can't let you through.'

Estelle glared at him, then rolled the window up and executed such a violent four-point turn that she almost ran him over. She drove them back towards Porth Enys with a sort of focused fury, making the tyres screech whenever she braked, throwing the Flying 8 around tight bends so that Olivia hit the door time and again with considerable force, and the overgrown hedge flowers and grasses whipped against the car's glossy body as they zoomed down the narrow lanes. Daddy would have a fit, Olivia thought, if only he knew. She thought of him on the train, chugging back upcountry, every minute getting further away.

As they turned down the lane towards Raginnis, they found the road blocked by a knot of official-looking camouflaged vehicles and Estelle swore in vehement French, which Olivia mentally noted down for future use. 'Now what?' her mother said crossly, and drew the car up closer to find out.

A tall man in battered corduroys and a holed jersey detached himself from the crowd and loped over to them. 'Afternoon, missus,' he said.

'Good afternoon, Jago. What's going on?'

'POWs, Mrs Kitto. They brung a contingent of 'em over from St Columb to work on the farm, now the Ministry's demanding higher yields.'

'Prisoners of war?' Estelle looked aghast. 'Working in the fields? Won't they escape?'

Jago laughed. 'We'll keep a good eye on them, don't you worry. Where they going from here at the end of the world? They going to swim to France?'

'Chance would be a fine thing,' Estelle said shortly.

Olivia thrilled at the idea of foreign prisoners, beaten enemy combatants, captured by their own troops. 'Can I see them?' Without waiting for an answer, she flung the passenger door open and ran to where armed soldiers were ushering a small group of men in khaki fatigues out of the trucks.

If she had been expecting horns and hooves or any other denominators of otherness, she was to be disappointed: they looked much like any men, if a bit thinner and shabbier. The POWs looked around at their new surroundings with little interest, and Olivia could hardly blame them for that; they were vanquished and far from home and the Roberts' farm was a sprawling, untidy affair with a big open farmyard strewn with rusting machinery, an austere farmhouse (since the farmer's wife had died it was a bleak place) and a series of ruinous barns and outhouses that ran with rats. Bad luck for them if they were being accommodated there, and knowing how mean Farmer Roberts was, they surely would be. No doubt they'd be tasked with hunting and killing the rats, too. She remembered watching Leo and Nipper and the others baiting lengths of drainpipe with poisoned meat, and bludgeoning the creatures they caught, and shuddered.

Now the last of the prisoners climbed down out of the truck and paused to look around him, taking in the rolling farmland, the distant sea, and the group of onlookers. His skin was a rich chestnut brown and his eyes were bright with curiosity. Olivia sucked in her breath as his gaze passed over her.

'Oi, Darkie, get along!' One of the guards gave him a whack with his rifle and shoved him in the direction of the other POWs. 'You ain't here on holiday!'

A moment later they were herded through the gate and out of sight, and soon after that the soldiers returned to their vehicles and drove off towards Porth Enys. Olivia got back into the car.

'Don't go running off like that!' Estelle said fiercely. 'You're not a little girl any more. I don't want you spending time on the farm now, not with those men stationed up here. You must be careful, do you hear?'

Olivia nodded, but she knew she'd disobey.

Back at the house they were eating a supper of cold cuts from the previous day's extravagant roast dinner – 'a final blow-out!' as Tony Kitto had triumphantly declared, slapping the illicit cut of beef down on the marble slab in the scullery – when the phone rang in the hall. Estelle put down her knife and fork with exaggerated care and said to Olivia, 'Go and see who that is, will you? Call me if it's your father; otherwise say I'm not here.'

Olivia belted down the corridor and grabbed the receiver. 'Good evening,' said the telephonist at the other end of the line. 'Is that Penzance 272?'

Olivia confirmed their number and accepted the incoming call. 'Hello?' she said into the hissing vacuum. After a long moment a female voice said, 'Hello, is that Chynalls? Is Mrs Kitto there? Mrs Estelle Kitto?'

'I'm awfully afraid she's out,' Olivia lied under instruction, in her best telephone voice. 'Might I take a message?'

There ensued another long silence. 'And when is she likely to be back?'

'Oh, not for ages I shouldn't think.'

'I see.' A sigh. 'I was told to ring this number, by Mr Kitto.'

'By Daddy?' Olivia felt herself go hot, then cold. 'I mean, by Captain Antony Kitto? Are you sure? Is he all right? Has something happened to him?'

'Something's happened all right, but not to him,' the other voice said coolly. 'Look, tell Mrs Kitto we'll be on the train to Penzance tomorrow.'

'What?' said Olivia, shocked into rudeness. 'I mean, I beg your pardon? Who'll be on the train?'

'My name is Mrs Ogden, Winnie Ogden, and I'll be bringing Mary on the midday train. It's all arranged. I would give you a number for Mrs Kitto to call back, but there's nothing much left of the house, you see.' She gave a mirthless laugh.

Olivia frowned. 'Sorry? Which house? Where are you?'

'Exeter, dear. Didn't you hear the news? We took a terrible bombing the day before yesterday.' The voice on the other end of the line – Winnie Ogden's (what an awful name) – said with a trace of exasperation, 'Anyway, please just tell Mrs Kitto it's the midday train. Have you got that?'

'Yes,' said Olivia uncertainly, and the line went dead. She stared at the black Bakelite receiver, then dropped it back into its cradle as if it had bitten her.

Her skin prickled. Some deep-seated instinct told her that she had just stumbled upon the cause of her parents' rift this morning, and that her mother was not going to be happy with the message she was about to relay.

Feeling oddly unsteady on her feet, Olivia made her way back to the kitchen, rehearsing her words, gripped by dread that her world was about to change for ever.

5

Becky

BACK AT CHYNALLS I LAY THE LIST ON THE TABLE UNDER
the sharp eyes of the woman in the portrait, who is quite
clearly, now I have met her, a younger version of Olivia.
I regard the strong-jawed young woman blocked out in
bold oils with unexpected affection. In the space of a short
hospital visit she has wormed her way into my heart.

'I promise,' I tell her aloud, 'to do whatever I can for you.'

I have made a big decision on my way back from Truro.
Whatever it takes, I must help Olivia get home. I cannot
have her wither away in a hospital as my poor mother
did. I wonder how I am going to explain my prolonged
absence to Eddie. And then I note that it is not the absence
itself that concerns me. Which is in equal measure interesting
and disturbing.

I look at the list again. It is daunting.

BRICK UP THE CELLAR (TOP PRIORITY)
FIND LOCKET
GIVE GABRIEL REGULAR EXERCISE

BILLS and BANK
INDOOR BATHROOM
DOWNSTAIRS BEDROOM

The first item seems an odd requirement, but Olivia was insistent. 'And DON'T let anyone poke around down there.' I am going to have to find the world's most incurious builder.

Numbers five and six are obviously the most vital tasks to be undertaken in order to get her home, but they are oddly not her first concern. Number three should be fun... not, and as for the locket, it came back into the conversation again and again. Olivia has described it for me in great detail: engraved and with a secret catch on the back that I am not, under any circumstances, to press. I wonder why, then, she has told me about it. Occasionally, while we discussed something else, she would pat her bare neck and give a little wail – *Oh, where is my locket?* – as if for a few peaceful minutes she had forgotten all about it.

It seems the easiest thing to start with. I go from room to room looking for it. For a time I get distracted – unusually, there is a lot of rather good original art on the walls of the house. In the room Olivia has been using as a bedroom there is a striking semi-abstract seascape depicting a line of silver light trapped between dark sea and dark sky as if marking a break where the fabric of the universe has split apart. I look at it for a long time, feeling a degree of connection. It has been executed with a great deal of texture, the wrinkled waves delineated by precise strokes of a palette knife, and a minuscule boat is breasting those textured waves, dwarfed and swamped by them. My heart clenches and tears fill my eyes.

On the opposite wall is a painting of a dark headland against a tumble of clouds, brooding and pent-up, a landscape waiting for a storm to hit. It's not a very restful picture. I'm not sure I'd want it in my bedroom.

In Gabriel's room, miraculously spared from his own abstract displays, there is a large painting of the bay beyond the house, the tranquil symmetry of sea and sky punctuated by the presence of a trawler making its way out to the fishing grounds. It has an eerie quality to it that I can't quite pin down.

Two ghostly spaces on the opposite wall mark where pictures were hung for a long time, then taken down, fairly recently, given the deeper colour of protected wallpaper from their faded surroundings.

I resume my search for the locket upstairs. In the front bedroom that I am using I open the top drawer in the dark wood chest against the wall and am almost knocked sideways by the smell of camphor. Inside is a collection of mothballed jumpers, thermal vests and pairs of hand-knitted socks.

In the wardrobe, I find tweed jackets, shirts and slacks, a pile of practical, flat-soled shoes, garments so sexless as to be ungendered. On top, there is a hat box, but when I lever the top off, I find it empty. In the drawer of the bedside table is a collection of notebooks, biros, a pair of reading glasses in a tooled leather case, batteries, a light bulb, a ball of elastic bands, and a string of dark red beads. The latter I pull out for a closer look. Despite the quest for the locket, Olivia Kitto doesn't strike me as the sort of woman who bothers with feminine fripperies. Is it a necklace? It is too short to go over any but the tiniest head. A bracelet?

It slips over my hand and sits prettily though too loosely on my wrist, the silk tassel that joins the ends hanging down in an ornamental but impractical fashion. I turn my hand, admiring the warmth of the colour against my pale skin, and wonder what it is. When I lift my hand I become aware of a faint smell: spicy, a little resinous. I close my eyes and breathe it in. Sandalwood? Is it a keepsake from a foreign trip? Or a rosary? The word pops into my mind. Rosaries are prayer beads, aren't they? Could Cousin Olivia be Catholic? I've seen no Bible or prayer book anywhere, though I scanned the bookcases with some care, fascinated by her eclectic library. I have always associated Cornwall with Nonconformism – Methodists and chapel folk, sternly opposed to louche behaviour, adornment and anything foreign. Apart from anything else, given Olivia's use of bad language it seems rather unlikely. Whatever it is, I like the silky feel of the beads against my skin. It feels comforting, like a human touch.

In the back bedroom the chests and cupboards are bare and the room has a cold and melancholy feel to it, as if it has not been occupied for decades, since some long-ago tragedy. At the door, I catch a whiff of perfume. *Je Reviens*, the sort Mum wore. I experience a thrill of recognition, followed by something that may be dread. Prickles run down my back. I turn around, gripped by the sensation that someone is watching me, but there's no one there. The scent has faded now, even when, like a dog, I sniff the air. I must have imagined it, been subconsciously thinking about Mum. But Mum has been here, several times: in her letters Olivia called it 'your second home' and said she was always welcome 'if things get too difficult to bear on your own'.

There was no date on that particular letter. I wonder now if it referred to the divorce or if it were more recent and that maybe Mum had confided her illness to Olivia. How strange and upsetting that she may have discussed it with a distant relative and not me.

The box rooms are packed with old furniture and boxes containing old clothes, old curtains, *National Geographic* magazines. No locket.

Down I go again. The bureau in the reading room is stuffed with paperwork. I riffle through it and extract the obvious official letters and demands, of which there appear to be an alarming number. I feel my stomach tightening, even though these debts are not mine. When you have been poor, the sense of impending financial disaster is never far away.

In the little drawers of the bureau I find two beautiful fountain pens, bottles of ink, a packet of charcoal sticks, hard wax and a heavy little paper-embossing press. A sheet of paper on which Olivia has written her name again and again and again, with very slight variations. Was she having some sort of identity crisis? Paperclips and old stamps. No locket.

Gabriel eyes me warily from his cage as I stalk around the sitting room, searching on the bookcase, the television table, the coffee table, behind the television. He bobs on his perch and whistles at me. 'Messy moose key!'

'Messy, certainly.'

I go back into the old woman's temporary bedroom and hunt under the camp bed and through the pile of blankets and clothing, making a mental note to take them all to the cleaners as soon as I have transport. I lift the hurricane lamp. Nothing. The table on which it is set is made up of a metal tray balanced on a chunk of wood. Putting the lamp to one side, I remove the tray, and find that the table-stand is carved on one side with a rough face which gazes up at me out of blind eyes. There is a kind of primitive power in the raw simplicity of its carving. When I turn it round I find it bears a second face, this one high-cheekboned with a long, straight nose and solemn, heavy-lidded eyes. Its expression is quizzical, the lips turned up in a slight smile. The face on the other side is more dour, the brows drawn together, the lips turned down. Is one face male, the other female? Or are the carvings two aspects of the same person? Turning it upside-down, I find the base is hollow and stuffed with paper, but something in its depths rattles. Did Cousin Olivia stash her precious locket in here and forget where she'd put it? I draw out the crumpled-up newspaper and something drops with a thud to the floor.

But it isn't Olivia's locket. It is a large iron key.

I weigh it thoughtfully in my hand, wondering if it has always been inside the table-stand and I am the first in decades to disturb it. It's a fanciful thought, but it's that sort of key. Something about it – its age, the manner in which it has been so carefully hidden – sends a shudder of sensation up my neck, as if I am being watched again. I feel compelled to put it back, and this I do, stuffing the bits of newspaper in after it.

The tassel of the bracelet caresses my hand, as if it approves.

I am just setting the hurricane lamp back on top of the

table when I hear voices, shocking me to the gut. Running out into the corridor towards the sound, I find a pair of large middle-aged men in grubby puffa jackets and baggy jeans taking up a great deal of room in the hallway.

'Ma sent us up to see what you wanted doing.'

Rosie's sons.

I stare past them into the garden, searching for the words to get them out. Saul – the thinner of the two, by a shade – turns to follow my gaze, then grins at me. His teeth are yellow and uneven and his fingers are stained with nicotine: I can smell stale smoke on him at several paces. 'Maybe rebuild the porch, huh?' he says hopefully.

'I think just clear it away.'

They look disappointed.

Ezra stares around the hallway with the sort of expression garage mechanics take on when about to tell you your big end has gone. 'This place is going to take a heck of a lot of work to put it on the market.'

'It's not going up for sale,' I say shortly. 'It just needs a bathroom putting in downstairs for when Olivia comes home.'

Ezra sucks his teeth. 'Bathroom won't come cheap. It'll mean plumbers and qualified electricians and all.'

'Yes,' I agree. 'It's a big job.'

The two men exchange an unreadable glance. Then Saul says, 'I'm sure we can find plumbers and electricians and all.' He grins at me. 'Ma'll never let us hear the end of it if we don't give you some help. She said to be sure to see what we can do. Olivia's practically family.'

'I'll need to get several quotations. It's not my money and it'll need signing off. In considerable detail.' This pair strike me as back-of-the-envelope men, however good their intentions.

Ezra shrugs. 'Better have a good look around then.'

Olivia's instruction gnaws at me, but it would be rude to throw them out when they're trying to help. 'OK,' I say, and they march past me, leaving a smoky trail in their wake: not just cigarettes, but the sweet whiff of something more herbal.

They spend half an hour poking around desultorily, making no notes, taking no measurements. Ezra opens the sitting room door and recoils. 'Fucken hell.' He closes it again quickly.

'Yes, I know,' I say with a sigh.

In the kitchen I suggest I may put a modern cooker in.

Saul raises an eyebrow. 'Ma cooks for Miss Olivia. She likes the old range. 'Tis proper Cornish.'

'It would be easier – for the carers, you know, and for me too.'

'You going to live here, then?'

It seems too complicated to explain that I'll be here while the renovations are being carried out and when Olivia comes home: it's all so nebulous. I am noncommittal. 'Maybe.'

'Bit isolated, isn't it?' Ezra says. 'Bit lonely for a woman on her own.'

His jowly face is impassive, his tone flat. It's an echo of what his father said yesterday: they have probably talked about me.

'Olivia seems happy here.'

'Well, she ent really alone, is she?'

'How do you mean?'

From the drawing room there comes a sudden shriek, then a long whistle, followed by a squawk of, 'Messy moose key! *Blaaack!*'

The two men take no notice.

'Besides,' I go on, 'it's so beautiful here, this stretch of coastline. I love swimming, and walking. I can't wait to get to know it better.'

Saul shakes his head. 'You be careful. Cliffs round here are unstable. Half soil, half stone. Water gets into the soil and they slip, don't they? Coast path is a nightmare. Some woman fell down it last year, just before Kemyel.'

Ezra nods. 'Broke both legs. Had to send in the air ambulance.'

Eventually they seem to get bored. We decide at last that they will, for cash in hand, clear away the rubble of the fallen porch. I help them load the detritus into the back of their flatbed truck, up and down the steep steps with armfuls of it. By the time we have finished we are all filthy, covered in dust and flakes of wood, and I am forty pounds lighter in the purse. I watch their truck roll away down the track, as relieved to see the back of them as to get rid of the rubble, as if they are carrying my sin away. It slipped my mind to tell Cousin Olivia what happened to her porch, and now the porch is gone. I will tell her next time I see her. I have already resolved to hire a car rather than suffer Rosie's terrifying driving, as soon as I find the locket and am able to it take to her.

The light is fading. I glance reflexively towards my left wrist, which always used to bear a watch before the recent acquisition of a smartphone made it redundant... and realize with a start that it no longer bears the little bead bracelet. My stomach lurches. I scan the cleared space in which I stand. If I dropped it out here while helping Ezra and Saul with the rubble then it is surely gone for ever. I run down the steps to the track below, but there is no sign of it. I *have* to find it: it was tucked away in Olivia's drawer like a precious object. I put my head in my hands and give a howl of rage and sorrow. I am a walking disaster area. I cannot be trusted with anything – with mothers or porches or jewellery.

Buck up, Becky! Mum's voice in my head is soothingly calm. *Retrace your steps.*

Back into the house I go. In the room where I found the bracelet, the room I now think of as my bedroom, I scan the wooden floor, the threadbare Turkish rug, the corridor outside, each stair on the way back down. I check the downstairs rooms, the camp bed, blankets, clothing pile, the totem table – no sign. I walk back down the hallway, checking there are no holes into which it can have fallen. At the pair of doors in the corridor opposite the longcase clock I stop. The smell of the men's smoke is strong here, but there's also a trace of something beyond the tobacco and marijuana, something more... foreign which draws me. I try the handle again, without success. Then I reach up to the lintel and my fingers touch something cold and metallic: a key. I suppose it's the logical place to keep it. Even though the bracelet cannot possibly be down there, I unlock the door, flick on the light switch and go down.

The cellar is about twelve feet square and full of boxes, tins, tools, shelves with paint cans on them – everything you would expect to find in such a space. I can't see any obvious reason for bricking it up: there are no cracks in the floor, or the walls, or the ceiling. It's cold down here, really cold, and it smells of damp, and stale smoke, and the sea, and something aromatic that I can't quite place.

Behind the shelf unit there is a door. I thread my arm into the narrow gap and pull on the handle, but it won't open. When pushed it remains solidly closed.

There is, however, a keyhole beneath the handle. A keyhole designed to take a large iron key.

6

Olivia

OLIVIA GLARED ACROSS THE TABLE AT HER UNWANTED guardian. The horrid woman behaved like an aunt but was only a housekeeper. She had been evacuated down here with an infant from the bombing in Exeter. Soon after which Mrs Kitto had been called up to work in London, leaving Olivia in her clutches.

Winnie Ogden fixed her difficult charge with what she considered a maternal look, though it did not come easily. 'Now really, dear, do you need another slice? Remember: a moment on the lips, a lifetime on the hips.'

Olivia was by no means fat, and always hungry. But even if neither had been the case she would have done what she now did, which was to snag a second piece of toast and smear it liberally with butter. Feeling the disapproval of Winnie's gaze upon her, she levered herself semi-upright and stretched across the table for the pot of strawberry jam the older woman had placed just out of reach. Eschewing

75

the jam spoon, she rudely dug her butter knife into it and juggled a whole berry onto her toast. This was her due, she thought. *I am being held captive by enemy invaders.*

Across the table five-year-old Mary gave an exaggerated groan of disgust and rolled her pale blue eyes.

Mrs Ogden tutted. 'You little savage! Did your mother never teach you any manners?' She sniffed. 'I suppose the French have different standards.'

Olivia gave her a death-stare as she swallowed the last of the toast. Then, because she enjoyed provoking Winnie, she said, 'I'm still growing. If I close my eyes and concentrate I can hear my bones creaking as they stretch in the dark. It's just like forcing rhubarb.'

Mary stared at Olivia in horror.

Winnie pursed her lips. 'No need to be fanciful, Olivia. We all have to tighten our belts these days.' She patted her flat stomach complacently.

Yes, thought Olivia, *there's nothing there, is there? Not an ounce of fat, or love, or joy. That's how you'd have the whole world.* It was impossible for her to imagine Mrs Ogden ever having married, made love with a man, given birth. Impossible. She still did not believe there had ever been a Mr Ogden. And if there had been he was probably, judging by his offspring, a hobgoblin.

'When are they arriving?' she asked.

'Afternoon train.' Winnie sighed. 'Wretched creatures. What does Farmer Roberts want with London girls anyway? They won't know one end of a cow from the other.' She gathered the plates and cutlery. 'In the village they said a Land Girl on the farm at Perranuthnoe got herself in the family way. They don't know how to keep their knees together, these city girls. They've got the morals of snakes. I know you have some of your mother's French blood, and goodness only knows what French girls get up to, but don't you dare go fraternizing with them!'

Olivia regarded Winnie's scrawny back murderously. 'It would be jolly hard to fraternize with them, given that they're female. Also, snakes don't have legs.'

Winnie turned, her lips set in a hard line. 'Mary, you may leave the table. Go upstairs and make your bed.' She watched as the child climbed down off the chair and reluctantly left the room. As soon as she was out of earshot, Winnie placed her hands on the table and leaned towards Olivia. 'You think you're better than us, that's your trouble, my girl, but I shall make it my business to teach you otherwise,' she said with quiet menace.

Olivia pushed herself away from the table, taking perverse pleasure from the scrape of the chair legs against the floor. 'You're quite right,' she said beneath her breath. Louder, she said, 'I'll go down to the station with Jago when he goes to fetch them in the car.'

'He'll be taking the cart. They aren't royalty.'

Olivia made a face. 'They'll think we're peasants.'

'They'll just have to take us as they find us.' Winnie cleared the table, denying Olivia the chance at a third slice of bread. 'Besides, you have chores.'

'They won't understand a word Jago says. I can translate for them.'

'They can't expect everyone down here to speak Received Standard. Now get along and make up their beds. Beat the rugs and put water in the ewer. I've cut one of the old towels in half – you give them one each. There isn't any soap: they'll have to get used to our backward country ways.'

She swept out of the room with an armful of crockery. Olivia glared after her. 'It's pure slavery,' she muttered.

Outside in the orchard she took her frustration out on the rug, giving it a thrashing that raised clouds of dust that eddied in the sunlight and made her sneeze. A pair of cats – escapees from the neighbouring farm – watched from a safe distance, eyes narrowed to golden slits, curious as to what their favourite human was doing and hoping she might stop it soon so that she could filch them some bacon rinds. With one particularly solid thwack the beater did exactly what it had been threatening to do from the start, the head splintering away from the handle, to dangle like a dead thing. Olivia looked at it in disgust then threw it aside and loped round the back of the house, past the tumbling nasturtiums, their gay orange and yellow trumpets fat with tiger-striped caterpillars, past the outhouse to where the garden rakes, hoes and apple-pickers were stacked. She selected the sturdiest rake and finished the task with some gusto, imagining Winnie Ogden begging for mercy with each strike – shoulders, bum, backs of legs.

When she looked back towards the house, she saw a face at one of the upstairs windows, watching. Mary: the resident spy. No doubt the tale of the broken carpet-beater would already be on its way to her mother. It was a survival technique the poor thing had acquired to curry favour with a mother who didn't seem to give two hoots for her, but it didn't endear her to Olivia.

There must be more to life than household chores and

running errands, something more challenging, more exciting. She imagined Mummy up in London, the collapsed
buildings and running people, the fire sirens and stretcher
bearers, the searchlights and the shrill of falling bombs
with a sort of horrible thrill. Oh, for some adventure, for
that sense of a life lived on the bright edge between the
daily grind and dark extinction. It was so dull down here.
Nothing ever happened. Perhaps, Olivia thought with
a gleam of hope, she'd be allowed to go up and join her
mother. She might get a job at the bank and wear a suit and
shoes with heels, and a little hat adorned with a feather like
Mummy, not the handknitted tam Winnie made her wear
everywhere to contain her unruly mop.

Bolstered by this pleasant fantasy, she whipped through
the rest of her chores, waited till Mrs Ogden was engaged
in some business with the warden, and slipped out of the
house and away down the lane, where she waited at the
junction for Jago to come by with the cart.

'Mistress din't say nuthin' bout thee coming.' Jago
squinted at her suspiciously. She hated it when he called
Winnie that. Still, she smiled her most winning smile and
produced a small bar of Bournville, which she had been
keeping for just such an occasion. The horse nickered with
interest, straining its head towards her. Olivia rubbed its
nose with her free hand. 'Sorry, old thing. Next time, eh?'

Jago's eyes gleamed as he took the chocolate from her.
Then he tapped his nose. 'Not a word, eh, bird?'

'Loose lips sink ships.'

They laughed. It was one of Winnie's favourite sayings.
Olivia hopped up beside him.

'Toovum furriners?'

Most Cornish folk were content to use this term for those who came from beyond the natural border of the River Tamar. Jago applied it to anyone who came from east of Camborne.

Olivia nodded. 'Yes. I don't know their names. Tuppence and Ha'penny?'

Jago grinned, his teeth dark with Bournville. 'Fatty and Nora?'

They made up names for the Land Girls all the way to the station. Olivia's favourite was Dandelion and Burdock, which Jago had rudely rendered as Piss-Pants and Sticky Bobs, the local names for these plants. Olivia was still giggling as they trotted along the seafront at Penzance, even as she thrilled at the idea of being in the presence of people who came from where her mother was working, who might even have met her, been served by her in the bank. And there was no difficulty identifying the two Land Girls amongst the homecomers and the men in uniform, who eyed Olivia with more curiosity than her Aertex shirt and baggy shorts warranted. They stood looking around uncertainly outside the station: one of them tall and willowy with elaborately sculpted blonde hair, a slick of scarlet lipstick and a pair of heeled shoes; the other a short girl with a cloud of brown curls.

'Shoulda bet on Fatty and Nora,' Jago said unkindly.

Olivia snorted, and ran over to them. 'Are you the Land Girls for Treharrow Farm?'

The dumpy one grinned, showing a wide gap between her teeth. 'Hello, ducks. I'm Beryl Hopkins and this is Marjorie Allison.' The blonde inclined her head but didn't say a word, as if she deigned to speak only to aristocracy. Olivia took an instant dislike to her.

'I'm Olivia Kitto. You'll be staying at my house – Chynalls, in Porth Enys. That's a Cornish name, though there's hardly anyone speaks Cornish any more. Chynalls means the house on the cliff, and Porth Enys means the port of the island! It's just below the farm so it'll be easy for you to get to work. And this is Jago Sparrow, and the horse is Nell. One of you can sit up with Jago and the other one can come in the back with me. It's not too grubby, honest.'

Marjorie stared in disbelief at Jago and the cart, clearly feeling she had stepped into the Middle Ages. 'I shall sit up front,' she declared to Beryl. 'You can go in the back with the... girl.' Walking past Olivia, she handed her bags to Jago as if he were a porter at the Ritz and climbed up, with Jago eyeing her neat bottom for longer, Olivia thought, than was strictly necessary.

'Righty-ho,' said Beryl. She hefted her own bags into the cart and jumped up after them. 'Dad's a coalman. Bit of dirt dun' bother me.' She stared around at the view. The air was so clear you could see as far as the Lizard to the east and Penlee Head to the west, the sea glittering with spangled light. 'Ain't never seen so much bloomin' water in all me bloomin' life,' she said, wide-eyed, and Olivia grinned, proud that her home was showing itself off to its best advantage, decked out in its finest cerulean blue and gold.

'My mother's working up in London, on Threadneedle Street, do you know it?' she asked Beryl as they took the hill towards Gwavas.

Beryl grinned. 'That's the city. I come from Lewisham.'

This was disappointing. 'What's the bombing been like? Mummy doesn't tell me much: I don't think she wants me to worry.'

'Not too bad at the moment, ducks – I reckon our boys have seen 'em off. I got a young man in the RAF, not flying, but ground crew, and he tells me all sorts.'

'Beryl.' A sharp rebuke from the front seat.

'Oh for heaven's sake, Marj, it's not like she's a Jerry spy, is it?'

'Loose lips. And don't call me Marj, it's common.'

Beryl rolled her eyes conspiratorially at Olivia. 'Miss Hoity-Toity,' she mouthed.

Olivia determinedly imagined 'Marj' shovelling cowshit up at the farm, and smiled.

They passed the quarry and the workers' cottages at Roskilly, trotted briskly through the village, where heads turned to watch them, details registered to pass on to family and neighbours, and took the steep hill towards Chynalls. As they neared the junction something shot across the lane in front of them, making Nell shy so that the cart skittered sideways. Marjorie gave a terrified yelp as Jago hauled on the reins and brought the horse under control. Olivia clambered over the luggage to see what had caused the kerfuffle, and there was Mamie, Farmer Roberts' little girl, sitting on the other side of the track, howling. Her knees were grazed and there was goosegrass in her hair.

Olivia jumped out of the cart and ran to Mamie, brushing her tears away, pulling the goosegrass off her. She took her hands in her own but Mamie pulled them away and kept wailing.

'What is it? Tell me. Did someone hurt you? Did you fall over? Did someone push you? Tell me and I'll thump them for you.'

Mamie gazed up at Olivia shyly, then gave her a wobbly

smile. She dug in a pocket and held something out on her palm. A Callard & Bowser toffee.

'Who gave you this, Mamie? Was it Leo, or Nipper?'

Mamie's little black eyes widened. She threw the toffee at Olivia, leaped up and took off running.

Olivia glanced back at the cart to see Marjorie's pencilled eyebrows arched in disdain, Beryl with her hands to her mouth, Jago frowning. 'I'll make sure she gets home safely,' she said, and belted after Mamie. Best not to arrive with the Land Girls anyway, given Mrs Ogden's prohibition.

She gazed both ways at the junction, uphill towards the farm, down towards the village, but there was no sign of Mamie in either direction. The girl had a knack for disappearing and she knew every hedgerow and pathway, every hiding place and animal track, which was why Olivia was concerned. Someone had upset her. She decided to walk up to the farm.

It was late afternoon and the sun was dipping, but its heat had banked itself up in the earth; it made the air in the narrow road fuggy and hard to breathe, charged the lively hedgerows, the singing birds and bright foxgloves, which leaned out on either side like an honour guard. Olivia both loved and hated the countryside around Porth Enys. It was familiar and beloved, the changes brought by the seasons intimately known to her, documented with every step. She knew when the elderflower came out and passed over, when the briar rose blossomed and honeysuckle twined; when the wheatears and swallows arrived and when they flew the scene. She knew the best places to lie in wait to watch fox cubs play and baby rabbits lollop out of their burrows; where the badgers made their holts, where the weasels looped and ran. She knew where the setting sun spread its rosy light upon the sea; she knew the secret ways down to hidden coves and sunbathing spots along the coast. To see her beaches now rimmed with barbed wire, the pillbox at the end of the Crackers, to watch young men – important and soldierly with their guns and binoculars – marching all over her beloved places made her both furious and sad. They were supposed to be there to guard against invasion, and yet to Olivia their very presence was an invasion.

Of course no one else saw it quite the same way. That was also why she hated being here. Here, many people tended to look no further than their noses, became incensed about tiny things, were fascinated by other people's business, and on the lookout for nasty rumours rather than good news. Some people were warm and kind and helpful, but others were sharp-tongued and prescriptive, always harking back to some nostalgic 'better time' when people were nicer, days were longer, bread was cheaper and cream creamier and the place wasn't overrun by foreigners.

After Dunkirk, Robbie Borlase and Jethro Sparrow, Jago's nephew, along with Jeremiah, his son, had gone down to Falmouth to watch the French refugees come in to harbour. They'd gleefully taken spoiled food meant for the pigs with them and had boasted on their return to any who would listen, 'We give 'em a right good pelting.' Robbie had sought her out to beg some 'Frog language' off her before they went, knowing her mother's provenance. ' "Lâche, lâche!" ' we yelled at 'em,' they'd told her the next day, proud of their stand. 'Damn cowards, leaving our brave boys to die defending their own bleddy soil that they all up and left, running like rabbits.'

Jethro added, 'They can fucken go back to their own country. We don't want 'em. They shoulda stayed and fought rather than come begging here. They was supposed to be our allies, fighting Hitler and all. Now they'll come and live in houses that should go to proper Cornish and eat food we can't spare. Fucken furriners.'

'Fucken bastards,' six-year-old Jem had echoed gleefully.

Olivia had been shocked. 'But they're escaping the Nazis. We're offering them sanctuary – they're refugees!'

'We got enough a them a'ready, fucken emmets.' The village had welcomed an entire Jewish school from London's East End.

But she was only a girl: what did they care for her views? They just laughed at her and called her unpatriotic, which had incensed her. 'Well, you're blasted idiots!' she had shouted after them, unable to use the forbidden word and knowing it to be an inadequate response. Shortly after this, on their eighteenth birthdays, the two older lads had enlisted in the navy and soon after Jethro had been lost when his cruiser had gone down, torpedoed in the Mediterranean. Witnessing the grief of his family at the remembrance service, Olivia had regretted her outburst. Eighteen was too young to die, for your country or anything else. But another part of her whispered that at least Jethro had got to see something of the outside world she was so hungry to glimpse for herself.

There was still no sign of Mamie when she reached Treharrow. The cows were out in the big field, black-and-white shapes moving placidly against a carpet of green; beyond them a tractor moved in the potato field, dragging the haulm topper behind it. Soon the harvesting would begin: one of the reasons the Land Girls had been drafted in. They'd be kitted out with wellies and potato sacks and set to work. She hoped to heaven she didn't get sent up here too. It was this thought that kept her from knocking on the door at the farmhouse to ask if Mamie had come home; besides, she had an idea she knew where the girl might hide. Skirting the farm buildings, Olivia ran behind the byre, making for the leafy footpath that led down the steep hillside towards the coast path. In the hedge beside the wildflower meadow there was a hollow in the roots of the hazels that was Mamie's favourite den.

Olivia crept along the hedge, ducked through the gap into the meadow and came quickly to the den, but it was immediately clear when she knelt and stared in that Mamie wasn't there. Inside was a bizarre collection of objects. A candle stub in a painted tin, a box of matches, a little pile of wrapped sweets, a potato sack used as a carpet, and a small wooden doll. Olivia picked it up and took it out into the sunlight for a better look.

In an almost uncanny echo of Mamie herself, its face was carved wide and flat, its mouth curved up in a sweet smile. It wore a neatly sewn dress of pale cambric. Looped around its neck and body, like a crossed bandolier, was a string of dark red beads joined by a silk tassel.

Across the field, in the shadow of the elm, the man watched as Olivia emerged from the hollow with the doll in her hands. He was struck by the intense concentration of her downturned gaze as she turned the object around in her hands, ran her fingers down the carved face and along the beads. He held his breath. Would she take it away? Would he have to go after her to take it back? It struck him that he did not want to do that and yet he might have to. And so he stood there, invisible, balancing on the balls of his feet, his muscles trembling with intent.

Then she bent and replaced the doll inside the hollow. He watched her stand there for a long moment looking back inside the little shrine, then turn and walk back the way she had come, her expression thoughtful.

7

Becky

THE IRON KEY HIDDEN INSIDE THE CARVED TOTEM FITS the lock in the door from the cellar to the tunnel with fairytale ease. With mounting excitement, I click on the torch app on my phone, open the door and shine the cool beam into the void. It illuminates a flat area that runs for a few feet, but after that the darkness is impenetrable. I wedge the door open with a heavy tin of what must be paint, though it has lost its label, irrationally terrified that it may somehow close behind me, then scuff along the flat section, playing the beam of the torch in all directions to make sure I don't fall down an unseen hole, or knock myself out on an outcrop of rock.

I can see that the tunnel is not a natural feature – there are the marks of tools – it must have been mined as an escape route from the house or a secret ingress up from the cove. As I step down something catches me painfully on the shoulder, and I yelp. I pat at the rock and compacted earth and feel the protuberance: thin and cold and hard. A spiky little stone, it comes away in my hand. Without thinking much about it, I stow it away in my jeans pocket, a little keepsake of my adventure.

Down I go, feeling the darkness gather at my back like a cold weight. And, God, it is really cold down here, the sort of chill that goes right to the marrow of you. It's probably just what comes of being in a lightless place where sea-ethers and seeping water permeate, but it feels a bit uncanny: all the little hairs on the back of my neck are stirring.

I think about rockfall, about getting trapped down here; I think about tripping and falling down all those steps; I think about someone entering the house, moving the paint pot and closing the cellar door against me.

So often in the past years I have opted not to do things. I have not braved the world. I have hidden myself away, avoided sex with the lights on, looked away from mirrors. I have even hidden from my own creativity. I have not picked up a paintbrush in years. I have been in the studio only to watch Eddie sitting at the wheel, moulding clay to his will, and even this quiet skill seemed to me like oppression. But getting on the train down here was a turning point: I am taking back some control over my life. I press on through the narrow cave, squeezing past the pinch point, and at last emerge into the clear light of the cove.

Feeling light-headed with relief, I dance a kind of victory dance, stamping my feet on the shingle, kicking bits of seaweed here and there, twirling round and round with my phone held high in triumph. Now, the beach really is mine, and mine alone. I have private, secret access to it, albeit rather dark and scary access.

And there is the sea, sparkling and turquoise, the waves lapping in with tender invitation, and in a sudden access of daring I strip down to my knickers and run across the beach, across the painful pebbles to where the wet sand squelches between my toes, and into the shallows, sucking in my breath at the change of temperature, lifting my knees high, then launching myself forward in a clumsy half-dive. I laugh in shock: the water is heart-stoppingly cold. My breath comes in a series of stutters as my whole body seems to constrict, and then I am swimming, my arms and legs moving jerkily, buoyed up by the Cornish sea.

Such a sense of freedom! I tread water, laughing out loud. I have taken myself by surprise. I am capable of more than I had thought, stronger and wilder than I knew. I swim up and down, making my muscles work and my limbs coordinate. I turn onto my back and let the sun bathe my face and torso, trusting the sea to keep me afloat. Despite everything, at this moment in time I am still alive, still myself. Rebecca Young. Daughter to lost parents, sometime artist, sometime lover. I resolve to go down into the village this afternoon to call Eddie. I may even invite him down here…

No, I won't. Even as the thought occurs, I shoo it away. For now, until Olivia returns, Chynalls is my special place. I do not want Eddie coming down and spoiling it. Besides, he has his show coming up. He would think me mad even to suggest it.

I flip over… and become aware of a dark head a few feet away from me. Another swimmer, in my cove? But no, it's a dog, a black dog. I paddle my legs, turning to look for its owner, but there is no one on the beach, and when I complete the circle the dog has vanished. I must be seeing things. But then the head pops up again, closer, and I see it is a seal. Sun gleams off its mottled, glossy head and its large black eyes. Its gaze radiates cheerful curiosity. Then it slips beneath the water and a moment later I feel it brush against my belly, a cool, slick touch that seems to convey friendliness and the wish to play, yet not to upset my equilibrium.

My whole body becomes a smile. I take a breath and duck my head underwater and open my eyes in the strange green light and there she is, waiting for me. We swim little circles around one another, the seal graceful and strong, and I feel graceful and strong as I match her, until at last she suddenly refines her bodyshape and torpedoes away from me, and that is the end of our game. I am sad, but swollen with delight. I kick to the surface and am just about to strike back towards the shore when I hear a shout, and looking back I see a small boat, its outboard motor burbling as it slows. There are two men in it. They are shouting at the seal, swearing at it, driving it off. And then they see me, and they stop. I recognize them as Saul and Ezra, Rosie and Jem's sons, and the strength starts to go out of me. All of a sudden I can feel the tiredness in my muscles. Panic starts to make me heavy, awkward, less buoyant. I thrash the water, swallow a huge mouthful of burning seawater, snort and choke and begin to sink. I force my arms into an ugly crawl, heading back to the beach slowly, so bloody slowly. Pride drives me on, pride and vulnerability.

At last the seabed scours my toes. Another stroke and I am able to stand with the water rippling against my chin. I turn to watch the boat. It has not moved. Ezra and Saul are still watching me. What are they doing out there? I see no fishing rods. Are they towing lines for mackerel? Are they checking crab or lobster pots? It must be something fish-related if they were trying to drive the seal off, I reason.

The boat bobs up and down with the waves. They must

have turned off the outboard motor, as if they are waiting for something. Perhaps they are waiting to watch me emerge. I think about my pale body in its clinging underwear and my teeth start to chatter, great shudders of cold running through me. What matters more – saving myself from hypothermia or guarding my modesty? *Get a grip, Becky*, I tell myself in the voice of my mother. *Walk out of the sea and put your shirt on. What does it matter what they think?*

Turning my back on the boat, I start to walk to the shore. The water drags at me, reluctant to let me go. I forge forward till the sea lies at my waist, the breeze chill on my shoulders, and I shove my way through the waves till I am clear and walk as quickly as I can without breaking into a run. I swipe up my clothes, shrug my shirt on over my head, cursing myself for not having undone the buttons before taking it off. It sticks to my wet skin, rucks up over my chest and I haul it down hard, glad that it is baggy enough to cover my knickers and skim my thighs, which are drying in the breeze, prickly with salt. I turn to face the sea and the boat is still there, just beyond the necklace of rocks guarding the cove. I wrestle my jeans back on and zip them up and feel armoured once more.

'I hope you enjoyed the show!' I yell, knowing the sound will never carry as far as the boat. I hope they detect my anger. I hope they see they have not cowed me. I aim my phone at them and snap a photo.

I decide not to return to the house via the cave. Not wanting to surrender my piece of secret knowledge to the onlookers, I take the earth steps up to the sea gate. By the time I reach the track there is no sign of the boat.

Inside the house I heat water in the scullery and have

a stand-up wash in the copper bath to get the salt off. I dunk my head and have to use the yellow bar of soap I have found for shampoo. It stinks of bitumen, the hot, nose-stinging smell of road mending. I wonder what it will do to my hair, but remarkably it leaves it glossy and tangle-free.

The wardrobe in my room renders up a Guernsey sweater in thick blue wool. Moths have been at it, but the holes aren't too noticeable; besides, there is no one here to see me. I drag it out, and turn with the jersey under my arm. The long mirror on the inside of the wardrobe door throws my image at me. There is little worse in life than being caught unawares by your reflection, before you've made the small adjustments all women make – I have avoided mirrors for so long that I have forgotten to look out for them – and there I am, thin and white and strangely shaped with concavities where there should be curves, ugly purple marks and puckers of skin where it should be smooth.

Shocked anew at the carnage, I trace the scars left by my treatment. A double mastectomy and lymphadenectomy. This small round lump just beneath my collarbone my implanted chemo port; this dark mark where the drain exited (I can still remember the crawling sensation of it being drawn out again, wormlike, foreign). I did not opt for reconstruction: it seemed to me then a pointless distraction from the matter of life or death, a foolish vanity. I did not want fat carved off my belly or buttocks or back. I did not want fake nipples sewn or tattooed onto me. I think my mind was not in the right place at the right time to make these decisions, being still awash with primal fear.

And now I am afraid again, afraid of the 'something' that

has been seen on my latest scan. Afraid of the kindness in my consultant's voice, carefully calibrated not to scare me away. Afraid of the possibility in my tenuous future of the words 'recurrence' and 'incurable', maybe even 'terminal'. I am three hundred miles from London, having run as far away from it all as I can without falling off the edge of the world.

I take in my reflection, this sexless patchwork of a woman, remembering the first time Eddie saw me after the surgery, how he could not disguise his horror and repulsion. He had always loved my breasts – like apples, like peaches, he would say as he kissed them, gathering them into his hands. He used to draw me naked. He was not a fine draughtsman, but he had a good sense of form, as you'd expect of a potter. Those soft pencil sketches showed someone female, proportionate, seductive. The breasts were lovingly rendered, shaded to give a sense of mass and heft, while the face remained sketchy – profile, eyes downcast, hair curling around the shoulders. Everywoman.

I turn and the light strikes me full on and gilds the surfaces, smoothing the imperfections, showing that my scars are less livid. And suddenly I see myself with a painter's eye: the form has a certain elegance to it, interesting, beguiling even, suggesting a withholding of self, a house of secrets. I press my fingers gently against my skin and feel no lumps beyond the familiar scar tissue, but what do fingers know? They are not scanning devices. And yet the fear is diminishing as a thought begins to take hold and I start to see how I might draw myself. It is a little shocking, but exciting. It is something I would never have thought to do before. My mind wanders to the discovery of the packet of charcoal sticks. Some other artist has been here before me. I wonder who it was?

Creativity is a curious thing. For years I took my own for granted. It defined me, gave me the personality I always felt I lacked. I would paint or sketch every day, fitting it in around the necessities of getting by in a city that cost too much to live in. When I was working, in a succession of temping jobs, I would get up early, taking sketchbook and pencils with me on the train to arrive at the river while the dawn light slicked the surface and the birds sang all around me. I would draw early morning mudlarks scanning the low-tide shores, the way the light shone through the canyons of the City's towers. I found lost gardens and drew them through the bars on the gates that shut me out of them. I drew birds courting, and sly cats lying in oblongs of sunlight on backstreet pavements. I drew reflections on the river and the dazzle of sun-freighted air filtered through cherry blossom. And then I would pack my drawing things away – all the visions of the delicacy and dreams – and trudge to the tyranny of work. By the time the financial crash hit and there were no temping jobs to be found, I had squirrelled away a reasonable sum, enough to tide me over for a few months. That summer, I gave myself over to painting, taking buses all over London to pockets of untouched parkland, to bird sanctuaries and commons. I painted people picnicking on Primrose Hill and swimming at the Ladies' Pond on the Heath. I painted statuary in Highgate Cemetery and fallen angels in Nunhead. I met other artists and exhibited with them. I sold some paintings, each time feeling such disbelief and wash of gratitude towards the purchaser that I wanted to halve the price, or give my work away. I ploughed my profits into new canvases and paints. It was during the last month of my freedom that I exhibited at the art fair and met Eddie. And everything changed.

For a while it was like being in a dream, all life's edges blurred into soft focus, except that Eddie was in centrefield and sharp focus, blocking everything else out of my view, with his flag of black hair falling across his forehead, the sharp curve of his lips, his wild energies and single-minded creativity, desperately seductive.

I take my phone and go in search of a signal. There is none in the house. I go out into the garden and hold the phone high. Not a single bar of reception. I consider heading for higher ground but the woodland behind Chynalls looks dense and unwelcoming. I will go down into the village, where I can also ask about good workmen capable of undertaking Olivia's project.

The village of Porth Enys was once described by an eminent poet as the loveliest in England, and you can see why. Its cottages cluster around three sides of an oval harbour in which boats bob on sparkling water and children play on the crescent of golden beach. Take away the cars and dress the people in period costume and it could be a snapshot of a bygone age. But then your eye is drawn by the bright kayaks ranged against the harbour wall, the defibrillator unit on the wall of the harbourmaster's office, the brightly coloured plastic buckets and spades outside the shop.

The next day, at the railing overlooking the harbour, at last I get a signal and suddenly missed call notifications cascade across the screen. Eddie, Eddie, Eddie. All from Eddie

– I spot a curt *Where are you, Becks?* and then *WHERE THE HELL ARE YOU*, all caps, no punctuation. I delete them all. I am so tempted to take the coward's way out and text him. But conscience won't let me. I call him. It rings and rings, then: 'Yes?'

'It's Becks.'

'I can see that from Caller ID. Where the bloody hell are you?'

'Cornwall. I told you, in my messages.'

'You know I never bother picking up messages when I'm working. If it's something important people always call back. But you didn't!'

'I didn't have a signal—'

'Don't be ridiculous, Becky, you can always get a signal. It's not the bloody moon!'

'I'm at my Cousin Olivia's. There's no signal there. I—'

'Who the fuck is Cousin Olivia?'

I explain the situation and there follows a long silence. Then Eddie says, 'I need you *here*.'

For a moment, I am engulfed by warmth. Eddie has never admitted to needing me.

'So when are you coming back? The house is a mess, and there's nothing in the fridge. You know it's my show next week and I need you here!'

His peremptory tone puts my back up. 'Sorry, I'm going to miss it. She's in hospital. The old lady.'

'Well, I'm sure she's being perfectly well looked after there, whereas I'm bloody starving, living off crisps!'

'Christ, Eddie, she's ninety-two and she's broken her leg and they're threatening to put her in a home unless she modernizes her house.'

'I've never even heard you mention her before. How do I know you're not just making her up? Whereas I—'

'Whereas you are unbelievably selfish! I don't exist solely for your convenience, you know.'

There is a pause. I have shocked him. Indeed, I have shocked myself.

'Oh, Becks, I've been so worried about you, I've hardly been able to concentrate on the show at all.'

For an instant, I almost believe he's sincere. But then I feel my heart grow a fine, hard layer of shell. 'I'm sure you'll manage. I mean, we live next door to a kebab shop – you're hardly going to starve, are you?'

'But when—'

'I have to go – you're breaking up.' The last thing I hear as I close the connection is my name, uttered on a rising wail. I have to admit to a little frisson of pleasure. I always felt Eddie was too good for me – too handsome, too successful, too confident. I've gone through paroxysms of anxiety that he will a) cheat on me, b) leave me c) get knocked down by a bus or d) get a terminal illness. Now, I experience an unexpected sense of freedom.

A seagull screeches overhead and when I look up I am dazzled by the golden light haloing its wings against the sky; and all at once Cornwall saves me.

'Chynalls, you say?' The woman behind the counter at the general store and post office is a middle-aged blonde with a sharp haircut and kind eyes.

'Yes, up at the top of the hill.'

'I don't know any house by that name, lovey.'

'Olivia Kitto's place,' I prompt.

'Oh, you mean the Cliff House! You must be her cousin from London, right?'

Goodness, I think, nothing is secret in a village. I can imagine Rosie coming in every day for milk and bread and a natter, trading gossip as she picks up her pension. 'That's right.' Suddenly I feel guarded. 'She needs a bathroom put in for her when she comes out of hospital: she's only got an outdoor loo at the moment.'

The woman laughs. 'That generation: tough as nails! Imagine living all this time with an outdoor loo!' She shakes her head. 'That's quite a big job. I'd recommend Chris George normally but he's off in the Seychelles at the moment. Not much good to you if you need something doing now. How about trying Jeff Holmes? I've heard he's very reliable. Not cheap, but reliable.'

'Not Ezra and Saul Sparrow, then?' I ask and she bends forward at the waist as if the force of her amusement has winded her. 'Oh, no,' she says. 'Not Saul and Ezra.'

I take down the number for Jeff Holmes.

On the noticeboard outside, among the adverts for t'ai chi, crafting classes and the farmer's market there is a printed card advertising a general builder and plumber: 'Let us solve your problem. No job too small'. Someone has written something below this and someone else has crossed this out in biro. I gaze at the scribble and make out the scratched-out remark. 'Go home Paki. Leave means leave!'

I feel so incensed I take down the number and call it right away.

★

Jeff Holmes is the first to turn up. 'Blimey, lead pipes, bird.' He scratches his head. 'That's a heller job. They'll all need replacing. I never seen anything like it since doing up my nan's place.'

'But it's possible?'

'Well, yes, but I'm very busy. I can probably fit you in around... November?'

I stare at him. 'November? But my cousin's in hospital and can't be discharged till she has facilities at home.'

He looks vaguely guilty but determined to stick to his story. 'Sorry, got a lot of work on. I could pencil you in in case we get a cancellation.' We agree on this, though I know we are just going through the motions, and off he goes, whistling, relieved to escape.

Dejection edges in. Of course it is going to be a nightmare. No one appears to have touched the house for a century. It's probably a job only for a property developer, someone with plenty of ready cash and their own workmen. What have I got myself into? Rather than give in to despair, I visit Gabriel with a peace offering of the grapes Olivia rejected. He glares at me balefully from his cage. 'If I let you out you have to promise me you'll go back in again without a fight,' I tell him. He bobs his head as assent, but I suspect it's to get a better view of the grapes. 'Go on then.' I open the door and he hops onto his doorstep, ruffling his feathers as if preparing for flight.

'Ala, ala,' he says and gives a soft whistle. 'Esme hand.'

'I haven't the faintest idea what you're on about,' I tell him.

He gives me a sardonic look, then steals the grape and

flaps off to the bookcase. 'If you stayed you could've had three grapes,' I tell him.

I refill his water and seeds and make a solemn vow to take on the cleaning of the room while he regards me haughtily, then tucks into his treat as if to demonstrate that one grape in the talon is worth more than two in my hand.

I am still grinning as I shut the door on him and walk out into the hall to find a figure peering through the stained glass. I can't help but give a little yelp. The figure takes a step back. I remember the postcard, and hurry to open the door.

'I did not mean to alarm you.' His brown eyes are wary.

I offer my hand. 'I'm Rebecca Young,' I say.

'Reda,' he replies, taking my hand. Then he places his other hand on his chest and gives a tiny bow, strangely courtly. 'Reda Medjani.'

'You're the builder I called?'

'I'm the plumber and general builder. My brother Mo is in charge but he is working in Penzance at the moment.' His English is clear but accented. He sounds French, looks Mediterranean.

I like him immediately. He is polite and solemn and goes from room to room, making notes, quiet and thorough. I take him down to the cellar and explain Olivia's instructions to brick it up. He shakes his head, puzzled. 'Why would she want to do that?' He touches the wall, examines his fingers. 'It seems dry: a good place for storage.' He looks around. 'I would have thought it a useful addition to the house.'

'I think she's concerned about safety,' I say. 'There's some instability in the area.'

He raises his eyebrows. 'I doubt shutting the cellar up

will solve that.' But he goes around, looking at the floor, the ceiling, making pencilled notes. 'We could put acrow props in, and then breeze-block up the doorways if that's really what she wants. But I wouldn't have thought it's your top priority.'

We go back upstairs, which feels a relief after the chill of the cellar. There's something oppressive about it – maybe just the idea of the whole weight of the house bearing down above me, maybe I have claustrophobia. Reda takes out a laser measuring device and goes to make more detailed notes on the required conversion, so rather than spy on him I take myself off to strip the guano-encrusted covers from the sofa in what I know I regard as Gabriel's room, under the watchful eye of the parrot, who has miraculously allowed me to entice him back into his cage. I will wash the covers by hand as a first step, I decide: too shameful to hand them over to a laundry in their current state. I take the filthy bundle outside into the garden and shake the covers out, careful to be upwind of the noxious dust clouds that billow off them. I leave them to detoxify in the sun and go back in, almost walking right into Reda, since the contrast between the sunlight and the interior has rendered me half blind. From his fingers dangles the lost bracelet.

'I found this,' he says. 'It looked as if it had been lost.'

It is such a relief to see it again that I all but snatch it from him and close my fingers over it. As I hold it a wave of warmth suffuses me, as if someone has told me all will be well, that all bad things will pass like a storm, that the sunshine will return. I hug it against my breastbone, smelling its faint, reassuring scent, then slip it back over my wrist.

When I look up he's watching me curiously. 'You are Muslim?'

The question is so unexpected I burst out laughing. 'No, why?'

'That's a *misbaha*.'

I am none the wiser.

'Muslim prayer beads,' he explains. 'They look very old, beautifully made. It's hard to find such nice ones nowadays.'

'They belong to my cousin, the old lady who lives here.'

'Is she Muslim?'

I wrinkle my brow. 'No...' How odd. Then I remember something. 'But she's well travelled. She mentioned that she had walked in the Sahara.'

His eyes become curves of shining light. 'She sounds like a remarkable person. May I?' He reaches out and takes my hand in his, turns it to examine the beads. A warm thrill runs through me and I feel myself blush. 'Imagine,' he says, 'how much work went into the making of this *misbaha*. How much love and attention. We have lost the ability to craft things in the modern world. No one has the time any more, or the money to pay for that time. Where I come from there is still a strong artisanal culture. People still make things and pride themselves on the perfection of their craft. But it's becoming a dying art even there.'

'Where's there?'

'Just outside Oujda.'

I have to admit I have no idea where Oujda is.

'In the north of Morocco,' he informs me. 'My family are still there and across the border in Algeria.'

'Do you see them often?'

'The Moroccan cousins, yes, but it's more complicated to

see my Algerian family – the border has been closed since the sixties.' He looks away, suddenly shy.

'What brought you to Cornwall?' I ask. Who is this unfamiliar woman, falling into easy conversation with a stranger?

'Oh, this and that,' he says, eyes on his notepad. 'Family, mainly.' I follow his gaze, half-expecting to see his notes running from right-to-left in the Arabic way. But instead his writing is neat and even upside down I can pick out such English words as *pipes* and *drains*.

'I've come down from London,' I say, pushing my envelope, but just then his phone rings. Goodness, a handsome, apparently capable, plumber with phone signal!

'I have to go,' he says after exchanging a few words in a language I do not recognize and closing the call. 'Look after that *misbaha*. I'll text you an estimate. We'll do a separate one for the conversion and the plumbing, and one for the cellar work.'

'You think it's all possible then?'

'Everything is possible. It will require hard labour but Mo and I are not afraid of that.'

'And if I accept your quote when could you start?'

He gives me the most devastating smile. 'Right away.'

As I watch him pick his way back down the path my thumb plays over the smooth wood of the *misbaha*'s beads and it feels as if a missing piece of the jigsaw of the world has been fitted back into the puzzle, bringing the whole design together.

My good mood continues until I get ready for bed that

evening. When I peel off my jeans something falls out onto the floor – a stone. The one I found a few days ago, that poked me in the shoulder as I made my way down the tunnel from the cellar.

It is a sort of off-white, a couple of inches long. I bend and pick it up and peer at it curiously. It is lighter than I had expected, and smoother too. It feels rather nice as I run my thumb down it. Until it flexes, then bends in the middle.

Pebbles are not jointed. Pebbles do not articulate.

A crab claw, I tell myself. That's what it must be.

But crab claws are pink, aren't they? Or is that only when they're cooked?

I know it is not a crab claw. I drop the object as if it is fire-hot. It lies on the threadbare Turkish rug pointing accusingly towards me.

It's a bone. A finger bone. A human finger bone.

My mind runs in frantic circles, jabbering crazily. There are human remains in the tunnel under the house. Is it part of a skeleton? Is it ancient, historic? It is rather disgusting, but also rather fascinating. I wonder if there's a local museum I can take it to for dating.

Then I remember Olivia's instruction to BRICK UP THE CELLAR and I go cold from the crown of my head to the pit of my stomach.

Oh, Olivia. What have you done?

8

Olivia

1943

THE SUMMER WAS PASSING EXTREMELY SLOWLY, AND
Sundays were the worst. Olivia hated Sundays. Who on
earth thought it was a good idea to have a day of rest and
then make you get up early to go to church?

For a long time she lay in her narrow bed contemplating
exactly how much trouble she would be in if she sneaked
off through the sea gate for a swim. It was so tempting.
Sunlight was piercing the edge of the blackout blind: it was
going to be hot. Her mind wandered to her conversation
with Mummy on Friday evening. Just three minutes – it was
all you ever got because of the need to keep the phone lines
clear. How evasive she had been when Olivia had asked
when she was coming back. 'Not for a while, darling, but
I'll do my best to be back for your birthday. Sixteen: I can't
quite believe it. Do you know, last week a young man I met
thought I was twenty-five? Sweet boy. He looked so smart
in his uniform—'

'Can I come up to London to see you then?' Olivia had cut in desperately, before the time ran out. 'I won't be a nuisance. We could go shopping.' She had been saving her clothes ration, just in case.

'Not right now, darling,' her mother said briskly. 'Let's talk about it next time. Must go. Tell Jago to turn the engine of the Flying 8 over, won't you? Toodle-pip, Olivia.' The connection cut.

Toodle-bloody-pip, Olivia thought. Such a ghastly phrase. She supposed it was very 'London'.

Hearing the sounds of the rest of the household stirring, Olivia threw herself out of bed and rolled up the blind. The sun hit her full in the face and she closed her eyes and bathed in it. Beryl and Marjorie would be bickering over who got to use the hot water first, not something that much concerned Olivia. 'Have a lick and a spit,' Daddy would say. It was impossible to think he was back in North Africa with his life in danger again.

By the time she appeared at the breakfast table everyone was seated, sipping their tea, or in Mary's case, yesterday's milk: Sunday was the only day Olivia didn't run up to the farm for fresh milk. At the sight of her, Marjorie burst out laughing. 'Heavens! What are you wearing?' Even Beryl suppressed a smile. When the Land Girls had first arrived Olivia had harboured hopes that Beryl might be an ally in her war of attrition against Winnie but Marjorie and Winnie had seemed immediately to be on one another's wavelength, and Beryl was too much in Marjorie's thrall to step out of line.

'Go and change at once, Olivia!' Winnie puckered her lips.

'What's the matter? It's all clean.'

'You can't wear trousers to church.'

'Other people do.'

'Men wear trousers, not young ladies.'

Olivia shrugged. 'They're comfortable, and it's too hot for stockings.'

'Well, put some socks on then.'

'My legs rub together when it's hot.' When it was hot her thighs chafed, a reminder of her weak and inferior femaleness with every step: something she didn't feel at all when she wore sensible clothing.

'You shouldn't eat so much,' Marjory said snippily.

'If you ate a bit more you wouldn't have to stuff your bra with cotton wool.' Olivia took no prisoners. Leaving them mouths agape, she ran back upstairs, ate a couple of biscuits she had squirrelled away for such emergencies (since Winnie's punishments largely took the form of Olivia being shut in her room without food, which seemed to happen with inordinate regularity, no doubt to stretch the rations) and savagely tore through her wardrobe and chest of drawers, emerging at the last moment in a formal cotton dress she hated, sun hat, plimsolls and ankle socks. And underneath her skirts a pair of French knickers she had filched off the washing line. They were Marjorie's and (apparently) expensive. Their disappearance had caused a great to-do and accusations levelled at the postman, the ARP warden and even Jago, while Olivia sat uncharacteristically quiet, giving her task of potato peeling her entire attention. She came down the stairs now, keeping her skirts tight as she descended so that no flash of the white silk would give the game away, and off they went up the hill to the church at St Pol de Leon. Winnie considered herself too posh for chapel, not even Mount Zion, which was Wesleyan.

Olivia's eyes wandered across the congregation. Such a diverse, yet unrepresentative, collection of folk, people whose paths under normal circumstances would never have crossed. Land Girls from London, Yorkshire, Suffolk, and even as far as Cumbria, lipsticked to the nines, since you never knew which young men might be home on leave. Four of the POWs were seated at the back, with Farmer Roberts and his son Leo flanking them as if on guard. The farmer was responsible for his prisoner workforce, on and – as on this rare occasion – off the farm, but down here at the end of the world it was unlikely any of them could escape: there was nowhere to go but Penzance station or the sea, and you'd never get as far as the former without a couple of hundred pairs of eyes on you and a hundred busy tongues reporting on your whereabouts. She sneaked a glance at the Dark Man, as she thought of him, which seemed more polite than the names the farm lads called out – *Oi, Blackie*, and worse. She was not the only one watching him: two of the Land Girls from Gwavas Farm were shooting him looks from under their lashes, then catching each other in the act and dissolving into giggles. But he appeared oblivious to their attention, and sat there staring into space, his expression closed and unhappy. He did not, Olivia noticed, join in with the hymns, or the congregational responses, and while the vicar gave his sermon, he closed his eyes. Olivia liked his face – a narrow wedge defined by sharp cheekbones and a long straight nose. Clean lines, she thought, easy to draw. She committed the shapes and planes of him to memory and wondered again why he was here. He didn't look European, but neither was he as dark as some of the American GIs stationed over at Hayle, whose arrival had caused a stir among the local populace who had issued dire warnings about little brown babies and social exclusion. He must have quite a story to tell but all she knew was that he'd been interned at the St Columb camp and passed on to work at the farm, where everyone avoided or insulted him because of his difference. Even Leo was pressing himself hard against the end of the pew rather than risk touching his side.

Winnie dug her in the ribs. 'Sit up straight!' she hissed. 'And pay attention.'

Mary, sitting ramrod-straight with her carroty hair tucked behind her ears, gave her a smug smile.

I am paying attention, Olivia thought but did not say. *Just not to the bloody vicar.* She crossed her legs and felt the cool silk whisper to her inner thighs.

The other POWs consisted of two German mariners picked up after their destroyer was sunk in the Channel and an Italian music teacher interned when his country had entered the war, no doubt for the crime of teaching young ladies from Truro to play the piano badly. The rest of the congregation consisted of those who were left when the young and fit went off to war or – like Olivia's mother – to bolster the war effort in London: the older people of the community, the local children, and the evacuees sent down here from upcountry to avoid the bombs. Conspicuous by their absence were the Jewish children repatriated from London: a temporary synagogue had been set up for them in the church hall, but anyway, Sunday was not their holy day, but Saturday, which they called the Sabbath. They had proved a useful resource for Olivia, who had gleaned all sorts of snippets of useful information about London from them: where the Penzance train came into, how to get to Threadneedle Street, which parks you might pitch a tent in. Because she had a plan. Or as she liked to think of it, A Plan.

Back in her room after a lunch of mutton and boiled potatoes Olivia counted her coins out, her brow furrowed in fierce concentration. A small pile of shillings, a stack of sixpences, a tower of thruppenny bits, a handful of pennies and ha'pennies. It wasn't just the cost of getting to London by train (one-way ticket only, of course) but a matter of surviving once she got there, and she was nearing her self-imposed financial goal.

For the past few weeks she'd been taking commissions for a few pennies here and there, but it added up. She had drawn Mrs Scoble's terrier for her, and the Hicks baby for Lily to send to her husband; one of the chaps manning the lookout had paid her a whole shilling to do a sketch of him to send to his sweetheart in Norfolk ('It's more romantic, more personal, like, than a photograph.'). Jeannie Blewett had paid her to draw her two boys in their navy uniforms before they were deployed. But this afternoon's sketching would be for her own pleasure.

She made her way through the potato fields that ran along the coast, slipping down through the quillets and into the woods below Kemyel Farm to scramble through gorse thickets and stands of hazel and privet, whose flowers smelled like warmed plasticine in the sun, till she reached the little boulder beach where she rolled her shirt up under her brassiere to allow the sea breeze to daringly caress her skin, and watched the clouds drifting across the sky. Taking her drawing charcoal and sketchpad out of her rucksack, she closed her eyes for a long moment to recapture her subject and then set about the task she had been looking forward to all these hours.

How long she sat there drawing and dreaming she could not say. She lost herself in her creation, using a fine edge for the detail, smudging the shadows to soften the skin texture. She embellished the reality, filling in detail to suit her own imagination of the exotic stranger, imbuing him with qualities from the stories she best loved. Truth was not, in this case, her quest as it was with the portraits she did on commission, when the subject had to look exactly the way they did in life, or at least in photographs; now she let her unconscious mind guide her hand. The Dark Man was subtly transformed from the slight, rather shy prisoner who went about his tasks at the farm with quiet acceptance, to an exiled Arabian prince, a Saracen warrior like the one in Sir Walter Scott's *The Talisman*. By the time she had finished she was half in love with the face she had conjured and the clouds piled up on the horizon were stained by the sunset, her limbs were chilled and her bottom was decidedly numb.

Olivia got to her feet and shook some life back into her legs. She was going to be in fearful trouble, skipping out on her chores for so long. She had better pick some blackberries to eat on the way back: she was sure to be confined to her room with no tea. She took a last lingering look at her sketchbook prince, then stowed her art materials in her rucksack.

And that was when she heard it, a series of low crumping noises – like far-off detonations, one after another, away to the east. Shading her eyes against the sun's dying light, Olivia gazed out across the bay. Spirals of dark smoke rose like trembling towers over the town.

They were bombing Penzance! The Germans were bombing Penzance! Why on earth would they do such a thing? Plymouth – sixty-odd miles away on the county's border with Devon, had been bombed many times, but Plymouth was one of the country's key naval bases. There was nothing of strategic importance in Penzance – just houses and shops and banks and down on the promenade hotels where people went to tea dances. Outraged, she slung her rucksack over her shoulder and ploughed a path back up through the woods, panting hard by the time she reached the top of the first potato field.

Another crump, much louder, made her breastbone judder, and looking back towards Porth Enys she saw a great plume of water surge up near the island, then another, and then a plane banked hard and seemed to be coming right at her, far too low: a roaring monster trailing a churning black wake of smoke. She turned her head to watch it till her neck ached; then it was past, and she saw a tiny parachute, like a seed from a dandelion clock, white against the darkening sky.

The impact as the plane hit rumbled through the ground, through the dark soil and the tubers and roots and leaves of the potato plants nearing their second cropping and into the soles of her feet, travelled up her leg bones and spine into the very heart of her, as with the land she absorbed the crash.

Until that moment, the war had seemed theoretical to Olivia – one of Daddy's tales, or something you heard about on the wireless; a distant conflict with limited direct effect upon Cornwall, let alone Porth Enys. But this was war: here and now. She stood with her heart beating fiercely. Then she was off and running, her feet kicking up the earth as she cut a straight line through the crop to the top of the hill.

As Olivia crested the rise she could see the blaze of the crashed plane two fields over, sending great columns of black smoke up like beacons from hell. By the time she reached the crash site it seemed as if the whole of Treharrow Farm was there: Farmer Roberts and his son Leo, Tom Madron and Jimmy Blewett and Jack Scoble, armed with spades and hoes and shotguns, some of the POWs; a gaggle of Land Girls; Jago arriving on the chugging Fordson with Jem and Nipper Martin. The farm dogs bounced around yapping wildly, keeping well away from the heat of the downed aircraft.

'Get back, get back!' Jago roared. 'The bombs will explode.'

'I saw it drop its bombs on the island,' Olivia called out, breathless from her climb. 'And I saw someone eject with a parachute!'

This caused great consternation. Mr Trembath, head of the Home Guard, and two of his men arrived at a run and were left to control the growing crowd around the hulk of the German plane, which had come to rest, or been stopped by, one of the ancient Swingate standing stones. It seemed far larger now that it was on the ground than it had in the sky. Through the flames and choking smoke Olivia could just make out flickers of the black-and-white cross near its tail fin, and seeing the Nazi symbol right here in front of her in a potato field half a mile from her home made her shiver.

'Messerschmitt 264,' Jimmy announced with some authority.

'Nah, it's a Stuka – see, it's got Junkers engines,' said Leo, pointing.

'How come you know so much? Secret Jerry, are you?'

They almost came to blows until Farmer Roberts grabbed his son by the arm, and took off with him and Jago on the tractor at dangerous speed so that it lurched precariously over the uneven ground, then disappeared from view.

Night was falling by the time the local constable and a contingent of uniformed men arrived to disperse the crowd, but by then there was really nothing to see, though Jem Sparrow swore he had seen a man looking out at him from the wreck of the plane. 'His face was like a skull! And his eye sockets were full of flames.'

One of the Land Girls burst into tears, but Olivia was intrigued. 'Did you really?'

Jem looked sheepish. 'Might have done.'

She met Marjorie and Beryl in the lane. 'What's going on?' Beryl asked, and Olivia told them the bare details, and watched their expressions shade from horror to fascination. Beryl was desperate to know more, but Marjorie took Olivia firmly by the arm, her nails digging into the flesh. 'You're in big trouble,' she told Olivia with grim pleasure. 'Mrs Ogden is in a complete bate. You were supposed to be helping her with the floors.'

'But Sunday's a day of rest,' Olivia said with mock piousness.

'The devil makes work for idle hands, that's what Winnie said,' Beryl added.

Olivia was unrepentant. She had seen an enemy, an actual German, floating above Kemyel Hill. The knowledge thrilled her. War had come to Porth Enys and she was the sole witness. She took her punishment from Winnie meekly when it came and went to her room, her spirits buoyed by her secret knowledge. Lying in her narrow bed, her blood beating around her body, she slipped her hand between her thighs and rocked quietly back and forth against her slippery fingers, visions of a dark prince in her head.

9

'IS MISSUS IN?'

For a brief moment Olivia felt a combination of annoyance and amusement, then she registered that Bert Blewett was holding a telegram discreetly at his side, and her knees started to tremble.

'Who's it for?'

'Mrs Ogden. Is she in?'

Olivia experienced a wave of relief like a warm wash through her innards, but a blink later doubt set in. If something had happened to her parents might the telegram still not be addressed to Winnie as the only actual adult at the address? Better grasp the nettle. 'I'll go and get her.'

Winnie was in the scullery, giving her daughter a wash in the copper tub. Mary stood as naked and skinny as a shorn lamb. She fixed the intruder with a chilly gaze. Olivia could swear she changed her eye colour at will, like a cat. 'Out of here!' Winnie flicked a soap-laden hand at her. 'Give the girl some privacy.'

Olivia moved to the doorway and turned her back. 'The postman—'

'Out!'

'—a telegram.'

There was a long beat of silence followed by a splash as the bar of Wright's Coal Tar soap fell from Winnie's hand, then the housekeeper pushed a towel into Olivia's hands. 'Finish her bath and get her dry.'

Olivia flipped the towel around Mary's shoulders with a hissed, 'Stay there!' and ran back down the corridor to make sure she didn't miss anything. It was very quiet in the hall: no one was saying a word, but she could just see Winnie reading the bit of paper the postman had given her.

Please, God, don't let it be Daddy, Olivia prayed wildly; then, feeling guilty, *Or Mummy, either.*

Winnie scanned the contents of the telegram for a final time then stowed it in the pocket of her apron. Bert was still lingering on the doorstep. 'If you want to reply, it's nine words for sixpence.'

'You can say "Up on train tomorrow, Winnie". That's five, I'll expect change,' Winnie said crisply, dropping a coin into his hand.

He jotted the message down, grumpily conceded her a couple of coins, then tipped his cap and trotted back down the path. Winnie stood there for a long moment, staring out into the grey morning, before shutting the door after him.

Olivia, frustrated at this withholding of information, scooted back down the corridor, only to find Mary standing at the scullery door shivering dramatically. Grabbing her more firmly by her thin shoulders than was strictly necessary, Olivia steered her back inside and started rubbing her fiercely.

'Ow, you're hurting me!' Mary wriggled under Olivia's rough attentions, looking pleadingly at her mother as she entered the room. 'Olivia left me and I got cooooold,' she whined.

But for once her complaint went unremarked. Winnie took the towel from Olivia and absent-mindedly dried her daughter. 'I'll have to leave Mary with you,' she said after a while. 'My mother is very ill.'

Olivia, who had been about to protest vehemently, closed her mouth. 'I'm sorry,' she said, but she was relieved the bad news had nothing to do with her parents.

Mary pulled at her mother's arm. 'I want to go with you!'

'An old woman's deathbed is no place for a child.'

'But Olivia's horrible to me!'

Winnie gave her a little shake. 'You must be a proper grown-up girl, Rosemary, and do whatever Olivia tells you. Now, take your things upstairs and let me think. Olivia, get her dressed, will you?'

For once Olivia did not talk back. Up in the nursery, the child became stiff and uncooperative, bending her arms at awkward angles as Olivia tried to put her cardigan on. 'I hate you!'

'Well, I hate you too, so we're even.'

She was ridiculously strong for a five-year-old. Olivia was sweating by the time they had finished. The idea of Winnie going away was a joyous thing but the euphoria was easily counterbalanced by the responsibility of having to take care of Mary. *I shall bloody well lock her in the cellar if she plays me up*, she thought savagely. It was a tempting prospect, but she knew she wouldn't. Mary would probably manage to get the sea door open and go stumbling off down the smuggler's passage to drown, and just think how much how much trouble *that* would cause.

The next morning the weather matched Olivia's mood as she watched Winnie make her way down the steps to the lane where Jago waited in the lovely Standard Flying 8, little puffs of smoke emanating from the car's exhaust. *Poor old girl*, Olivia thought, *neglected for so long and then made to go out on such a rotten day*. An idea occurred to her. It might not be The Plan, but as consolations went, it was *a* plan. Imbued with sudden energy, she ran to the kitchen and washed up the breakfast things, leaving them to drain as she was never usually allowed to do. Then she locked a protesting Mary in her bedroom, pulled on her mackintosh and sou'wester, filled her pockets with what she needed and made her way up through the woodland at the rear of the house to the small barn they used as a garage. She did not have long to wait before Jago returned.

'Did you catch the train all right?'

Jago wound the window down and regarded her curiously. 'Aye.'

'I thought I'd save you the walk down to the house,' Olivia said brightly, raindrops dripping off the brim of her sou'wester. 'I'll take the starting handle and put it back in its box. You know, to keep it out of the hands of the enemy, like the Ministry says.'

Jago parked the car and gave it and the key to the garage

over reluctantly. Olivia smiled sweetly. No doubt they both had the same idea. She waited till he disappeared up the lane to the farm before doubling back to the garage, opening its creaky old doors wide. The Flying 8 sat there, its long dark bonnet as warm as the belly of a slumbering animal – a dragon, she thought, alarmingly huge. Could she even remember how to start it? She climbed in, feeling the heat of Jago lingering in the hard leather of the driver's seat, assured herself that the handbrake was on and that it was out of gear. Then she pulled on the start cord, expecting it to rumble to life, but nothing happened. Bother. She got out and walked to the front of the car, feeling rather awed by its waterfall grille and shiny louvres, and dragged from her memory her father's careful instructions about not getting her thumb caught as she cranked the starting handle, turning it good and hard twice and feeling for the sweet point before giving the handle a firm extra swing... Her heart beat wildly as the engine caught with a fearful roar. She half-expected it to emit a bolt of fire.

Tremulously, she drove the car out onto the gritted lane, made a shaky ten-point turn to get it facing in the right direction, and went chugging off down the long hill, the Flying 8 picking up speed as the incline increased, then the road swept in a long parabola down past the farm cottages and Carn Dhu, where a contingent of soldiers was billeted. She kept her foot on the brake all the way down into the village, where the streets got narrow and things got a lot more tricky, especially if you met anyone coming the other way. But her luck was in: people were saving their fuel for emergencies. She parked on the road by the chapel above the old quay and got out, feeling at once trembly with nerves and triumphant. A wild scheme came into her mind. She could drive herself to London! But reality smothered this mad idea before it could grow legs and run away with itself. Of course she couldn't. It was hundreds of miles to the capital and such a journey – even if she could negotiate it – would use every drop of fuel stashed in the stonehouse. Also, her parents would quite simply kill her.

And she had left Mary locked in her room... Olivia did not feel entirely guiltless about that. She resolved to purchase Mary some sweets as a peace offering out of the housekeeping money Winnie had left. No doubt the child would be compiling a long list of woes with which to regale her mother by the time Winnie returned. Maybe she should hold back her bribes till later in the week, when they would be fresher in the memory.

The rain clouds had drifted east by the time she got out of the car, leaving clear blue skies in the west and the sun falling in great slanted shafts of gold. She spent a cheerful half hour pottering around the harbour, chatting here and there to the local women taking a break from their chores, watching the children jumping into the sea from the Gaps with shrieks of delight. She even treated herself to a sherbet dab from the shop and sat on the harbour wall, swinging her legs and waving away the seagulls that watched her every movement with their cold predatory yellow eyes.

Then, feeling very grown-up, she bought four mackerel for a few pennies at the quay – a proper bargain, and not rationed – followed by a fresh tinloaf, a saffron cake, a small tin of Nestles cream and a large tin of cling peaches (since Winnie, being congenitally mean, still had the relevant ration stamps), which came to over three shillings. She was going to have to be very careful from now on with what remained of the housekeeping money.

Making her way back to the car she came upon an altercation, someone crying out in a harsh, penetrating voice, another person speaking low but urgently. As she neared the small group of people she heard someone say, 'I won't have it in my house!' It was a fat woman in a print dress, her feet planted squarely, finger wagging at a man with a hangdog expression and some large object in his arms.

'Bugger off, arsehole!'

Olivia sucked in her breath. What shocking language! It wasn't as if the words were unknown to her – you couldn't hang around a farm when hard physical labour was going on without hearing these and worse – but in the middle of the village, with children in earshot? For a moment, the little crowd parted and she saw a sudden glimpse of startling colour: a parrot, shaking out scarlet wings! A swearing parrot in a cage!

Delighted, Olivia inserted herself into the crowd. 'He begged me give un to 'ee, missus. It were his last wish.'

'Stupid old fool – what do I want with a foul-mouthed bird? I wouldn't have such a filthy thing in the house. I won't take un.' The woman folded her arms across her stout bosom.

The man looked pleadingly around the crowd. 'A dying man's wish,' he said almost in a whisper, but they weren't having any of it.

'You could probably eat un, Joan,' one of the women said. 'Reckon it'd taste just like chicken.'

The man held the cage tighter. 'I couldn't let you do that,' he said. ''Twouldn't be right.' He looked around the gathered group. 'Won't someone take un? He's right companionable, and very young. I'm sure you could train him out of his ungodly ways. He's been among sailors, you know. It's not his fault.'

People started to peel away, dragging fascinated children behind them. 'Please,' he said again. He sounded utterly defeated.

Olivia stepped forward. 'I'll take him,' she said.

From its cage on the passenger seat of the Flying 8 the parrot eyed her warily. She had not thought to ask its name, even when handing over the ten shillings the man had demanded at the last moment – 'for the cage' – following which the sailor had vanished with suspicious speed. So that was the last of Daddy's money and a bit of the housekeeping besides.

Olivia held its gaze. 'You behave yourself, Parrot, and we'll get along just fine.'

The parrot cocked its head and emitted a soft caw.

Olivia drove the car with exaggerated care back up the hill. The combination of the freedom of the road and the presence of her passenger was intoxicating, as if some wilder, more brazen, aspect of her personality had been released into the world. She found herself driving right past the turning to the garage and carrying on up the hill through the farmland. So what if Jago saw her? She would just say she had Pa's permission. Laughing out loud, she wound the window down and began to sing, '*Keep Saturday free for me, Saturday in your heart. Though we're far apart, it's always Saturday in my heart for you...*'

Every so often the parrot would punctuate the song with a whistle or a click; Olivia was enchanted.

She drove past the top fields where yet more potatoes were being harvested, seeing lines of bent backs and hemp sacks. Beryl and Marjorie would be amongst them, anonymous at this distance in their khaki Land Girl togs, and the POWs too – all hands were needed to get the harvest in before the ploughing could begin. These fields would be turned over to cereals next year and this should all have been finished earlier in the month, and would have been had they not been so short-handed.

She rounded the bend at the top of the hill and changed gear with a crunch. She would, she decided, passing the stump of the road sign, which had been taken down to confuse the enemy, go down just as far as the old mill and turn around there: better not to use up any more fuel.

On her return, as she ghosted down the road back to Chynalls, four men emerged suddenly, one after another, over the stone stile out of the potato field into the road – Leo Roberts and Nipper Martin, with two men in POW overalls: the Italian music teacher, and a blond man she had not seen before. With a start, she realized he must be the survivor of the German bomber and felt a cold frisson run through her. An actual Nazi was standing right in front of her, looking remarkably matey with Leo and Nipper, as if he were on bloody holiday, rather than held prisoner. He accepted a cigarette out of Nipper's packet of Woodbines and waited for the farmhand who lit it for him with a strange deference, as if their positions had been reversed. As the blond man took a draw on the cigarette, the sunlight hit his face full on, delineating sharp cheekbones. He was, she thought suddenly, like a negative version of the Dark Man, black made white. But whereas the Dark Man gave her a warm feeling, despite his good looks this man left her chilled to the bone.

Leo stepped into the road and held up a hand and Olivia drew the car to a halt.

'What you doing fossicking about in that car?'

Olivia affected a nonchalance she did not feel. 'I had errands to run. Too much to carry up the hill.'

'Standard Flying 8, int'it?' Leo ran a hand over the gleaming paintwork as if he had every right to do so. He peered in. 'What the bleddy hell you got there?'

By way of answer the parrot let out an earsplitting squawk that made Leo jump back in shock. The others laughed at him and Leo told them to 'Shut up! Shut the fuck up!'

'Shut the fuck up!' echoed the parrot gleefully, and that made them double up.

'Got a right one there, Olivia. Where you get un?' asked Nipper.

'It's all rather complicated,' Olivia said vaguely.

'Can I have a go in the car later?' Nipper pushed past Leo. 'Mebbe we can drive down Love Lane, eh, Livy? That's where the soldiers go.' He made kissing noises at her, saliva slicking his red lips, then turned to the pilot and winked.

Olivia felt a bitter taste come into her mouth, and not just at Nipper's crude suggestion – she was used to that, and worse. What she wasn't used to was seeing him being so pally with an enemy, an actual follower of Adolf Hitler. She revved the engine.

'Don't even think about getting fresh with me, Stanley Martin.'

'Oh, go on, you know you'd love it.' He dug in his pocket, brought out a couple of sweets and pressed them into her hand. She looked down. Callard & Bowser toffees. 'No thanks,' she said, pushing them back at him. 'Must dash.' She felt four pairs of eyes on her as she let out the handbrake and pressed the accelerator, making the vehicle hop and splutter, and then, thank goodness, she was out of their sight.

'But I don' like mackerel,' Mary moaned. The child had been angry and obstinate ever since Olivia had returned, which was not entirely a surprise. The fish spat and hissed in the pan as if in fierce agreement about not being eaten but Olivia was not to be swayed.

'They're fresh off the boat and good for you. Your ma said you were to eat them twice a week.'

'You don't usually take notice of what Ma says,' Mary pronounced sullenly.

They were sitting in silence eating the mackerel with bread and butter when the front door banged and there came the sound of voices.

'Don't you dare say a word,' warned Olivia.

'What'll you give me?'

The tempting answer was 'a jolly good hiding', but Olivia restrained herself. She wished she had gone to the sweetshop after all, or even taken Nipper's toffees – not that he'd have got anything by way of exchange. The idea of his overly wet, red lips making kissing motions at her... ugh.

'You can have some pear drops.'

'When?'

'Later.'

'I want them now.'

The bargaining was interrupted by the arrival of the Land Girls. 'Did you catch his name?' Beryl was saying, going to wash her hands in the bowl of water.

'I believe it's Michael or something,' Marjorie said. 'Pronounced in some awful foreign way.'

'Ah, Michael, like the archangel, with his lovely yellow hair and piercing gaze. Not too much of an angel, though: I swear he was undressing me with his eyes.'

'Oh for heaven's sake, Beryl!'

'He called me Rita Hayworth,' Beryl said dreamily. 'He pointed to my hair.'

Marj snorted. 'Must've lost his glasses in the crash.'

'I'm quite sure pilots have perfect eyesight,' Beryl replied sharply.

'He probably wasn't the pilot,' Marjorie said, 'just aircrew. And how you can find him in the least attractive I can't imagine. He's an enemy – a Jerry! Where's your patriotism? They destroyed half of Penzance. We'd probably both be dead if it had been the night before.'

'He does look rather dangerous.' Beryl gave a secret smile. 'He's got that sort of mouth – you know, what do they say, chiselled? But anyway, he ain't a Jerry, he's Austrian.'

'How do you even know that?'

'I asked Nipper.'

Marjorie made a face. 'I'll never understand men. It's like Nipper hero-worships him, stupid beggar. It just isn't right. Besides, Hitler is an Austrian. You keep away from him, Beryl Hopkins.'

'Why? Want him for yourself, do ya?'

Olivia could hardly believe her ears: she'd never heard Beryl confront Marjorie in such a way before.

'Don't be absurd. I have far better men chasing after me; young men fighting for our freedom, not some wretched Nazi. Now, calm down, Beryl. Let's make some tea and have a quick game of whist before supper and say no more about it.'

She set about briskly boiling the kettle and assembling on a tray the teapot, cups, saucers, tea strainer, milk, sugar, and the saffron cake Olivia had been earmarking for herself and forgotten to hide. Damn. As Marj warmed the pot then carefully dropped two teaspoonfuls of the precious loose leaves into it and covered them with hot water, Beryl said, 'Let's have our tea in the parlour, since Mrs Ogden in't here to tell us not to. We can pretend we're grand ladies.'

'I think there's a concert on the wireless,' Olivia said quickly, trying not to sound desperate. 'And it's much grander in the dining room – the parlour's very dusty.'

'Don't be ridiculous, Olivia,' said Marj, as if noticing her for the first time. 'It's *Farming Today* on the Home Service at the moment and I for one have had quite enough of farming for today.'

'There's a surprise in the parlour,' said Mary. Olivia, holding her by the arm, dug her fingers in harder.

Marjorie fixed the child with a cool gaze. 'Is there now?'

'Yes.'

'Time for bed,' Olivia said hurriedly.

'It's too early for bed.'

'I don't think it is.' Olivia hauled Mary out into the corridor, the child fighting her all the way.

'... parrot!' Mary shouted.

'What was that?' Beryl came to the doorway, looking puzzled.

'Oh, nothing. She's just developed this craving for carrots,' Olivia called back over her shoulder and launched Mary up the stairs and into her room, where they stared at one another hotly. 'No sweets for you,' Olivia said.

'Don't care. You're going to be in big big trouble.'

Olivia shut the door on the awful child and crept along the landing, listening. The inevitable scream came seconds later, followed by loud avian cackling, and Beryl came bolting out into the hall, eyes out on stalks. Marjorie followed on her heels, lips compressed, tea tray firmly in both hands. The cups rattled: she was shaking. 'Beryl, go into the dining room. We'll play cards in there.'

Olivia sauntered down the stairs as if nothing had happened and as Beryl scuttled past, weeping, Marj fixed her with a gimlet stare. 'Well, look at you, little Miss Butter Wouldn't Melt. You can't possibly keep that vile thing. I shall ask Jago to get rid of it tomorrow.'

'It's mine and I'm going to keep it,' Olivia returned. 'This is my house, and you have no say here.'

Into the beat of silence that followed as Marj mustered a furious response there emanated from the parlour a distant but distinct, 'Bugger off, arsehole.'

10

Becky

THE NEXT MORNING, HAVING NOT SLEPT AT ALL, I AM sitting cross-legged in the snug with several of Olivia's books spread on the floor around me. It is remarkable, I think, how dependent people have become on the Internet in any quest for knowledge. Under normal circumstances I would simply key the words 'human finger bone' into Google and wait for a torrent of information. But of course there is no signal here.

And so, stymied and disturbed, I paced the corridors of Chynalls in the early hours until the book-room beckoned me and there, amongst the cornucopia of travel guides and memoirs, books on photography and art and architecture, encyclopaedias and classic novels, histories (in both English and French) of Morocco and Algeria and the Second World War, anthropological tomes about world cultures and field guides to birds, butterflies and wildflowers, I found on a high shelf a medical volume and a human anatomy manual. Quite the library, Olivia has. Not what you might expect to find in the house of a batty old lady.

The medical volumes are opened to pages showing illustrations and descriptions of the human skeleton.

There can be no doubt as to the nature of the artefact I have found. But nothing I have come upon in my research can reveal the age or identity of the human being to whom it once belonged. And that's really rather crucial, isn't it? Yet I don't know if it was part of someone male or female, child or adult, prehistoric or rather more recent. And I cannot take it anywhere for analysis because of the suspicion and terrifying legal consequences that might fall upon my frail, old cousin, already struggling to survive in Treliske Hospital.

And so here I am now at seven in the morning, with my eyes sore and gummy and my mind fuzzy from lack of sleep, wondering if Olivia has murdered someone, or is covering up for someone else who has murdered someone, or if she is completely innocent and even maybe unaware of the presence of human remains below her house and wants the cellar and tunnel bricked up for some other, unknowable reason.

I know I am not thinking straight. But who would under such circumstances?

At last I stir myself. I put the medical volumes back on the shelves and gingerly pick up the bone with a piece of tissue and take it into Olivia's old camp-bed room and hide it away in the hollow of the carved totem, where I found the big iron key. I stuff balled-up newspaper in after it till the totem doesn't rattle. After that, I feel better. Out of sight, out of mind.

I make myself a mug of coffee and some toast and Marmite, and thus restored, arm myself with the torch, my phone – in case I need to take photos (it being precious

little use in any other capacity without any signal) – and
the big key. I have also purloined a small metal trowel that
I rescued from among the other paraphernalia caught up in
the collapsed porch. Down I go into the cellar, feeling not at
all like an explorer but more like a grave-robber. My heart
thumps unhelpfully: I can feel panic coming on at what I
must do.

Calm down, Becky. Take deep breaths.

Who do you think you are? I ask silently. *My mother?*

I take deep breaths and feel the panic recede a little. I
have to know, I tell myself. I have to know what I'm taking
on here. Because if there is a body...

A corpse, whispers the unhelpful voice in my head.

If there is a... If there are human remains, the likelihood
is it will involve the police, and I will have to consider my
position.

This sounds so pompous even as an internal monologue
that I almost laugh out loud. *Consider my position.* As if I
am a corrupt politician, caught out by the newspapers. All I
am trying to do is help my poor old cousin, I tell the universe
silently. I'm trying to do a good thing here, so please don't
make it any harder than it needs to be, OK?

I drag a heavy paint pot across the dusty floor and wedge
it up against the cellar door, so that I can run for my life if
I have to. Then I fit the key into the lock. Iron, cold iron.
Didn't people used to believe iron stopped magic from
working? Which is why they hung horseshoes everywhere?

The door creaks as I open it. I push the shelving units
clear of the door and manoeuvre another paint pot across
the cellar floor, making sure the tunnel door is also securely
wedged open. Then, with my torch beam playing alternately

on the rough walls and the uneven stairs of the tunnel, I descend into the darkness to where the bone tapped me on the shoulder.

Is it my imagination, or is it even colder in here than it was last time? Is that my breath I can see in the air, or the remnants of some early morning mist that has drifted up from the cove? My muscles feel tightened by fear, by the anticipation of what may be lurking down here, and my brain is constricted by the weight of everything it may mean. I run the torchlight over the spot where the bone fell from. The wall appears to comprise irregular blocks of some sort of grey stone that may be slate and compacted earth. Here and there small pebbles are embedded, some dark chunks, others paler than the surrounding bedrock. There is no immediate sign of any other part of a hand, or of the body to which it was once attached. On the ground, though, there is some debris to mark the spot where it fell to earth – a scatter of soil and tiny stones, but no other bones. I move a step further down and examine the wall there, which is completely solid and undisturbed. I go back up a step.

I touch the tip of the trowel to the wall and a little more soil crumbles away. Scrape, scrape: more earth and a spill of tiny pebbles. The sound they make as they skitter down onto the steps is whispery, eldritch, and I shiver. When I dig a little deeper there is a sudden small gush of debris and I leap out of the way in terror: what if I bring the whole wall down? I dash back up the stairs, shaking with dread, but no collapse follows and I make myself go back to examine the wall and shine the torch into the small hole I have made, but there is nothing to be seen but rock and earth.

My shoulders drop with relief. Perhaps the bone is just a tiny remnant of a bygone age. Perhaps it was just a buried finger! The result of an accident, or some arcane punishment. Being honest with myself, I must admit that I don't really want to know, because the more I know, the more I will be implicated if this all comes to light. But then, I reason, if there's nothing important to be known, I can go ahead with the renovations. Inter the bone out in the orchard, maybe even say a few words over it for what good it will do, and get Reda and his brother to carry out Olivia's instructions and think no more about it.

I play the torch one last time over the wall, and still see nothing incriminating. I do the same with the opposite wall and find it safely and innocently solid.

Right, then. I scurry back up to the cellar and lock the tunnel door against the darkness and flee back up into the house, turn off the light and breathe.

Then I walk into the village, take a bus to Penzance and hire a Renault Clio from the cheapest hire company I can find.

I do not drive the car directly back to London, which is probably what I should do (if the old banger would make it that far). Instead I drive to Truro, tackling the bends and roundabouts with rather more care than Rosie Sparrow. I am fuelled by determination, though my moral compass spins between panic and common sense. *Just ignore it and get on with the practical work*, my common-sense voice tells me; but panic interrupts: *Your cousin is a murderer and she's making you an accomplice after the fact!*

One way or another, I must get to the bottom of this mystery, must persuade the old woman to be honest with me, so that I can proceed with a clear conscience; or run away and preserve myself.

But as I enter the ward and present myself at the nurse's station a doctor who was bent over the computer screen straightens up and asks if I am Olivia Kitto's next of kin. A bolt of cold electricity jolts through me. 'Is she OK?' I ask, fearing the worst, and quickly confirm that I am indeed designated as her next of kin.

'Would you mind if I ask you a few questions?'

She leads me to a little side room, and closes the door behind me. This feels ominous. I do not sit down.

'We ran tests on Mrs Kitto and some of the results were a little strange,' the doctor says, leaning back against the deck, and some of my fear evaporates. She has grey shadows under her eyes. I wonder how long she's been on call. 'So I wondered if I might ask you a couple of questions about her lifestyle?'

'Lifestyle?' Whatever could she mean? Her haphazard living arrangements, the filth in the house, her penchant for digestive biscuits?

'Tell me, does Mrs Kitto have a history of drinking?'

'What, like an alcoholic?' There isn't even a corkscrew in Chynalls: I'd bought a bottle of Merlot from the local shop and had to push the cork in with a hammer and a bit of kindling: amazing how the need for wine can drive you to invention.

'Not necessarily. Lots of things can cause the liver's function to be impaired, but of course alcohol is the first thing we check for. We asked Mrs Kitto, but—'

'I can imagine.' I smile. 'But no, I don't think she drinks at all.'

'We were concerned that it might be cancer or NAFLD' – she unpacks this for me as 'non-alcoholic fatty liver disease'– 'but when we scanned her we couldn't find evidence of either.' She shrugs. 'Every body's full of secrets, and she's in remarkably good shape for her age. We've put her on some medication and we'll keep an eye on her. We've explained all this to her but she's quite—'

'Irascible?'

The doctor laughs. 'Bloody-minded was what I was going to say.'

We grin at one another like conspirators and abruptly I feel disloyal. 'She's very independent. I don't think she takes well to being cooped up.'

'If we can stabilize her and she passes her assessments she can go home. Once the works have been carried out. Social services will take over from us at that point, and they may be able to provide a certain degree of support, but I think when Mrs Kitto does go home she's likely to require full-time care.' Her shadowed eyes fix me with a penetrating gaze.

'Well, I'm not going anywhere,' I find myself saying, and feel myself go hot, then cold.

She leans forward to squeeze my arm. 'I'm so glad. Despite everything, we've become very fond of her.' Then she is all business again and ushers me back to the ward.

At the door, I excuse myself, and flee to the toilets. I sit on the hard plastic seat inside a cubicle with my throbbing head on my knees. What was I thinking? My life is in London. Eddie is in London. My consultant and his team are in London. And there may be a corpse buried under Olivia's house.

I dig into my handbag and roll some of the lavender stress-relief oil I keep there over my pulse points, losing myself in the scent for a minute or two. *I am not committed to anything*, I tell myself. *I have all sorts of good excuses for not doing this.*

Just take it a day at a time, darling. Don't run at everything like a bull at a gate.

My mother was always coming out with things like this. She knew me too well, knew how easily I let myself become panicked and over-stressed. And again I remember Evie calling me 'so fragile' and James recalling how Mum used the excuse that I already had 'enough on my plate' for not telling me she was ill. I roll my shoulders and get to my feet. It's time to take some responsibility for a change, to try to do some good in the world, to help my elderly cousin as I was never able to help my own mother. I push the thought of the bone away. Of course Olivia has not killed someone and buried them under Chynalls. Of course it's historic, and maybe not even human.

Yes, you tell yourself that, Becky.

'So we thought we could make a hole in the wall in your sitting room to lead into the old scullery and put your new bathroom in there, then you won't have far to go to get to the loo. And we'll make the doorway wide enough for a wheelchair—'

'What nonsense! I don't need a wheelchair!'

I glance at her cast, which she seems to have forgotten. In the corner of the cubicle is a walking frame that the nurses tell me she refuses to use now that the break has knitted.

We talk for a time about the practicalities of the build and she uses my phone to call her bank manager in Penzance. There is a lot of back and forth, during which she says, 'Power of attorney?' in response to something he has just said. 'Of course I'm not giving her power of attorney: I haven't entirely lost my marbles.' I stifle a chuckle.

There appears to be back-tracking at the other end of the phone and explanations no doubt as to why these formalities are necessary, before Olivia cuts him off with, 'I've banked with you for over seventy years. When your father worked in the branch he had a rather ill-advised affair with a friend of mine.'

A passing nurse catches my eye at this bellowed declaration. It soon transpires that the bank manager is sufficiently convinced that Olivia is indisputably herself and acting of her own free will, so is prepared to sidestep the usual security requirements. He must have said something about losing his job if anyone finds out, for Olivia says loudly, 'Don't be such a wimp! Things were different in my day.' She thrusts the phone at me.

'I'm so sorry,' I say into the phone. We agree a time for a meeting, then I cut the call and raise my eyebrows at my cousin, but she is entirely unrepentant. 'It's my blasted money,' she says mutinously.

Just as I am about to frame a response to this my phone buzzes and I see I have a text from a number I don't recognize. When I open it I see it's from Reda, along with a photo of him with another man, a bit balder and wider, who must be his brother, giving me the thumbs-up: Mohamed has accepted the job.

'It's from the builders,' I say.

'I hope you're not using Saul and Ezra,' Olivia says fiercely.

I can't help smiling.

'That's a very secretive smile.'

'Look,' I say, angling the phone towards her. 'This is Mohamed – he's the builder I found – and his brother, Reda, who's the plumber. They've just texted to say they're going to do the work for you.'

Olivia looks at the photo for a long time without saying anything and I can't help but brace myself for the inevitable racist remark, but she doesn't say anything. I lean over her shoulder. 'They're Moroccan,' I tell her.

Olivia is fiddling with the screen so that the image shifts in and out of focus. 'Oh, these wretched things!' she huffs. 'I can't be doing with these modern gadgets.'

I expand the view for her and Olivia brings the phone up almost to her nose. 'Would you like your reading glasses?' I ask, but she shakes her head.

'Moroccan, you say? Not Algerian?'

'From Oujda, Reda said that's in Morocco.' Belatedly I remember him saying something about Algerian cousins, but it seems too complicated to add.

She sits up a bit straighter. 'I went to Morocco once, you know.'

'Did you?'

'I rode a camel through the desert.' She looks wistful, then intensely sad.

'I'd love to hear about your adventures. I remember you said in your letter to Mum that you walked across a desert.'

She shoots me a look. 'Have you been reading my correspondence? It's private! Nothing to do with you. Where's your mother? She should be here!'

I shake my head, rendered wordless.

'Oh yes, she's dead. I remember now. Not going doolally, not quite yet. Oh well, we all decline to dust, don't we?' She gives a great sigh, then asks briskly, 'And how is Gabriel?'

'He's doing very well.' I tell her about his antics and make her laugh, then dig into my bag and bring out the string of beads.

'I didn't find your locket, but I did find these.'

Olivia stares at it, then snatches it out of my grasp.

'Reda told me it's a *misbaha*. He says they're Muslim prayer beads.' I watch her but she closes her eyes as if deliberately cloaking her thoughts. I wait for her to open them but a minute later she starts to snore. Cartoon snoring – the snort, the pause, the whiffle. To test her, I touch the string of beads as if I might take them back again, and as soon as I do, her fingers close over them.

You old fraud, I think, rather admiringly.

I get up, gather my things, push my chair back out of the way, making sure she can hear all this preparation for departure, then walk away, letting my flip-flops clack loudly against the soles of my feet. At the ward's door, I stop, step aside and look back. For a long moment Olivia does not move and I begin to think I may have misjudged her, then she lifts the *misbaha* and lays her cheek upon it. Her shoulders jerk: she is crying.

★

A few days later I drive the Renault Clio into Penzance for my appointment with Olivia's bank manager.

As I wait outside his office I very much hope he won't take his affront at Cousin Olivia's rudeness out on me. I haven't always had a good relationship with banks: for me it was a relief when the system became depersonalized.

The door opens to reveal a tall, thin, ascetic-looking man of sixtyish, with swept-back silver hair and a pair of half-moon spectacles halfway down his nose. He looks like a kindly consultant, the one come to break bad news as gently as possible. He ushers me inside, looking down the corridor and closing the door quickly behind me, as if engaged in some illicit action.

'This is very out of the ordinary,' he tells me as we both sit down with his big paper-covered desk between us.

'It is Olivia Kitto we're talking about,' I say, with a smile to indicate I know what he's up against.

'Indeed. She is... rather a force of nature.'

'She's asked me to take over paying her bills. I have her cheque book, but some companies don't take cheques any more, so I'm not sure how she's been managing.'

He runs a hand through his hair. 'She used to come in every week or so and take out cash to pay them in person, but these companies have gone online now, so after that she would come into the branch and have one of the team help her on the computer.' He sighs. 'It was very time-consuming, but she simply wouldn't learn how to do it for herself like everyone else. The problem is now, Miss Young... well, has she not let you read the correspondence?'

I look at him blankly. 'What correspondence?'

'We've been sending her letters for about six months now, but she hasn't been replying.'

'How's she been paying her bills? The utilities are all still on at the house, so I imagine she must have been somehow.'

He leans forward, and all but whispers, 'Rosie Sparrow.'

I nod. 'Oh. OK. So she's been getting Rosie to come in.'

The bank manager shakes his head impatiently. 'No, no. Rosie has been paying the bills herself.'

I feel my eyebrows shoot up. 'Really? I thought Rosie was her cleaner? How can she afford to do that?'

Now he looks agonized, then says, 'I'm afraid there have been some irregularities in your cousin's account. I took the liberty of printing off her current statement.' He pushes a couple of pieces of A4 across the desk towards me.

I pick them up and scan them. I hate bank statements, but I know an overdraft when I see one. I gaze up at him, aghast.

'We've honoured her outgoings so far, but I've been writing for the past few months to say that we really can't continue to do so. She is way, way over any permissible overdraft level for a woman of her age without a regular salary or assets.'

My head is spinning as I try to process this. 'But what about the house? Could she not...' I dig for the grown-up words. '... apply for equity release?'

'We did send a chap around to value the property, but he came away saying she wouldn't let him in – in fact he said she was rather rude to him – and that the place was falling down around her ears, so he couldn't recommend it as collateral.'

I take a deep breath. 'We're addressing the state of the house – putting in a proper bathroom, mending drains and windows...' I look at the bank statement again, then turn it over. There is the debit for the cheque Olivia gave me, but there is no sign of the one I gave Mohamed and Reda to start the work. I look again. 'Um, how long does it usually take for a cheque to clear?'

He pauses. 'If there are sufficient funds in the account, usually three or four days, sometimes a little longer.'

'I gave the builders a cheque for two thousand pounds,' I say, dreading his response.

He looks down at his desk. 'Ah. Yes, well that is a bit of a problem. Of course, if you were to put a stop to... ah... certain outgoings from the account and make sure she's getting all the benefits she's surely entitled to, I might find a way for such a sum to be honoured.' He nods at the paper I hold in my hand. My eye is drawn by the regular appearance of a number of noughts – three thousand pounds paid out on the fourth day of every month. To the account of Mrs R. Sparrow. My head comes up.

'Three thousand pounds? For cleaning and gardening?'

'Indeed,' he says grimly.

'But that's criminal!'

'Miss Kitto herself validated the payments.'

I stare at him. 'I don't understand.'

He gives me a tight smile. 'Neither do I. It's why I've written to her several times, but she has replied to none of my letters. Maybe you can find out what's going on.'

'Can I cancel the standing order?' I ask after a pause while I try to take in the enormity of it all. How will we pay for the work to the house? If Olivia can't return to her own house will she have to go into a home? And if she does, will we have to pay the fees? What if we have to sell the house? It all seems terrifying and cruel, endless ramifications piling up into a huge black thunderhead cloud.

'Yes,' he says slowly. 'But be prepared for repercussions.'

Sitting in the hire car in the car park off Causewayhead, I wonder what he means by this, and find I am trembling. Suddenly, I am afraid to go back to Chynalls, afraid to see the lovely builders and face their dismay. I cannot *not* tell them. There are people who teeter through life on the brink of financial ruin, brazenly lying, borrowing wildly, buoyed by the phrase 'it's only money'. I am not one of them. All my life money has been tight: I have worried how I will pay every bill, let alone cope with unforeseen emergencies. Money – or lack of it – keeps me awake at night.

What have I got myself into?

11

Olivia

1943

OLIVIA WALKED A PROTESTING MARY TO THE VILLAGE
school with her drawing things in a satchel. She intended
to sketch the crashed plane in the field with the standing
stone. It would make a striking composition: the serene
sea and wide horizon, and the great hulk of burned and
twisted metal in harsh counterpoint in the foreground. The
wreckage was being towed out the day after tomorrow
to be melted down for the British war effort, and so that
ploughing could begin in that field, so it was now or never.

The raid on Penzance had done a lot of damage, but
the death toll had been relatively low. More than seventy
houses and businesses had been destroyed by incendiary
bombs, and fires had raged all night and into the next
day. It was hard to reconcile those dramatic scenes with
these tranquil hedgerows, dotted with red campions and
bindweed, agrimony and honeysuckle. The spikes of the
foxgloves stood tall and emptied, the excited droning of the

summer bees no more than a distant memory whispering among the husks left on the spent stalks. There was a dusty stillness in the earth, a long-hoarded build-up of heat, like a lull before the storm, as if Nature were waiting for some catastrophe to occur before making a final burst of effort ahead of the dying season.

Up at Treharrow the ploughing was under way. The local farmers had grouped together and were going from homestead to homestead with machinery loaned from the Ministry of Agriculture. It was faster and more efficient to have the work done by experienced hands than to let youngsters and prisoners loose with the harrow, as Farmer Roberts – always one to pinch a penny – had found out the hard way the year before when a runaway team had crashed through the fence and run riot through the kitchen garden.

Once the milking was done and the cows put out to grass much of the workforce was at more of a loose end than usual, except the girls, who had been put to work churning in the dairy. Olivia made her way through the farmyard, not taking much notice of her surroundings. She was clambering over the second gate beside the cowshed when she heard a small muffled cry, and then someone said, 'Just hold still, you stupid cow.'

Someone attending to a sick animal, was her first thought, but walking along the back of the cowshed, she could see in through the narrow opening that served as a window that it was empty – except for three figures in the furthest corner. She could easily have missed them, for shadow concealed their forms, except where a missing slate in the roof allowed the sun to penetrate like an accusatory finger, illuminating a startling glimpse of white flesh. Olivia knew with a flash of recognition that something very wrong was occurring down in that grubby corner of the shed, in a place none but cows should be.

Two men stood on either side of a small figure draped over a stone trough like some sort of sacrifice. The one facing Olivia was holding down the figure's arms and Olivia recognized him as Nipper Martin. The other man moved and obscured her view but as he shrugged his top half out of the prisoner overalls he wore and stepped into that finger of light, she saw that his hair was blond, and that the figure bent face-down over the trough, into whom the half-naked man was now pushing himself with grunting thrusts, was Mamie Roberts.

Before she could think, she yelled out. 'Mamie! Oh my God, Mamie!'

Nipper's head shot up and he said something. Mamie in that instant found the strength to squirm away from him and fell away into the straw. The blond man – the Austrian airman, Olivia realized in horror – turned around, not making any attempt to hide his erection. His gaze penetrated the space between them and Olivia felt suddenly both violated and complicit, a victim and an accomplice, afraid and guilty, a voyeur and an object of lust. Out of the corner of her eye she saw Mamie pull down her dress and run for the door at the other end of the shed. The two men exchanged words, and then Nipper followed Mamie, with a purposeful stride. The blond man stared at Olivia, and then he smiled and her stomach lurched.

She looked around but there was no one she could call to for help. Dropping her satchel, Olivia turned and ran back down the alley, hurled herself over the first gate then pelted for the second. She could hear heavy footsteps behind her, but she dared not look back. As she threw a leg over the top bar of the second gate, a hand closed on her other ankle. She felt a scream rise, but her throat closed tight and dry and nothing more than a squeal came out. She clutched hard to the gate, but the Austrian pulled her backwards and she fell awkwardly, knocking her head against the wall.

The man laughed and said something she could not understand as the blood beat in her ears. He bent and picked her up and crushed her against him, immobilizing her with one arm as his other hand tore at her shirt and brassiere, squeezing her breasts till tears of pain filled her eyes. His face, as he pushed it at her, was flushed, his narrowed eyes dark with lust. Olivia let his mouth come at her, then wrenched her head back and smashed her skull into it, connecting with a satisfying crunch. For a moment his grip slackened enough for her to wrench free and take off running.

Olivia ran wildly, desperately, her feet slapping the ground, her brassiere displaced, her breasts loose and uncomfortable. She pelted into the farmyard, shrieking, 'Help! Help!'

There was no one around.

She ran till her lungs were raw, and then threw up into a drain, with her legs trembling like jelly, the hot sun on the back of her head and black stars dancing in her vision. 'Buck up, Livy,' she told herself. Dragging in deep breaths, she readjusted her bra and tucked her torn shirt in. Staggering across the yard, she hammered on the door of the farmhouse and waited, but there was no answer. She peered in through the windows at the familiarly shabby interior, but could see nothing. 'Mamie!' she called through the letter box. 'Mamie, are you in there? It's me, Olivia, are you all right?' No sound.

Sitting back on her haunches, she watched the open ground between her and the distant cowsheds, but there was no sign of either Nipper or the blond man. She needed help, needed to tell someone what she had witnessed, but first she had to find Mamie.

Mamie was thirteen years old. She had been simple from birth but was sweet and good-natured, never any trouble. If you told Mamie to do something, she would do it without question: and that was clearly a problem now that she looked like a grown woman. Olivia's hands balled into fists. Fear for herself turned to cold anger. The child's mother had succumbed to an infection two years ago and there being no penicillin available to civilians had failed to fight it off, leaving Mamie's father, Farmer Roberts, a widower with a farm to run and a family to raise – their eldest son, Albert, who was now off fighting somewhere in the Western Desert; Leo, who had been granted an exemption from active service to work on the farm; and Mamie. To be honest, Olivia hadn't thought much about what it must be like to be Mamie, raised among unthinking men too busy with the farm and their own concerns to be thinking of her protection, let alone her difficult transition into womanhood. It had probably never even occurred to Farmer Roberts that she could ever be in danger, because he simply saw her as a child. As for Nipper Martin… Olivia could hardly breathe for her fury at his betrayal. How could he ally himself with an enemy, a Nazi, against a little girl, and one who was as near to his sister as made no difference? Nipper was practically one of the family, living at the farm, away from his mother in Newlyn who had taken to drink when her Frank went down on his trawler in a storm before the war.

Olivia stomped around the yard till she found a pitchfork, and headed for the barn. Inside, nothing stirred except a few swifts up in the eaves. They would be off soon, cutting through the cooling air on their way back to Africa. How she wished she could go with them.

Up in the hayloft she found Mamie, weeping silent tears into the fur of a compliant tabby cat. 'Oh, sweetheart.' Olivia scaled the remaining rungs of the ladder, flung the pitchfork down and enfolded both child and cat in her arms. The tabby, deciding this was too much to bear, disengaged itself and fled, renewing Mamie's tears.

Olivia's heart clenched. How could they have done this to a child? She could hardly bring herself even to consider the word 'rape'. It was taboo, extreme. Rape was the act of fiends and monsters. She'd known Nipper Martin since they were infants at school together: he'd always been annoying and rude, but was he a monster? Could she have misinterpreted what she had seen in the gloom? She summoned back the smell of the cowshed and the soft, scared mews of the girl; the grunts of the man. No, she was not mistaken: it was rape. Certainty turned to determination.

'Come with me, Mamie. Let's go and find your da.'

Taking Mamie by the hand, Olivia led her up to the top fields, holding the pitchfork like a standard bearer marching into battle. If she saw the blond man, she would ram the tines right into his guts. The image was so clear, so visceral, that she rather terrified herself.

A knot of men were gathered at some distance from the abandoned Fordson tractor, which sat in the middle of an unploughed row. Nothing but fire, plague or flood would stop Farmer Roberts in the middle of a row. She began to walk faster, hauling Mamie so fast that the child stumbled on the rough ground.

'There she is!' someone called, and the knot broke apart. Olivia was alarmed to see both Nipper and the blond man in the group, along with Farmer Roberts, Leo and four or five men from the farms at Kemyel and Kerris, who had brought the teams of horses. Eyes turned on them. Hostility burned in the air. Mamie started to cry.

Olivia took a deep breath and planted the stave of the pitchfork in the ground. 'Farmer Roberts, can I talk to you for a minute?'

The farmer pushed back the cap he habitually wore, revealing a stripe of pale skin. 'What about?'

'I meant, in private. It concerns...' She gave a small nod towards his daughter.

'I've heard all about un,' Farmer Roberts said, glowering.

Behind the farmer, Nipper Martin was watching her with an unreadable expression.

'Get over here right now, Mamie!' the farmer shouted.

Compliant as ever, Mamie let go of Olivia's hand and walked towards her father. Olivia followed, but the farmer jutted his chin at her.

'Get thee gone! Kittos were always witches' spawn. What your mam thought she was doing leaving you here to run wild I can't imagine. Don't you ever come near my girl or my land again.'

Outrage swelled in Olivia's chest. 'It was Nipper and

him!' She pointed to the Austrian. 'I saw them, raping your daughter!' The forbidden word filled the space between them.

'Have you no shame, you harlot?' His face, always florid, went purple. 'Telling such ungodly lies!'

Leo took a step forward. 'You got a bleddy nerve, Olivia Kitto. Everyone knows you're a liar and a whore, taking your pa's car out like some like some fancy madam, flaunting your cash around the village, buying fancy food and exotic birds and the like. Where'd you get the money for that then? Offering handjobs for a shilling a go, that's what I heard, and God knows what else. I was there myself when you suggested taking Nipper down Love Lane, and now you're corrupting my little sister who don't know no better. You're filth, you are.'

Something wet hit Olivia's cheek and she realized he had spat at her.

'How dare you, Leo Roberts! I know what I saw and you're either in league with these bastards or you're as thick as mud.'

Leo raised an arm as if to strike her, but his father caught it, turned and frogmarched him and Mamie away.

'She's your sister, Leo, for God's sake! Don't you care?' Olivia yelled after him.

Nipper leered at her triumphantly, then went back to the group.

Violence hung in the air, a tangible cloud of male hostility as if the real war had suddenly revealed itself as having nothing to do with geographical boundaries and international politics but was instead the age-old battle between men and women. Olivia wondered what might happen if she stayed. Almost the worst possibility was them seeing her cry. Turning on her heel, she dug the pitchfork furiously into the ground with each step, feeling their eyes on her back. Catcalls followed her all the way back down the field.

Damn them. Damn them all. She would run away, pack a bag and take the train to London. But then she remembered Mary, and the parrot, one responsibility that she had not chosen, another that was self-inflicted, and that made her curse again.

She retraced her steps to the cowsheds with the intention of retrieving her satchel, but it was gone, its absence signalled by a single pencil lying in the grass by the side of the path where it had spilled from the bag as she fled. She scoured the area without luck. It seemed that her day was to be one of loss after loss after loss: loss of all her favourite haunts, of Mamie, of reputation and innocence, and now this. The angry tears became sobs of genuine hurt, sobs that doubled her up and stole her breath.

When someone touched her elbow, she shrieked.

It was the Dark Man. He took three or four steps back and put a hand up. In his other hand dangled her satchel.

'Qu'est-ce qu'il se passe? Qu'est-ce qu'il y a? Vous êtes blessée?'

She was so surprised – by his presence, by the French, by his obvious concern – that she stopped crying at once.

'No, no I'm not hurt… je ne suis pas blessée.'

His expression was that of someone who has been given an unexpected gift. 'Mais vous parlez français!'

'Not very well,' Olivia sniffed.

'C'est à vous?' He held up the satchel, asking if it was hers.

She nodded.

'*Vous êtes une grande artiste.*'

He must have looked in her sketchbook, and he liked her art. For a moment, she revelled in the compliment, then... That meant he had probably seen the romanticized portrait she had made of him just ten days ago. Something inside her shrivelled.

He held the bag out and she took it from him gratefully, though he kept his hand on the strap as if to detain her. 'Thank you,' she said stiffly, unable to meet his eyes.

'*Pourquoi vous pleuriez?*' Why were you crying?

Olivia shook her head. '*Je ne peux pas...* I can't talk about it.'

He said something in fast French that she couldn't quite catch. 'I don't understand. I'm sorry, I must go.'

Still he did not let go of the satchel. 'Bad men here,' he said at last. 'Yes?'

'Yes,' she said simply. '*C'était Mamie, la petite fille du... fermier.*'

'*Qui l'a fait?*' His face had gone very still.

'Nipper Martin, *et le Nazi...*'

He burst into words that were neither French nor English. They sounded angry. Then he turned – in the distance voices could just be heard.

'Go,' he said. '*Yallah!*'

He let go of the satchel strap and she took off running. Taking the tracks made by foxes and badgers she made her way down through bracken, thorn and gorse towards the coast and came out close to where she had seen the plane fly overhead on that fateful day, and from there headed east to the lookout post. By the time she reached Chynalls, the sun was starting to dip, sending long fingers of red light out across the bay. Mary sat in the porch, looking forlorn.

'Oh, I'm so sorry,' Olivia said, all enmity towards the child forgotten. 'Have you been here long?'

'Ages. Ages and ages and ages,' Mary said, sounding more exhausted than belligerent.

Before the war, everyone would leave their doors unlocked, but with every year that passed paranoia had grown. Olivia dug in the satchel for the key and they went in together.

12

Becky

THEY SAY IT NEVER RAINS BUT IT POURS, AND THAT NIGHT it pours. Lying wakeful, thoughts churning, I am suddenly shocked by something wet hitting me in the face. It takes me a while to realize that it's raining, and that the bloody roof is leaking.

I switch on the light and watch mesmerized as the next raindrop bulges out of the ceiling, gains heft and with infinitesimal slowness releases its hold and falls. I grab the pillow before the raindrop hits, then haul at the bed. Its big brass feet drag across the bare wooden boards, making an unholy noise. When I have managed to shift it by a couple of feet, I squeeze in behind the bedhead and shove it until it's out of the way of the leak, kicking aside the detritus that has been lurking beneath – a rolled-up eiderdown, a heavy cardboard box, a small suitcase, a roll of cartridge paper (*Ooh, cartridge paper!* my artist brain cries in glee, undeterred by the unfolding disaster). I place the ewer from the dressing table underneath the leak and the drops plink noisily against the china.

Light is greying the edges of the curtains but I feel wide awake thanks to my impromptu shower. I examine the box of books. Old paperbacks on the top – thrillers by Wilbur Smith and Alistair MacLean, their covers faded, their edges foxed. Underneath these a photo album and a shallow-lidded box covered in gilded paper worn away at the edges by years of repeated handling, tied closed with a ribbon.

I am not by nature a snoop. I respect other people's privacy. Going through Mum's things felt like an invasion, but Cousin Olivia is, like Chynalls, stuffed with secrets, and I feel compelled to find out what I can. I open the first album.

Black-and-white photos on textured paper with deckled edges. Most are stuck down on the soft black card with little transparent hinges – the sort used by stamp collectors – some spill out as I open the pages. I can recall their slippery feel before I even touch them, and their gummy taste. James and I had a childhood passion for stamp collecting, fed by a sudden spate of postcards and letters Mum received from travelling relatives. I think I learned more geography from looking in an atlas to see where the stamps came from than I ever did at school.

If I was hoping for candid shots of family life, maybe even some of Olivia with my mother, I am to be disappointed. Most are artistic shots of landscape, recognizably local. Atmospheric, sometimes dramatic, the contrast bumped up by whoever developed them: silver light on the sea, storm clouds over headlands, ever-receding hills, endless horizons. The sort of photos you take in preparation for paintings, I think with a jolt of recognition. There is the cove below the house, and a small boat rowing in. There is the sea gate, clean and bright and oiled and unencumbered by vegetation. Briar rose has colonised its curved top bar. In colour this would make a beautiful greetings card; in black and white it looks austere and rather mournful.

I skip through the album. Fishermen on a quay mending nets, making crab pots, splicing ropes. Women in stained aprons; barefoot children. A young woman sits primly in a chair with a basket of roses on her lap. I am struck by something familiar about her eyes, which are narrowed, almost hostile. I pull at the photograph slightly and it comes away from the page. On the back in pencil it reads, *Mary's wedding day June 7th, 1955*. Her bridegroom, with his long face and lantern jaw, his hair slicked back with Brylcreem, looks uncomfortable in a suit.

I am juggling the loose pictures at the back of the album when one falls out onto the floor. It shows a girl staring straight into the camera with an expression of outrage, her well-muscled arms folded. Turning this over I find it labelled *Olivia betrayed. 1946*. With a shock, I recognize it as a study for the portrait downstairs. So this is what my cousin looked like when she was young. She is striking, handsome rather than pretty, with a strong face and large, capable hands, her shoulders thrown back, chin jutting.

I shiver. *Betrayed*. I wonder what the betrayal was, and who the perpetrator.

There are photos from foreign trips – Venice, Paris, a city with narrow alleyways full of stray cats and tumbling flowers. It looks Mediterranean – Greece maybe, or Corsica. Robed people shopping in a market. Sand dunes covered in striated patterns, sinuous and endlessly replicating towards a distant horizon, stark contrasts in the light – another study, maybe, for an abstract painting. Olivia herself in that desert, in a sort of flowered turban drawn up over her nose so that only her eyes are visible – but I know those eyes now. She is leaning towards the camera, her eyes full of laughter, as if she is trying to retrieve the camera from whoever is taking the shot. There is one of a man in a burnous and turban, looking profoundly out into the landscape with a fierce profile, the lines on his face as much a part of the desert landscape as the patterns in the dunes.

The last pages of the album are empty as if she never got around to sticking anything more in. I now apply myself to the gilded cardboard box, taking note of how the ribbon is tied so I can do it up again in the same way. The act of pulling the bow apart feels much more transgressive than the opening of the photo album. The tied ribbons signals intimacy, the barring of strangers. Even as the ribbon falls slack, I hesitate.

Then the lid comes off.

'Rebecca?' There is a knock at the bedroom door. My head shoots up. I stagger to my feet, my hips stiff from inaction. 'Coming!' I shout, panicked. 'Hang on.'

This is meant as a warning, to buy myself time to put on some clothes, but it doesn't work. Reda sticks his head around the door, takes in my near-naked state and looks quickly away. I grab the nearest thing to hand – the old paisley eiderdown – and haul it around me.

'Sorry, I did not mean to disturb you, but there was no sign that you'd been up – no coffee cup in the kitchen – so I was worried about you. And I need to ask you something.'

Oh no, here it comes. I grasp the nettle. 'Reda, is it about the cheque I gave you?'

'Ah.' He looks embarrassed. 'Not that, in fact, though Mo was going to mention it to you later.'

And yet they have still turned up and, judging by the state of Reda – cement dust and paint all over him – have been working away for some time. 'I'm afraid Cousin Olivia's finances are not in a good state,' I confess. 'It's not her fault – she thought there was more in her account than there is. But I went to the bank, and made an arrangement: if you present the cheque next week they promise it will clear. The problem is, I don't know how I'm going to pay you the rest.' I almost choke on those last words.

There is a long beat of silence, then he says gently, 'Is it really that bad?'

I nod, feeling tears well up. Reading Olivia's letters from my mother – so many of them, going back years; intimate letters, about her fears about her marriage, the discovery of my father's affairs, the final confrontation and divorce, and then his death; answers to letters in which Olivia must have admitted to fears about her bouts of awful weakness and sickness – has made me rather emotional.

Reda comes into the room and, rather than loom over me, perches his tall frame in the little armchair. He gazes at the ewer, which is almost full of rainwater. 'That answers the question I came to ask. After the downpour last night I wondered if the roof would leak. We had better deal with that quickly.'

'But, the money?'

'You will find the money,' he says confidently.

'I don't know how.' Everything seems so hopeless. I am infused with my mother's despair, with her loneliness and fears.

'In our country we say, "God will find a way."'

How nice, I think, *to have such faith*. My confidence in the world has been sorely tried. 'I can't have you working without being paid. It would make me feel terribly guilty.'

He considers this quietly. 'Let us at least make the house weatherproof,' he says at last, 'and then we will give you time to think about what happens next. We have a job in St Buryan we can get on with in the meantime.'

I nod mutely and Reda gets up and goes back downstairs, closing the door quietly behind him.

Mo and Reda work all day on the roof, replacing tiles, repointing cracks in the chimneys. At last, Reda finds me while I am scrubbing the carpet in Gabriel's room while the parrot looks on sardonically. On seeing the builder he perks up, hops from one perch to another and lets out a great squawk. '*Ba-lack! Ba-lack! Zamal!*'

Reda splutters with laughter and for a long while cannot speak. At last he wipes his eyes and looks at me. 'It seems you have a North African parrot.'

'What?'

'That was Darija he was speaking, our local dialect of Arabic.'

'What did he say?'

'"Get out of the way", and then something very impolite.'

'I want to know!'

He repeats the word. '*Zamal*. It's a strong insult where

we come from, how you would say, "paedophile". "Paedo". Someone who does bad things to children, yes? Sorry. I think that's the best translation, pardon me.'

As if on cue, Gabriel chuckles and repeats the word over and over with obvious glee, bobbing his head up and down. And then punctuates the brief silence that follows this little display with a vast oral fart.

'Oh my God, he's a monster!' I cry, mortified, but Mo has now turned up at the door, and together the brothers roar with laughter.

'Wait till I tell Amina,' Mo says.

Amina is his wife. She runs a little deli in Penzance. They have two children, a boy and a girl, and Mo became a British citizen last year, a fact of which he is inordinately proud. He carries in his wallet a photo of himself signing the citizenship register in front of a portrait of the Queen and brings it out at the least excuse. Reda's status is rather more hazy. He holds a French passport, but I think there may be a wife back in North Africa. Or maybe she is here and he just doesn't mention her. Actually, I have no idea of his immigration or marital status. I haven't liked to ask: it seems too personal. And as a result I have never mentioned Eddie either.

When they have gone, I think about calling Eddie. I really should, I know, but I haven't felt the desire to do so, which is odd. While I was ill I thought Eddie was all that was tethering me to the world of the living, that I would die if he left me. It would be useful to discuss the situation I find myself in now, for if there's one thing Eddie's good at it's money, but I feel a reluctance to do so. I don't want to share Chynalls and Olivia with anyone else. *Something will turn up*, I tell myself, remembering Reda's words, and my mind shies away from these insoluble difficulties.

I go back to the noisome task of cleaning the parlour carpet, using bucket after bucket of soapy water and an ancient scrubbing brush, until the whole place smells of wet sheep and coal tar soap, which is only marginally better than the stink of parrot poo.

Then someone raps on the window.

It is Rosie. Seeing her unleashes a riot of feelings in me – anger, confusion, trepidation. I stalk to the front door and stand there, barring her way. She won't know yet, I think, that the standing order has been cancelled. She stares at my crossed arms and I realize I still have the rubber gloves on. All the better to strangle her with.

'Yes?' I say. 'Do you need something?'

'Got a phone call,' she says, looking affronted. 'From the hospital.'

All the steel goes out of me. 'Oh no.' I step back and let her in.

She heads straight to the kitchen and puts the kettle on the range as if she's the one at home and I'm the visitor.

'Is she… Is Olivia…?'

'She had a stroke, poor old dear.'

I sit down heavily on one of the chairs. 'Oh no,' I repeat. Rosie, meanwhile, potters about the kitchen, opening and shutting cupboards and drawers as if looking for something.

'Hasn't gone yet, though. Tough old bird.' She sounds resentful.

A little of the crushing dread lifts. 'What did they say?'

'A stroke in the night. She's on oxygen, though I told them she doesn't want all that, but apparently my word doesn't count for anything. They aren't sure she'll pull through so you might want to go and say goodbye.'

I stand up, move the kettle off the hot plate and take her by the arm. 'I'll go right now,' I say. 'No time for tea.'

'Suit yourself. I would come with you, but Jem's a bit under the weather,' she says spitefully, throwing the tea strainer into the sink. 'I can drop you at the station if you want.'

'It's fine, I have a car,' I tell her and watch her eyebrows lift.

I pull the door closed after us and turn the solid new key in the new lever lock. I see her looking at it, but neither of us says anything and in that moment we both take stock of a changed situation. Rosie's hand goes to her neck, and her face goes tight. Then she turns and trundles off down the path like a malevolent Mrs Tiggywinkle, while I take the path up through the woods to the garage outside which the hire car is parked.

The nurses on Phoenix Ward greet me brightly. 'She's out of ICU, we're very pleased with her. She's still on oxygen, but she's breathing for herself. It appears to have been a stroke, and there is some paralysis, but she's a tough one. Don't get your hopes up too high though, she's not out of the woods yet.'

I hurry towards the cubicle they indicate. They've drawn the curtains around her and she appears to be asleep. Machines tick and blip; tubes run from them to her arm; an oxygen tube lies across her face, little prongs slipped inside her nostrils. I sit on the edge of the bed and take her frail hand in mine. 'Olivia?'

Her papery eyelids flutter. I squeeze her fingers. 'It's me, Rebecca. Geneviève's daughter. Rosie told me that you—'

The eyes flicker open and pin me. So dark, almost black. The eyes in the photograph, and in the portrait downstairs. Her fingers grip mine. She looks over my shoulder and her mouth moves but no sound comes out.

'It's OK, Mrs Sparrow's not with me,' I say gently, and her grip relents. 'How do you feel? The nurses are very pleased with your progress.'

'Tough as old boots,' she says.

She's still in there, I think. 'You are! What did you say to me? "The women of our family have lots of gumption."'

She gives me a lopsided grin that almost breaks my heart.

'Oh, Olivia, you have to pull through this. Promise me you will. There's so much I want to ask you. So much I want to share. You didn't tell me you were an artist. I'm an artist, too. Or I was...'

It's hard to read an expression when only half a face moves. 'Locket,' she says.

'Your locket?' She just won't let it go. I must try again to find it.

'Lock. It.' She separates the syllables with great effort. 'The cellar.' Her fingers on mine are vicelike. 'Brick it up.'

It feels cruel to press my advantage, but I must. 'Olivia, I found a bone. A human bone. Down in the tunnel that leads out of the cellar. Can you tell me anything about it?'

She looks away from me, very deliberately closes her eyes, and then, with more effort, her mouth. I sit there waiting, waiting, willing her to say, 'Oh, that. It is nothing.' But she remains silent and at last a nurse comes to make her observations. 'Don't tire her out,' she admonishes as she removes the blood pressure cuff. 'Eh, Mrs Kitto?'

Olivia does not even respond to this provocation.

When the nurse goes, the old woman draws a ragged breath. 'I never...'

'What?' I grip her hand, feel her fluttery pulse beat beneath my fingers. Her eyes are open but she is looking off into empty air.

'Olivia?' Her hand is slack in mine.

I stay like this for a time, watching her as she stares into space, as if she is sleeping with her eyes open, but when I make as if to leave her grip tightens again and her gaze comes back to me.

'Rebecca...' The black eyes bore into me. 'I never told him.'

'Told who what?'

'Close it up. Promise.' She clutches me with such ferocity that her knuckles are white.

'I promise, but you must tell me, Olivia: whose bones are down there?'

She turns her face to the wall. For the rest of the half hour I spend with her, this is how she stays. She does not utter another word.

I visit Olivia every day. She's still not speaking. The nurses are worried. I take photographs of Gabriel and of the house to encourage her recovery. I play her a recording of Gabriel saying, 'Bugger off' and 'Messy moose key' and *Bal-lack*. This, at least, makes her smile. I tell her how much I love her paintings. She looks wistful, but she still won't talk to me.

'Rosie has said she'll visit,' I say at last, seeking a reaction.

The black eyes open wide. 'No,' she says. 'No.' Her pale lips firm into a straight line. 'I'm not sorry about any of it,' she says. And she goes back to sleep.

It feels strangely empty in the house without Mo and Reda there. I keep hearing noises. Half the time it's Gabriel, whose repertoire is impressive. I sit in the parlour with him most evenings with the TV on in the background. Every so often he will whistle or chuckle or say something I can't quite catch and I will smile and say something nonsensical in return. We're like an old married couple, taking comfort in each other's company but with nothing of any great importance to say to one another. The rest of the time, I don't know. Old houses make odd noises and the acoustics in Chynalls have changed since the downstairs rooms have been remodelled. At times I am sure someone has been smoking downstairs. I catch the scent of an acrid, strong tobacco, and sometimes a sniff of spice, as if someone has been cooking something exotic in the kitchen. The house is full of secrets, and sometimes they come out and whisper together in the night.

I lie in bed, on the edge of tumbling over into sleep, and I'm sure I hear voices below, or out in the garden. Half a dozen times I have got out and gone to have a look but there is never anybody there.

I feel the weight of the knowledge of the excavated finger bone weigh down upon me and imagine its owner stalking through the empty rooms and corridors in search of the missing piece in its skeleton.

Superstitiously, I keep the marble rolling pin from the kitchen under the bed.

13

I PULL DOWN THE ATTIC LADDER AND CLIMB UP INTO the musty darkness. The builders have told me there's quite a lot of stuff up here, though most of it doesn't appear to have been damaged by the roof leak.

Tapping the torch app on my phone, I scan the cavernous space. There are cardboard boxes up here, an old treadle sewing machine, some bulging bin bags that Mo and Reda have moved to the side. I check the contents desultorily and find exactly what you'd expect – old clothes, curtains, books, board games and jigsaw puzzles; a set of *Pictorial Knowledge* encyclopaedias, an old Bakelite phone – pre-war, with a circular dial and a heavy handset, its frayed brown cable wound around and around its base unit. Briefly, I wonder if it will still work if plugged into a phone socket. *Of course it won't, Becky.*

At the far end of the attic, up against the eaves, is a large rectangular object shrouded by a sheet, and cobwebs. I make my way gingerly from joist to joist and twitch a corner of the sheet off to reveal what looks to be a piece of hardboard. I turn it around, then sit back on my heels, hardly able to breathe.

The shrouded objects are a nightmare to get through the ladder-hatch, and I wonder why Olivia went to so much effort to hide them up here. It would surely have been a lot easier to have left them in one of the spare rooms. Or burned them, but I am fervently glad she did not. In the light on the landing I examine them with my heart in my mouth. Here, unframed, on stretched canvas, is an exquisite painting of the sea gate, with blowsy roses twining over its curved bar, just like the black-and-white photo I found in the album. The colours are muted, the last gasp of summer, the paint on the gate sun-faded, the grass at its feet sere as straw; behind it the sea is a wistful grey. Petals have fallen from the overblown roses and lie like old confetti, browning at the edges. It is, I think, one of the loveliest and most melancholy paintings I have ever seen, a testament to times past, times lost. I put it to one side and turn my attention to the second canvas – and burst into shocked laughter.

A naked man faces away from the viewer, the taut muscles of his thighs and buttocks almost warm and tangible, despite the semi-abstract style of the painting. The light gilds his raised hip – a slick of confident golden brushstroke – as he reclines on a bed, propped on one elbow, looking at what is clearly the view out of the window in my bedroom. He is portrayed as a male odalisque: an exotic object of desire, his beauty marred only by a mark on the canvas, spoiling the smooth skin beneath his ribs. And the bed appears to be the same as the one in my room. The decorative ferrules and cannonball post-tops are polished to a deep bronze sheen that closely matches the shade of his long back.

Well, well, Olivia Kitto, you dark horse!

You can almost smell the testosterone in the room, the scent of sweat and musk. They have clearly just made love. There is a languor in his posture that speaks of deep satisfaction. Out of nowhere, I feel a pleasant hot twinge low in my abdomen. This painting is seriously sexy. I would like to climb up on the bed right now and fit my form to these curves of muscle, slip my hands around him and hold his smooth back against my breastbone, the flat planes of his chest against my palms. I imagine him turning his head to me, smiling, and he has Reda's face—

Oh, for heaven's sake, Becky! Don't cast the poor, unsuspecting plumber in your sex-starved fantasy.

It has, I realize with a start, been a while since Eddie and I slept together. How long is 'a while'? I reach back, searching ever deeper memory. It's beyond weeks – months... Yet when we started it was sex that bonded us. I remember the first time we slept together, on a mattress in his shared studio, surrounded by easels and sacks of clay, unframed canvases, unfired pots and the smell of white spirit and slip, and how when Eddie kissed me the powerful orange blossom scent he likes to wear – an expensive Serge Lutens fragrance – obliterated all else, just as his tongue and hands brooked no resistance from my protests that it was too soon and we were just friends; how he had spread me wide and left me sore yet aching for more, although nowadays I'm not even sure it would count as consent, and certainly if I hadn't been so inexperienced and easily swayed, I should have beaten him off and fled home, alone. But there was obviously something in me that craved his hunger, his greed for me – after that, we rarely passed a day without sharing our bodies. Until I became sick. But now that I think about it I can't even recall the last time we held one another, let alone had sex. I appear to have been sleepwalking through my life. I know that illness stole my mojo, my chemo-induced exhaustion morphing into a long, grey depression. It was during my third month of that that Eddie cheated on me. He didn't even bother doing much to cover his tracks – he would slink in at three in the morning stinking of wine and sweat and perfume. I've tried not to think about this betrayal in the year that has passed, but now it hits me in the gut. What decent human being runs off to have sex with someone else when their partner is engaged in a life and death struggle? Why am I still with a man who did this to me – and it wasn't the first time, either – and who could not even be bothered to come to my mother's funeral? These are questions I cannot answer rationally. At the thought of Eddie I feel a brief, warm flutter of desire, even now, but that's just not enough, is it?

I take a deep breath and sit back on my heels, shocked anew, taking in this painting in front of me that has been made with love, and trust, a canvas that represents a painful contrast to where I am in my own life.

Who is this handsome man? Was he Olivia's lover? Well, of course he was: her painting style is unmistakable, and he's clearly not just an artist's model – every lick of paint has been laid on with adoration. I wonder when she painted it. When I look on the back I find there's no date on it, just a simple 'OK' in pencil, like a faint appreciation, or an administrative tick. *Olivia Kitto*. With a jolt, I realize that the letters are of course Olivia's initials. Suddenly my brain itches and I get a flashback to an article I read years ago in

The Fine Artist magazine – Eddie's subscription; I thought it pompous and self-serving – which referred to 'the OK Painter'. It had amused me at the time that anyone would adopt this as their moniker to avoid public exposure. Surely, as Eddie said, getting to be well known was what art was all about? If people didn't know who the artist was, there was little value to their art. The market was all about the brand, and recognizability. 'No one serious buys paintings just because they like them,' Eddie had said, sneeringly. God forbid. Paintings were investments, like gold bars and antiques, to be traded in when their value matured. Except that 'the OK Painter' had, I seem to remember, acquired a certain cachet. My skin prickles. I damn the lack of mobile signal at Chynalls: how typical that I can't go online and check out the story.

Little mysteries surround me, deliberately withholding themselves, trembling on the edge of revelation.

I will go into Penzance and call Eddie and get him to unearth the article before I drive into Truro. I carefully rewrap the paintings and stow them in my bedroom, then grab my handbag, phone and keys and have just reached the top of the stairs when I hear the ratchety old doorbell rattling away – three, four, five times – insistent and peremptory. I stick my head over the banister and can just make out three figures outside the door. It is, of course, Rosie Sparrow. And flanking her, her sons, Saul and Ezra.

I know immediately why they have come. I should go down and angrily demand why Rosie has been siphoning money from Olivia's account. But I find myself sitting on the top step of the staircase, hoping they will go away. I can hear them muttering, keeping their voices down. Then one of the men peels away and disappears from view. I know where he will have gone: round the back. But there is no back door into the scullery now – indeed, no scullery – and the new door out of the kitchen and all the windows are fitted with new locks, thanks to Mo and Reda. And so I sit here, hugging my knees, the euphoria about the discovered paintings draining away like water out of a holed bucket.

Someone gives the front door a kick that makes the glass rattle. The voices outside are raised. I remember Ezra saying how isolated the house is, about the accident that happened to the woman walking the cliffs. Being here alone is one thing, being here without a mobile signal or working landline quite another. I must do something about that.

I rest my head on my knees and wait. Would the Sparrows really have the gall to break in? I listen and listen. There is silence out there now, and at last I summon the strength to get my feet and make my way into my bedroom to peer out of the window. There they are, nearing the gate at the bottom of the path. Thank heaven, they've given up. But I know they will be back.

I duck away from the window as one of the men stares back at the house. I sit down on the bed, shaking, wondering what would have happened if I'd let them in. A shouting match, or something worse? Should I go into the police station in Penzance and report them? But I have no proof of malfeasance – even the bank manager said Olivia had set up the standing order herself.

Instead, I wait another half hour then creep up the path through the woods to where my hire car is parked and drive very slowly into Penzance, on the lookout all the way for Saul and Ezra's truck, of which thankfully there is no sign.

In the car park I call the general number for BT and wait to get through to the right department. I explain the situation – old lady on her own, coming out of hospital, existing line, the need to be reconnected – and wait while they consult their records, or maybe just twiddle their thumbs. At last the woman on the other end of the line says, 'We'll send an engineer out to you…' and gives me an appointment in six weeks' time. I explain, through gritted teeth, the urgency, but the woman is unmoved, and in the end I cut the connection. In a very bad mood, I march down the hill to the main street.

The Cornish Hen feels too exposed in its prominent position opposite the bank, so I slip down the side streets to the Honeypot Café opposite the Acorn Theatre and sit with my back to the wall, comforting myself with a large cappuccino and a wicked-looking almond croissant. The signal is iffy, but at last I get through.

A woman's voice: Evie. My heart sinks. 'Is James there?' I ask.

'Good lord, Rebecca, we've been worried about you,' Evie scolds. 'It's not like you to go running off. Poor darling Eddie, he's been at his wits' end.'

Poor darling Eddie? I ponder this as she goes to fetch my brother.

James is also brusque with me. 'Where on earth are you, Becky? Eddie said you'd run away! He thought we might know where you were.'

I should have told James, I know, but what is Eddie on about? I told him where I was – in Cornwall helping Cousin Olivia. A flicker of rage boils up. How dare he make it all about him again? I can just imagine his wheedling complaints to James and Evie that I've run off, left him at his most vulnerable and busy time. A cold blade enters my chest. Is Eddie thinking of coming down here? To do what – fetch me back? James is talking again but my anger and anxiety have erased some of what he is saying.

'—been selected as a Conservative candidate to fight the next election. Imagine that, Evie running for parliament. Isn't that fantastic?'

I do not have a high opinion of Tory politicians but suspect Evie will make rather a good one. 'Good grief,' I say, trying to rally my thoughts. 'Yes, well, you must be very proud of her. Sorry, can we go back to Eddie? What exactly did he say?'

There is a disgruntled pause at the other end of the phone. I have punctured James's boastful balloon. 'He suspects you're having an affair.'

'He *what*?'

'He thinks you've run off with a lover. I told him that was utterly absurd—'

'Oh, thanks. I might have done, you know: it's not impossible that someone might want to run away with me.'

Now it is James's turn to be shocked. 'You've got a lover?'

'I haven't, of course I haven't. I've no idea why Eddie's come running to you. I told him I've come down to help out an elderly relative – Cousin Olivia, Olivia Kitto – remember the one that Dad called completely batty? He refused to have anything to do with her and took you fishing when Mum and I went to see her.'

'Oh… that one. Pa called her "that awful woman". She's a hermit or something, isn't she? Shut herself off from the world. House smelled terrible. That's all I can remember.

Can't believe the old bat's still alive. She must be a hundred.'

'Not quite. And she's amazing, James! A wonderful character, and in her time a great painter – her work is just wonderful! But she's in a bad way now, and she'd written to ask Mum to come and help her – I found the letter amongst the stuff I went through at the flat. So I came instead. Look, James, the reason I called is I think there are some people here who've been preying on her.' I lower my voice, but no one in the café appears to be paying me any attention. 'Taking money out of her account and stuff. They turned up this morning and were threatening and I'm a bit worried.'

'Call the police!' James says fiercely. 'Or, even better, come away at once. You don't want to get caught up in some awful feud – these things can go on for generations in these out-of-the-way places. And besides, we don't want any family scandal coming out of the woodwork with Evie standing as an MP.'

'I can't leave. Olivia's in hospital and I'm trying to get the house ready for her to come back to… but I've run out of money, and there's nothing left in her account.'

'Oh, Becky, always taking on lame ducks. First Mark, then that tree man, then Eddie—'

I'm taken aback to hear him casting Eddie as a 'lame duck'. I'm sure he'd be extremely resentful to know my brother despises him so. I wonder if I have unconsciously sided with the losers in life, those who find the world tricky to deal with, who fear failure so much that they flee the fight. As I know I have done for so much of my life.

'You can't really say Olivia Kitto's a lame duck; she's an old lady on her own, and a feisty old bird.' I take a deep breath. 'Look, James, I called you for some practical help. First of all, can you lend me some money? And secondly, isn't your mate Jonathan somebody high up at BT? I need to get the landline connected as quickly as possible and they're telling me they can't do anything for months...'

'Crikey, Becks, I can't just call in favours to buck the system for you—'

'Well, if I end up battered or disappeared...'

'Don't be so dramatic.'

'I'll leave a note, so everyone will know that I called you and you didn't do a damn thing because you were more interested in Evie's career.'

'For heaven's sake, Becky. Look, I'll see what I can do. Give me the address of the property.'

'And promise you won't tell Eddie the address?'

There is a pause at the other end of the line. Then he says, 'Oh really, Becky, that places me in a very difficult position.' He sighs and then I hear muffled sounds as if he has placed his hand over the receiver. After a few moments his voice is clear in my ear again. 'Evie says you're not being fair on Eddie.'

My hackles rise. 'It's nothing to do with Evie.'

'Don't be so snippy.'

I force myself not to swear. 'Look, I'm sorry, it's all very stressful. What about the money?'

I can hear him sucking his teeth. 'Things are a bit tight now. I'm waiting for something to come through so maybe next month—'

'James. I need it right now. Olivia needs it. She's your relative too, you know.'

'Do you think her paintings are likely to be valuable?'

Why, oh why, did I mention the paintings? Now he's regarding them as collateral.

'I really don't know. Anyway, she's not dead yet, so don't be so venal.'

'All right, all right. How much?'

I take a breath. 'Ten thousand pounds.'

Deep silence at the other end of the phone. 'I hope you're not getting out of your depth down there, Rebecca.'

I am, but there is no going back. I wait.

'Well, I can't possibly give you ten thousand pounds. Maybe I can manage three thousand. Email me your bank details and I'll make a transfer. You can pay me back – with interest – from your share of the sale of Ma's flat when it gets sold, though I should warn you there's a fair chunk of the proceeds that'll have to go back to the equity release company, which means there won't be a huge amount left over so don't go wild.'

I finish the call and text James the details he's asked for. At least I can pay Mo and Reda some of what I owe them. Having them back at the house will be a relief. Not that I can duck confronting Rosie Sparrow and her thuggish sons for ever. The waitress arrives with a second coffee and I relish it quietly while I google "Olivia Kitto". I find a number of other women with the same name, but no Cousin Olivia. I search for 'the OK Painter' and amid a slew of irrelevant nonsense find an article on the website of *The Fine Artist* about modern anonymous artists. I scan it avidly, and when I scroll down, the image with which they have chosen to illustrate the article makes me catch my breath. It is the painting I have just retrieved from the attic, the one I called in my mind *The Sea Gate*. I read the relevant part of the article with great attention.

The painting in question disappeared from the sale room the day before the auction, so it was never involved in the bidding on the day, although it does appear in the catalogue and had raised considerable interest, bearing as it did the moniker 'OK' on the rear of the unframed canvas, although unlike the previous works sold by the auction house in 2003 and 2004 – namely *The Girl in the Orchard* (1951) and *The Pilchard Fishers* (1953) it was not dated. There has been considerable speculation as to the identity of the artist of these works, and critics have drawn parallels with paintings made by artists grouped under the St Ives School of Art, though the style is somewhat more painterly than most works by the more abstract artists in that loose confederation. There is also some mystery as to why these paintings have only recently come onto the market, whether they have been deliberately withheld for sale to increase the value, or for more personal reasons.

The curator of the Tideline Gallery, which specializes in handling the works of Cornish painters in the post-war period, says, 'No one knows the identity of the artist in question. Some have posited that these paintings may be unfinished works by the artist Oscar Kendal, who lived and worked in West Penwith during his latter years. But others argue that although the textures share the boldness and confidence of Kendal's best work, the focus and colour palette suggest a more feminine sensibility.'

Others still argue that the initials do not comprise a signature at all, but are a joke at the art world's expense, or the administrative flourish of an artist or his assistant selecting works for sale.

Whatever the truth of the matter, the OK Painter remains a delightful enigma and an anomaly in a market that is driven by brand names.

I send myself the link via email, and then turn off my phone, feeling as if I am engaged in some work of deep espionage. There is no doubt at all – to me – that Olivia is 'the OK Painter'. Probably just as well I wasn't so sure about this when I spoke to James: I am a hopeless liar. Now I want to know why, with the wonderful talent she had, she wanted to remain incognito. She does not strike me as a shrinking violet, or an overtly modest person either. And her paintings are everywhere around the house. I must ask her, if she is strong enough to answer, when I visit.

At the hospital I go to Phoenix Ward, and find Olivia's bed empty. Panic clutches at my heart. My despair must be palpable, for a nurse passing through the ward wheeling a trolley of meds stops and says, 'They've moved Mrs Kitto up to Wheal Jane: she's doing a lot better.'

Upstairs, I find the nurse in charge and ask about my cousin's recovery. 'Oh, Mrs Kitto,' she says, and rolls her eyes. 'I think the occupational therapist will be very glad to see the back of her. I've never heard such bad language from an old lady.'

'Sorry,' I say reflexively.

'No need for you to apologize,' she says. 'We can't choose our family, can we? I should tell you we'll be starting the discharge process shortly. She's being assessed by the reablement team, and we'll arrange a visit to her home by social services to look at her needs, and go from there.'

The tiling, lighting and final fixes in the bathroom have yet to be done; the walk-in shower needs grab rails and a stool; the doors have to be made and fitted; a hospital-style bed and adjustable chair have to be bought; the new bedroom could do with painting; and a floor surface that won't trip her up... The realities of the situation begin to unspool in my head: all that, and cooking meals... heck. I have not thought this through. And then there is the cellar...

I give the nurse manager my contact details and explain the signal problem at the house. 'Ah yes,' she says, looking at her notes. 'We have Mrs Sparrow down as the back-up contact.'

Rosie.

'There will be a landline soon,' I say hastily. 'Please take Mrs Sparrow off your contact list.' Recklessly, I give her Reda's mobile number. He's a kind man: I hope he won't mind. I'll clear it with him when I call.

'She's in the TV room at the moment.'

That's where I find her, sitting at some distance from the other patients, who are watching *Bargain Hunt* turned up loud. When I call her name she does not respond and when I get closer I see she has stuffed cotton wool in her ears.

It sprouts out of her head like some weird tufted plant. She appears to be deep in a book. When I tap her on the shoulder she looks up, and I feel the force of her annoyance as she turns her eyes on me, then her expression relents and with some effort she pulls the cotton wool out and winces at the volume of the television.

'Oh, it's you. Thought it was somebody come to disturb me again. They can't bear that you should have a moment of peace in this place, as if a bit of silence might kill you.'

I am getting better at understanding Olivia's mangled speech. One side of her face droops, though am I imagining it, or is it drooping a little less today? Her left hand rests on an upturned book. 'What are you reading?'

She makes a wonky face and shows me the cover. 'Got it off the library trolley.' Daphne du Maurier's *Rebecca*. 'I've read it before and it's a bit lightweight, but reasonably entertaining.'

'Mum called me after that.'

'Strange, she was not a nice woman, the Rebecca in the book.'

I had read the letter from Mum from amongst the many in Olivia's under-bed cache:

Dear Cousin Olivia

Well, goodness, now I understand why you never had children: what an awful to-do pregnancy is. I have felt trapped in my own body these past months, hauling around a burgeoning alien. Really, I can't wait for these heavy little souls to be born so that I can regain my life again. There isn't anyone else I can tell this to: everyone is so relentlessly thrilled for me. That's what they say:

'You must be thrilled.' 'Aren't you so thrilled?' 'We are so thrilled for you.' 'Isn't it utterly, utterly thrilling?' Well my dear, it utterly, utterly isn't. My body is like an elephant and I am sure my husband is having an affair. He returns at all hours of the day and night smelling of cigarettes, and you know he has never smoked, so I think you were right when you said to me after meeting him not to trust a man with a roving eye. I cannot leave him – not in my current state – so I am stuck in my choice and must make the best of it.

Thank you so much for the book you sent me. I so loved it and shall seek out Daphne du Maurier's other works.

Would it be wicked of me to call my unborn daughter Rebecca? It is, after all, a very pretty name and it will always remind me of Cornwall...

'I miss my mother,' I say.

Olivia pats my arm. 'I miss her too.'

'They said you'll be coming home soon.'

She gives me a smile, and yes! I am sure it is a little less lopsided. Goodness, what remarkable recuperative powers she has. A tough old bird, indeed.

'I just want to get back into my house again and be surrounded by my own things and all my memories.'

This would surely be a good moment to raise the matter of the paintings, and the bone in the tunnel. I open my mouth to ask that very question... then close it again. I no longer want to know about that bone. I just want to brick it all up and forget about it. So instead I say, 'Cousin Olivia... I went up into the attic – the roof was leaking but the builders fixed it – and I found some paintings up there. Some wonderful paintings.'

She stiffens.

'You didn't tell me what a marvellous artist you were.'

For a moment a small, secretive expression of satisfaction twitches one side of her mouth. Then the shutters come down again. 'I don't know anything about that.'

I turn on my phone and find the photo I took of *The Sea Gate* and show it to her. 'It's so beautiful, and so sad. Tell me, Cousin Olivia, are you the "OK Painter"? It is you, isn't it? I found an article online…'

The eye closest to me fills with moisture and I watch a solitary tear swell and spill and roll down her withered cheek. 'I'm sorry, I didn't mean to make you cry,' I say, gently wiping it away. 'You mean the world to me.' Another tear follows the first, and I feel cruel.

I pull a tissue out of the carton on the bedside cabinet and she blows her nose noisily. 'I would have done things differently,' she says after a while. 'I wish I'd had the courage.'

'To do what?' I prompt, but she shakes her head.

'No good comes of digging up the past. It's a fool's game. Read me the next chapter.'

She thrusts the book at me, and I do as I'm told. Another visit in which I can't bring myself to press her for answers. But there is always the next time, and the time after that. As Olivia herself would no doubt say, *softly, softly, catchee monkey.*

Before I head back to Porth Enys, I call Reda and am hugely relieved when he answers. 'I've got some more money coming through,' I tell him. 'Enough to pay you and Mo for most of the work you've done.' This makes him very cheerful.

'You see? I told you God would provide.'

We agree that he and Mo will come back tomorrow. 'We want to finish the job and make the old lady happy,' he says. 'And you, too.'

It seems there are still some good people in the world.

The house appears peaceful and secure when I return, but when I press the key into the front door and push, something stops it from fully opening. I shove the door and squirm inside, to find something jammed between the doormat and umbrella stand. I bend to examine it, and spring back. It is a huge dead rat. Someone has squeezed it through the letter box; the force of this has made its nose bleed and bits of its guts have extruded past its yellow teeth at one end and out of its anus at the other.

Maybe Gabriel can smell it, or has sensed the violence of the act, for he is shrieking in the parlour, jumping from the low perch to the high one and back again. Forcing my gorge down, I pick up the rat's corpse on a shovel and take it to the overgrown orchard. By the time I get there it does not disgust me any more; rather, the act that robbed it of dignity in its death tears at me, and I am suddenly furious. I dig a hole for it, channelling my anger into each strike of the spade, and stamp the soil down as if I am stamping on Saul and Ezra Sparrow's faces. I have no doubt at all that they are responsible for this atrocity.

Then I wash my hands and take Gabriel the treats I have

picked up for him in Penzance. I let him out of his cage and he flies around the parlour for a few minutes, his wings clattering. I only have one mess to clear up – not too terrible before it dries – and he goes back in meekly as if making a great effort to be polite.

But when I go to the door and turn the light off he croaks, 'Evil old bitch.'

He sounds just like Rosie Sparrow.

14

Olivia

1943

THE TELEPHONE WOKE OLIVIA FROM A DEEP SLEEP. DOWN in the quiet cavern of the hall it rang on and on and on. When it became clear that no one else was going to answer it, she hauled on her pyjama bottoms – discarded, along with the top, in the mugginess of the night – and ran down the stairs, convinced that the phone would rattle its last before she reached it.

The black Bakelite receiver trembled in her hand. 'Is that Penzance 272?' an unfamiliar voice enquired.

'Yes.' Olivia's heart beat faster. She sat down on the bench, her knees wobbling. It was still dark outside, though shades of grey had begun to filter through the panes flanking the front door. Who would ring so early? Perhaps it was Leo Roberts or Nipper Martin, intent on terrorizing her. Or maybe Winnie wanting to speak to Mary. Perhaps something had happened to Mummy up in London...

All these thoughts and more ran through her head as she heard the operator say, 'Putting you through.'

'Darling?' Her mother's voice, sounding very far away. 'Is that you, Olivia?'

'Mummy! Oh, Mummy, I was so worried about you. Are you all right?'

'Hush, darling. I'm afraid I've had some terribly bad news...'

Olivia held her breath. Not Daddy. Not Daddy. Anyone but Daddy. No. No. No. She would bear anything – Aunt Winnie, Mary, Farmer Roberts, going to church, doing her chores without complaint, or any other bargain with the Almighty that could be made – if only Daddy were safe.

'Are you still there, Olivia?'

'Yes,' she said in a tiny voice, as if quietness could lessen the impact, or shrink the truth.

'I wish I was with you, darling, to tell you properly...' Her mother's voice was clipped and controlled, as if she knew she was being overheard. 'If I could have come to you, I would have... but, it's all rather complicated.'

The blood buzzed in Olivia's ears. She knew what was coming and she did not want to hear it.

'Olivia, dear, I'm so sorry to tell you like this, but I'm awfully sad to say that Daddy has been killed in action.'

'No...' The word in her head was a wail; what emerged was barely a whisper.

'He died a hero, darling, not that that makes any difference in this wretched war. I really am so terribly sorry to tell you like this, Olivia, but—'

The operator's voice cut in with, 'Three minutes, please, caller.'

'Tell Mrs Ogden to make you some cocoa!' Mrs Kitto called down the line. 'I love you, darling. I—'

The phone went dead. Olivia sat there, staring at the receiver, as if it were the traitor that had broken her world apart. Then, very slowly, she replaced it on the base unit and sat with her hands in her lap staring at her bare feet planted on the cold tiles of the hall floor. Brick-red, black and cream, replicating patterns of fleurs-de-lys, black on red, red on black, black on white, more of them illuminated as dawn broke outside. What was the matter with her? Daddy was dead, yet she couldn't cry, couldn't shed a single tear. Her feet were brown against the tiles: it had been a hot summer and she had spent a lot of it shoeless and outdoors, 'like an urchin', as her father would have said, tousling her hair.

He would never say that to her again. She would never ever hear his voice again.

Now the tears came, huge, silent tears drawn from deep inside her as if she were weeping with her heart's blood. Daddy was dead. *Killed in action.* Daddy was dead and Mummy couldn't be with her and there wasn't even Winnie Ogden here to make her cocoa.

'Why are you sitting half-naked by the phone?' Marjorie's voice was sharp with suspicion. She came down the stairs at speed now, slippered feet thudding. 'Leo Roberts told us all about what you've been getting up to, Olivia Kitto. You're nothing but a little whore!'

Olivia stared at her with hot, seeping eyes, and for the first time ever could not find a word to say.

'For God's sake cover yourself up! You're absolutely shameless. Been on the telephone to one of your beaus,

I expect. Well, Beryl and I are not sticking around to get tarred with the same brush. We're packing up this morning and moving to the farmhouse on the request of Mr Roberts, so give us back our ration books and we'll say good riddance.'

Olivia stood up, feeling the thundery air swirl over her naked skin. Like an Amazon she stalked past Marjorie and up the stairs, using every ounce of her willpower to hold the tears till she was out of sight. Reaching her room, she put a pillow over her head and wept and wept.

'What are you doing?' An accusing voice.

Olivia unearthed herself and stared at the intruder.

'You've been crying!' Mary announced with unholy glee. 'Is it because Marjorie and Beryl have gone?'

'Go away.'

'Shan't.'

'Go away and leave me alone.'

'I want my breakfast,' Mary said mulishly.

'Get your own breakfast.'

'No!'

'Well, go hungry then.' Olivia turned her back on the disobliging little beast.

'I'll tell on you.'

'Good luck with that,' Olivia said wearily.

Mary stared around the room, full of malice. Spying Olivia's sketchbook, she grabbed it up and started ripping pages out of it.

Olivia sat bolt upright. 'You bloody little savage!' She flew across the room and gave the child such a clout that

Mary ended up against the dressing table, howling as if all the demons in hell had been unleashed.

Olivia was unrepentant. 'Never, *never* touch my things again, do you hear me? Or you'll get worse than that.'

Mary bawled, nursing her sore jaw, on which a large red mark was blossoming.

'My father is dead,' Olivia said fiercely. It sounded surreal to say the words aloud, as if by uttering them she had made it true.

'Good,' said Mary. 'I hope you die too.'

Olivia took the child downstairs and applied cold compresses to her face with controlled fury as if by doing so she might erase the deed along with the bruise.

'I'm going to tell on you,' Mary declared again, sniffling.

'I really, really don't care. Nothing matters any more.'

Robbed of her leverage, Mary glowered. 'I'll make you sorry you hit me if it takes the rest of my life.'

Olivia walked Mary to the village school in silence, the child dragging her feet unhelpfully. It was a long walk for her, but Olivia kept up an unrelenting pace, feeling hollowed out, her mind elsewhere. Where *was* Mummy? Why couldn't she just get on a train from London and come to comfort her only child? You'd think, Olivia reflected angrily as she stomped back up the long hill towards Chynalls, that she'd care *that* much about her. Surely the bank could grant her compassionate leave, especially with her daughter alone here in Cornwall, hundreds of miles away. Of course, Mummy didn't actually know that Winnie Ogden wasn't there. Olivia had been rather vague about that the previous time Mummy had called, but even so. It was clear she didn't really care, despite all the soothing words and 'darlings'.

Olivia kicked a stone up the hill with ever increasing degrees of violence. Darn her! Well, she was on her own now, that much was obvious. She would just have to fend for herself. Olivia against the world!

Back home, she took in the drab interior with rising dismay. There were feathers and splatters of guano all over the parlour and dust on every visible surface. Marjorie and Beryl had left the remains of their breakfast scattered over the dining room table, their dishes and cutlery defiantly unwashed. No doubt they'd left their rooms in a state too. The kitchen was already a shambles. Olivia hated housework and without *Oberleutnant* Winnie to keep her in line she had let things slide. She rolled up her sleeves. This was her domain now: she would take charge of it.

For the rest of the week, Olivia dusted and mopped, pummelled, scrubbed and pressed through the mangle everything that could possibly be washed. The monotony of all this domestic work kept her mind from circling around her deep-seated grief, but in the depths of the night it sought her out and found her, burrowing up to the surface to torment her with all the knowns and unknowns of her losses.

The weather remained heavy, lowering clouds trapping sticky air between the sky and sea. In the mornings a livid line of light showed across the horizon, held prisoner between the elements. Olivia could not stop looking at it: it called to something deep inside her, that stripe of light trapped in darkness. She sat with her father's treasured Leica for a long time in her hands, imagining she could smell his scent on the leather case, and when she pressed her eye to the viewfinder, she thought about how the last eye other than her own to look through that tiny window had been his. It was oddly comforting. She had taught herself how to use it, wandering far and wide along the coast to take photos with this expensive piece of kit while Mary was at school, taking a malicious pleasure in trespassing across the edges of Farmer Roberts' land. She had rigged a studio in Marjorie's vacated room, where the blackout curtains came in useful, and learned how to develop the film from absorbing her father's photography books, and a lot of trial and error.

Exposure errors became deliberate style statements, the photography print papers lending different textures and finishes to her creations. She was rather pleased with some of her efforts, but most she destroyed. She was, she told herself, developing her own artistic sensibility. Her favourite images she essayed in the medium of oil paint. When money for supplies ran out, she mustered new-found courage and went to see Mrs Harvey, who ran the down-chapel hall, and offered to give drawing classes for a shilling a class. She took her sketchbooks with her. Mrs Harvey looked through them dubiously. 'You do know there's a war on, don't you, bird?'

'It's a good way for people to escape from all that for a while,' Olivia said doggedly.

And so on Tuesday just before midday Olivia took up residence in the hall, bringing a roll of cartridge paper she had bought in Penzance with what was almost the last of the grocery money, a handful of drawing pencils and some erasers. She had cut up some of the hardboard used to floor sections of the attic into drawing boards and gathered whatever bulldog clips she could find. She set the hall chairs in an optimistic semicircle and put on each one a board with a piece of paper clipped to it. From her duffel bag she brought out a piece of driftwood scavenged off the foreshore beneath Kemyel, some sea-smoothed stones with interesting markings – rounded pebbles of quartz-speckled granite, lumps of folded slate bearing unusual striations – apples from the orchard in various states of wellness and decay, and a mackerel, which was beginning to smell, but which offered a tantalizing exercise in the use of light and shade.

It was distinctly chilly: Mrs Harvey had refused to light the fire in case no one came. 'We're running low on coal; it's not Buckingham Palace, you know.'

Olivia pulled the cuffs of her cardigan down over her hands and stomped around the hall to warm her feet, her steps booming in the emptiness. Then she sat down and regarded the fish. Picking up a board and pencil, she lost herself in the intricacies of the mackerel's tiger-striped skin.

'Why, you're a natural. I should hardly think you need lessons at all!'

An elderly lady was peering over Olivia's shoulder. She wore a thick navy jersey and a large silver pendant and Olivia recognized her as Mrs Hocking, whose daughter ran the grocer's.

Despite this, she felt suddenly shy. 'Actually, I'm giving the class.'

Her only other student lurked in the doorway looking belligerent. It was Mrs Harvey's daughter, Judith, who had been two classes below Olivia at school in Penzance. 'Ma said I had to come.'

No doubt to make sure she wasn't smuggling naked live models into the chapel hall, Olivia thought, and stifled a laugh.

Mrs Hocking had brought her own set of watercolours, the tubes gnarled and the paint within uncooperative. 'It's been years since I had these out, not since my Jackie died.' She tapped her necklace in some complicated manner and a mechanism made the front of the pendant spring open like a hinged bivalve. Within lay a tiny black-and-white photo of a man with not much hair but a huge moustache. Olivia was fascinated, having never before seen a locket.

Mistaking her interest, Mrs Hocking said, 'A fine-looking man, my Jackie.' Her voice was burred with emotion. 'Been gone twenty year now and I never so much as looked at another man since then.'

Olivia got them both drawing, and was surprised to find Judith had a fair touch with a pencil and a good eye for line and perspective, and the girl beamed at her praise, but it was the older woman who astonished her, producing a mackerel in dabbed and silky watercolour that looked as if it might swim off the paper back into the sea. Mrs Hocking smiled rather sadly. 'Jackie and I used to take our paints and sketchbooks wherever we went, but he lost the use of the fingers in his right hand during the Great War and it didn't seem right to outdo him after that.' She paused. 'He had no joy left in him when he came home from the front. He never laughed, he'd hardly even speak. War is a terrible thing: it drains all the humanity out of a being.'

She fell silent, patting her necklace. Then she drew it over her head, popped it open, took out the little photograph and slipped it into her handbag. She handed the empty locket to

Olivia. 'For you, dear. You've reminded me to do something for myself again, and not to live for ever in the past.'

'I can't take it,' Olivia protested. 'It's much too precious.'

The old woman laughed. "'Tis pewter, my bird. It shines up well, but it's not silver. You take un: you've given me something much more valuable.' She tapped her fish. 'Now I've started I won't stop again.'

Olivia allowed Mrs Hocking to hang the necklace around her neck. She thought, *I will find a photograph of Daddy and put it in there*, and that made taking it feel better.

The following Tuesday she had five students; the week after that seven. But in between, everything changed.

15

THE YEAR HAD TURNED TOWARDS WINTER. FOGS WRAPPED
the coast, clagged the trees; cloud hung heavy over the
headlands. Birds' cries sounded mournful and distant, eerily
like the cries of children. Sometimes the fog did not lift all
day and the hedge and its sea gate marked the limits of her
vision.

Chynalls felt like an island and Olivia could imagine
herself a figure out of legend, a castaway or exiled warrior
living beyond the bounds of normal society. Despite this,
she treasured her isolation, swimming in the cove beneath
the house even when the temperature of the sea made
her teeth chatter and her heart clench. She felt as if every
dip toughened her up, tempered her, added new layers of
protection. She was Achilles in the Styx; the Gorgon on
Sarpedon. But one day when returning through the sea
gate with her hair in long snaky locks, she came upon the
postman on the steps up to the house and the sight of him
reversed the Medusa effect so that she was the one who felt
turned to stone. Was her mother dead now too?

But Bert Blewett grinned at her. 'Something special for you,' he said, holding up a brown-paper parcel.

It was addressed in her mother's clear handwriting, but she could not make out the franking stamp. When it became clear that Olivia was not going to open the parcel in front of him, or share the contents, Bert sniffed and went on his way, muttering. Inside the brown paper was a cardboard box in which a small cornucopia of treats had been packed between wood shavings. Olivia pulled out a Chanel lipstick, a small bottle of Givenchy perfume, a packet of candied almonds, a beautiful ruby-red beret, and a set of Caran D'Ache drawing pencils in the full spectrum of the rainbow. A small card accompanying these gifts read, *For my beautiful grown-up girl on her 16th birthday, with all my best love, Mama*, and three kisses.

Olivia sat with the treasure box on her knees, and burst into tears. She had completely forgotten that it was her birthday.

As a gift to herself she walked up to the garage and took the car out, up the hill, past Treharrow Farm, ignoring the catcalls of the men in the yard as she whizzed past. She had never returned to the scene of the assault but all the time had been aware of it as a dark weight, lurking just up the hill. It felt good to whisk past it in the Flying 8 and leave it all behind.

At the crest of the hill she turned right, then left onto the road towards Land's End, passing through the dark wooded valley that led down to Lamorna and winding back up onto the tops again, where the mist was beginning to thin. Just past Boleigh Farm she drew the car up on the verge and jumped out, leaving the engine quietly ticking over.

Climbing over the old stile, she made her way up through the field until she reached the ancient menhirs known as *Dans Maen*, the Dancing Stones, or Merry Maidens. Mist drifted between the stones, floating just above the unmown grass. She knelt, feeling the chill moisture soaking through the knees of her trousers – a pair of Daddy's, too big, but held up with one of his stout belts – and took several shots with the Leica. Then she stood up and slung the camera over her shoulder and started to walk widdershins around the circle, touching each stone in turn. When she touched the fourth stone she drew her hand back sharply as if burned: some energy between her and the granite had arced, literally shocking her. Hesitantly, she reached out and laid her hand on it again, but whatever electricity it had collected had been discharged and it felt simply like a cold, damp stone. Even so, she was shaken.

The legend ran that the circle represented the remains of a group of maids who had defied the rule of the Sabbath and danced to the music of two local pipers, all of whom had been punished for the transgression by being turned to stone. It had always seemed a silly tale to Olivia, annoyingly moralistic, but right now, engulfed by the mist, still tingling from the contact with the petrified dancer, she shivered.

Continuing her passage around the stones, she trailed her fingers across each one till she came back to her starting point. Should she make a wish? It was another local custom, another silly superstition. But why not?

Olivia walked on to the fourth stone, laid her palms on its rough surface and closed her eyes. For a time her mind remained blank. Then a single fleeting thought crossed it and she smiled. That would do: it was so absurd it could never ever happen so it was perfect for a mad sixteenth birthday wish.

Back in the car again, she drove on slowly through the narrow lanes, praying not to meet a tractor, since reversing was not something that Daddy had got around to teaching her. And now he never would. Tears blurred her vision, but she was in luck, for there were no other vehicles on the road. On the hill above Sennen, isolated shafts of sun were breaking through the low cloud as the end of the land came into sight. The light rendered the scene with such contrast and sharp clarity that it looked, she thought, like a daguerreotype, the sea all silver plate and mercury, fixed with a solution of common salt. She drove as close to the cliff as she could then abandoned the car and walked along the furze-covered cliffs, taking photographs of the stark granite sentinels against that silver sea. She passed lookout stations and mounted Bren guns and men in uniform who asked her not to take photographs of their positions, and eventually made her way back to the car, realizing with a start that so much time had passed that she would have to drive directly into Porth Enys to collect Mary from school. As a result she drove faster than she should have, and just as she was taking the corner down to Raginnis, she lost control of the vehicle and, panicking, turned the wheel in the wrong direction and worsened the swerve, sending up a spray of earth and stones and taking the Flying 8 over the verge and into the hedge. The impact sent her head-first into the steering wheel and the horn went off with a fearful blare.

'Bugger!'

Olivia rubbed her forehead and got out to examine the damage. The front of the Flying 8 was well and truly embedded in the hedge. She looked around. Of course, it had to be on Treharrow land. Before anyone could arrive to berate her for her reckless driving, she got back in and tried to reverse out. The car grumbled and the wheels spun uselessly. She pressed the accelerator harder and the engine shrieked, then died. She employed the pull cord over and over, to no effect.

Someone rapped on the window, making her jump.

'Need some help?' It was Jago.

Relieved, she nodded and wound the window down. 'I can't get it out,' she said piteously.

'Can see that. We'll need to bump you out of the hedge.' Turning on his heel, he strode off down the road before she could reply, disappearing through an opening in the hedge.

Olivia sat there, torn between running away like a scared child, and accepting the consequences of her actions like a grown-up. In no time, Jago returned with two of the POWs. One was the blond man. Olivia felt her guts shrivel. She sat rigid in the driver's seat, her hands clamped on the wheel.

'Put 'er in neutral,' Jago said through the open window.

Like an automaton, Olivia changed the gear, keeping her eyes on the hedge, but a moment later the blond man was fully in her vision, leering in at her as he and the other man pushed and bumped the Flying 8. Olivia fixed her gaze on the small square of bonnet that ended before the blond man's hands and clenched her teeth. The car bounced and juddered and suddenly rolled backwards out onto the road.

'*Splann!*' declared Jago. He leaned his head in through the window again. 'Do 'ee want to leave her here with me and I'll get her back to the barn with the lads? You can walk back from here, can't 'ee, bird?'

Olivia shook her head desperately. She could not leave the vehicle: she could feel hot urine pooling beneath her on the leather seat. 'One more try,' she pleaded.

She pulled the start cord again, but the engine did not respond.

'Ar, well give me the starting handle and I'll give her a go with that,' said Jago.

Olivia handed it over without a word and watched as he cranked and cranked – to no avail. She was almost crying now. If it wouldn't start she'd have to walk, and that meant getting out of the car in front of all of them with the tell-tale stain on her trousers. She couldn't, simply couldn't. She should have kept her wish from the stones for now, she thought miserably. And then, a miracle, the engine caught and roared to life, and she put her foot down and rocketed away from them all without even a thank you. In the rear-view mirror she saw the three figures standing in the road, ever dwindling, and raced on.

Mary was at the school gates, bundled in the too-large gabardine coat that had been Olivia's own. Olivia flung the passenger door open for her and she climbed in, looking suspicious.

'Where did you get this from?'

'It's Pa's,' Olivia said shortly.

'Does that mean it's yours now he's dead?'

Olivia said nothing.

Jago brought her back the starting handle later that night and she stowed it in the box in the hall where Pa had always kept it and swore she was never going to take the car out again.

★

Two nights later there was an immense thunderstorm with winds that made the glass rattle in the window frames. Olivia, reading a book in the kitchen under the flickering light of the hurricane lamp, jumped as the first crump of thunder sounded overhead, as loud as German bombs, as loud as the downing of the crashed aircraft. She went to the front door, opened it and stood in the porch, watching the slanting sheets of rain battering the plants in the overgrown garden. The moon lay over the sea, trapped between thick clouds. It sent a small silver disc like a spotlight onto the brazen surface of the sea below like an SOS, then disappeared again from view, casting all into darkness, until a fork of lightning split the sky, illuminating everything with a flash of harsh light that left jagged after-images on her eyeballs.

Olivia loved storms. As a child she would stand on a chair at her bedroom window, mesmerized by the elemental power, as thunder raged and lightning zigzagged. She had had to be restrained from running out into the wild weather, arms wide, mouth open to catch the rain. She itched to be out in the elements now, running down the path to the cove, leaping into the lightning-seared waves. The sea was warmer during a storm, it would be wonderful—

Someone called her name, breaking the spell, and she turned. At the top of the stairs Mary sat like a small ghost, her face almost as pale as the white nightclothes she was wrapped in.

'I don't like it.'

'Go back to bed. It's just a storm.'

'My night light's gone out.'

With a sigh, Olivia came back inside.

As she relit the little candle with one of the precious matches, the child grasped her arm. 'I heard someone outside. They're coming to get me.'

'Don't be silly. It was just me, checking all was well before locking up.'

'When will it stop?' Mary whined.

'The storm? Soon, I'm sure.'

'The horrible war. When will Mummy come home?'

It was weeks now since Mrs Ogden had gone to Bristol to see her sick mother and in all that time there had been no word from her. Olivia had come to the reluctant conclusion that she had abandoned Mary and would never return. This theory had been bolstered by the fact that Winnie had taken all her money with her. Olivia knew this, as she had checked the blue ginger jar where Winnie kept it, from which Olivia had occasionally helped herself to the old shilling, feeling no sense of guilt at all.

'I'm sure she'll be back soon. Now go to sleep.'

'Will you stay here till I'm asleep? There are monsters in the shadows.'

Olivia laughed. 'There's no such thing as monsters. Don't be such a baby.'

In the pale circle of her face, Mary's eyes glittered furiously. 'There are monsters! There are lots and lots of monsters, everywhere.'

As Olivia turned to leave, the child whispered, 'And you're one of them.'

★

Olivia was still smiling to herself as she made her way down the stairs, but then her smile faded. She had failed to draw the blackout curtain over the front door when she came back inside, and now she was certain she could see a figure out there in the porch. She froze, holding her breath in the pitch dark. She could hear the rain hammering on the porch roof and blowing as hard as hail against the front windows, the sound of the wind buffeting the chimney. Another rumble of thunder sounded, further away. It was just the storm: a trick of the light.

She relaxed and started down another stair when the shape outside moved – and just as it did lightning jagged across the sky for an instant and Olivia saw, as clearly as if taking a flashlight photograph, the blond man.

A small mew of horror escaped her. Preoccupied by Mary, she had come straight in and gone upstairs. She had not locked the front door. In a sudden pause in the noise of the storm she heard the handle turn, and then he was staring right at her, his hair a pale beacon in the darkness.

An internal voice was telling her to *run run run*, another to *think think think*. She could not get past him to the front door: he filled the space like an ogre. If she was fast she might get out the back. Had she locked the back door? Her mind was a blank. She thought she had, but was that just a memory of the hundreds of times she had done so before? If she had locked it he would surely catch her while she scrabbled for the key in the scullery. Even if she got outside he would surely catch up with her. He was fast, and rough, that much she remembered, and her breasts ached from the memory of his hands on them. If he ran upstairs, she could lock herself in the bathroom. But then he would find Mary.

Did she care about that? Oddly, she found she did. Then she thought: the cellar! If she could get to the cellar steps she could throw the bolt on the cellar door and escape down the tunnel to the beach and from there run up through the sea gate and along the lane to sound the alarm and bring help...

All these thoughts tumbled through her head in the split second in which it took the blond man to step through the door.

'I see you,' he said.

Olivia felt her guts knot. She tried to run, but her muscles wouldn't obey. Suddenly she found herself sitting on the stairs as her knees gave out. A coward! She was such a coward! Where was her Achilles, her Medusa, her warrior self when she needed them?

He hauled her upright and she felt something hard and cold at her throat: a knife. She could smell the nicotine on his fingers, and his sweat. He was speaking in German now – hard, guttural words. Her eyes were riveted by the sight of his grey lips working in the gloom. She couldn't move a muscle. Petrified, she thought. Now she knew the true meaning of the word, and the true feeling of it. The poor dancing maidens, she thought. Being turned to stone was horrible. Knowing you were going to die, unable to do anything about it.

He repeated his demands. She shook her head, trying to clear her thoughts. Then: '*Auto*,' he said, and made a cranking gesture with his free hand.

Her relief was so great she almost wept. He needed the starting handle. That was all he wanted: to escape in the car. It occurred to her he must have already located the garage and broken in if he knew the starting handle was not there. All she had to do was give it to him and he'd go away.

'Go away,' she said. It came out as a child's whisper.

He smiled and his teeth were like bright stars in the darkness. '*Schnell!*' he barked at her, but still she could not move. He repeated his demand, more angrily, and she felt the knife push against her skin, wet and icy: rain, or blood? Her legs began to shake. When he pulled at her, her feet slipped on the polished wood and she fell the last two stairs, knocking him off balance, sending them both to the ground. Olivia heard the skitter of metal on tile, and when she flicked her eyes towards the sound she saw where the knife had spun away towards the front door. Purpose broke through her paralysis. She got her knees under her and crawled towards it, managed to get her fingers over the haft, but he was fast. Taking hold of her trailing leg he hauled her backwards across the smooth tiles, fell on top of her and pinned her flat, his weight on her ribcage so oppressive that she could barely breathe. Then he inched his thick body up her till his hand was on her wrist, and beat it again and again on the hard floor.

She would not let go! She would not! Gritting her teeth against the pain, Olivia clung on. She writhed and took a deep breath and tried to buck her spine against him, but it was as if an ox had fallen on her. And then her grip failed and the knife fell from her fingers. With an almighty act of will, she flicked at it as it went, sending it skittering against the skirting board and down the hall corridor. The blond man roared in frustration and knotted a hand in her hair.

He was going to smash her face into the ground. She could imagine with precise repulsion the way the bone and cartilage in her nose would crumple as it contacted the hard tiles, the tang of blood on her tongue, down her throat; her teeth cracking, her tongue severed by her own jaws. Terror filled her with preternatural strength. She managed to drag her knee under her and push back with her head, hitting him squarely on the chin. Everything stilled and in that moment she writhed free and scuttled like a shore-crab scared out of its hiding place, down the hall, scooping up the knife on her way, hurling herself into the first room she came to: the parlour.

There was, of course, no lock on the parlour door. She knew her error as soon as she'd made it. Slamming the door shut, she shoved the couch towards it as a barricade, but only got it part way across the opening before he was there on the other side, pressing door, sofa and her backwards in his fury. She remembered being inside the car with his taunting eyes fixed on her, his mouth twisted in a half-smile as he pushed her out of the hedge.

There was no half-smile now. The moonlight from the uncurtained window shone into his mad eyes – no blackout in here during the winter because the only room she used was the range-warmed kitchen – and 'I kill you!' he growled, and she knew he meant it.

Despite her fear, she wondered where he had learned these English words, and if he had used them before: on Mamie, maybe, or during whatever incident had enabled his escape from the farm.

Thunder rumbled outside and the window glass rattled as the wind pushed at it and sounded across the chimneys like a moan.

Then a hoarse voice yelled, 'Bugger off!' and the blond

man stopped dead, the whites showing all around his eyes. The parrot jumped from perch to perch, rattling the cage on its stand and shrieking, 'Bugger off, arsehole!'

Once he saw it was only a parrot, an insignificant distraction, the airman turned his attention back to Olivia, laid both hands on the couch and pulled it away from the door. Olivia's feet skidded on the rug and it rucked up behind her. Acting before her brain told her not to, she leaped up onto the couch and right at him, stabbing at him as she went. The blade snagged on the fabric of his coat and she put all her weight into the blade and he cried out in what she hoped was pain, but then he roared and shoved her and she flew backwards, losing her grip on the knife and landing heavily on her back.

In a blink he was on her, laughing in mad, gleeful rage.

The clouds parted and moonlight spilled in, illuminating his ghastly face, all teeth and eyes like a wild animal. Her arm was painfully twisted behind her; it felt as if her shoulder might spring out of its socket as he pressed down on it. Then his hands were around her throat and she was choking. Awful sounds filled the dark room as his hands bore down on her and she tried to drag in oxygen. Dark stars buzzed in her eyes, the pressure on her throat as hard as a stone.

Olivia peered piteously past the Nazi airman's face, not wanting it to be the last thing she saw, and something moved into her field of vision. It was a figure, a man in silhouette, and he reared above them both with a bulky object in his hands. 'Ba-lack, zamal!' the newcomer cried and 'Ba-lack zamal!' another voice echoed. In the recesses of her mind, Olivia realized that the echo was the parrot: she could hear the bars of his cage rattle as he jumped from perch to perch in agitation.

The airman looked around, and in that instant the man hit him. Something hot spattered on Olivia's skin, then something small and hard hit her face as the blond man fell away from her. She moved her hand to her cheek and took the object in her fingers. She could make no sense of what it was, then with a start she realized it was a tooth and threw it down, revolted.

Olivia coughed and rolled sideways. Beside her the airman was groaning and scrabbling with the other figure on the floor, both roaring out words she could not make out, matched by the alternate barking and shrieking of the parrot. She got unsteadily to her feet. The knife. Where was the knife?

The clouds had closed over again; she could not see anything. Who was the figure who had come to her aid? The two men were indistinct shapes, entwined in their struggle, a pale head on top, then a dark head.

It was the Nazi who found the knife. The blade rose in the air in an arc of muted silver and came down and the other figure cried out and Olivia was seized by a fresh wave of ter-ror. The blond man was invincible, a monster; he was going to kill the man who had come to save her, and she would be next. It was absurd, surreal, she almost wanted to laugh. She was going to be killed in her own home, in the house where she had been born, by an enemy combatant while the rest of the war was a continent away, and the only witness to her violent demise would be a foul-mouthed parrot.

Never had she more wanted to live, never had it seemed more likely that she would die. She turned to run, barked her shin on something hard, almost fell – the bulky object with which the newcomer had hit the airman. When she picked it up she recognized it as a log from the wood pile in the porch. Possession of it made her braver. She turned back to the struggling pair. But the blond man was on his feet now, the knife in his hand. Instinctively, she held the log between them and thrust it towards him as the blade came down at her. The jarring impact drove her backwards. Her foot caught in the rucked-up rug and she staggered and lost her balance. Her agonized cry came as a hoarse whisper out of her tortured throat, then she landed hard, and the world went still.

16

Becky

I WAKE UP WITH MY HEART POUNDING AND EVERY HAIR on my body standing on end. I am more than awake: I am super-alert, hypervigilant. I lie there, stiff as a corpse, sending my senses out into the house to report back their findings. Rain thrashes against the window: perhaps that's what woke me? At least this time it's not pouring through the ceiling, though I have to put the light on and scrutinize the ceiling to be sure.

Gradually, I take deep breaths and feel my pulse rate beginning to settle.

Pull yourself together, darling! My mother's voice, kind but exasperated.

I was prey to nightmares as a small child – the thrashing-limb, howling-banshee kind that dragged Mum from her bed in the small hours of the night to calm me, which usually involved waking me up then holding me till I stopped wailing and could be persuaded that no monster, bad man or Dalek was pursuing me.

I look at my phone: it's four a.m. Rather than try to go back to sleep, which I know will be fruitless, I go downstairs to make myself a mug of cocoa and potter around in the kitchen. Work hasn't started in here yet. I'm getting used to the vagaries of the old range so have decided that putting in a new oven can wait. I grab a digestive biscuit and my mug of cocoa and head upstairs. I will read in bed until I get sleepy again.

As I step up onto the first tread, I hear a noise. My ears strain. Rain slapping the path beyond the front door, but beyond that something else. In the house, most definitely in the house. The clink of something hard – metallic? – on stone, then something sounds like the scuffle of feet on a gritty floor.

There is someone else in the house.

Trapped by indecision, I hover on the stairs. I could retreat to my bedroom, put a chair under the door handle, get under the duvet and listen to the rain, and wish all the bad things away. Downstairs, there is scary reality, the possibility of confrontation, even violence.

Buck up, Becky.

I turn and step down again into the hall, my feet making a soft slapping sound on the bare tiles. How can anyone have got into the house? Have they broken in? But the front door appears untouched: no panes of glass are broken and I know I locked it before going up. I hold my breath and listen. Now I can hear nothing but the rain rattling against the glass. Have I imagined it? I make my way quietly back towards the kitchen, listening, listening. Maybe it was just Gabriel that I heard? But I'm sure I put the cloth over his cage last night, which makes him go to sleep, or at least become quiet.

I am about to check on Gabriel when I hear the noise again.

My heart trips and thumps. As if to confirm my suspicions, a finger of light flits across the hall, then disappears. It came, I am sure of it, from the bottom of the door to the cellar.

There is someone in the cellar.

God, what am I going to do? And why didn't I take Olivia at her word and get Reda and Mo to brick it up before they started on the rest of the work?

I stand there, paralysed, all my senses questing and terrified. And there it is again, low and grumbling: men, talking quietly, furtive but not nervous. Are they planning to come up the cellar steps and through the door into the house? After me? But the door is locked. Isn't it? I creep towards it, reach to the lintel. Yes, there it is. Now the key is in my hand. Quietly, quietly, I insert it into the lock. If there is a duplicate they won't be able to open it from the other side. That buys me some time. My heart is knocking, knocking.

The sensible thing would be to creep back upstairs, get dressed, grab my keys and flee the house. That's what I should do.

Instead, shocking myself, I find myself turning the key, pulling the door open and flicking on the light switch.

Below are Ezra and Saul Sparrow.

They freeze, blinking in the flood of light. My eyes take in the trails of wet footprints, the oil drum lying on its side. Ezra has a large package in his hands; Saul carries a black torch – its beam made redundant by the unshaded cellar 100-watt bulb – but it looks solid enough to be used as a weapon.

Behind him, I can see the tunnel door is ajar: they must have come up from the cove. Do they have a key? Did I leave it open? I remember the day I swam with the seal, the small boat that was clearly about to put into shore, and was prevented from doing so by my presence. What are they doing? Hiding something? Something illicit – otherwise why would they be so furtive?

The moment lies suspended between us: me with my hand on the cellar door, looking down; them, caught in the act, staring up at me. I think: anything could happen. They could rush me, hurt me, lock me in the cellar, drown me at sea... anything. I am an idiot for confronting them, for giving the game away. What on earth did I think I was doing? The image of the rat flickers through my mind, its lips drawn back in rigor, its extruded guts...

I slam the cellar door shut on them and turn the key in the lock.

'I'm going to call the police!' I yell through the thick wood.

I hear heavy feet on the stone steps, then one of them hammers on the door. 'You got no signal, you ent calling anyone!'

Ezra Sparrow, I think. The fat one.

I start to shake. What if the door does not hold?

The door rattles and rumbles as Ezra kicks it, but it is sturdy and shows no sign of giving way. More swearing; more kicks. Then the sound of footsteps retreating.

Should I run out of the front door and down the lane till I get a signal and call the police? But if I leave the house, might they not run down the tunnel and come up through the sea gate and chase after me like the monsters in my dreams? What if they come up the path and break down the front door? They cannot let me go, having seen what I've seen.

I must run up through the woods, get in the hire car. I dash up the hallway. Keys, where are the keys? The keys are not in the bowl on the hall console. Where are they? Oh God, they're still in my handbag, upstairs. And I'm barefoot, in pyjamas.

A screech splits the greying air. '*Ba-lack! Ba-lack!*'

Through the parlour door I can see that the cloth I drape over Gabriel's cage at night has slipped off and he is jumping in an animated fashion from high perch to low perch and back again. 'What are you doing? Get off me!' he squawks, followed by, 'Die, you mad old bitch!'

I stand there, my heart jumping faster and faster. The first phrase the parrot uttered in Olivia Kitto's recognizably plummy tones, the second perfectly mimicking Rosie Sparrow. Did Rosie try to hurt Cousin Olivia? Is it how Olivia came by her broken leg? The thought chills me.

What a monstrous family they are. Dangerous. Violent. I cannot stay here.

Up the stairs I run, fast as a rabbit, snatch my handbag – give it a shake: yes, keys, thank God. Mobile phone, for what good it is. Grab the marble rolling pin from under the bed – might need a weapon. Shove feet in trainers, try not to trip over the laces as I hammer back down the stairs again, grab my coat and shrug it on (it is pouring out there). I am standing at the front door shuffling through the keys to unlock it with my handbag slipping off my shoulder, trying not to drop the rolling pin jammed under my armpit when the rain, quite suddenly, stops.

The silence is oppressive. My brain seeks to fill it, searching for noise, but I can't hear anything at all. Outside the sky is greying. I press my nose to the glass and gaze out at the burgeoning dawn, as the sun creeps over the horizon, gilding the clouds a rich, deep gold, shooting red streaks across the eastern sky.

Red sky in the morning, shepherd's warning, I think.

Everything is still. Even the seagulls, usually in full cry at this hour of the day, are quiet. Through the stained glass panel to the right of the door I spy in the orchard the tip of an elevated orange tail – one of the local moggies on an early morning hunt, the rest of him obscured by the long grass. Swallows swoop upon insects down near the sea gate; by the path, a blackbird is hauling a worm out from amongst the montbretias. Life and death in the natural world: a constant cycle.

With the light, reality returns and panic recedes, a little.

Armed with the rolling pin, I go back to the cellar door and listen. Nothing at all, not even breathing. Holding my weapon high, I quietly unlock the door and crack it open. No one jumps out at me. I peer around. No murderous man comes charging up the steps at me. The light is still on: I stare into the brightly lit space below. It is empty. Spilled tins lie strewn around on the scuffed and dusty floor, a scatter of tins and paint pots: the shelving unit has fallen over. They seem to have gone, but I have no intention of going down to check, not on my own. I close and lock the door again.

They'll be back, of that I am sure.

I return upstairs and gaze out. I cannot see from here what state the tide is, whether it is in, trapping them in the tunnel below me, or whether they have managed to get to a boat. There are some small boats out there on the sea. Does one of them belong to the Sparrow brothers? Have they motored out through the rock arms of the cove? I hope so.

I wish I had some binoculars. I stare and stare, as if hoping might make it so.

Wings spread wide, a small crowd of seagulls follow a small fishing boat on its way in to Newlyn to land its catch.

It all seems so normal, as if nothing has happened.

I should report the break-in to the police, I think. Drive into Penzance and file a report, tell them my suspicions about the Sparrow family. Should I dig up the rat and take it in as evidence of their menaces? And what about Olivia's broken leg? Had it really been the result of an accident, an old lady simply losing her balance on the stairs? Or had Rosie Sparrow pushed her? Was Gabriel parroting a scene he had heard, or witnessed, or was he simply regurgitating random bits of noise, maybe even dialogue from the television, recast in familiar voices? Could parrots do that? It was hardly evidence, was it? I pictured myself in court, Gabriel balanced on my hand, spreading his wings to show off all his splendid scarlet feathers, telling the judge to bugger off...

Get a grip, Becks.

I will go into town later anyway. No point in rushing off in my pyjamas, looking like a loon. Check all the locks, make some coffee, then write everything down and get it into some semblance of sensible order, dig up and take a photo of the dead rat, and go and talk to the police. They can come and have a look at the cellar and see if there is any sign of illegal goods there.

I go around the house making an inventory of all the possible points of entry and find them all secure, and at last make my way into the kitchen. I am busy making coffee the way Mo and Reda like it, the way I have now come to prefer it – in a little stove-top espresso pot on top of the range – when a shadow passes the window onto the back alley.

I jump back with a yelp. Somehow, I manage to knock the espresso pot over and a thick black ooze of coffee grounds sizzles and burns on the hotplate so that the kitchen is filled with a bitter, searing stench.

It's probably the postman, I tell myself, trying to settle my racing heart. But I know it's too early for the postman or anyone else on bona fide business. Too early even for Mo and Reda. It is, I know with horrible certainty, Saul or Ezra Sparrow, come back to do me harm. I remember their threatening words, the disgusting rat shoved through the letter box. But I also remember the thousands and thousands of pounds their thieving mother has extorted from a vulnerable old lady, and Gabriel's mimicking of an attack on her, and my fear transmutes into some sort of anger.

Rolling pin in hand (I swear I will keep it with me all the time – 'Weapon? Of course not, officer, I'm a keen baker.'), I tiptoe to the window and catch the flick of a dark coat just disappearing around the corner to the right of the house. I imagine the intruder skirting the wall on the other side of Olivia's suite, picking his way between the overgrown flowerbeds there, rampant with weeds and brambles. I have not yet got around to tidying up the garden.

I run down the hall corridor and wait by the front door, obscured by the stained glass panel, until the inevitable shadow falls across it. Then I turn the key, haul the door open and leap snarling through it, brandishing the rolling pin. If the Sparrow brothers are determined to have a battle, they will get one!

The figure in the dark coat falls away before my fury and when I look down Eddie is looking up at me in bewilderment.

Relief is swiftly replaced by confusion. How can Eddie be here? He's three hundred miles away. And how on earth has he found me...?

Goosegrass and stinging nettles are wrapped around the leg of his smart black jeans. His Armani raincoat has slipped off one shoulder, revealing his favourite black cashmere sweater: both are covered in dust. Sprawled on the cracked concrete apron where once the porch stood, he looks as I have never seen him before: inelegant and uncurated.

'What the hell are you doing here?'

He gets to his feet, looking aggrieved. 'I've come all the way down from London to find you, on the fucking sleeper train – or should I say the "so-called fucking sleeper train", since I didn't get a wink – and that's the best you can do? We've been apart for weeks! I thought you might be missing me. Or at least want to know how my show went.'

I completely forgot about his show, and I don't even feel guilty about it. 'How did you get this address?' But I already know. Bloody James, bloody male solidarity. Or bloody Evie, doing a favour for 'darling Eddie'.

'Aren't you pleased to see me?' He isn't even looking at me, more concerned with dusting off his coat and removing the weeds from his jeans. I take some small satisfaction at seeing him wince as one of the stinging nettles gets him and he jerks his hand away and sucks it like a child.

'No, I am not pleased to see you.' I lower the rolling pin. 'Why are you here?'

He cocks a look at me from underneath his heavy black fringe, and there is mischief in his eyes, his confidence returned: for how could any woman resist him? 'Don't I even get a kiss?'

He comes at me and crushes me against him, rolling pin and all, and bends his head to mine. 'Oh, Becks,' he breathes into my neck, and then he is kissing me there, my ear, my cheek, my mouth. 'I've missed you.'

My knees start to weaken in that old familiar way. 'Hey, stop that!' I wrench my head away.

But Eddie thinks my evasion is some sort of game. He pulls me back in and I am engulfed by that familiar scent of musk and orange blossom and it is as if each breath I take erases another degree of my hostility and soon his arms around me feel like a haven rather than a threat, and then all I can think about is sex.

There's something about Eddie. He casts a spell. It's easy to say that men like Eddie are 'good in bed', but when Eddie makes an effort you become the centre of his world, the focus for every iota of his attention. This proved intoxicating for someone like me, who'd never thought much of herself. It was a novelty to see myself through his eyes – he who worshipped beauty, who caressed my body the way he caressed his pots. He made me feel ultimately desirable. Suddenly, I remember standing in front of Courbet's *L'Origine du Monde* in the Musée D'Orsay in Paris with no one else around to make me embarrassed at examining some other woman's hairy nether regions, going weak at the knees as he breathed into my ear, 'That's you, that is: the essence of woman, the origin of the world. I can smell her cunt, can't you? I can smell yours. Let's go back to the hotel and fuck till dawn.'

Uncouth but somehow irresistible.

It's been a long time since I felt desirable, let alone desired.

I can feel his hardening cock pressing against me, hot and insistent, and his tongue is in my mouth, the musk of him all around me, rising up through the orange blossom...

I lead him into the house and up the stairs. In seconds we are naked and tangled together on the big old brass bed.

17

Olivia

1943

LIGHT GREYED THE ROOM. A PRETERNATURAL QUIET HAD fallen outside: no wind, no rain. The storm had blown over. Even the parrot was hunched and still as if the violence had shocked it into silence.

Olivia sat with her knees drawn up to her chest, watching the Dark Man warily. He put his hands up as if in surrender. They were covered in blood. He said something in French, but Olivia was too shaken to make sense of the sounds. Her head throbbed, her throat and shoulder smarted. There was blood everywhere – splatters of it, and a widening dark pool like a black halo around the airman's head. She could not stop looking at his staring eyes – the pupils vast and fixed, haloed by a fine ring of grey iris.

The Dark Man sat back against the wall, breathing heavily, a hand pressed to his side. Olivia watched in horrified fascination as blood pulsed between his fingers.

Yet more blood. 'You're hurt,' she said hoarsely. 'Sorry. I can't think of the words in French.'

He looked up with difficulty as if his head was heavy. She had to do something or there would be two bodies in her parlour. She got to her feet, feeling sick and dizzy. Concussion, she thought, then pushed the word away. Bandages. She needed bandages, to stop the bleeding. She had to clean the wound. She fixed on this idea and made it move her feet, past the corpse, past the Dark Man, past the couch and out into the hall. She left a bloody handprint on the door jamb, and another on the kitchen door, saw them both as she returned with clean linen tea towels, a bowl of water, the bar of Wright's Coal Tar soap and the kitchen scissors.

When she re-entered the parlour she found the Dark Man sitting beside the body, his hands close to the dead man's head, his fingers working in small, clandestine movements. His face was downcast, his lips moving silently. When she approached he looked up. He held a string of beads in his hand and she recognized it with a start.

'*Une prière, pour le mort,*' he explained. A prayer for the dead. He put the beads away in his trouser pocket, wincing as the movement caused his wound to leak again.

Olivia could not move. She recognized those beads. The light was not yet bright enough to see the colour of them, and yet she retained an image of redness, a dark cedar-red, just like the string she had seen on Mamie's doll in her hedgerow lair. Was the red from the blood? Why would he have Mamie's beads?

Her suspicion must have shown on her face for he was

looking at her intently, all the lines of his handsome face focused into her eyes, boring in.

'Where is Mamie?' She forced the words from her damaged throat and watched as he listened. A great sadness came over him.

'I have made... *prière*... for the dead *deux fois*, two times today,' he said softly. 'The first was hardest.'

Olivia's fingers opened and she dropped what she was carrying, the bowl sloshing, the soap and scissors clattering onto the bare boards, the tea towels floating down to cover them all like a shroud. 'She's dead? Mamie's dead?'

'He kill her... *zamal*.'

'What happened?' Olivia sank onto the couch, feeling hollow.

'*Tempête... tonnerre*, scare animals... *vaches*. Door not shut... they push past farmer and men and...' He gestured, indicating the widespread dispersal of the cows. 'Mr Roberts he fall, *blessé*, Mikael, he escape.' He nodded towards the corpse. 'Big confusion, *grand bruit, confusion*, running here, there. I go after Mikael *mais trop lentement, trop tard*.' He shook his head.

'And Mamie?' Olivia pressed, despite not wanting to know, an awful dread growing inside her.

'Don't know how he find her, *elle jouait avec sa poupée...*' She was playing with her doll. 'He pull her *dans la cour du ferme*' – into the farmyard – 'he have knife, *mais elle lutte*, she fight, and when he see me he—' He made a brutal gesture, a finger across his throat. 'He push her at me and we fall.'

'Oh God, oh God.' That poor little girl, who never did

anything bad to anyone. How could she die like that? The world had gone wrong, it was all awful, a nightmare. She wanted to wake up from it, to walk into a clean dawn with nothing worse before her than the household chores.

'I try stop *le sang*' – the blood – 'but so lots. And she, gone, like that. *Elle est morte, je peux pas le croire.* I not believe it. Mamie, *la mignonne.* I shake her,' he demonstrated, 'but she gone. I put her down, close her eyes. I take her *poupée* and put it in her hands and say *prières* for her, and then they come, Leo and Nipper, and they see me. They think I kill her! And the prayer beads on the doll – I take them...'

Olivia's mind felt scrambled. His gaze was open, earnest. 'Are you telling me the truth?'

'I swear to merciful God that I am. *Alhamdulillah.* I run then. *J'ai couru.* No explain. They not believe me. And I know Mikael, what he want. You, your car, *la voiture.* So I go after him. He talk *voiture* a lot – he see you in car two times, he like. He ask why you in it, not man, if no man in your house, *aucun homme chez vous.* Leo, he talk too much, *il aime le pilote, comme il est un grand hero*, big Luftwaffe man. They all laugh, say now you no allowed visit farm no more, have to go to village for your milk and eggs, *faut chercher vos choses ailleurs*, you alone *toute seule*, in house now *les filles, Marj et Beryle*, come to farm. And Mikael, *il écoute.*' He fell silent, listening. 'They come here soon, I think, looking.' Then he winced and blood oozed from his side.

Did she believe him? She did not know. Her brain wasn't working. She picked up her first aid things and concentrated all her thoughts on cutting the fabric into strips and dealing with his wound, trying to remember what she had been taught of anatomy, and whether there were organs just below and left of the ribs, trying not to think that he too might die. But the hole was shallower than she'd thought and with some effort the wound was soon cleaned and plugged. He did not make a sound through it all. Despite herself, she thought him very brave. '*Merci*,' he said at last, and repeated it as she addressed his lacerated hands. 'I go. After move him, I go.' He shook his head. 'He kill that child. *Zamal*.'

'No,' she rasped fiercely. '*We* will move the body and *you* will stay. *Il faut rester.* They will kill you otherwise. *Vous tuez.* Besides, you saved my life.' She grabbed a cushion and shucked the cover off it, then pulled it over the airman's ruined head. It was a relief not to have to see those staring eyes any more.

In life Mikael had been heavy; in death he was as immovable as a menhir, but somehow together they half-dragged, half-carried the corpse into the hall. They sat him at the top of the cellar steps while Olivia fetched the hurricane lamp. While the Dark Man held the cellar door, Olivia gave the body a shove with her foot. Down it went, tilting into a graceless forward roll, limbs flailing, contacting steps and wall in a series of grotesque acrobatics until at last it came to rest in a crumpled heap in the gloom far below. 'I'm afraid you'll have to go down too,' Olivia said quietly. 'Can you make it? *Vous pouvez le faire?* There's a rope rail, *une corde*, here.' She guided his hand to it and down they went, the leaping light making their passage ever more nightmarish. Olivia crossed the cellar and opened the door there with a large iron key.

She wondered if the tide was in, and if they could get

the body all the way to the cove, but she knew the local currents only too well: even if they could get it through the pinch point and manoeuvre it out to the waves it would bob out as far as the encircling rocks, get caught in an eddy and linger accusingly. The hope that the sea would swallow the evidence was a vain one, too easy a solution to a hard problem. Sins and secrets were not so easily hidden.

Between them, they pushed and dragged the corpse across the dusty floor and out into the chill of the rock tunnel. Olivia closed the door behind it, locking it again with the big iron key.

'Stay here,' she told the Dark Man. '*Restez ici.* I must clean the blood away upstairs before Rosemary gets up.'

'Rosemary?'

'There is a child in the house,' she explained. '*Il y a un enfant ici.*' She felt calmer now that the airman was out of sight. 'I'm going to lock the door up there, but only to stop anyone finding you. I will knock three times. *Je vais frapper trois fois*, like this,' she demonstrated. 'If anyone else tries the door up there *utilise le clef*, use this key to go out into the tunnel.' She handed him the iron key and watched as he took all this in, feeling like a character in a book – *The Thirty-Nine Steps*, maybe, or *The Riddle of the Sands*. Except that this wasn't fiction, and Mamie was dead. The murderer had died in her own parlour. It seemed surreal.

Exiting the cellar, she locked the door at hall level, put the key up on the lintel and took in the scene with dismay. There were wide smears of blood across the tiles, and a glimpse of abattoir through the door into the parlour. Picking her way down the clean margins of the hallway, she closed the door on the horrible vista within. At least Mary was scared enough of the parrot that she wouldn't go in there: she could clean that up later.

She ran to the kitchen, gathered a pail of water, a scrubbing brush, some Oxydol and an old towel and worked her way down the hall, expunging the evidence. The blood was not yet dry, it came away easily, leaving the tiles gleaming, but even so the water quickly swirled pink then rusty red and she had to empty the bucket down the butcher's drain in the scullery three times. She had just cleaned the parlour door and handle and was hefting the final bucket back towards the scullery when a small voice said, 'What are you doing?'

Mary's head had appeared through the rails of the banister, her eyes pale holes in her white face.

'I spilled some milk,' Olivia lied easily.

The child regarded her suspiciously. 'No you didn't.'

They locked eyes.

'I drank the last of the milk in my cocoa before I went to bed,' Mary said. 'And why are you whispering?'

Olivia went hot and cold. 'I kept some back for breakfast,' she said, trying to speak normally. 'But unfortunately now there's none left. I think I have a cold coming on.' She walked to the kitchen door, away from that penetrating gaze, then noted with horror her bloody print upon it and quickly placed her hand over it.

'I heard noises in the night.' Mary had followed her down the hall. The soles of her slippers left little half-dry patches on the damp tiles.

'It was probably the storm. It was very noisy.'

'I heard voices.'

Olivia laughed, a little hysterical. 'You ninny, of course you didn't, you must have been dreaming.'

'I'm not a ninny!' Mary said furiously. 'I did. I heard people shouting.'

'That was probably the parrot,' Olivia rasped. 'You know how he is when he gets upset.' Before Mary could say anything else, she added, 'There's a little bit of cream left. You can have it in your porridge.'

Mary looked disbelieving. 'Really?'

'And some jam. Run back upstairs and have a very good wash – I shall check behind your ears – and put on your pinafore and your lace-up shoes' – that would keep her occupied – 'and I'll make the porridge.'

As soon as Mary had disappeared back upstairs, Olivia wiped the handprint off the door, then swiftly returned to the scene of the crime.

The parrot sat hunched on his perch, looking shell-shocked. Olivia stuck a finger through the bars and stroked his head. He was too miserable even to try to bite her. 'I'll bring you treats later, I promise.'

Olivia took in the devastation of the room, then pushed the couch back against the wall, rolled up the ruined rug and shoved it underneath. A large stain remained in the middle of the floor. She pulled the big wool rug they used as an antimacassar off the armchair and laid it over the mark. It would have to do till she had time to give it a proper scrubbing. She removed the worst of the spatters of blood, stuffed the killing log into the grate and dumped the knife with which the monster had murdered poor Mamie into her bucket.

She had just shut the door on it all when she heard voices outside.

18

OLIVIA WENT TO THE DOOR. OUTSIDE STOOD SERGEANT Richards and a man in a trilby, whom he did not introduce. 'I don't mean to alarm you, Miss Kitto, but two of the POWs from up Treharrow escaped last night and we have reason to believe they're highly dangerous. Just want to make sure all is well here and to assure you we're doing everything we can to apprehend them.'

Olivia said nothing, aware of the second man's gaze on her, so intent she was sure he saw her guilt and fear. Or perhaps there was blood in her hair – unconsciously, her hand rose to her head.

'Have you seen any strangers?' he asked, his voice curiously high and light for a man his size.

She shook her head. 'We haven't seen anyone.'

'We?'

'Just me and Rosemary Ogden, the housekeeper's little girl.' It came out as a rasping whisper. 'Sorry – sore throat.'

'Some nasty colds around the village,' Sergeant Richards said sympathetically.

'We believe the men headed this way last night, and it appears someone tried to break into the barn up the lane – that's one of your outbuildings, isn't it?' the second man said.

'It's where my father keeps his car.' Kept. The immensity of his death hit her anew. Her eyes began to burn.

The sergeant looked pained. 'Sorry, bird. I heard about your da.' He turned to the other man. 'Miss Kitto's father was killed in action.'

'I was aware of that. My condolences.' He removed his trilby and she saw that underneath it he had a bald patch as wide as a monk's tonsure. 'They didn't take the car?'

'I keep the starting handle in the house.'

'Very wise. It's a nice car,' Sergeant Richards said. 'A Standard Flying 8, I believe?'

She remembered passing him when running Mary into school one day and fervently hoping he would not stop her and ask to see a licence. She knew he knew she hadn't got one, but driving tests had been suspended since the start of the war, so it wasn't really her fault. Still, the guilt welled inside her. He gave her a little smile, then turned to the other man.

'Might we not station one of the lads here to keep an eye out for the young ladies till the bastards – beg pardon, bird – till the escaped prisoners are caught?'

'Oh, we're fine,' Olivia said, a little too quickly.

'I'm not.'

Mary appeared at her elbow, scrubbed and dressed in her school pinafore. On one foot her shoelaces trailed: she still hadn't mastered the art of tying them, but trying and failing several times had clearly slowed her down.

'I hardly slept at all for all the noise.'

'She means the storm,' Olivia explained, putting an arm around Mary's shoulders.

Mary tried to wriggle free. 'I do not. There was a lot of noise. I was afraid.'

Olivia's grip tightened. 'You were dreaming, dear.'

'Wasn't. I heard shouting.'

Olivia felt sick. 'The parrot,' she said. 'It got very upset by the thunder.'

The men exchanged glances. 'You have a parrot?' asked the nameless man, replacing his trilby. He looked austere and sinister with it on, like the villain in a film.

Olivia opened her mouth to answer but Mary said, 'Yes. I don't like it. Will you take it away?'

Sergeant Richards smiled. 'You want me to arrest the parrot, do you?'

'Yes,' said Mary. 'It's rude.'

'Do you mind if we take a look around?' the other man asked. 'We feel you may be in particular danger.' He did not explain why.

She could hardly say no. Olivia moved aside to let them in, then followed, holding Mary's hand tightly. She opened the never-used smart sitting room for them, watched as they took in the bureau and bookcases, the formal chairs and the dust coating the ornaments and coffee table. They would have to look in the parlour next, it was unavoidable. Her heart skipped and thudded as she walked in ahead of them, standing carefully on the antimacassar so they could not kick it aside. Luckily, the parrot demanded attention at once, bobbing up and down on its perch, squawking and whistling.

'Hello,' said Sergeant Richards, walking up to the cage to regard the bird eye to eye, and it promptly gave him an ear-splitting wolf-whistle.

The sergeant took a swift step back. 'No call for that!'

The trilby-wearer raised an eyebrow. 'A very unmannerly creature,' he observed. 'I hope he didn't learn it from you,' he said to Mary, who looked deeply offended.

'*Ba-lack!*' the bird screeched.

This was the word the Dark Man had uttered last night before bashing the airman's head in with the log. Olivia was revisited by that apocalyptic moment, her terror, the feel of the heavy body, the smell of the blood, and felt faint.

'Black?' Sergeant Richards said, frowning. 'Is that what he said?'

The trilby man frowned. 'It sounded to me rather like the Arabic word for "out of the way".'

Olivia's mind worked furiously. 'I bought him from a sailor,' she said. 'I expect he's widely travelled.'

The man gave her a long, appraising look. She did not like his eyes: they were large and dark but strangely dull, like the eyes of a blue shark she'd seen brought up on the quay. She held his gaze, and at last he turned away and began to walk around the room. He sniffed the air like a dog. Olivia wondered if he could smell the blood, if he were some sort of special investigator brought in for his peculiar skills. Then he walked over to the couch with its hastily rearranged cushions, and dropped to one knee to look underneath it. Olivia's heart stopped.

He pulled at the rolled-up rug, tapped it, then unrolled the nearest corner. Olivia's stomach turned over. She took a deep breath to keep the rising bile down and forced out a laugh. 'Did you think there was a body stashed in there? I rolled it up to save it from the parrot. When he gets out he can make rather a mess.'

'He's disgusting,' Mary added firmly. 'And he smells.'

'Cark!' the parrot yelled as if in agreement. He made the sound of a log hitting a skull, though perhaps only Olivia recognized it as such.

'I really must make Mary some breakfast before she goes to school,' Olivia said, hoping this would hurry them along, but they seemed in no great rush.

'May we go upstairs?' the trilby-man asked, abandoning the rug and pushing himself to his feet. 'Just to make sure no one got in while you were asleep.'

'Yes, please do.'

'Is there an attic, miss?'

Olivia explained the dangerous tendencies of the attic ladder to them, then towed Mary into the kitchen and made porridge, adding to Mary's a spoonful of cream and precious jam. As she did so her hand shook, so that the teaspoon jittered against the glass of the jar. She added hot water into the teapot onto yesterday's leaves and poured out the pallid results and sat quietly as Mary scraped and swallowed and the floorboards upstairs creaked under the men's feet.

'What are they doing?' Mary asked, once the bowl was empty.

'Searching for some people who escaped from the farm.'

'Marjorie and Beryl?' Mary asked, her eyes brightening with interest.

Olivia choked on the vile tea. 'No.' She did not elaborate.

The policemen reappeared. 'All clear,' Sergeant Richards declared cheerily.

Olivia got to her feet. 'I really must get Mary off to school.'

'You shouldn't be going out with that cold. We'll be driving back down into the village in a mo – we can drop her off if you like.' The sergeant beamed, and Mary looked at him, suddenly very alert.

'Won't people think I'm a crinimel if they see me in your car?'

Sergeant Richards smiled indulgently. 'You can tell them you've been helping us with a very serious case.'

Delighted, Mary ran to fetch her satchel.

As they followed her out into the hall, the man in the trilby stopped suddenly, and laid his hand on the cellar door's handle, tried it and seemed annoyed when it did not open. 'What's in here?'

Olivia was tempted to say it was just a broom cupboard, but she knew Mary would correct her. 'Oh, just the cellar. We never use it.'

'I'd like to check it anyway,' he said.

Olivia laughed. 'No one could get in that way.'

'Even so.'

'Rather safe than sorry, eh?' Sergeant Richards said. 'Let's just have a quick peep.'

The other man rattled the handle harder as if the doorknob itself were resisting him. 'Do you have a key?'

'Maybe there's one in the kitchen,' Olivia said faintly. She turned her back on him. The key was on the lintel, but she would have to buy some time. In the kitchen drawer there was a collection of strange old keys: she brought them all back and tried them noisily in the lock. Then, 'Sorry,' she said, 'I just remembered. Daddy used to keep it up there, out of reach.' She indicated the lintel. 'I wonder if it's still there.' Actually, what she wondered was whether the Dark Man had heard all their noise. She couldn't risk knocking, and anyway, what if he'd passed out, or fallen asleep? They would find him and then the bludgeoned airman, and how was she going to explain that? She would go to prison for obstructing justice and lying and murder. She would be put away for life…

The trilby-wearer retrieved the key and opened the door. 'Is there a light?' he asked.

Olivia shook her head. 'There are candles somewhere,' she said.

'No matter.' He took a small flashlight out of his coat pocket and dread rose in a cold tide up through Olivia's chest. He shone it down the stairs. Dust motes danced as he took a step down and swung the torch beam around. Cobwebs, hundreds of them. It was like entering an undisturbed tomb.

'I do so dislike spiders,' the man said, drawing back.

'Let me,' said Sergeant Richards. 'Bleddy ol' lobs don't frighten me.'

Down he went, the flashlight picking out small circles of detail. Olivia closed her eyes. *Let him not see the blood, the drag-marks.* She saw again the clumsy tumbling of the body, the flailing arms and legs, the graceless fall to the dusty floor…

Standing at the top of the steps she forced herself to stasis, though she was poised for flight. If they found the Dark Man, she thought, she would shove the trilby-wearer down the stairs, lock the door behind him, grab the starting handle for the Flying 8 and make a run for it. She would need money, and whatever petrol she could carry in the car. Frantically, she calculated—

'Nothing down there,' Sergeant Richards announced, reappearing. 'Though it appears you have mice, Miss Kitto, or maybe worse.' He cast a glance at Mary.

'Rats,' Olivia less delicately supplied. 'Yes, I know. They eat the labels off the tins. Sometimes you open one thinking it's corned beef and it's condensed milk!'

They laughed, except for the man in the trilby. 'I do hope you're not hoarding food down there.'

Olivia tried to look shocked. 'Of course not. It's just the emergency rations Daddy put down there in case the Germans invaded.'

The two men exchanged a glance, then the official cocked his head towards the front door.

The sergeant took Mary's hand. 'Off to school, young lady. Shall we leave Miss Kitto in peace, Mr White?'

Olivia had the clear impression this was not the trilby-wearer's real name. She wondered who he was.

By way of an answer, Mr White took a notebook from his pocket and scribbled down a number on it. He tore the page out and handed it to Olivia. 'I notice you have a telephone. Call me if you're ever concerned,' he said.

Olivia saw them out, feeling exhausted. Then she went into the kitchen and made a pot of tea with new leaves (though there was no milk), cut two slices of bread off yesterday's loaf and piled a tray with plate, knife, mug, butter, sugar, teaspoon and honey,. along with a candle in a wonky pottery holder she had made at school at the age of eight, and carried it down to the cellar.

She rapped three times on the tunnel door. For a long time nothing happened and she heard no movement. Then there was the grating of the key in the lock on the other side and very slowly the door opened and the Dark Man peered around cautiously. Seeing Olivia standing there with the tray, illuminated by the candle flame, his face relaxed and he slipped around the door and closed it on the darkness beyond.

'What's your name and how did you come to be a prisoner of war?' Olivia asked as they sat on upturned paint pots and she watched him add three teaspoonfuls of sugar to his tea. She had found her French again and suggested that for the time being it was better he stay down here, in case the police returned. 'My name is Olivia. Olivia Kitto, and this is the house where I was born.'

He held out a bandaged hand for her to shake: very formal. 'My name is Hamid. Let me tell you my story. I am known as something of a storyteller where I come from. Even there, where people know that tales take their own time to be told and go at their own pace, just as donkeys move slowly down the old tracks on their way to market, I have sometimes to beg patience of my listeners.' He spoke slowly and carefully, and cast a brief smile at her before gazing down into his teacup as if to retrieve something. His eyelashes cast deep shadows on his cheek. Then with a single swift action he drained his cup and replaced it on the tray. 'So I apologize now for starting at a beginning that seems distant from the question you asked, and hope you will forgive me.'

19

Hamid

'I WAS BORN IN A VILLAGE IN NORTH-WEST ALGERIA IN the foothills of the Atlas *udraren*. My people are an ancient race known as the Imazighen, or the Free Ones; the French refer to us as *Berbères*, after the Egyptians who called us "outlanders". We have lived in North Africa for thousands of years, before the Romans, before the Arabs, before the Andalusi or the Turks. But it was the French who tried to change us. My father's family are from across the border in Morocco; my mother, she is of mountain stock. She has tattoos here and here.' He touched his chin and forehead. 'The eye of the partridge, for beauty; the *nuqat*, or *ddar*, for safety and home. My first language is Tamazight; after that Darija, our local dialect of Arabic; then French. I think English is very hard to learn. There is,' he frowned, 'no logic to it at all.

'When I was a boy I thought I would do as my father had done all his life – herd our goats and sheep in the mountain pastures, moving them down the valley in times of drought, up into the peaks in the wet season, so they could feast on the best grass. I thought I would lie back in the embrace of an old tree, breathing in the scent of thyme and lavender and watch our animals spreading across the ground like a living cloud, the kids and lambs play-fighting and butting heads and jumping from rock to rock, the females calling them to move along. But there were years when no rain fell, and no grass grew and the animals got as thin as sticks and we had to sell them for their hides and meat before they died and had no value. I hated that, for I had come to know them all by name.

'From the age of nine I spent weeks at a time in the hills. Then I would come home and my older brothers Ibrahim and Nazir would take over from me, and Omar and I would go to school in their place from eight in the morning till five in the afternoon. My parents were never keen for me to go – after all, the school was several valleys away from our home, and worse, the teacher was French – but if they stopped me I moped around the house and did my chores so badly that my mother would end up throwing spoons and slippers at me, and my father said I might as well go and fill my head with something other than air.

'I loved school. I loved the long walk with nothing to do but take in the rocks and plants and clouds; I loved to sit in the classroom among books and pencils. All those things to learn – it was as if the teacher were rolling a magic carpet out as he told us about the world. I did not know there was anywhere beyond Oujda, Aurès or Oran, and I had never visited any of them – they marked the boundaries of the real world for me; though the imagined world ran as far as the tales in the Qur'an and One Thousand and One Nights, from whales in the bottom of the ocean to the harems of sultans. Our teacher came from Nantes, and oh, how he spoke, with a beautiful accent: it sounded like music to me, who was used to the sound of Tamazight, the growls and the spitting noises of it; to the bellowing of rams and the howls of jackals. It demonstrated to me that there were other ways to live. He did not wear a frayed djellaba or go barefoot like me and my brothers. Even though he lived in the school house in no better surroundings than we did, he always wore a white shirt and a tie, and pleated trousers held up by a shining leather belt, and proper shoes, and a woollen coat in the winter. I wanted to be like him, with his gleaming hair and his clean-shaven chin and clipped, precise vowels. It became my dream, my aim.

'And so when I heard from a travelling medicine-salesman that the French administration in the city of Oran were hiring young men to act as translators and *passe-partouts* and said that I should try my luck there, I went to my father and told him I would like to go. I thought he would be angry. He is a fierce-looking man, his dark skin stitched and seamed by wind and sun, his eyes like flints, his thick beard as black as night. When I said my piece to him he did not shout at me. We sat together and he gave me the first tea from the pot, pouring it from a great height...' He mimed with Olivia's little brown teapot, holding it aloft and tilting it so that she feared its lid would shoot off and break on the hard floor. 'Poured in this way the tea wears a crown of pale bubbles that we call its turban, or *shesh*.' His teeth shone white in the gloom. 'Then he poured a glass for himself, and sat down cross-legged and drank it, all this without uttering a word. Then at last he said, "When some eaglets fledge they never stray far from the eyrie and pickings are made hard for the whole brood. When the stronger ones take flight for more distant hunting grounds, everyone prospers."

'"I will send all the money I make back to you," I promised. My father was a virile man: my youngest sister had been born only three months before.'

'How many of you are there?' asked Olivia, with the wonder of an only child.

Hamid grinned, his eyes gleaming in the flickering light. 'Ten,' he said and she whistled, which was not very ladylike. Her father had taught her to whistle: her mother had disapproved. He reeled off their names, a cascade of foreign sounds. 'So I set off for Oran. "Just go downhill," my father told me, "and keep going until you reach the sea."

'"Have you ever seen the sea?" I asked him. All I had seen were black-and-white photos in a French textbook. *La mer, la Méditerranée.* It looked like a wide mountain meadow dotted with sheep; except that the sheep were boats.

'"Once," he said. He stirred more sugar into the pot. "Just the once. I wept: it was too big." That frightened me, that anything should overawe my rough, tough father so; a man who was used to the wild vastnesses of mountain and sky. "It was beautiful," he said wistfully. "The most beautiful thing I ever saw." He paused. "Apart from your mother on our wedding night." It was hard for me to think my mother beautiful: she was as thin and dark as the mountain earth, her hair fell in ringlets like the wool on the biggest ram, and her eyes were like a buzzard's.

'It took me four days to reach the coast, and another half day to come to the outskirts of Oran. I sat on a hill overlooking the city when I came down out of the forest, where a local farmer told me the last two Barbary lions in

Africa had been killed, and marvelled at it. The sight of it took all my words from me. All white it was, the houses and the roads, and the sea was so blue, bluer than the sky, bluer than new lavender, bluer than gentians, and touched with green, as if it hid secret underwater meadows. It was huge. There were perhaps thirty houses in our village, and they were all made of *pisé* – of mud and straw – and roofed with baked earth; they were of the ground on which they stood, a part of the unchanging landscape. But Oran shone grey and white and full of glass, and the streets were full of cars. I had never seen a car: where I lived if you needed to travel to the *moussem* or the market you saddled up a donkey.

'I had set out wearing my best djellaba, which was foolish. After four nights of sleeping in it, of tearing it free from thornbushes and prickly pears, it was dusty and tattered and creased. How was I to get a job in such a shining city dressed like a poor peasant? So at first I stayed on the edge of town and worked in the souk there, running errands, helping stallholders – for a loaf of bread here, an apple or an orange there, or the share of a *tajine* – for all the men working there cooked for themselves. I learned all manner of things from the people in this market, for many of them travelled from one quarter of the city to another. There was the strawberry man and the lemon seller, the herb man and the perfume seller; and the man who repaired and sold old clothes. It was he who procured for me a shirt and trousers like those my teacher wore, though re-hemmed, with mismatched buttons and a little patched. I put this new costume on at once and thought I looked like a foreign prince. The herb man laughed and clapped me on the shoulder. "One of my best customers, the wife of a French administrator, lives in a great house in the Nouvelle Ville," he said. "Come with me when I deliver her next order. Be respectful and polite and show a little of your learning and maybe she will know someone who has a job, in the *douane*, the customs, maybe, at the port."

'The man on the next stall overheard this and spat loudly into the dust. "Stay here among good Algerians, that's what I advise. You don't want to get involved with those—" and here he used a foul word I cannot repeat, but he meant the French. "They treat us all like slaves, as if we come from the jungles. I've heard them call us black with my own ears, and laugh about our language and our habits. Don't fall into the trap of thinking they're special or better than us; for all their fancy ways they are no better than savages themselves."

'The herb man rolled his eyes as if he had heard this many times before. "Leave the lad alone; all he wants is to make some money for his family."

'It was not all I wanted, but I nodded to that.

'The next week I found myself in the Nouvelle Ville, inside a great white house with shining marble floors and light everywhere. I could hardly believe my eyes. It was more richly furnished than our local mosque, with all its fretted wooden screens, its great china vases and silver goblets. All the paintings and mirrors were framed with intricately carved wood, acanthus leaves twining around and around, as if the wood was still alive. I liked to whittle while I sat by the campfire telling stories to my brothers at night in the mountains, keeping watch for jackals and foxes – but all I ever made were dollies for my sisters, or crude pots for my mother. Now, I wished fervently that I could use a knife more delicately and learn to make such art. I was so mesmerized that I found myself drawn to the largest mirror to lay my fingers to its frame.

'"Please don't touch!" The woman's voice was shrill and angry and I stepped back, feeling like a bad little boy.

'"I am sorry, it is just so beautiful, like a mirror out of the old stories. I think a djinn might try to bewitch me through it, or an ensorcelled princess might appear to beg for her release."

'The woman laughed and turned to the herb man. "I see what you mean, Omar – he really is quite charming, and his French is excellent." She looked back at me. "Can you read and write?"

'I told her I could, and started to list my accomplishments. She held up a hand. "And work with figures?"

'"My teacher has praised my understanding of arithmetic, though I have to admit I have only just begun to understand algebra. Did you know that was an Arabic word – algebra? It comes from the Arabic *al-jabr* and it means the reunion of broken parts. I like that, 'the reunion of broken parts': it's poetic, don't you think? I like mending things, and my teacher said algebra was the unifying thread of mathematics, so I intend to devote time to studying it more closely."

'"I don't think an advanced understanding of algebra will be entirely necessary to what I have in mind," the woman said drily.

'They left me then and after a while the woman returned alone. "Where is Sidi Omar?" I asked. She did not reply to that question. Instead, she took me to another part of the house and showed me a small room.

'"My husband works away a lot, but he will be back in

due course and I think you will be useful to him. This will be your room and you can help me till he returns. My name is Madame Duchamps. I allow my special friends to call me Marguerite. Maybe one day I will let you call me that."

'I was very confused by this, but I set myself to working hard at every task she set me. I went to the market for her, I tended the garden, and that day I was cleaning out the bowl of the courtyard fountain and repairing the mechanism that was clogged with silt so that it spouted joyfully again. I had taken off my shirt so as not to spoil it with dirt, and sang while I worked, the songs I sang for the goats in the mountains, when I had the feeling of eyes upon me, and when I turned Madam Duchamps was watching me. I felt like a mountain hare under the eyes of a jackal. I stopped what I was doing.

'"Come with me, Hamid," she said, and put out her hand.

'She led me not to the kitchen for tea, nor to the servants' quarters, but up the stairs.' He looked at Olivia under his lashes. 'But I think that is a story for another time, and you would not like to hear it.'

Olivia, who had sat rapt throughout, lulled by the cadence of his lovely French and the gently unrolling story, said at once, 'Oh, I would!' and he laughed.

'Well, I will keep that one to myself, for now, I think. We must all have our little secrets. It seemed that Madame and Monsieur Duchamps had many secrets from one another, for I heard from Mariam, who did the cooking and the laundry for them, that monsieur would often return from his working trips with smudges of cosmetics and unusual scents upon his clothes. She had been snappy with me at first, Mariam, and said, "Oh, another one, how she runs through them," which at the time made me try harder to please, since I thought it was because previous employees had not worked hard enough. I was, how you say, *naïf*. I had noticed for myself that when Monsieur Duchamps returned he and his wife were extremely polite together, like people who do not like one another much but have made some sort of arrangement to share the same space. My mother could be like that with my father's mother, who lived in our house and was always criticizing, even though she did not do any work herself.

'Monsieur Duchamps took me with him to his office in the business district of Oran. He worked in procurement, supplying French ships with all they required when they put into port. Before the war these had all been merchant vessels, but things were different now and he was much busier: he had a whole battalion of young Algerians running here, there and everywhere between La Blanca and the Nouvelle Ville to get the best price on everything from vegetables and cigarettes to pomegranates and girls. Me, I specialized in the paperwork – I'd be the go-between for the vendors and Monsieur Duchamps' office staff, but sometimes when we were really busy I'd help with deliveries to the ships. And that was how, on the afternoon of the third of July 1940, I found myself on board a French warship named the *Strasbourg*, which had put into Oran's port – Mers el-Kebir – along with a number of other battleships in the *marine nationale*, delivering crates of oranges and lemons, and some brandy for the captain. We were in his cabin, haggling over the final payment for this latter item (my master always overcharged outrageously and left it to me to calm the buyer down), when there was a lot of noise outside, and he swore and shoved the full sum of money at me and ran up on deck. I ran after him, because he was severely overpaying and that seemed wrong to me, but when I got outside I could not believe what I saw! The sky was full of planes. I know now that they were British aircraft, but at the time I was entirely uninformed. The war was something that was happening in other places, not close to my home. I knew that France had surrendered to a country called Germany and was now run from a government in somewhere called Vichy, but I could not even point to any of these places on a map. I had only ever seen one map and that had been pinned to the blackboard at school, and it made no sense to me at all that the whole world could be represented like that, for the world as I knew it was rough and steep and full of mountains and the valleys were deep and verdant – and how could you show all that on a flat sheet of paper? I could not understand how Algeria could be all around us, yet be a small shape drawn at the top of a continent called Africa, or that it could contain a thousand colours within the vista I could see out of the window, but be rendered in a single shade of blue alongside all of France's other "colonies". There were a great many colonies in Africa, though I could not understand how a country could "own" another country.

'I must apologize to you, Miss Olivia, but I didn't even know the words *England* or *Great Britain*, let alone have the first idea of where they might be. When they told me I was in Cornwall when they took me prisoner, they might as well have said the moon. But I am getting ahead of myself… And perhaps you would like a break?'

'Not at all,' said Olivia briskly. 'I want to know what happened.'

Hamid dipped his head in assent. 'So there I was out on deck with sailors running all around me, and these British planes strafing us and dropping mines and bombs and the ships' anti-aircraft crews firing back. It was deafening. That makes it sound as if I knew what was happening but to be honest it was chaos: I did not even know whose planes they were. All I wanted was to get off that ship and back onto dry land as fast as I could, but the boat I had come out to the ship on was gone, and I did not know how to swim.' He saw Olivia's expression. 'Where I come from water is scarce – it's not a skill we learn. I can run down a scree slope or climb a cliff – I've had to do both to rescue stray sheep – not the goats, though: they are the most surefooted of all creatures. I've seen them scale sheer rock faces no man could ever climb.

'I gazed down into the dark water, wondering how hard swimming could be, when there was an almighty explosion. I turned to see a great tower of smoke and flame, and water as solid as a wall rising from where the ship nearest to us had been. Even the sea was burning, and so were the men who had been thrown off its decks into the water.' He dropped his gaze. 'I will never forget their screams.'

Olivia was horrified, picturing the poor sailors on fire in the oil-slicked waters with warplanes screaming overhead. He had painted a less-than-heroic picture and suddenly she found herself wondering how and where her father had met his end. Against her will she started to cry, then began to sob uncontrollably.

Hamid was alarmed. 'I apologize most sincerely, I did not mean to upset you with my story. I am an idiot. I should not have elaborated with such grim details.'

Olivia raised swollen eyes to him and sucked in a breath. 'It's not that. It's... everything. It's all come together – my father's death, Mummy not coming home, having to deal with Mary, and all the bills, the trouble at the farm, Mamie, and what h-happened last night...' Some of this came out in English, some in broken French. She sniffed hard, but failed to stop the tears and at last sank her head in her hands and let them come.

For long moments Hamid sat there, not knowing what to say or do, then he reached out a bandaged hand and gently laid it on her shoulder. 'I did not know about your father,' he said. 'I am so sorry. And you're so young: it's all too much. You shouldn't have to deal with so much.'

Olivia blew her nose into the dust one nostril at a time. Mummy would be horrified, she thought, blowing her nose on her sleeve. But Mummy wasn't there, so what Mummy thought didn't count. Her chin came up. 'I'm sixteen,' she said in English, 'and we are at war, so I've just got to buck up.' And then had to explain that supremely British concept to him. 'Please carry on with your story.'

'So that was what happened to the warship *Bretagne*, nearly a thousand crew dead or dying, just like that. I sat down on the deck, I was so shocked, and the ship I was on, the *Strasbourg*, started its engines and powered her way out of the narrow harbour. How we did not hit any of the mines the British planes had dropped I do not know, but God must have been smiling on us.'

'But I don't understand,' Olivia said quietly. 'Why would the British bomb these ships? The French are our allies.'

'I understand no more than you; it seemed as if the whole world had gone mad. But as we left Oran and Algeria behind us – my country, just a shadow on the horizon, then vanishing from view – I heard from the sailors around me that the British must have taken the decision to bomb the French fleet rather than let it fall into enemy hands – the Germans', I suppose. Because the French government had capitulated and the new government in Vichy was cooperating with the invasion force, and if the new government had ordered the admiral to surrender the fleet, he would have been obliged to do so. It all seems very complicated to me.

'The next day we sailed for Toulon, and as we came in to the immensely busy port a man came to stand by me and spoke in my native language, though some of the words and inflections were slightly different. We exchanged names and greetings and he told me he lived in Marseille, but that his family came from a town on the coast of Morocco called Salé, near Rabat. "My family have been sailors ever since the seventeenth century," he told me. "Some called us pirates then, more politely corsairs. The sea is in my blood and I have no loyalty to any but my family and my people, and I believe you're Amazigh, like me. But, my friend, you have no papers, I think?"

'I didn't know what he meant by this, so he explained at length. "But won't they just let me go home to Algeria?"

'He barked out a laugh. "I think not, my friend. They'll throw you in a prison camp. Or more likely just shoot you: feeding prisoners is an expensive business."

I must have looked utterly despondent, for he put an arm around me. "Don't despair. I know people. Don't disembark with the rest. I will show you where to hide and I'll come back and find you as soon as I have seen them. Do you have any money?"

Ah, so now we came to it. I had the captain's brandy-money tucked away, but I am not a complete fool, so I said nothing, waiting to see what else he would say.

In the end, he shrugged. "Well, no matter. If you can't trust another Berber, who can you trust?" He showed me to a cup-board – it was barely more than that – and told me to stay there and not to open the door for anyone unless I heard the word *baraka*. That made me smile: it is our word for bless-ing, for good luck. I stayed there, in the dark, for the rest of the day and through the night – so you see, I am used to these conditions...' He grinned, his teeth bright in the gloom, and waved a hand to indicate the confines of the cellar.

'I was ready to give up on my new friend coming back for me, and was starting to curse my bad luck when I heard someone outside in the companionway. There was a long silence. I held my breath and then someone said "*Baraka*". It was not my friend outside, but another, older, man who also spoke my language.

'"*Salaam aleikum*," he said, and handed me a flask of black coffee as thick as oil, and a still-warm almond pastry wrapped in newspaper. I ate and drank like a starving man as he talked. He could not, he said, find me passage back to Algeria, or even Morocco: there was too much "activity", as he termed it, in the Mediterranean. So, he had brought me papers in the name of his dead cousin, a fisherman on a boat that worked out of Toulon.

'"I'm no fisherman," I told him. "I'm a shepherd."

'He just shrugged. "I was no smuggler till this war broke out. I ran a little hotel. But that was requisitioned by the bastard Germans, so what can you do? You've got to make a living, got to take care of your family, don't you?"

'"That's what I was trying to do in Oran," I said woefully. "But I'm so far away from them now I wonder if I will ever see them again."

'The older man laughed. "Of course you will. We'll take care of you. Play your cards right and you'll make far more than what you are getting doing whatever you are doing now."

'"It sounds dangerous."

'The man made a face. "Danger, it's everywhere now. But better the sort of danger you choose than getting sent to your death by some bastard officer who hasn't a clue what he's doing."

'"What do I have to do?"

'"You crew on one of my boats," the man said. "I'm the admiral of my own little fleet. We run up and down the coast, buying and selling, if you take my meaning."

'"Smuggling?"

'"We never use that word, *mon cher*. A little black market action. *Sous le manteau*." Under the coat. "Some cigarettes here, brandy there, cheese, soap and coal. Guns. Whatever people want but can't get hold of, we supply it."

'It didn't sound too different to what I had been doing these past weeks in procurement. I thought, rather guiltily, of the large sum of money in my pocket, and swore one day I would return it to M. Duchamps, with interest.

'For the next few months I worked with these *contrebandiers*, going up and down the French coast, making drops by dead of night in unlit harbours and secret coves, sometimes meeting other vessels at sea, sometimes transferring goods in caves or leaving them in crab pots sunk off the coast. My French improved considerably, and soon I was able to send Monsieur Duchamps his money, via relatives of my employer, and the same amount again back to my family. I thought I was the cat's whiskers. I had a job, I had money, I had a tribe – that was how it felt working on the boats. We had *esprit de corps*. Forged by danger and the celebration of our survival day by day. I even found my sea-legs, but I never learned to swim. Luckily, there was never any need to, until...'

'Until?'

'Our operations took us further and further north. We were heading back to France one day with a load of Welsh coal when we hit a mine. My God, I thought I was dead. I thought we all were. I could not swim, I went down, but someone pulled me up, and I caught some wreckage. I was the only one who was fished out by the crew of the minesweeper that was clearing the waters for a British convoy. If it had gone through half an hour earlier we'd have sailed right through the eye of a needle. I don't know what happened to the rest of my crew. I'd like to think some of them survived...'

He went quiet, took his prayer beads out of his pocket and played them through his fingers for a minute or two, while Olivia waited.

'Our lives are in God's hands.'

'*Entre les mains de Dieu*,' she echoed. Did she believe this? She hardly knew what she believed any more. But to have survived last night... Surely someone was looking out for her. Yes, someone *was* looking out for her: this man right in front of her. He was her guardian angel. He hadn't had to come after the Nazi: he could have made his own escape and left her to her fate. He might be a foreigner

– the most foreign foreigner she had ever seen, let alone met – but he had saved her life. She felt a powerful swell of gratitude towards him; a sort of awe. 'So they arrested you and interned you,' she finished for him.

He nodded. 'I had no English then, they had no French, and I look the way I do.' He shrugged. 'My papers went to the bottom of the sea along with every other thing I owned. So now I am back to being Hamid again and here I am.'

Olivia leaned forward. 'Thank you for coming here, and for doing what you did. If you hadn't...' She closed her eyes, thinking of Mamie.

'They say there is no such thing as true evil in the world,' he said, 'but that man, Mikael, was the closest thing to pure evil I ever encountered. He boasted that he came from the same place as Hitler, that his family had supported him in his rise to power. He said Hitler is brilliant, a visionary leader who will purify Europe. He told them all this at the farm, telling them they would be safe under his rule. "You are all Aryans," he told them, "the true Europeans. There is no good reason for us to be at war with one another: we are just the same. But the deficient" – and by that he meant that poor little girl – "and the foreign and dark-skinned" – and obviously by that he meant me – "they are no better than animals and will be removed. We are the master race," he said, "and we will remake the world in our own image and take back control." He flattered those boys up at the farm: they were lapping up his words like camels at an oasis. Wherever you go in the world, it seems to me, there are gullible people ready to be manipulated by those who are cleverer or more malign. They mould them into followers and do whatever they will.'

Olivia thought of how they had faced her down in the field above the Swingate Stones when she went to confront them, to tell Farmer Roberts what had been done to his daughter. Even him, she thought, even he was swayed – if not by the airman, then by the weight of opinion of all the rest.

For a moment it seemed as if the world shifted on its axis and she felt like a foreigner in her own village. They were so wrong, so dangerously wrong, and she had been right all along. They hadn't believed her because she was just a girl, a silly female. But now they would believe Hamid was responsible for the death of Mamie. It suited the stories they told themselves about the dark-skinned man, the foreigner, the outsider, the Muslim.

Olivia was not used to feeling righteous – she was usually in the wrong – but now that also swelled up inside her, and with it a powerful determination. Whatever it took, she would keep this man safe and repay the debt she owed him. She would shelter him from the authorities, from the easily misled people who could not see past what was right before their eyes – people like Beryl who had been taken in by the airman's handsome looks, his boy-blond hair, his piercing blue eyes, his clear-cut profile – and failed to recognize the dangerous predator in their midst. It would not be easy to keep Hamid out of their hands, safe and hidden, but by hook or by crook she would do it.

He broke into her thoughts. 'We must get rid of the body. Do you have a pickaxe or something like it?' He motioned working with such a tool.

Olivia saw him stifle a wince. 'What, bury him here? In the cellar?'

'I spent a fair bit of time out in the tunnel. There is a section between seams of rock where I think I could dig. I think the area is large enough to hide a body. And if it is not, then we will have to cut it up.' He saw Olivia's horrified expression. '*I* will have to cut it up. I've had to butcher hundreds of sheep and goats,' he lied, making light of it. In fact, he had never butchered one. He knew them all by name, every single one of them; he had left the job of death and dismemberment to the butchers in the villages where he had taken them to be sold, and taken a little less for each animal as a result.

He knew Mikael by name too, but by Allah that would not stop him.

20

Becky

'REBECCA? REBECCA, ARE YOU IN THERE? ARE YOU OK?'

The handle rattles, then the bedroom door opens, and Reda's head appears. I stare at him but his gaze has already slid to the half-naked shape of Eddie beside me, soundly asleep amid the rumpled sheets. There is no ambivalence to this image, none at all. I have never felt so mortified in my life.

We speak at the same time. 'Sorry, I—' 'No, oh God, I—' and then he's gone, closing the door quietly behind him.

For a moment, I lie there feeling as if I have been stripped not only of my clothes, my modesty, my dignity, and self-respect, but of everything that makes me me. Then I shoot out of bed, haul on my jeans and T-shirt – no time to struggle into my carefully constructed prosthetics bra – and hammer downstairs after him.

'Reda, wait.'

When he turns to me, his face is a careful blank, the face of an artist's manikin, waiting to have the features delineated.

'I don't know what to say,' I say lamely.

There is a thread between us, drawn hot and tight and painful. Neither of us can look away.

'It's my ex, he just turned up.' Is Eddie my ex? It comes out automatically, not a conscious lie.

Reda shakes his head as if shedding my pathetic excuse. 'It's none of my business.'

'I didn't mean to sleep with him. I'm such an idiot.' *Just keep digging that hole, Becky.* I can't stop gazing at him piteously as if somehow I expect him to fix this horrible situation just as he and Mo have fixed the house. But his eyes are shuttered and distant. After all, what is he to me? A professional who's come here to do a job, a job that is very nearly complete. One to whom I owe a significant sum of money.

I want to tell him he means so much more than that but I can't even begin to articulate it to myself, let alone to him.

I watch him turn away from me, mumbling something about a skirting board, and then the thread between us frays apart and he's gone. I grip the banister, feeling on the edge of tears.

Oh, buck up, Becky, I tell myself fiercely, and for once it's my own voice in my head, not Mum's. Mum has gone: I know that now. I must rely on myself.

Leaving the problem that is Eddie to catch up on his lost sleep, I muster my determination and resolve, go out into the garden, dig up the disgusting rat corpse, clean the earth off it with a handful of grass so the full horror of its squashed and tortured state is revealed, and take several photos with my phone.

Then I take the path up through the woods to the old

barn and stonehouse. Mo and Reda's truck is parked in its usual space, considerately to one side, but a shiny red BMW has blocked me in. Some bloody tourist, I think, gone off to walk the coast path.

Not in the best mood to begin with, I stomp over and stare into it. Strewn on the back seat are an old panama hat and a big black Dunhill umbrella and a striped toiletry bag suspiciously like the one I bought for Eddie at TK Maxx. My suspicions are confirmed by the presence of a reusable ceramic coffee mug with a rubber top that I last saw on our kitchen counter, now jammed into the cupholder between the front seats. There is a Hertz sticker in the window, and the hire leaflet left upside-down on the parcel shelf is printed with a London phone number.

What the—? Why on earth would Eddie have lied about taking the sleeper train?

Anger makes me all the more determined. I get into the Clio and although it takes twenty minutes of sawing back and forth, widening the angle by tiny increments with each manoeuvre, at last I manage to squeeze past the BMW, leaving a small but distinct dent in its rear passenger door. I can almost hear Eddie telling the hire company *it wasn't me, I've no idea how it happened* – and then I'm off up the lane, onto the road that winds through the village of Sheffield, past the turning to Chyenhal and St Pol de Leon, and down the long hill into Newlyn and thence to Penzance.

Just as I am parking at Greenmarket the heavens open, soaking me to the bone. Drenched, I dash into the bank to check the balance in my account on the indoor cash machine, surreptitiously wringing out my hair and T-shirt. At least James has kept one promise, even if he couldn't keep his mouth shut. I go to the counter and take out half the money as cash, stuff the thick envelope deep into my bag, and run back to the car with my handbag over my head as cover from the rain, convinced that someone will mug me for it. Then I make my way to the police station.

There isn't anyone available for me to make a statement to – 'So many cuts,' I am told by the young man at the counter, who is clearly not impressed by my dishevelled appearance. 'You have to go to Camborne now if you want to report a crime in person.'

'But that's miles away!' I remember coming through Camborne on the train. It seems like months ago.

He nods lugubriously. 'Eleven police front desks have gone. It's a nightmare. You can call 101 if it's not an emergency, or fill in a form online.'

I look at him askance.

'Yeah, I know. Sorry. You could talk to one of the community support officers?'

'Can they do anything, like arrest someone?'

He makes a face. 'Not really.'

I scroll through the phone, show him the rat. He recoils. 'Bloody hell.'

'It was shoved through my letter box; then last night they were in my cellar—'

'Rats?' he says dubiously.

'No. Two men. They were doing something in the cellar, stashing something, or,' I think about it, 'taking something away.'

'So... is it a theft you want to report?'

'No! It's intimidation and... well, I don't know exactly. Maybe smuggling. And I think their mother may have pushed my elderly cousin down stairs. So it's the whole family, really. The Sparrow family, from Newlyn.'

It's as if a shutter has come down in his eyes and I wonder if he knows them, or whether he's beginning to see me as a bit of a nutter. He hands me a leaflet. 'Look, here are the details you need. Just call in your concerns or go to the address online and fill in the form there. Sorry I can't help any more.'

Feeling deflated, and dreading a return to a house with Eddie still in my bed, I drive to the auction house on the edge of town, pull up in the car park out front, and ring the bell. The rain is just coming down in random scatters now, flung drops as from the leaves of a windswept tree. I stand as close as I can to the door to shelter under the tiny porch.

There is a long delay and I'm beginning to think there is no one here, when a tall young man in chinos and a crisp pink shirt appears on the other side of the glass door. His curly dark hair is in disarray; I wonder what he has been up to amongst the antiques.

'Hello, hello,' he greets me. 'Awfully sorry to leave you out in the rain, I was cataloguing some stuff that's just arrived. What can I do for you? Are you here to check the lots? Come in, come in.' He has a delightfully casual manner despite his cut-glass accent and expensive clothes.

I follow him up a flight of stairs into a chaotic office, where he clears a pile of papers off a chair and gestures for me to sit down.

'I came to ask you about a painting by a local artist,' I say carefully. 'I wonder if you know anything more about it than I've been able to find out.' I reach across the desk and show him a photo of *The Sea Gate* on my phone and watch as he scrutinizes it, zooming the screen in and out, peering at it closely, then flicking to the next image – 'Do you mind?' I do not: the next photo shows the auction house label still attached to the back of the painting. I see his eyebrows shoot up, then he returns to the original picture and looks at it again for a considerable time.

Then he runs a hand through his mop of hair and regards me solemnly. 'Good lord,' he says. 'Where on earth did you find it?'

'So you remember the painting?'

'Of course. It came in to us about…' he looks off into space, calculating, 'oof, ten, twelve years ago, I think. I was helping Pa, learning the trade, you know, and at the time I didn't think much of it – just an old gate, rather pretty, a little romantic in style for my taste, not my sort of thing, really. I was a callow youth back then.' He flashes me a grin. 'But Pa knelt down in front of it and looked at it for, I don't know, ten minutes? I thought he was having some sort of episode – an absence, or something, he was so still. I was babbling away, asking all manner of nonsense, and he just held a hand up and said, "Do shut up, Stamford, and pay attention: this is special."'

'Did he know the artist?'

Stamford shakes his head. 'Honestly? No, though we'd sold a couple of previous paintings and they went for more than expected.'

The Girl in the Orchard and *The Pilchard Fishers*, I think, remembering the article I'd come across. I decide against mentioning them: don't want to alert him to the fact I know about the OK Painter.

'Do you have any idea who brought it in?' I ask innocently.

He lets out a big breath. 'It's a long time ago. What I do remember is it was a surprisingly hot day, at the end of the summer, and I only had a couple of weeks left before going back up to London. I remember being frustrated – it would've been a great day for going to the beach with Peter. So...' He leaps out of his chair and goes to the bookcase, unwinding his long frame to its full height to reach a morocco-bound volume from the top shelf. He blows a cloud of dust off it, sets it down on the desk and riffles through the pages. 'Aha! I remember that table, hideous thing, went for a fortune, some people have no taste... Thursday... Paintings, *Female nude* by Gillian Jenks, *The Gaps* by Tom Davies, *The Sleeper* and *Trereife House* by Henry Rook... Ah, here we are, *The Sea Gate* – no artist attributed, but there's a signature...' He examines it for a long moment. 'Nope, can't make it out.'

He passes the ledger over to me, his finger still marking the place.

There is an elaborate scribble in the vendor's column as if someone was trying to disguise their handwriting. But when you know what you're looking for no amount of disguise can hide the truth.

'Thank you,' I say grimly. 'Do you mind if I—' I snap a photo of the page before he can stop me.

'Oh I, well, I'm not sure you should—'

'It's fine, I know the auction house has done nothing wrong,' I assure him.

'It went missing,' he says. 'An hour or so before the auction.'

'Someone broke in?'

'Well, not exactly.' He looks embarrassed. 'People come

to view lots they're interested in before the auction starts formally and well, there was this chap, I was showing him some of the French mirrors, nineteenth century, quite expensive; he was keen and I thought I was going to make some good commission... and he was rather good-looking.' He grins, remembering. 'And then I took him to look at some chairs I thought he'd like and when I came back...' He spreads his hands.

'It was gone?'

He nods. 'Tell you what though, we were just making our way back downstairs when I passed the window and saw this awfully swanky old car pulling out of the gates with an elderly lady at the wheel. Proper antique – the car, I mean, ha ha! Definitely pre-war, whatever it was. And I remember thinking, I bet that's worth a fair bit.' He taps his lip thoughtfully. 'You don't think she could have been the thief, do you? Where did you come upon the painting, remind me?'

Sneaky old Cousin Olivia, I think.

'I'm afraid I can't tell you, not right now. But I promise I'll explain if everything works out. You don't happen to make house visits for valuations, do you, just in case?'

He is puzzled but polite about my refusal, and gives me his card. 'Not as a matter of course, but I have to say you've piqued my interest. I do love a good mystery.'

We shake hands and he shows me out. I can feel his gaze follow me as I turn the Clio around and drive onto the road out of Penzance.

★

When I arrive back at Chynalls, Mo and Reda's truck has gone and my mood sinks. Now it's just me and Eddie and I am going to have to grasp that big old nettle...

21

Olivia

1944

THE SNOW CAME SWIRLING IN GREAT FLURRIES, COATING the ground instantly. Olivia stood there with her hands spread on the sea gate, watching the flakes fall in a silent, drifting blizzard. Out on the horizon the far, dark shapes of vessels showed against the heavy grey cloud: shipping on the Atlantic convoy. It was all so peaceful, impossible to imagine that, the week before, a German submarine had ghosted into Mount's Bay and laid mines, one of which had blown up a trawler setting out early the next morning, despite the efforts of the dawn minesweeper. Impossible, too, to imagine a war going on across these waters, on the continent just twenty-six miles away, men pinpointing one another in gunsights and ending another human life with a squeeze of a trigger.

She shivered, thinking first of her father, then of the life that had ended in her own house. Weeks on, it seemed like an episode in a lurid novel, or the vestiges of a nightmare. She touched the gate's top bar for luck, remembering her grandmother's stricture never to touch wood with legs on it for fear her luck would walk away. Trust the Cornish to make their superstitions extra difficult. Granny had been a mine of such rules: don't put your shoes on the table; don't pass on the stairs; don't let your knives cross; always leave a little food on your plate for the knockers; always stir your tea clockwise, never widdershins; never sweep out the dust on a Monday morning. You could hardly turn round without invoking some ancient law. She couldn't recall anything to do with snow, though. It was such a rare experience in Cornwall: it never settled. This snow was settling, though. She watched it in wonder as it covered a bramble runner in delicate increments till the branch began to bow. Snowflakes were beginning to settle on her jersey, her eyelashes, her fringe.

She shook her head, picked up the milk churn and ran back up the steps to the house, aware of eyes on her from the bedroom window.

Even so, she was shocked when the front door opened.

'Stay right there—'

A click, a whirr, and then Hamid was laughing, waving the camera at her. 'I caught you! A princess from a fairy tale, a wild creature in the snow…'

'Get back indoors, someone will see you!' Olivia pushed him inside, closed the front door with a bang and took the Leica away from him. 'Why are you so reckless? If anyone sees you—'

He stopped her words with a kiss and Olivia felt the familiar tide of heat rise through her, robbing her of thought.

The milk churn gave a dull ring as she set it on the hall tiles and then they were racing upstairs, giggling like children.

Afterwards, lying on her back, reduced to liquid happiness, Olivia watched the snow drifting past the window. It was coming down in great, twisting curtains of white. Perhaps we'll be cut off, she thought drowsily. It was an enchanting thought, having the house to themselves without fear of interruption or discovery, able to laze like this for hours as if they were the last people in the world.

How strange life was, she thought, that she should lose her virginity to a man from Africa whom she would never have met had there not been a war, and who would never have been interned, let alone working up at the neighbouring farm, had it not been for misunderstandings and xenophobia. And yet here they were – male and female, brown and white, the epitome of difference, united in a warm afterglow. She lay bathed in this sense of wonder till it occurred to her that she was not, in actual fact, all that warm, and that despite the low, regular breathing that showed he was deeply asleep, Hamid's skin was coming up in gooseflesh. How she wished she'd stopped to light the fire up here. But although it was made up ready for emergencies, she hesitated: coal was scarce and what little firewood she had was downstairs. Rather than disturb him, she slipped off the bed and opened the bottom drawer in the chest, was almost knocked backward by the smell of old mothballs, then hauled out the blanket. It was the one her mother had always put on her bed on winter nights. She remembered as she hugged it to her naked body the bewilderment she had felt as a small child at its juxtaposition of sensations on her skin – the rough scratch of the wool, the cool slipperiness of the satin selvedge. Straightening, she glanced out of the window at the swirling snow, then down at the transformed garden, its shapes and zones camouflaged by the blanket of snow. And then something broke into the whiteness.

Her heart stopped, then beat rapidly.

'Hamid! Hamid!' She shook him by the shoulder and he came instantly awake, like a cat that had been drowsing with one eye half-open.

'*Les autorités!*'

He sat bolt upright. 'Where shall I—'

'Under the bed, hurry.'

He took his clothes with him and she rolled the pink blanket and pushed it after him, thrust on her clothes and pulled up the bedcovers, then cast herself downstairs, where she stood for a moment, breathing heavily, in front of the hall mirror, raking her fingers through her dishevelled hair. Her eyes were over-bright, her cheeks flushed. *I'd know exactly what someone who looks like this had been up to*, she thought, and that made her pinken further.

The ratchet of the doorbell spun her away from the mirror and she ran to open the door.

'Afternoon, Miss Kitto.'

It was Sergeant Richards and the man in the trilby. The policeman's helmet was crowned with white and snow had gathered in the longitudinal dimple on the other man's hat and on the shoulders of his gabardine.

'Sorry to bother you, miss. You remember Mr... White?'

The name seemed even more contrived against the backdrop of snow.

She tried to smile, managed a tight grimace. 'Won't you come in? I'll put the kettle on.'

'Very kind of you,' said the sergeant, stepping inside. He took off his helmet and shook the snow off it into the porch. The trilby-wearing man followed, not bothering to remove his headwear. Despite wiping their feet, they still tracked wet snow down the hall behind Olivia.

At the threshold of the kitchen, Olivia stopped dead, remembering. *Hell and damnation...*

'Won't you need this?'

Mr White was holding up the milk churn Olivia had abandoned in the hall.

'Oh, silly me!' she trilled. 'I'll forget my head next!' She took it from him and lugged it onto the kitchen counter, filled the kettle and set it on the range, then poured some of the milk into a jug. Lucky it was a cold day. Even with her back to them she could feel their eyes travelling around the dingy room in the gloomy snowlight, looking... for what?

'We're doing the rounds again,' Sergeant Richards explained, 'since we've not yet apprehended the escaped prisoners, and we still have no witnesses to their disappearance. Can you tell me, miss, if your car is still in your barn up there?' He indicated the way up through the woods with a tilt of the chin.

'Yes, yes, it is,' Olivia confirmed, feeling deep guilt at her behaviour in the hour before they had arrived. 'Would you like to see it?'

'We'll be passing the garage on our way up to the farm,' Mr White said. 'Perhaps you could let us have the keys so we can check it for ourselves, and we can drop them back to you after we've talked to Mr Roberts again?'

'Of course,' said Olivia. The kettle started to whistle: she turned to attend to it.

'And you've seen no strangers this past fortnight? No one suspicious?'

'No one at all,' Olivia replied, pouring hot water onto the meagre tea leaves in the base of the pot.

'I don't like to think of you here in this big house all alone,' said the sergeant.

'Oh, I expect my mother will be back any day soon,' Olivia said airily.

The men glanced at one another. 'I don't believe she will,' Sergeant Richards said, and Mr White frowned at him as if he had spoken out of turn.

Olivia put the kettle down carefully. 'What do you mean?'

The sergeant reddened. 'I'm sorry, miss, I misspoke. Don't alarm yourself, nothing's happened to her.'

The trilby-wearer was giving him a hard stare, then he turned his flinty gaze upon Olivia. 'We're considering billeting some officers with you,' he said. 'To give you some protection.'

Olivia's gut clenched. 'It's really not necessary; we're perfectly all right on our own, Mary and me.'

'Even so, it's a big house, and everyone's got to make sacrifices if we're to win this war.'

'I've already lost my father, thank you very much,' Olivia said sharply, and turned away to pour the tea before he could see how rattled she was. 'Mary is very distressed by her abandonment and I really don't think having strange men in the house would help.'

'Abandonment?'

'Her mother went upcountry to look after her sick mother and we've heard nothing from her since.'

If Mr White had been a dog his ears would have pricked up. 'And when was this... a fortnight ago, maybe?'

'Much longer than that – back in the summer,' Olivia said and enjoyed the way his face fell.

'Do you know where she went?' asked Sergeant Richards.

'Bristol, I think.'

'And her name?' He got his notebook out and wrote something in it.

'Winnie Ogden. I don't know her mother's name or address, I'm afraid, but Mrs Ogden and her little girl were evacuated down here from Exeter after their house was bombed.' Olivia hesitated. 'At least, that's what she said.'

Mr White was watching her suspiciously. She wondered if it was in his nature, this distrust. How unlikable he must be if so. She wondered if he were married, or had a sweetheart. It seemed unlikely. Fancy sleeping with such a cold fish— She pushed this unwarranted thought away. Since she had started making love with Hamid, which had happened all of six days ago – but goodness, how many times a day? She had lost count – she thought about sex all the time. Truly, what a slut she was...

'And this Mrs Ogden, was there anything... foreign about her? No letters from abroad, no accent or anything?'

Olivia almost laughed out loud at the idea of Winnie being some sort of Nazi collaborator or spy. 'Really no, not at all.'

'Did she visit the farm? Did she know the escaped men?'

'She'd have seen them at church. Up at St Pol de Leon, not down-chapel.'

Sergeant Richards wrote this down.

'We'll look into it,' said Mr White. 'You never know. People can be very... cunning. Perhaps we should interview the daughter?'

The sergeant looked appalled. 'She'm only a little 'un,' he said, remembering the sombre child they had dropped off at the school.

'Leave no stone unturned,' White said, his tone implying the repetition of an order from on high. He took his cup from Olivia and gazed into its pale contents dispassionately. 'And how did Mrs Ogden travel to Bristol – did she have a car?'

Olivia shook her head. 'She took the train: Jago dropped her at the station. Jago Sparrow – you can ask him.'

Mr White gave a deep sigh; Sergeant Richards jotted this down, then took a sip of his tea and grimaced. 'Sorry to ask, bird, you don't have any sugar, do you?'

Olivia explained that her ration did not stretch this far, and the sergeant looked melancholy. 'The sooner this war's over, the better.' He glanced back at his notebook, frowning. 'How two foreign POWs can vanish in this close-knit community, I can't fathom,' he said. 'There's something odd going on. They've not stolen a car or a boat, and they didn't take the train. So either they're sleeping rough or they've swum for it and drownded.'

'Or someone has taken them in.' Mr White fixed Olivia with his unblinking gaze.

'Maybe they've grown wings!' the sergeant offered with a chortle, but his companion did not crack a smile.

Olivia trembled. 'Gosh, it's cold, isn't it? I'm afraid I'm running out of coal.'

'If you were to have the officers billeted with you, you wouldn't have to worry about such things,' Mr White said nastily.

She forced a smile.

'We're still waiting to hear about deployments – we'll come back to you.' It sounded like a threat.

The two men drained their tea swiftly (it tasted like dishwater) and moved out into the hall, their eyes still roaming. Olivia knew they were scanning for clues, a man's hat on a hook, a too-large pair of boots, two teacups left on a table. Thankfully, there was nothing. But as they passed the parlour door, Mr White stopped suddenly, then walked in. He looked under the couch. 'Wasn't there a rug rolled up under here last time?'

Olivia's breath caught. The rug was down in the cellar now, making Hamid's living quarters a little more comfortable. He had made a decent job of getting the worst of the blood out of it with a scrubbing brush and a bucket of cold water, but you could still see the stains if you looked.

'Oh, it started to smell very bad – from the parrot, you know – so I dragged it outside to clean it and then left it to dry, and then, the snow...' She spread her hands. 'Well, I wasn't expecting it.'

Sergeant Richards laughed. 'That'll take some drying out, but least it shouldn't smell so bad when you get it back in!'

They took one more look around, then headed for the door. The parrot jumped from his perch to the bars of his cage to get a better look at them as they passed, his claws rattling against the metal. 'Fuck the fuck off!' he cried to their backs.

Mr White stopped dead and the sergeant had to step smartly aside to avoid cannoning into him. Olivia put a hand to her mouth.

'What disgraceful language. There's a war on: there's no food to spare on pets! I shall have to file a report.'

'Oh no, you mustn't! He's my only company!' cried Olivia piteously, looking to Sergeant Richards for support.

He patted her shoulder. 'I'm sure he only eats waste, don't he?'

'Yes, yes, hardly anything, really. It's probably why he's so bad-tempered. But I do love him.'

At the porch, Sergeant Richards paused and let his companion go ahead of him. He turned back to Olivia. 'Don't worry about the parrot,' he said softly, and tipped his helmet to her.

'We have to be more careful!' Olivia said. 'It's your life at stake!'

Hamid nodded ruefully. 'It's my fault. I was excited about the snow.'

'Not just the snow, I hope,' Olivia said, pulling a face.

They kissed. Olivia held his skull between her hands: so round, so heavy, his hair so springy and coarse, so different to her own. Yet she felt she knew him better than she had ever known any other human being in the world. They had talked for hours, down in the cellar, where she had set up the little camping stove which ran on methylated spirits, and boiled water in the old tin kettle. She kept all the tea and sugar she could for Hamid – he liked his tea sweet and he drank it constantly. It was pretty down here in the candlelight, romantic even, if you forgot that just on the other side of the door a corpse was buried.

Over Hamid's shoulder her gaze inadvertently slid to the door. 'Oh!' She slipped from his embrace and stood up, reached out and ran a hand down the edge of the tunnel door. 'That's... lovely.'

Hamid lay back among the cushions, the candlelight gilding the fine-boned planes of his face. He smiled enigmatically.

The carvings were like a sort of alphabet, she thought, the shapes deliberate and significant: she could feel the power in them. It was as if her fingers tingled. She remembered that day up at the Merry Maidens, the strange shock that ran through her when she touched the stone. But this was wood and even she – who had been terrible at school physics – knew that wood didn't carry a charge. 'Does it mean something where... where you come from?'

Hamid gazed back at her, his eyes dark as night. 'You could say that. Where I come from, patterns hold power and I've carved these on both sides of the door. The points of the triangles, they are there to put out the evil eye. The black is protective against djinns and... the dead.'

Olivia stepped smartly away from the door with a shudder of revulsion. She gave a shaky laugh. 'That's just superstition, though, isn't it? That the dead walk?'

Hamid's smile became tight. 'I'm sure it is. But to be so close...'

'I know, I know. But it's really the only safe place in the house. You know, if they search it. At least if they insist on looking down here I can say I've made it comfortable for me and Mary in case of air raids...'

'I understand. But sometimes it's hard to be so far away

from you. I think of you lying in the bed upstairs, when I want to hold you in my arms.'

Tears sparked in Olivia's eyes. 'I think of that every night. I fall asleep imagining we are together, with me lying on my side and your arms around me.'

'If we were in my country we would be married and you would wear a silver crown.'

'A crown?'

'Studded with little gems in red and green.'

Olivia laughed. 'Crowns aren't really my style,' she said, gesturing down at her workaday trousers – a pair of her father's, cut down rather roughly and unevenly because even necessity didn't make her a more attentive needlewoman – and her old wool jersey.

'To me you always look beautiful. But sometimes I see you in a long silk kaftan edged with silver embroidery and a wedding crown upon your head, and your eyes...' he ran his fingers across his own eyes, 'outlined in kohl, and I pray that one day we will live such a moment.'

Such a vision stirred Olivia's imagination. Accompanying it were billows of incense, palaces with forests of marble columns and starlit pools with golden fish swimming in their dark-green depths, wicked viziers and genies trapped in lamps. She smiled a little wistfully. Of course real life wasn't like that. She couldn't see a future for the two of them, not here, or anywhere, so she tried not to think about the future at all. 'Maybe one day. When the war is over,' she said, cupping his cheek.

There was, she was relieved to hear, to be no further

deployment of officers in West Penwith. Sergeant Richards stopped her in the street on her way to her art class. 'Manoeuvres elsewhere,' he said, tapping the side of his nose. 'Don't worry about the parrot either, miss.'

She grinned at him. 'Did you manage to talk to Mr White out of filing his report?'

'Oh no, he wrote it, and gave it to me to implement. But let's just say it ended up in the round file,' he said cryptically. 'Best make sure you keep the beggar quiet, though, or it'll be me who gets in hot water.'

It took her most of the rest of the day to understand what he meant by 'the round file', and when she did, she laughed. Good old Sergeant Richards: what a nice man he was.

Days slipped by. Spring arrived with a fanfare of daffodils and hedgerows full of violets and primroses. When Hamid got too stir crazy, he would, after muttered prayers on the *misbaha*, make his way down through the tunnel to meet Olivia at the beach. She taught him to swim, and to hold his breath underwater – just in case – though at first he had been reluctant, remembering his terrifying ordeal when the fishing boat blew up. There were rocks to hide behind, the cove was sheltered and not overlooked from above and the navy had commandeered most of the fishing boats, so what sea-traffic there was tended to be far out towards the horizon in the convoy lanes.

One day, late in the summer of 1944 when Mary was on the little beach in the village with her friends, they watched a pod of dolphins out in the bay, leaping joyfully through the waves, the sunlight flashing on the whites of their bellies.

Once they watched two huge triangular fins slip past the outer arms of the cove, one large fin followed ten or fifteen feet later by a smaller fin. Hamid scrambled up onto a rock. 'Sharks!'

Olivia laughed at his panic. 'Just one shark,' she corrected him, and as she spoke it rose to reveal a body as long and grey as a miniature submarine, before submerging once again until only the shadow of it was visible beneath the turquoise sea. 'It's a basking shark,' Olivia said. 'We get them here at this time of year, chasing the shoals of little fish around the coast. It's completely harmless.'

'It's huge,' Hamid said, wide-eyed. 'I don't think I want to swim any more.' He scanned the waters of the cove in case other monsters lurked unseen.

They made love to the sound of gulls and kittiwakes, then Olivia lay back on the shingle, feeling the heat from the sun-warmed pebbles soaking into her body. She stared up into the wide blue sky as a pigeon beat past overhead, the feathers of its wings made luminous by the sun, and sighed. 'I wish every day could be like this.'

Hamid took her hand in his and began to sing softly. His singing voice surprised her – a sweet tenor, confident and tuneful. When at last the notes drifted away, she turned her head towards him. 'That was beautiful.'

'It's an Amazigh song called "The Dove and the Hunter". We never speak directly of love: it tempts the evil eye. You are my dove.'

'And you the hunter?' Olivia teased.

He chuckled. 'I would make a poor hunter,' he said. 'One glance from you would kill me every time.'

'Do you really believe in all that stuff, djinns and the evil eye?' What she really wanted to ask was, 'Do you believe in God?' But that felt like too big a question; a question that would open a vast gulf between them. Ever since Mamie had been murdered, maybe even since her father had been killed, Olivia had been questioning the faith she had been raised in. She had even stopped going to church, despite Mary's tantrums. The child was very narrow in her views. 'You'll go to hell,' she told Olivia, and spent her Sundays reading from the Bible and saying prayers to safeguard her own fate. In truth, Olivia avoided church largely because she could not bear to see Farmer Roberts and the rest of them. She could have walked down-chapel and changed congregations, but a stiff resistance to the whole tawdry idea of religion had grown in her.

Now, Hamid squeezed her fingers and said, 'Of course. There may be no physical djinns – what you call them here – little people?'

'Piskeys, they're the good ones, or spriggans, not so good,' Olivia supplied.

'But there is evil all around us. I would rather turn its gaze aside than confront it head-on.'

'But you did confront it head-on,' said Olivia, remembering that terrible night.

'I came to warn you, not to kill him,' Hamid said. 'I am no warrior, no hero out of a story, I'm just a… I don't know what I am. Just a man.' He fell silent for a long time.

'What are you thinking about?' Olivia asked eventually, spurred by eternal female curiosity.

'My family back home. Especially Samira.'

Olivia felt her heart dip. She was greedy for his attention: she wanted every iota of it. He had told her about his family, reeling off the names of his nine siblings like some sort of incantation. Ibrahim, Yacine, Amir, Nazim, Karim, Omar and Mehdi; Samira and Yasmine. Seven brothers, two sisters. He missed them all. He was right in the middle, after his brother Omar and his sister Samira. Whenever he said Samira's name he paused and looked sorrowful. Olivia had once asked if she'd died, but he said it was worse than that: she had lost all her babies to miscarriage or stillbirth and felt God had cursed her.

'I am worried that her husband Kasem will leave her, or take another wife.'

Olivia had never heard of such a thing. 'Can he do that?'

'Under Islam a man may take four wives.'

Olivia sat bolt upright, scandalized. 'Four?'

Hamid laughed. 'Imagine. As if one isn't enough trouble.'

Rather put out, Olivia went down to the edge of the surf and knelt to wash the semen, stiff now as dried egg-white, off her thigh. They were always as careful as they could be, and so far they had been lucky. But perhaps she was barren, like poor Samira? One part of her rather hoped so: raising Mary was a trial, and heaven only knew what would happen if she ever did fall pregnant. She remembered Winnie's condemnation of the Land Girl at Perranuthnoe and her 'brown baby' and something inside her twisted with fear. They should stop having sex, they really should. There were other things they could do that were almost as nice: they had tried many of them. She wondered if he had learned some of those things from Madame Duchamps, and went cold with jealousy. But she knew she wouldn't have the strength of will to stop: she was a slave to the sensation of Hamid moving inside her, hard and male, alien and yet so desired. She was addicted to him, even more than he was addicted to sugar.

'Better go in,' she said, retrieving her tangle of clothes.

'You're a tyrant.' He grinned, lying there uncovered, his hands behind his head, his skin as brown as a conker. Under her gaze his cock twitched once like a separate, live animal.

'Come along,' she said firmly, doing her belt up extra tight.

They crunched back up the beach to the back of the cove and kissed at the entrance to the tunnel. 'I hate going in here,' he said. 'It's like walking into the realm of djinns.'

He was half-teasing her, but also half-serious. She put a finger to his lips. 'I know.'

He gazed into the dark maw between the granite rock faces. 'When I get to the top my heart beats like a rabbit's. It calms only when I am on the other side of the door, though I think the spirits only walk at night. I must carve the symbols on the other gate, too.' He tilted his chin up to indicate the sea gate. 'To keep you safe.'

'Someone might see you.'

He balled a fist. 'I will do it at night. When the moon is next full.'

22

Becky

I FIND EDDIE IN GABRIEL'S ROOM, THOUGH HE'S KEEPING his distance from the parrot, which is watching him closely, claws and beak locked to the bars at the front of the cage. He's regarding the painting between the bookcase and the window, the one of the little fishing boat ploughing a lonely course out into the bay, his hands in his pockets, his head almost touching the canvas.

'Lovely, isn't it?' I say, and watch as he flinches, so preoccupied that he hadn't heard me come in.

'Not really my sort of thing,' he drawls, stepping back.

I know it is not a style of art he appreciates, so I am curious as to why he is taking such a close interest in it. But I reckon I can guess. 'I wonder who the artist is?' I say casually.

If he knows, he's hiding it well. He shrugs. 'Loads of artists doing this sort of semi-abstract landscape thing down here. It's all about the light.'

'I think it's lovely. There's a lot of texture to give the waves real depth and body, and the layering of colour is amazing.'

'Bit blah for my taste, to be honest.'

He runs a hand through his hair, lets his fringe fall across his eyes so that his expression is hidden. It's a familiar gesture and one I suddenly recognize for what it is: a disguise for a lie. Other occasions flicker through my memory. Oh yes, then, and then. I always knew, I think, subconsciously, when Eddie was lying to me, but I was never confident enough to challenge him.

He flicks the fringe back, open and smiling again. 'Cornwall's done you good. You look… different.'

'Clean air and sunshine,' I say. 'And getting away from London.'

'Getting away from me, you mean.' He laughs. It's supposed to be disarming. I'm meant to demur – *oh no, how could you imagine that?* I say nothing. See how it discomfits him. He shifts from foot to foot.

I suppose I do look different. I have more colour, my muscles are more toned. I've been more active than when I'm in London, with all the cleaning and the walking up and down hills, the steps, the swimming. I feel fit and well. I'm not used to thinking of myself in this way. So much of my time was taken up with the shock of illness, of hospitals and treatment, with endless blood tests and check-ups and scans. I've been a lump of meat on an operating table, a subject for medical discussion and examination, an invalid, a patient. Never really a person in my own right or on my own terms.

Other than examining my fading scars in the mirror, I've not given much thought to my cancer in the past few weeks. It wasn't that I didn't think about it at all – maudlin thoughts came to me at unexpected times, woke me at night, made me wonder whether it was worth buying a new tub of moisturizer – but getting away has been good for me, having a project and someone other than myself to think about. Oddly enough, the isolation has given me back to myself, made me stronger – perhaps even stronger than I have ever been. I daresay I will have to go and have that scan sometime, but at the moment I am listening to my body, which tells me – as the consultant did – not to panic.

'You know, Eddie,' I say, 'I think being away from you has been a real tonic.'

He looks aghast, then breaks into nervous laughter. 'Ha ha! Very good, Becks. You had me going there.'

'In fact,' I go on, 'being away from you has done me a power of good, as Mum would have said.'

His smile wavers, then he musters the tattered remnants of his old charm. 'Hey, let's not retread old ground, eh, Becks? This morning was great, wasn't it? Just like it used to be.'

'This morning,' I enunciate carefully, 'was a big mistake. I don't know why I let it happen, but I shouldn't have. I don't want to be with you any more, Eddie, and that's the plain fact of it. We're not right together.'

His left eye twitches, as it does sometimes when he's under stress.

'You are joking? Aren't you? Come on, Becks, this isn't like you. It's not like you at all.'

'That's probably because I've changed. I'm not the doormat I used to be. The one you wiped your feet on every day but otherwise hardly noticed.'

He looks astonished. 'You've gone mad. Are you on different medication or something?'

'Because I couldn't possibly be immune to your charm if I wasn't taking mind-altering pills? Don't make me laugh.'

'But this morning—'

'This morning happened because I was horny and you were there, OK?'

Blood fills his face. 'You bitch! You utter fucking bitch! You've stumbled on your own little goldmine here – big house full of valuable paintings, old woman at death's door – and you don't want to share it. I wondered why you weren't wearing your ring. And no doubt there's money coming from your mother's estate too, so you thought,' he puts on a grotesque female voice, '"I'm financially independent now, I don't need Eddie any more."'

'Oh, you remember my mother now, do you, the one who bought your studio for you? The woman whose funeral you couldn't be bothered to attend? Let's face it, Eddie, you're a nasty piece of work. You're one of life's takers, and you never give back. We've been together ten years and you've cheated on me at least four times during that time—'

'Well, who could blame me? You were so mimsy, so… bloodless. You'd just lie there and take it, so sweet, so passive, so desperate to please. Sometimes a man wants a bit of a challenge, a woman who puts up a bit of a fight in bed, someone who's a bit more fucking sexy.'

In the early days of our relationship Eddie would sometimes slap me in the middle of intercourse – usually just a tap, on the cheek, the buttock, the leg, but occasionally he left marks. It had perplexed and upset me, and had the opposite effect to the one he was after. I grew limp with confusion, withdrawing out of my body and into my head. Eventually he had stopped trying to goad me and, I suppose, gone elsewhere for the more exciting tangles he sought. Back then, it made me feel ashamed and diminished: now it made me furious.

'It's a bit hard to be "sexy" when your breasts have been chopped off and you've been injected with poison. Where were you when I came home in a taxi after four hours of chemo, feeling like a wrung-out rag, to an empty house, wondering where you were? You try being sexy when you're throwing up all day, thinking you're going to die. And all the time I knew something was going on. I noticed you suddenly taking an interest in your appearance: the weights that turned up in the studio, the mysterious disappearance of the grey in your hair – I know damn well it wasn't me sticking empty Just For Men containers in the bin! It was that trampy little waitress from the Cuban restaurant you used to take me to, wasn't it? Lola or Lulu, or whatever. What was she, seventeen, eighteen? You used to roll in at all hours reeking of cheap wine and sex. I may have been sick and knackered, but my sense of smell was stronger than ever on chemo. Did you think you had a free pass because I was so sick? Or that I was so "bloodless" that I didn't care? What kind of man does that to his partner at the worst time in her life?'

'A bad man. A weak man...'

The voice comes from behind me. Reda steps into the room.

'... and a thief.'

There is an object under his arm, a large rectangle bound in a bin bag, dripping with rain. I know instantly what it is.

'I saw him put it in the boot of his car,' Reda says conversationally.

Eddie glares at him. 'Who the fuck are you? And what the hell do you think you're doing fiddling with my car?' Then he gives me a nasty grin. 'I knew you'd run away down here with some...' he regards Reda contemptuously, 'some fucking wog. Met him at the kebab shop, did you?'

Reda puts *The Sea Gate* down carefully by the door and moves to my side. His expression is closed, his emotions controlled, but I can feel the heat coming off him in waves. 'It's OK,' I say, putting a hand on his arm. 'I can deal with this.' After all, I faced off the Sparrow brothers. At the moment I feel I could punch Eddie's lights out, lay him flat on the floor. It's an odd feeling for someone who has been so timid all her life.

'I thought I knew the worst of you,' I say very coldly. 'But I see there are depths to you I never imagined. You'd better leave. Before I call the police.'

Eddie laughs. 'You'll be lucky: there's no fucking signal! And I reckon I can take out loverboy here.'

'This kind man is not my lover: he's a plumber, helping me get the house ready for Cousin Olivia's return.' I glare at the man I wasted ten years of my life on. 'Tell me, Eddie, did James tell you about her paintings? Well, obviously he did and you put two and two together. Why else would you come all this way?'

He's thinking of denying it, is searching for a form of words that will somehow justify his actions – the hiring of a car, the long drive, no warning, the theft – then his eyes slide back to Reda and he sneers. 'There's nothing else here to bother with, is there?' he says bitterly. 'You've made that abundantly clear. Ten years, eh? Gone, just like that.' He snaps his fingers. 'Why don't you let me take the painting with me? As a goodwill gesture at the dissolution of our marriage? A proper clean break? I'll clear all my things out of the house and you can have it to yourself.' He licks his lips. 'Go on, Becks. Times are hard. The show didn't do nearly as well as I'd expected.'

He is so contemptible. I can't imagine now, seeing his mask slip, how I ever found him attractive, let alone depended on him to the extent of giving him power over me – my choices, my clothes, my emotions. I look at him, hanging on my every word, his eyes crafty.

'You're pathetic, Eddie. You're a conman and a creep. No, of course you can't have the painting. Even if it were mine to give – which it is not – I'd do anything – *anything* – to keep it out of your hands! All you care about is money and being seen as some sort of great man of the art world. You've never cared about anyone other than yourself, least of all me. You're a hollow, hollow man, and the worst of it is you think that everyone else is like you. Now clear off, before we make a citizens' arrest! I never want to see you again!'

I can feel Reda's grin in the air between us.

Eddie gives one more defeated glance towards *The Sea Gate*, as if calculating his chances of bolting with it, then shakes his head. 'I'm a shit, yes, I know.' He shrugs, then lifts his chin. 'But, hey, it took you ten years to work it out, didn't it? Plenty more gullible fish in the sea.' He holds out a hand. 'Shake?'

I frown. What a way to end ten years and a torrent of let-downs and betrayals. But I find myself offering my hand, if only to mark the ending. He takes my hand and his thumb plays over my palm, a final brief caress. Then his entire demeanour changes and suddenly he has his arm hooked

around my neck, pressing hard against my windpipe. With
his free hand he manoeuvres a knife out of his pocket,
presses the button in the handle and the blade flicks open.
He holds it out then tosses it in the air and catches it, a
nonchalant assassin.

'Out of the way, there's a good chap,' he says to Reda.
'Plumber, eh? I bet you'd like to give her pipes a good clean.
Shame about that.' He pauses. 'How about all that crap
about the hair dye? That was nasty, wasn't it? I didn't know
you had that in your repertoire, darling.'

Reda takes a step towards him and at once Eddie
transfers the blade to my throat, the tip pressing in painfully,
preventing me from making a sound. 'Oh, I don't think so,
do you? You need her to stick around or you aren't going
to get paid. No one does a job like this out of the goodness
of their hearts. Though I can tell she fancies you, it's all in
the eyes. Perhaps she's thinking about paying you in kind
– something got her all hot and bothered this morning. Bet
you want a British passport, don't you, with that accent of
yours? Shame you didn't get together with her before now.
You could have made off with the paintings, sold them for
a small fortune and set yourselves up nicely. Look at you,'
he sneers, 'desperation shining in your eyes as you try to
reckon the odds of taking me down without me sticking
this in her. See, that's the difference: you care about her and
I don't – and that's what gives me the whip hand. Now,
you're going to help me carry that painting back up to my
vehicle like a good little mule – I'm sure there are plenty of
those where you come from – and I'll just follow along with
Rebecca here, make sure you don't do anything that might
prejudice her health – what's left of it, anyway. You know

she's not all that any more, don't you, old boy? No tits, a scarred old chicken carcass. It's only a matter of time: she's just walking dead—'

'Shut your mouth, *putain*,' Reda says with quiet menace. 'Every word shows me the filthy rot that is your soul. This woman is a fine woman. She has strength and compassion, honesty and determination. She is worth ten thousand of you. What she ever saw in you I cannot imagine.'

'My cock, mate. She loved it. Even this morning when I gave her a final mercy ride, she loved every fucking moment of it.'

I can tell by the way his muscles subtly tense that he expects to shock Reda with this revelation, to goad him, but Eddie was asleep when Reda looked in and saw us, so he doesn't even get this small satisfaction. Reda just stares at him, his dark eyes like agates.

Eddie's knife sketches an insolent figure of eight in the air. 'Ah, well. No time to waste. I've got a bloody five-hour drive back up to London from this out-of-the-way shithole. Place for washed-up losers if ever I saw one.' He pauses. 'You can take that down as well,' he says, indicating the painting of the sunwashed bay, the little boat in a luminous cloud.

I cough and try to speak but Eddie just tightens his chokehold till I'm struggling for air.

Reda's mouth is a hard, flat line. He strides across the room and takes the painting down. Behind it, a rectangle of bright wallpaper is revealed in its pristine pre-war state and I can suddenly picture the room as it must once have been, elegant and sunny, vibrant with colour, the heart of a lovely family home. Its current degradation, despite all I have done to try to bring it back to life, seems so poignant that tears fill my eyes and spill onto Eddie's forearm.

The moment of distraction as Eddie looks down in confusion is all Reda needs. With a single neat spin he jabs the corner of the painting into the angle between Eddie's jaw and ear. Eddie screams and lets me go. Rather than run away, I turn and swing my fist into his face with a roundhouse punch that lands with astonishing force.

Eddie drops without a sound.

23

I CRADLE MY HAND. VIOLENCE IS NEVER THE ANSWER TO anything, but I've never felt so weirdly euphoric. My knuckles are red and already starting to swell, but even if I can never hold another paintbrush it will have been worth it. I expect I'll feel differently later, but for now I'm damn well going to treasure the moment.

Reda is looking at me in astonishment. He holds his hands up in a gesture of surrender. 'Don't hit me.' He grins.

We both stare down at the unconscious form of Eddie, but I feel nothing. Not regret, or hatred or even repulsion. Nothing at all. All my emotions appear to have burst out of me in that one punch. I imagine them flowing down my arm like Popeye's spinach, pumping up the muscles, exiting in a cartoon-bubble, POW!

'What shall we do with him?'

'Call the police,' Reda says without hesitation.

'Really? Can't we just put him in his car and let him go?'

'After what he did to you? After he came all this way to

steal from an old lady? If you let him go, what's to stop him coming back to hurt you again?'

'I don't know.' It's all so complicated. I rub my throat: my voice is hoarse.

Reda takes a pace towards me, moves my hand away and crooks his neck. 'Look at what he's done to you,' he says, and there is such tenderness in his voice that my knees start to tremble.

I step away. I want to step towards him, but I step away. Fear, confusion, embarrassment. I am fourteen all over again.

Eddie has not moved, but I can see his chest moving up and down, so I know he's not dead. Even so, I drop to one knee and place my hand in front of his slack mouth to be reassured by the rhythmic expulsions of warm air. Then his eyelids flicker and he stares up at me and groans.

'Up you get,' Reda says, heaving him to his feet, where he stands, swaying unsteadily.

'Shouldn't we check him for concussion?' I ask.

Reda shrugs. He holds a hand up in front of Eddie's face, little finger and thumb folded down. 'How many fingers?'

'Fuck off!' says Eddie.

'He's not concussed.' Reda turns to me. 'Phone the police?' He digs in his pocket, removes his mobile, thumbs the code into it and passes it to me.

'No signal.' I show him the screen. 'What do we do?'

'Go and open the cellar door,' Reda tells me.

I hesitate. Ever since finding the bone and making that single foray to check for more I have avoided the cellar and the tunnel down to the cove.

'We can keep him there till the police come,' Reda adds.

Eddie stares at him incredulously. 'You must be joking.' But he's still not quite with it and he's too slow to prevent Reda taking hold of his arm and jamming it up behind his back till he yelps.

I think of the Sparrow brothers down in that cellar, another thing I haven't told Reda. I wonder whether there are traces of their nefarious goings on down there. What if Eddie finds the drugs? What if he takes them? It all seems too surreal. I almost laugh hysterically, but I run and unlock the cellar door and between us we manage to get a struggling Eddie safely down the steps. At the bottom, he looks around, confused. 'Don't leave me down here!' he calls after us as we run back up the steps. 'It's fucking freezing! Ah, come on, Becks – I hurt you, you hit me – we're even. Just call it quits, eh? Just let me go. I'll leave and you'll never see me again, I swear!'

I turn back, unsure, but Reda hauls me through the door, locks it grimly and steers me into the kitchen. 'You need a cup of strong tea. And I also prescribe biscuits.'

I sit at the kitchen table beneath Olivia's portrait. I think today she looks rather bleak, disappointed in the shortcomings of humankind. Prompted by this, I tell Reda of my suspicions about the Sparrow brothers. I tell him about the rat. He stops pottering around with plates and biscuits and stares at me. 'They pushed a dead rat through the letter box?'

'I hope it was dead before they pushed it through. Poor thing. I buried it out in the orchard.' I take a sip of the tea he has made me. It is massively oversweet and almost undrinkable, but I drink it anyway. He has, for some reason, used the best bone china cups and saucers: my cup is prettily decorated with little blue flowers; his with roses and a sprig of rosemary. It looks ridiculously dainty in his strong workman's hands.

He takes a sip from his own cup, wrinkles his nose and sets it down. It chimes against its dinky saucer. 'I ran out of sugar,' he says. 'It tastes bad without it.' Picking up a digestive, he devours it whole.

'That's a good trick!' I try to emulate it and end up choking greedily. His delight at my idiocy lightens our mood and soon we're giggling like children.

When at last we stop laughing, I say, 'I want to explain. About this morning.' Was it really only this morning I slept with Eddie? It seems half a lifetime ago, and completely inexplicable.

He shakes his head. 'You really don't need to explain anything. Really. It's none of my business.'

'I feel I do and...' I hesitate. I was about to say 'and I'd really like it to be your business' but I just can't muster the words. 'Well, I'm sorry,' I mumble in the end. 'It was a mistake. A stupid, giant mistake.'

He's gazing at me intently and I can feel myself reddening. To hide my embarrassment, I get up and go to the cupboard and take out of it one of the mugs I usually use. I pour fresh tea into it but the sugar bowl is empty. In the cupboard above the kettle I find an old canister which when I shake it gives back the soft sifting sound of granulated sugar. I refill the sugar bowl, and am about to return the canister to the shelf when I see another tin shoved to the back of the shelf. I fiddle it down.

It looks ancient, the label obscured by repeated handling and oxidization, but even so I can make out the words 'Thomas

Harley Ltd, Perth' and 'for beetles mix with soft sugar', which makes no sense at all. Above this '… low phosphorus' and in capitals – 'RODINE' and 'PO…N'. A horrible thought occurs to me, and I fumble at the tin, which falls to the floor and rolls on its side across the slate tiles to fetch up at Reda's boot, dislodging the lid. He bends to retrieve tin and lid, sniffs the contents and recoils. He jams the lid back on with some alacrity. 'I think,' he says slowly, putting the tin down on the table and pushing it away from him, 'that this is rat poison. We use something like it back home.'

'What on earth is it doing in a kitchen cupboard?' I frown.

We look at one another. I can feel the eyes of the figure in the portrait upon me. Reda gets up and examines the bowl of sugar, then the tea caddy. He shakes his head. 'They seem fine. It's a strange place to keep rat poison, though.'

I remember something. Several somethings. My hand flies to my mouth. The somethings are beginning to join together in a distressing way.

'I found letters from my mother to Cousin Olivia upstairs, some dating back years. In some of them she must have said she'd been ill because Mum replied saying she hoped Olivia was feeling better.'

'She's an old lady,' Reda says slowly.

'Ninety-odd, yes, I know – but it went on and on, from year to year, that she was sorry Olivia was feeling under the weather, "hope you've got over this wretched tummy bug", "hope you're feeling more yourself"… and Olivia isn't one to complain: she's a tough old bird. And when I was visiting her at the hospital, the nursing sister said there was something up with her liver, they were getting odd test results…'

Reda shakes his head. 'I don't—'

'All this time... and that stuff – well, it looks pretty old. Do you think rat poison goes off? Loses its potency? Do you think you can build up some resistance to it? If someone's been trying to poison her, why isn't she dead?'

Reda blows a long breath out of his nose. 'Perhaps whoever it is doesn't want her dead. Perhaps it's some sort of punishment?'

'That's horrible.'

He nods. 'But who would do such a thing?'

I feel the eyes of the girl in the portrait on me, mocking now. I look at the dainty porcelain cups and a wave of revulsion rises through me. I look up at Reda, feeling stricken. 'No one will believe me.' I haven't even told him about the parrot's utterances and my suspicion that Cousin Olivia was pushed down the stairs.

Reda places the tin of rat poison in a plastic carrier bag and ties the neck. Then he undoes it and places the cups in there too. 'Greed,' he says firmly. 'It's at the heart of everything, isn't it? The house, the paintings. It's all about money.' He shakes his head. 'People are sadly predictable when it comes to money.'

As if in answer to this, the heavens open again and rain batters the window. It's getting dark. Reda checks his phone but there's still no signal. 'I'll run up the hill and try to call the police from there,' he says.

'No, please.' I put my hand on his arm. 'I'm feeling very spooked by all this. I don't want to be here on my own, not at the moment. Not with Eddie down in the cellar. Do you mind?' I shiver, feeling a distinct chill even though the range is fired up.

He nods. 'Come on then. Let's light the fire in the parrot's room and we'll see if I can teach him any more rude words in Darija.'

Gabriel likes Reda. He perks up whenever he enters the room, jumping noisily around his cage, trying to catch his attention with affectionate little trills and whistles. Today is no different.

'I should let him out for a bit,' I say, feeling guilty that he's not been let out of his cage for the past few days. 'I've been reading up – he needs to exercise his wings, and it'll make him happier. Body and soul. Makes sense – who would want to be trapped in a cage?'

Which is what I have been, these past years, I realize even as I say it. Fear has trapped me, rendered me immobile and powerless: fear of losing Eddie, fear of the cancer, fear of everything, really. I'd forgotten I even had wings, let alone how to use them.

'You think parrots have souls?' Reda asks, regarding the bird askance.

'I'm sure Gabriel does.'

'Do you, Djibril?'

The bird cocks his head at Reda, then bounces up and down as if in assent and lets out a piercing whistle. 'Djibril!'

'How did he learn that so quickly?' I am astonished. 'He's a genius.'

'It's his name.'

'Gabriel's his name.'

'It's the same, in Arabic.'

'But...' My mind spins. Not knowing what to make of this, I concentrate on opening the cage door. Gabriel

– Djibril – watches me closely. I have brought a handful of unshelled peanuts from the kitchen for him and I hand him one. He takes it politely in his hooked beak, holds it still with his talons and cracks it open efficiently. 'That beak is quite a weapon,' I laugh, as Gabriel plunders the nut inside.

The parrot, having disappeared the peanut, comes questing after another. 'Oh no, you don't!' I tell him, laughingly hiding the rest. 'How else am I going to bribe you back in again?'

He gives me a ceramic stare, then hops out of the cage onto my hand, unceremoniously claws his way up to my shoulder, then uses my head as a launchpad for his cold, scaly feet and sails across the room, giving us a magnificent display of his scarlet underfeathers.

Just as he touches down on the bookcase there is an almighty grumble of thunder outside and the rain redoubles its force. 'Whoo!' says Reda. 'Grandfather never said anything about weather like this here.' He grins at me. 'I'll light the fire.'

I am about to reply when there is a huge howl of wind, followed by a low hooting noise, like the sound made by blowing over the top of a bottle. It's eerie. I can see it's unsettling Gabriel, whose feathers are ruffled, and a crest has risen on his head. Reda takes no notice: he is building a little pyramid of kindling in the crate, arranging logs carefully around it. He takes some newspaper from the pile I use to line the cage, tears it into strips and rolls and twists them into pretzel shapes, then takes a lighter from his pocket and starts the fire as quick as magic.

'You're very good at that,' I observe.

'Up in the hills where my family come from they keep fires burning all winter long – you'd die if you didn't know how to light a fire!'

'I thought Morocco was a hot country, with deserts and stuff.'

'Morocco is all things to all men, from the poorest peasant to the richest lord. It has modern cities and villages where there's no electricity; superfast Internet and mule carts; there are mountains covered in snow all year round, and of course deserts. In some places the temperature can hit fifty degrees in summer, yet be minus ten in winter. You learn to be adaptable. It's not easy if you're poor – that's why we all send money home for the old people. It's why I'm here.'

He says something else but his words are drowned out by a particularly large rumble of thunder and then the ground shakes as if the land on which the house sits is convulsing, as if something in the world is shifting. I stumble against the door jamb and feel the wood trembling beneath my fingers as if it has come to life. There is a distant wail, muffled but distinct. Where did that come from?

I know it came from the cellar.

Gabriel squawks in panic and beats past my ear and out into the hall, because in the midst of all this the door has come open.

'Gabriel!' I go after him, as much for his own sake as in fear of losing him. I don't want him hurting himself in his panic.

Outside, the hall is freezing. Absolutely freezing. And silent. There is no sound of the storm; no trace of the parrot.

Reda joins me. 'What was that? An earthquake? A lightning strike?'

'I don't know,' I admit.

'There may have been some movement of the ground down there. We had better check on him.'

I notice he doesn't use Eddie's name. 'I just want to find Gabriel and make sure he's OK first.'

Reda nods and goes down the hallway towards the front door, making *tchhing* noises and calling softly, 'Djibril, Djibril!'

In the end it's me who finds the parrot, though he's not really hiding. He's perched on top of the longcase clock, watching the cellar door with a gimlet gaze. Just as I'm about to speak, the clock lets out a sonorous chime. It's the first time it's made a sound in all these weeks. I had thought it was broken: a beautiful, redundant antique. But it is ticking now, quite clearly, its pendulum telling out the seconds, the movement of its long hand unnervingly loud in the reverberating space of the hall now that the rain and wind have abated.

'I've found Gabriel!' I call to Reda. He rejoins me and watches as I dig in my pocket and lay peanuts on the palm of my hand for the parrot. For once, the creature doesn't show the least bit of interest in them, doesn't even move. His claws are splayed across the top of the clock as if he's holding on for dear life and the white rings around his dark pupils seem wider than usual. '*Bal-lack!*' he cries. *Get back!*

'Come on, Djibril,' Reda says, and offers his hand for the bird to jump onto but Gabriel just continues to sit there, unblinking. Reda murmurs something in Darija which sounds coaxing but the parrot is adamant.

'*Bal-lack!*'

'I think he's all right,' Reda says, stepping back.

'Look at his feathers, though, all fluffed up. He's scared of something.'

'All the noise, I think. Come on, we should check on him.'

I listen for the second time that day at the cellar door. It is as quiet as the grave and I can't see any light coming from under the door. Taking down the key, I glance at Reda and he nods: he is ready in case Eddie charges up the stairs. I turn the key in the lock and quickly push the door open. It is pitch dark and there's no response when I flick the light switch. The bulb must have blown – water in the electrics, perhaps. Or perhaps there was a lightning strike and the electricity down here spiked. Perhaps that's why Eddie shrieked. I wouldn't blame him.

'Eddie?' I call.

In response there is a sudden stirring in the air and a clattering sound and then Gabriel appears overhead, his wings beating furiously. I think for a startled moment he is going to swoop down into the cellar, but he lands on top of the door, tucks his wings in close and curls his talons around the wood of the frame, sentinel-like. Reda and I exchange glances. It's as if he's waiting for something.

Reda fetches a big rubber torch from his work kit, clicks it on and shines it down the stairs. Swirls of dust eddy in its silver-white beam in a complex atomic dance.

But of Eddie there is no sign.

We have to go down: there is no avoiding it. With Gabriel's eyes on our backs we head down, our steps ringing off the stone.

'Eddie?' I call again, but my cry is swallowed into the darkness.

We reach the bottom of the stairs and Reda swings the

torch beam back and forth across the cellar. The shelving unit has collapsed, spilling its contents everywhere: might that have caused the noise? For a moment I wonder if it's fallen on Eddie, but it appears to be lying flat. Behind the shelves, the door in the back wall is ajar, its leading edge pushed out into the deeper darkness of the tunnel.

'He's escaped!' I swear I can see my breath clouding the air. The atmosphere down here is eldritch: I have the strong sense that I don't want to be here, and that something doesn't want me to be here. That our presence is disturbing some long-established equilibrium reached between the house and its bedrock. I can, I think, smell something foreign – old cigarette smoke, the unfiltered type. Has Eddie taken up smoking again after years of giving it up? Maybe he found some of the Sparrow brothers' contraband. But it smells faint, not recent, like a scent-echo of something long gone.

Suddenly I feel the need of warm human contact. I take Reda's hand. His fingers close around mine and I can feel the pulse in his thumb: his heart must be beating as fast as mine.

Reda shines the torch over the tunnel door. The patterns around its edges seem more clearly delineated than usual in the focused white light, their points and triangles sharp, as if newly carved. 'Who did this?'

'What? Sorry, what?'

'These carvings.'

'I don't know. They're interesting, aren't they?'

'They're protective, not just interesting. They're here for a reason.'

'I don't know. Perhaps Olivia—'

'I know who made this. I've seen it before, exactly the

same.' He steps in front of me, takes a sharp breath and tries to push the door open further. There is a skittering, a pattering sound. Like rats' feet, I think, but as Reda's torch plays across the chaos beyond the door I realize that it is loose earth, and that the tunnel has become blocked by a rockfall.

'A landslip,' he confirms, pulling the door back and closing it firmly. He sends the torch beam jumping up to the cellar ceiling, to the junctions of its walls. 'No cracks. I don't think it's a major one.'

'What about Eddie?'

He shoots me a quick look, hard to make out his expression in the darkness. 'I don't know. Where does the tunnel go?'

'Down into the cove beneath the house.'

'Is there another way down?'

'Through the gate and down the steps on the other side of the lane below the house.'

'Come on, then,' he says grimly.

The moon is a silver sliver between scudding clouds, the intermittent light from it chancy and fitful. It makes the garden an alien place as it shifts in and out of full darkness. In the trees behind the house, the wind soughs as if the hillside is breathing into the night.

I use the app on my phone to light my way, though Reda swings the torch beam back and forth on the steps to aid my progress. Out onto the lane we go, where the air is almost still and the sea stretches charcoal to the horizon. We go through the sea gate, and when Reda reaches behind me to close it, the torch catches the carvings on its seaward side. His breath hisses in through his teeth.

'We should leave this till the morning.'

I stare at him, his face seeming as carved as the wood, and eerie, lit from below, his eyes agleam in cavernous sockets. 'We can't. What if Eddie is trapped by the landslip? He might die. I don't want that on my conscience.'

'You still care about him.' It's not a question.

'No... yes, well, not really. I wouldn't leave anyone down there,' I say lamely. 'Not if we can help him.'

'You stay here then,' he tells me, but I'm past the stage of being told what to do by men any more.

'No, if you go down I'm going with you, and if you stay here I'll go by myself.'

He shakes his head then mutters something in which I hear the name *Allah* pronounced several times. A prayer. The idea of Reda – this big, strong, practical man – praying before going down to the cove unnerves me far more than the storm, the fitful moon, the superstitious fear of the dark, but we have to go down: it's our human duty.

'It's a bit tricky in places,' I say. There is nothing for it but to go down on bum and hands, even though we're going to get filthy. I hear the shuffle and scuff of him as he follows me down. As we reach the cove I hear the susurrus and recoil of the waves, the rattle of pebbles as the sea sucks at them, but this soothing sound is punctuated by an intermittent clanging noise, discordant and doomy, like a cracked and distant bell.

The tide is halfway in – or out – but as we crunch up the pebbles the light from my phone shines on the stones to a certain point after which they appear duller, as if they are drying, so I think, and hope, it's on its way out.

At the rear of the cave we find the origin of the clanging sound – the iron gate into the tunnel has been left unlatched and gusts of wind are knocking it into the rocks. I wonder who left it like that – Ezra and Saul Sparrow as they made their getaway? Or Eddie?

Behind it, the tunnel beckons, a thin, sardonic mouth in the cliff face. I really don't want to go in, but I must. I have spent a long time running away from things, trying to ignore them, hoping they'll go away. *It's only a small landslip,* I tell myself. A geological accident. All the recent rain seeping into that softer seam of earth that made the construction of the tunnel possible. What was it the Sparrows said to me? *The cliffs round here are unstable. Water gets into the soil and they slip…* It seems both reasonable and rational, yet utterly terrifying.

Up the tunnel I go with Reda behind me, one hand holding out my phone with its arc of white light, the other pressed to the rock, which seems so very cold. Colder than anything I have touched before other than actual ice. My fingers begin to numb, the bones to ache. I can feel dank, salty air filming my skin, making my face and neck clammy. As we pick our way through the pinch point there is the first sign of rubble – earth and loose stones underfoot; then as we near the steps up towards the cellar we come upon thicker, more unstable debris. I move up cautiously but even so manage to dislodge a rock that skitters past Reda, knocking against the walls of the tunnel, the sound of its passage unnaturally loud in the dense silence.

'Eddie?' I call. There is no echo: the fallen earth swallows the word. I try again, louder, and we stand still, bending our senses towards the invisible door into the cellar. Unless he managed to get down the tunnel before the fall came, Eddie must be somewhere in the next fifteen feet.

'This place,' Reda starts. 'I—' His voice cracks: he is scared. I remember how I felt the first time down here, coming out of light and air into this chill blackness, aware of the rock pressing in all around.

'I know.' I turn and brush my fingers over his cheek and he shivers. My hand is cold, but even so I feel the warmth between us, life and hope and everything they stand for. And then he smiles, the reflection of the torchlight in the half-moons of his eyes, and I am smiling too, our joined gaze a gossamer thread that binds us in the darkness, a tenuous link that speaks of liking and desire but also of trust; a moment of lightness in the gloom. Then I break the connection and we forge on.

The last few feet of the tunnel are choked with detritus – floor-to-ceiling rock and earth and twists of pale roots and sticks. It is hard to make any further headway.

'Eddie?' How can he be under all this and have survived? It seems unthinkable. But how can he have got out? There was no sign of him on the beach or the rocks of the cove, and I know he cannot swim.

There is a faint noise. I don't know how to describe it. It's neither movement nor a word but somehow both at the same time. All the hairs along my spine start to prickle.

Reda touches my shoulder and I almost jump out of my skin. 'Go back. I'm going to use the mattock – I don't want you getting hit by falling rocks. If it does come down, just run, as fast as you can, back out to the beach. Get up the hill or down towards the village and call for help.'

'But what about you?'

He makes a minuscule shrug. 'I hope Allah hears my prayers. Go back, Rebecca, I don't want anything happening to you – this stuff is unstable.'

I move aside and he sets the head of the mattock into the fallen earth, pulls against the resistance and steps back to let the debris trickle harmlessly to the ground. Carefully, he repeats the exercise. I move to where I can see him: I cannot leave. More detritus, but no sign of Eddie.

The air gets chillier, if such a thing is possible. I hug myself, and the light from my phone is muffled against my body; only the torch, left on the ground, pointing up, breaks the wall of utter darkness.

Far away – as if in another world – I hear what may be a parrot's cry.

Another strike and this time rocks come bounding out and I have to dodge them. One goes rattling off down the tunnel. The other bangs up against my foot. I am about to look down when something buffets past my head, its swift progress as palpable as the air from beating wings. I think, *How did Gabriel get down here?* but then it is past, trailing behind it an appalling stench. A rotten reek, ancient filth tinged with the faint, acrid scent of old tobacco, fills the air. My ears ring from the sound of it, high-pitched between a wail and a whistle.

And then it is gone.

I stand there with my heart trying to smash its way through my ribs. 'What the hell was that?' I whisper. Reda looks back at me, his eyes wide. Then we both look down.

At my feet, liminal in the darkness, neither of one world nor another, lies a human skull.

24

HOW NEITHER OF US BREAKS AN ANKLE IN OUR FLIGHT down the tunnel back out to the cove, I will never know. We do not stop until we make it down to the water's edge and breathe in great gulps of the sharp salty air.

I am shaking now, half frozen, half scared to death. 'Did you hear it? Did you see anything?'

Reda's face is pale in the moon's shine as he shakes his head. The clouds have parted: the surface of the sea is spangled with scintillas of light.

'I heard something,' he admits.

'I thought it was Gabriel,' I say, and there's a question in my words.

'Whatever that was it wasn't Gabriel.'

'And the...' I can hardly bring myself to say the word.

'... skull? It was a skull, wasn't it? I wasn't imagining it?'

'Yes, it was a skull.'

'Reda... there's something I ought to tell you.'

He looks at me intently. 'Go on.'

'I found a bone down in the tunnel one day a few weeks

back. A finger bone. I suspected it was human at the time, but I was too worried to do anything about it, or even to mention it. I tried to ask Olivia about it...' My voice trails off.

He considers this for a long moment, then says, 'And you think this is why she wanted us to brick up the cellar?'

I nod mutely.

'Whoever these remains belong to has been down there for a long time,' Reda says.

'I suppose so. But Olivia is in her nineties...'

'We'll have to tell the police.'

'Yes, I know.' There's no avoiding it now that Eddie is down there too.

He shakes his head, then says, 'Look at you. You look so cold.' And he pulls me into an embrace and we stand close together, sharing each other's warmth, letting our heartbeats return to a more normal rhythm. Not entirely normal, because now I'm feeling something else: an awareness of his proximity, the tang of his sweat, which does not smell at all offensive, but makes me want to get closer to the source of it.

'I'll call the police,' I say at last.

Reda nods and hands me his phone. Miraculously, it has a signal.

Back up at the house, we find feathers scattered in the hall. I gather them up and cradle them against my chest.

'Oh no...'

While Reda bravely checks the cellar, finding nothing of note, I walk the length of the corridor, checking each room in turn. Everywhere is tranquil; the hall washed with the light of a gilded-rose dawn, the tiles patterned with red, gold and blue reflections from the stained glass door-panels. But of the parrot there is no sign.

I cannot help but remember that far-off cry before the churn of rotten air whistled past my head and my heart droops. 'Gabriel!' I call in vain the length of the hall, into the dining room, the kitchen, into the quiet comfort of the reading room, into Olivia's new living quarters.

All is serene in the parlour. Slanting tiger-stripes of sunlight pattern the wooden floor, reflect off the vases and ornaments, slick off the polished coffee table. In the grate, the fire has burned to embers that give off an aromatic woody scent. A tiny spatter of guano lies on the edge of the hearth, and instead of feeling a tremor of annoyance and disgust my throat feels tight with suppressed emotion and my eyes begin to burn.

'Oh, Gabriel.' I feel he was standing guard for us when we went down into the cellar, and maybe stood sentinel all the time while we made our way up through the tunnel. I remember him crying out '*Bal-lack!*' and it is hard not to interpret it as a warning, his way of trying to protect us against something he understood better than we did.

I am about to go and find Reda to report my lack of success when I sense eyes upon me. I turn... and a head pops up from the floor of the parrot cage.

'Gabriel!'

The cage door is closed, though not latched. It appears he took refuge in here and has – quite literally – been lying low. I reach in and stroke the top of his head with a finger and he pushes against me in what I like to interpret as affection. When I lay out on the cage floor all the peanuts in my pockets he casts a sardonic look at me in case this bounty is some sort of mistake then covers them with his huge feet and gathers them into his body, like young. Little peanut eggs waiting to be hatched. Relief bursts out of me in a torrent of laughter.

'Reda! Reda!'

He comes at a run, as if I sounded hysterical, which isn't completely surprising. 'Djibril, Djibril, you monster,' he chides the bird, then touches a hand to his heart and says softly, '*Alhemdullilah.*'

'*Alhemdullilah,*' echoes the bird piously, then he bends his head, cracks another peanut wide and attacks the contents with alacrity.

'Nothing much wrong with him,' says Reda, grinning.

The police arrive with remarkable speed, two of them in uniform: one very young and looking rather unshaven, the other a dark-eyed Cornishwoman in her thirties, who removes her chequer-banded hat and briskly shows me her ID card. They look around the tranquil house, bemused, after the drama of the call received to roust them at the crack of dawn and the urgent scramble to get to this remote spot from wherever they are stationed.

We explain who we are and how we came to be present in someone else's house and how my ex had turned up and tried to make off with valuables and been threatening when we tried to stop him; I show them the bruises and the cut on my neck, and then take them down to the cellar where we had shut him in, with its fallen shelves and dust and detritus. Reda takes the policeman down into the cove and shows him the tunnel choked with landslip, and the skull. The lad looks wide-eyed upon his return and accepts a cup of coffee with some gratitude.

'But no sign of your ex?' the female officer asks.

'None.'

She looks at me. 'Could he have got out before the earth movement?'

'I don't know. It seems unlikely – there would have been no way out of the cove when the tide was up.'

The two officers look at one another, then the woman takes some details from me and starts to speak into her radio, moving away out of the kitchen and out of earshot.

When she comes back her expression is grim. 'It appears your ex has a record.' She gives me a hard stare.

'Eddie?' It seems absurd. 'Surely not?'

She consults her notebook. 'He's been cautioned for possession of a Class B drug, found guilty of affray and of carrying a knife in a public place, and has a suspended sentence for handling stolen goods.'

'But I lived with him for ten years and I didn't know...'

Her lips press together as if she's trying to stop herself telling me how blind people can be. She must have seen it all, I think. I wonder how hard it must be for those working in the police force to form healthy relationships. It would surely undermine any trust you might have had in the goodness of human nature. 'They're sending over a sniffer dog, an excavation team and the local surveyor, to look for the missing man and make a risk assessment,' she says, then pauses. 'Can you tell me about the owner of this house, and whether they may have been involved in the importation or handling of drugs?'

I almost laugh. I explain about Cousin Olivia's age and how she has been in the hospital all these weeks, about the work we've been doing on the house to prepare for her return.

'Don't forget the rat poison,' Reda prompts.

'Rat poison?' The policeman looked up from the notes he has been taking.

Reda hands him the bagged items. 'I know it all sounds mad,' I say, 'but I think there's been something going on here for a very long time, a sort of campaign of intimidation, of bullying, against the old lady who lives here.'

I tell them what I know, and even what I suspect. When I mention the name of the Sparrow family the two officers give each other a long, meaningful look.

'We'll need you to come into the station to make statements and give your fingerprints,' the woman says.

'All the way to Camborne?'

She shakes her head. 'We'll make sure there's someone qualified on duty in Penzance. Can you do it today? The sooner the better.' She takes down our names and contact details, makes a couple of calls, then gives us both a card headed *Devon and Cornwall Police* on which she is identified as Sergeant Hephzibah Johns. 'Please call me at once if there are any further developments.' She turns to the young policeman and says, 'Let's call in the troops and make a little visit to Newlyn, shall we?'

We watch them disappear through the rain-sodden vegetation and down the garden steps.

★

A couple of days later I go into the shop in Porth Enys for bread and milk. The woman behind the counter gives me a delighted smile, and serves the other customers – a pair of German tourists – with accelerated speed, before leaning across the counter conspiratorially and saying without preamble, 'Someone said they found some remains.'

'Sorry?'

'Up at Miss Kitto's.'

Her curiosity makes me cautious. 'I don't know anything much. They're still sifting through the rest of the landslip.'

'You be careful the whole place don't fall down round your ears.'

'They've got civil engineers in to make a report. But they think the house itself is safe.'

'And there was someone in the tunnel, under the fall?' She is delighted to have got me cornered, to be able to cut through all the local gossip to get the real information from the horse's mouth and is holding on to my bread and milk as hard as Gabriel does to his treats.

'Mmm,' I say noncommittally.

They had found Eddie, remarkably still alive beneath the rubble. He had managed to slot himself into a recess in the tunnel where most of the debris from the landslip had sheered past harmlessly, but had trapped him inside it. 'I thought I was going to die,' he had wailed. 'It was like being inside a tomb! I shouted but no one heard me, and when I tried to dig my way out, more of the stuff fell on me and pinned me down.' His complaints were piteous.

The rescue team, encouraged by the reactions of the sniffer dog, had taken some hours to reach him and, after the engineers had propped the tunnel, to carefully remove the fall of earth and rock. When at last they did find him, he was curled in a ball, whimpering, able to breathe only the foul air where the corpse had been interred. The team had not only retrieved Eddie but also most of a skeleton, which had been removed for further forensic investigation.

Eddie was taken by ambulance, in handcuffs, accompanied by the police, to be checked out at the West Cornwall Hospital. I have decided not to press charges for his assault on me, feeling that my own retaliation had somewhat cancelled that out, but we each separately gave a statement about the attempted theft and because that breaches the terms of his suspended sentence it seems more than likely that that original sentence will now have to be served. The police sergeant told me that when she explained this to Eddie he had cried and had to be given a tissue but all he had said was that he couldn't believe he was still alive, and that prison would be a piece of piss after what he'd just been through.

'Probably one of the gang,' the shopkeeper says, looking knowing. 'I gather the Sparrow brothers have disappeared.'

'Disappeared?'

'Lots of rumours flying around. They've taken the Roscoff ferry to the continent, gone into hiding. Or they've been dealt with...' she slices a finger across her throat, 'by their gangmasters. Drugs is a dangerous business.'

'Surely not?'

'Everyone round here knows what they've been up to

for years. How else they got those big houses? You don't get to live somewhere fancy like that on honest fisherman's wages.'

I say that I have no idea where they live and the woman grabs her iPad from beneath the counter and with a few key taps shows me first of all a handsome granite building set in fine gardens – 'that's where the parents live' – and then a photograph of a vast glass-fronted architect-designed monstrosity which she says belongs to the brothers.

'God knows how much they bunged the local planning department to get that through,' she says darkly. 'They never even gave me permission to change my bleddy window frames.'

'Why didn't anyone ever shop them if it was so well-known?'

'Locals, ent they? We don't rat on our own down here, no matter how bad they are.'

Unfortunate choice of words.

''Sides, nasty pieces of work, the Sparrow family. You don't want to wake up one mornin' to your decapitated cat hanging off your front door, do you? 'Part from Jem – he's okay. Spent his whole life being bullied by his missus.'

'Rosie?'

'You ask me, she's the real brains in that family. Not from round here though. They say her mother abandoned her here during the war and Miss Olivia raised her, and then Miss Olivia's mother, till she died. Tragic that: far too young.'

How fascinating. I admit I know nothing at all about Cousin Olivia's mother.

'Died not long after coming home. Can't remember what

of – was it a fall or something? Anyway, rotten luck to die so soon after coming through the war.'

My mouth is so dry I can barely reply. Was that what Gabriel's cry was about, and not Olivia's fall after all? I pay for my milk and bread and hurry back to the car, my head pounding.

I stop at the gate to the Sparrows' house and stare up. Handsome, four-square, granite, the house is like a smaller, smarter version of Chynalls. The garden is stuffed with exotic plants – banana palms, tree ferns, yuccas, aloes, birds of paradise, aeoniums, and between them statues are plonked down incongruously – a terracotta Greek athlete, discreetly naked, crowned with laurel; a flamingo treading delicately in a concrete pond in which a huge laughing frog sits on a stone lily-pad; a pair of cherubs squat in the rosebed, their wings trailing strands of ivy; a cute fat dragon gazes up through the ferns as if begging for food. On either side of the front door sit two roaring stone lions that would be more at home guarding a manor house.

Having picked my way through this strange menagerie, I reach the front door. There is no doorbell and no door-knocker, and as far as I can see, no letter box either, and the glass in the panels is fortified with crisscrossed ironwork inside the house.

I am having misgivings about coming here, especially alone. Reda is finishing the job in St Buryan with his brother and I felt I had taken too much of his time to ask him to come with me. Now I wish he was here. But it's time for me to stand up for myself, and he has already done so much for me. He keeps dropping by on one pretext or another – bringing me his mobile so that I have a better chance of a signal at the house and don't feel cut off – he shows me the old Nokia he is using instead and programs its number into the Galaxy he has given to me. 'Just text me and I can be there in ten minutes!' He brought me cakes cooked by Amina, Mo's wife, each one beautifully shaped and set with its own jewel-like glazed almond; treats for Gabriel; a good sweater of his, since I have brought no winter clothes with me and the weather is turning so chilly. He has chopped a mountain of firewood and kindling, rehung the paintings Eddie tried to make off with.

'I can stay,' he said when at last I pushed him out of the door. He hesitated, two steps down the path and looked at me under his thick lashes. 'I'd like to.'

My head is full of the possibilities of him and me together, naked, clothed, laughing, solemn. Exhilarating possibilities; scary possibilities. But it is too soon. Too much has been going on. I need to clear my head, and my heart.

Even so, I have been sleeping in his sweater. There is a faint scent of him woven through the weft of the wool – slightly spicy, slightly musky. I have slept like a stone the past few nights.

Now, I rap sharply on the door, then take a step back, feeling like a naughty child. There is no sense of movement in the house. I am about to leave, when the door cranks suddenly open.

Jem stands there, framed in darkness. 'What do you want?'

He says this gruffly, but with more curiosity than hostility. I wouldn't blame him if he were hostile, after all, I have turned out to be his family's nemesis, come down here from London to meddle in their affairs, when everything has been rolling along so well for decades.

'I was looking for Rosie,' I say, forthright, sounding braver than I feel.

'She ent here,' he says shortly. 'Gone shopping.'

I suck in a breath.

'To Waitrose,' he adds. 'For food and stuff.'

'Oh, OK.' I turn to leave. 'I didn't even know there was a Waitrose down here.'

'Up Truro.'

A chill inches down my spine.

'Mebbe she'll call in at Treliske on her way back.'

'To visit your father?'

He stares at me. 'My da been dead thirty year.' Then he shuts the door against me.

All my fears crystallize in an icy rush and I turn and run down the steps as if all the stone beasts are in pursuit.

The Clio has a one-litre engine and has seen better days. Car after car overtakes me on the A30 even in its notional fifth gear and with the accelerator pressed to the floor. By the time I hit the backed-up traffic at the Chiverton roundabout the air inside the cabin is blue with every swear word I have ever known and several more compound nouns I have devised.

From there, the cars snake along the Truro road, snarling up at every set of lights. When at last I pull off at the hospital junction I am in a sweat. Two voices have been jabbering in my ear the whole way: one cool and reasonable, my normal unstressed voice; the other as mad as Gabriel's. The first one says, *Don't be ridiculous, what can an old woman do to*

*another old woman in a public place under the eyes of staff
and visitors?* But the other voice will not be assuaged: *She's
going to kill her this time, and you're not going to be able
to stop her! It's already too late…*

My feet slap on the corridor floors, upstairs, along
another corridor. I pass people moving slowly – on
crutches, in wheelchairs, pushing walking frames. Porters
stare curiously as I dash past, but no one says anything.
Hospitals are theatres of human drama, of triumph and
tragedy: the place where most of humankind enters and
departs this world. People are always in a hurry to meet
some crucial event – a death, a birth, the awful limbo in
between.

I push open the doors to Olivia's ward and stare
feverishly around. Everything looks just as a geriatric ward
should look: old folk lying quietly in their clean hospital
beds, sleeping or gazing into space, some chatting to visitors
as nurses go solicitously from bed to bed with clipboards
and blood-pressure machines. A burly blonde woman is
wheeling a trolley bearing a tea urn, cups and saucers and
biscuits. One old dear in the first bay is trying to unclothe
herself, as determined as a small child, despite the attempts
of two student nurses to stop her. 'Shan't, shan't!' she
squawks. 'Horrible dress! Horrible bra! Nasty pants!' She
catches my eye. 'They're trying to kill me,' she informs me
matter-of-factly. 'They kill everyone in here, but if you take
your clothes off they can't touch you!'

I smile apologetically at her, then at the nurses and duck
past. Olivia is not in her usual bed. I try not to let this panic
me: they do move the patients around from time to time
according to the urgency of keeping an eye on them. I walk

past each bay in turn, trying not to stare intrusively, but it soon becomes clear she is not in this ward, unless...

I twitch back a privacy curtain that has been drawn around the last bed. Inside, Olivia lies on her back with her eyes closed and her hands folded on her chest. She looks peaceful. But unutterably dead. Terror grips me. I dash inside and grab her hand.

Her eyes fly open. 'Oh, it's you.' She does not look pleased to see me. She frees her hand, makes a shooing gesture. 'Go away – you'll spoil everything!'

'Spoil what?'

'Isn't it obvious? I'm supposed to be dead.'

'Cousin Olivia, whatever do you mean?'

Her expression is crafty. 'I pulled the curtains round myself at the end of the shift. The new ones will find me here like this and cart me off to the morgue – or whatever they have in hospitals these days. Then I can slip out and get the bus home. I've got a five-pound note hidden in my knickers.'

'Olivia!' I press my hands against my mouth to stop myself laughing. 'I'm so glad you're OK, I was worried about you. There's been a lot going on.' How am I going to tell her about Eddie and his attempt to steal the paintings, and the small matter of the Sparrow brothers being pursued by the police, the Border Force, and the Coast Guard; and the landslip? I will have to explain the structural work that's going on at the house, the underpinning and the concreting up of the tunnel. There are going to be financial implications: there is some talk about the council making the entire hillside safer but there may have to be an insurance claim and I haven't been able to find any insurance documents anywhere.

But, most importantly, I have to ask her about the skeleton in the tunnel.

I help as she huffs herself upright and add an extra pillow for support, and I'm about to launch into this difficult subject when there is a rattle and a clank and the curtains part. 'Afternoon, Mrs Kitto!'

'Miss,' Olivia growls, as the tea lady sticks her head into the bay.

'Nice cup of tea?' she asks, oblivious to the correction.

Olivia grudgingly admits that a cup of tea would be nice.

'And how about your visitor – would you like one too?'

'I'm fine,' I say, and the head disappears back into the ward. I am sure I've seen her somewhere before.

'Chocolate digestive!' Olivia bellows.

'Oh, sorry, Mrs Kitto,' comes the disembodied voice. 'No choccy biscuits today. How about a custard cream or a nice garibaldi?'

Olivia grumbles and at last accepts that a custard cream is not the end of the world. I reach over and position her tray table, then take the cup and saucer and perched biscuit from the tea lady for her. I am about to pass it to Olivia when my nose picks up the faint scent of garlic. I bring the cup closer for a better sniff.

'Thought you didn't want one, dear,' the tea lady says, 'but we all change our minds, don't we?'

I hurl the cup away from me, spilling tea everywhere including over the tea lady who dances up and down, shrieking and brushing at her clothes. There is a momentary lull in the surrounding din in the ward which makes the shattering cup sound cataclysmic.

'What did you do that for?' asks Olivia crossly. 'I was looking forward to my tea.'

But I am on the move, grabbing the 'tea lady' by the arm. There is a scuffle, and the trolley goes scooting across the ward and bashes into an intravenous drip stand. An alarm goes off and suddenly everyone is running at me.

'What on earth is going on here?' demands the ward sister, helping the tea lady – who in the midst of all this has been poleaxed by her own trolley – to her feet. She is not, by any stretch of my wild imagination, Rosie, but a woman a good thirty years younger, her hair clearly her own, if badly dyed. Everyone is staring at me as if I'm some sort of axe murderer.

'I'm very sorry,' I say. 'I dropped the cup. I'm so clumsy. I do apologize. Are you all right?' I ask the tea lady, who is glaring at me uncomprehendingly.

'You threw that cup at me!' she accuses. She turns to the ward sister. 'And I was only doing my best for poor old Mrs Kitto. Her special tea always perks her up.'

'Special tea?' My suspicions fire up again.

'Her friend brings it in for her. Such a kind old soul – in this little flask…' She indicates a tartan-patterned Thermos that is now rolling around the bottom tier of the trolley. I swoop upon it, wrapping the sleeve of my sweater over my hand to pick it up. The tea lady curls her lip. ''Tain't hot!' she says contemptuously. 'That's how them flasks work – keep the tea hot on the inside while the outside say stays cool.'

'Very clever,' I say. 'What will they think of next?'

She fixes me with a hard stare. 'I do hope you haven't broken it. A person can get very poorly drinking tea with a bit of broken glass in it.'

The ward sister is watching this pantomime with her hands on her hips and a deep frown.

'Could I have a quiet word?' I ask.

25

THE FOLLOWING TUESDAY THERE IS A KNOCK AT THE DOOR. I go to open it and find a young woman in a navy blue jacket clutching a clipboard. She greets me with the determinedly brisk politeness of the professional who is forced to be pleasant in order to carry out an onerous task. 'You must be Rebecca!' She extends a small, well-manicured hand. 'I'm Terri Jones, from social services. Come to do the assessment for Mrs Kitto.'

'Miss Kitto,' I say under my breath. She looks about twelve. I usher her in.

'What a beautiful old house,' she says, standing there in the hall, taking it in, the brittle veneer giving way to genuine surprise – and suddenly I see it through her eyes: the gleaming wooden panelling, the lovely old banisters and carved newel post, the authentic wallpaper, the lofty ceiling with its original mouldings, the fleur-de-lys floor tiles, the light streaming in through the stained glass panels beside the door colouring the floor with pools of cyan and scarlet.

More light pours in from Gabriel's room, which is where I take her first.

'Oh,' she says, looking alarmed at the sight of the cage. She scans through the paper on her clipboard. 'I don't think I've got a tick-box for parrots. We do ask about pets, but by that we generally mean a dog or cat—'

She is interrupted by a long wolf-whistle from the incorrigible old bird, which takes her off-guard and charms her, especially when I say I am the one who will be taking care of him.

On the way to the kitchen we are met by Reda, who pops his head out of Olivia's suite, no doubt intrigued by the sound of female voices. 'This is Miss Jones, from social services,' I tell him; but 'Oh, do call me Terri,' she says, giving him her hand, which seems a slightly odd thing to do when meeting someone's builder. I half expect him to lift it to his lips, but he smiles and shakes it and says he must get back to work, he's just finishing the snagging. Terri walks around the suite, ticking boxes, checking the grab rails, asking if Olivia will need a frame to get up from the loo; also checking out Reda's handsome backside, snug in its dark overalls. I catch her looking and she gives me a conspiratorial grin.

She measures the doorways for wheelchair access, watches as I operate the controls on the hospital-style bed we have installed in Olivia's private room, asks whether I have noticed the old lady's remarkable improvement over the past couple of weeks. 'Ever since she knew she was getting out!' she declares, as if Olivia is being released from a prison sentence. Though hardly for good behaviour.

I have noticed. I've driven into Truro most days to see her and each time she has surprised me with a sharp observation, a stronger grip on my arm, a less pronounced limp as we patrol the corridors, building her strength. She utterly refuses any help in the bathroom – 'I can pull my own knickers up, thank you very much!' – and with the tip of her tongue poking between her lips as she concentrates on the fiddly coordination of fingers, buttons and button-holes, has proved she can dress herself (another box ticked on the reablement list) given a little time and patience.

Once back out in the hall, Terri Jones says, 'Lucky Mrs Kitto, having you two looking after her. Your husband is absolutely delightful: you make a wonderful couple. I can see she's going to be in very good hands.'

Dumbfounded, I watch her slip out through the front door and down the garden path.

Reda comes out, wiping his hands on his overalls. 'Husband, eh?' he says, and grins at me.

'Silly woman,' I say, but my insides are leaping.

Olivia gets discharged from hospital the very next afternoon. Such unwarranted efficiency must mean they are desperate to be rid of her, and as she waves her walking stick in the air and berates the poor paramedics labouring up the steps with her wheelchair, I can quite see why. 'Careful, careful, young man. Are you trying to kill me? Think of the paperwork.'

She looks up at me, standing in the doorway, and her eyes narrow. 'Where's my fucking porch?'

The paramedics guffaw: someone else taking the flak at last.

'It... er... fell down,' I say, berating myself for failing to garner the courage to prepare her for this shock.

'Porches don't just "fall down"!' she barks, surveying the strange absence, the pale stone revealed by the collapse.

'It was pretty rickety...'

'Did I tell you to put DEMOLISH THE PORCH on the to-do list?' she demands, but by now it's a rhetorical flourish.

I usher her and the paramedics inside. One of them, a younger man with a shock of yellow hair like a dandelion, gives me a sly wink as he passes, and I grin back. 'But see how much more light you get inside the house without it,' I cajole our charge.

Even though I can't see Olivia's expression, I can feel her taking in the changes that have occurred since she left. I have lost several layers of skin, many pints of elbow-grease, and put hundreds of hours of effort into making every square inch shine. The air smells no longer of parrot shit but of lavender floor wax and lemon polish. There is love in this house once more, where there had been bitterness and despair and hatred. I hope she can feel it.

I offer the paramedics a cup of tea but 'Bugger off, arsehole!' the parrot squawks, and I see them shoot a look at one another, then at me. 'Blimey,' says the older man, 'it's a madhouse.'

The dandelion-haired paramedic bears his shockingly white teeth at me in a grin that expresses both chagrin at his compadre's rudeness and enjoyment of my discomposure, then wags a finger at Olivia. 'Goodbye, Miss Kitto. Behave for this lovely young lady, eh?'

'Oh, bugger off. And you' – she points at me – 'help me out of this blasted chair!'

They beat a swift retreat, back to the quiet, safe space of their ambulance, parked down on the lane.

'"Lovely young lady",' Olivia echoes sardonically, and her left eyebrow twitches up. At first I think it's just an involuntary reflex, but no: it's a deliberately cocked eyebrow. My goodness, she has regained far greater control of her facial muscles in the past few days.

'I'm sure he says that to everyone,' I tell her dismissively, helping her to stand. She sways dangerously for a couple of seconds, then plants her stick firmly and heads towards the parlour. It is, I must admit, nice to receive a compliment and I feel a sudden warmth in my cheeks, but it is as nothing compared to the way Olivia's face is suffused with joy as her gaze alights upon the parrot's cage.

'Ah, Gabriel!'

Her dark eyes brim suddenly with tears as she leans on my arm, setting her handbag on the floor so that she can stroke his head tenderly through the bars.

I settle her on the sofa with her stick and her handbag within reach, riddle up the fire and bring Gabriel to sit with her. She is astounded at his good behaviour with me – sitting good as gold on my hand, allowing me to transfer him from cage to sofa arm without so much as a peanut by way of a bribe. I leave them together to catch up while I go to make tea, turning at the doorway to see the parrot leaning his head into Olivia's caressing fingers. He is making a sound I have never heard from him before, the sort of noise you'd describe as a purr, if parrots could purr. Perhaps he is copying one of the orchard cats; perhaps there was a pet one in the house once.

When I come back with a tray bearing cups – new ones to replace the flower-patterned ones – the fat brown tea pot emitting a curl of aromatic steam, a little milk jug and sugar dish I found in Penzance and a packet of chocolate digestives, she turns to me and beams. 'How lovely of you! I feel like a queen.'

'I'll show you around your new royal quarters after you've had your tea. I think you'll like it very much. I hope you will.'

I pour out a cup of tea for her and she takes it gingerly. The surface of the liquid ripples with the trembling of her hands, but it's not as pronounced as you might expect and she manages to set cup and saucer down on the little table without a spill. Then she sits back into the sofa and looks past me, around the room – at the polished surfaces and the steam-cleaned rug, the fresh flowers glowing in the winter sunlight; at her paintings on the walls. Her gaze settles on *The Sea Gate*, now taking pride of place where Reda helped me hang it.

'It's so beautiful,' I tell her. 'Cousin Olivia, you're a wonderful painter.'

'I was once,' she says wistfully. 'A long, long time ago.' She pushes herself to her feet, and with the aid of her walking stick shuffles across the room to examine the painting with me following nervously in case she stumbles. She reaches up and brushes the canvas with her free hand.

'Who carved those patterns on the other side of the gate?' I ask her softly. 'And the ones in the cellar?'

Her look becomes shuttered and she returns to the sofa to reapply herself to the tea and biscuits. I pass her a wet wipe. 'I'm not crying, you know!' she says fiercely.

'It's for your hands. After touching Gabriel.' I have been well drilled by social services.

'Gabriel is a pristine creature, aren't you, my darling?'

I snort at her wild lie and try a different angle. 'Is his real name Djibril?'

She freezes with a biscuit halfway to her mouth. 'Why are you asking me all these questions?' she demands, suddenly furious.

Not the time to raise the matter of the skeleton, then. I feel suitably admonished, and apologize, and we sit drinking our tea in an awkward silence punctuated only by Gabriel's happy whistles.

When she has finished her drink, her energy seems to drop, and a little while later her eyelids droop and soon she is asleep and snoring, her mouth half-open, like a child's. I reach over and smooth her hair from her cheek and arrange the cushions supportively around her, then reach my arm out to Gabriel, who hops onto it as if he is the best-trained bird under the sun.

Back in his cage, he shells his reward peanuts with deft flicks of his beak and does not seem to mind at all that I have latched his door and rendered him a prisoner once more. I clear away the tea things and wash them up in the kitchen and sort through the food purchases to make a choice for supper.

By the time I get back to the parlour, Olivia is on her feet at the window, her knobbly old hands braced on the sill, looking out over the tangles of garden vegetation towards the sea. When she turns at the sound of my entrance, her face is wet with tears.

'I'm sure you thought sometimes you'd never be coming back here,' I say softly.

She starts, then squares her shoulders and fixes me with a penetrating gaze. 'Nonsense. I always knew I'd be coming home.'

We gaze at one another. I can feel all those unanswered questions hanging heavy in the air between us, but I know I cannot ask them yet.

'Come and see your room,' I say to her. 'See what Mo and Reda have done to make you comfortable. I hope you'll like it.'

'I'd better.'

I escort her slowly down the hall to the new suite. The room is warm and welcoming. I have lit the candle in the hurricane lamp to complement the inset lights overhead, currently turned down low, controlled by a dimmer switch, and a small bowl of incense which sits smoking beside it, full of complex scents – roses, musk, perfume, spices: a gift from Reda. It masks the smell of gloss paint – we only finished painting the woodwork yesterday.

I show her the en-suite bathroom, with its walk-in shower-bath, high-level loo, and grab bars, and explain how the taps and the emergency cord work. The spare modern lines of the white suite have been offset by sandy travertine, and a huge metal and camel-bone mirror that Reda brought from home hangs over the sink and vanity unit. 'I think she will like it,' he said. 'It will make the room look less... utilitarian.' He beamed as he told me he had to go to his French/English dictionary to find this word.

His generosity left me speechless. And he was right: she does love it. 'So beautiful. It brings back so many memories.' Her voice drops almost to a whisper. 'I remember walking through the bazaars and seeing lovely things just like this, all handmade. You know, you could see them displayed for sale and walk a few paces away around the back of the stall and find men squatting on the ground, beating out patterns in brass and silver with these little hammers, cutting tiny shapes out of ebony and camel-bone and piecing them together like a jigsaw. I could watch them all day, they were so skilled, so intent on achieving perfection. I love the way those craftsmen worked – just think how many hours it took to be created by such clever hands.'

She caresses the inlays in the carved frame, her expression withdrawn and distant as if she is connecting with her memories. At last she gives a little shake of the head and grimaces at her own reflection. 'For a moment,' she says, 'I thought I was young again, but look, there I am – utterly decrepit.'

I grin. 'Cousin Olivia, you look quite splendid to me.' But I can see she's not convinced.

Back in the main room the hospital bed has been disguised with the lovely old paisley quilt from upstairs. The incense masks the slight smell of mildew on it, though I aired it in front of the range – or maybe it's just the scent of long-ago times. Olivia runs her hand over the quilt: another fragment of her past.

On the bright walls, set beneath new picture lamps, hang more of her paintings – the self-portrait from the kitchen, the trawler ploughing away into the shimmering sea. They look gallery-worthy – handsome and important, commanding this clean space – and I am proud of my selections and their staging, but Olivia glares at the last one she comes to.

'I don't want that old portrait of me in here,' she says at last, glaring at the girl with the black eyes. 'It's just a painful reminder.'

Olivia betrayed. I berate myself for not making the connection.

'What would you like there instead?' I ask.

Her gaze goes faraway. Then she gives a shrug. 'I don't know. Anything else, really. Something cheerful.'

'There is...' I start, and hesitate, then make myself go on. 'There's a painting I found upstairs that would look marvellous there.'

She looks at me suspiciously, her eyes very bright. Then her eyes go very wide and I can see she knows exactly which painting I mean.

'Nosing around my things!' she accuses.

'It was up in the attic when there was a leak in the roof. I moved *The Sea Gate* so it didn't get damaged.' A useful half-truth. 'I love the portrait I found with it,' I add gently. 'The colour in it, the warmth... the love.'

Her gaze narrows and her mouth firms. 'I don't know which painting you mean.'

'The one of the naked man,' I can't seem to help myself going on, though I know I am treading on dangerous ground now. 'On the bed in the upstairs bedroom... Will you tell me who he was... one day?'

She shoots a pained look at me, then grabs her stick and scuttles quickly across the floor, so quickly that I am terrified she will be overtaken by her own momentum and fall, but she reaches the door and holds the jamb, breathing heavily.

I have gone too far. I scoot across the room after her and take her elbow. Together we make our way back to the parlour, where she sinks heavily back onto the sofa. I take a seat in the armchair, trying and failing to find a way to apologize.

The silence stretches on and on. At last she says, 'Are there any sardines?'

The next day I take Olivia a cup of tea to waken her. I have prepared my careful words of apology and made a promise to myself that I will not harangue her. Balancing the breakfast tray in one hand, I rap on her door and then open it, hoping she has spent a comfortable night.

As I take a step inside the new suite, she emerges from her bathroom with her hair swaddled in a colourful length of cloth she has wound into a great onion of a turban. She looks exotic, otherworldly. For a moment I stand in the doorway with the tray in my hands, taking her in. She smiles – less lopsidedly. What unevenness there is to her features now seems less evidence of disease than an abundance of character.

Seeing me gazing at her, she pats the turban.

'Hamid taught me how to do it.'

'Hamid?'

'The man in the painting.'

A frisson runs through me. I cross the room and put the breakfast tray down on the dresser before I drop it. Olivia subsides into her chair, crosses her bare feet and regards me catlike and amused. I must be careful, let her tell me what she wishes to tell me, at her own pace, in her own time.

'It suits you.'

'He always said that.'

I wait, determined not to press.

She looks away from me, thoughtful, then sad. I can see her physically withdrawing from me, as if she is bodily slipping back in time. She glares down at her hands – the swollen knuckles, the liver spots, the blue veins snaking just beneath the surface of the papery skin – as if they do not belong to her.

After a long time, she raises her head. 'I loved him so much. We made our own little paradise together, a secret world, just like Adam and Eve before the Fall...'

'Oh Olivia, how romantic.'

'His name was Hamid and when I first knew him he was only twenty years old, and the handsomest man I ever saw.'

'And you only drew his back?' I grin at her.

She tsks. 'Of course not. I made dozens of sketches of him. There were photographs too.' She looks wistful.

I admit that while searching for her missing locket I have scoured the house but not come across these portraits. Her chin comes up. 'They were all burned,' she says.

'Here? In the house? Was there a fire?'

'In winter there is always a fire,' she says cryptically. 'I saved only one.'

'Can I see it?'

She looks away. 'It's gone now.'

'Can I ask how you met?' I am, I know, pressing my luck.

Olivia folds her lips. 'Breakfast first. What is there?'

We settle on scrambled eggs and toast, and I go out to the kitchen to prepare it, and a fresh pot of tea, while she dresses herself, since she has steadfastly refused any aid. Under instruction, I take the breakfast things into the parlour and remove the cloth from Gabriel's cage, and when Olivia comes in, turbanless now and with her hair dried into a silky white froth, he bounces up and down, bright-eyed and delighted, as if her return has given him a fresh lease of life.

I can hardly eat for curiosity, but I make myself chew and swallow as she works her way through her breakfast, taking her time. I am sure she is spinning it out: every so often she shoots me a sly look.

At last, she folds her napkin. 'I've never spoken about this to a living soul, you know,' she says in a somewhat combative tone. 'I'm only telling you because you have that look in your eye. That family gumption. The never-give-up look. But it's private: you understand?'

'Of course.'

She sits back, cradling her tea, takes a long sip from the cup, then begins. 'It was during the war.'

I do not need to ask which one: the date on the back of the painting of the naked man reads '1945'.

'Hamid was an internee up at the farm. He'd come off a trawler that hit a mine, smuggling, I think. He was an Algerian, so not really an enemy, but at that time all you had to do was speak with a foreign accent and they'd put you in a POW camp. So he was working up at the Roberts' farm: they put prisoners of war to work, you know. There was a labour shortage and the country needed all the food that could be grown. There were a number of them working up at the farm – no guards or anything: you didn't need them down here at the end of the world. Once you were here there was nowhere left to go, except into the sea!' She laughs mirthlessly.

'One night there was an escape. An Austrian airman whose plane came down in the field up by one of the Swingate Stones – have you walked the upper footpath to Lamorna?'

I admit that I have not yet ventured out in that direction, except to walk to the bench overlooking the sea past the lookout point, a tranquil spot where you can watch the sun burnishing the sea.

'It always seemed so shocking to me that such evil could occur against such an enchanting backdrop,' she says. 'Or that it could look so... clean-cut. The Land Girls who stayed here thought he was a proper looker: blond-haired, blue-eyed, very proud of his Aryan heritage. He held some sway over the boys at the farm, too. People are so gullible, aren't they? They fall for appearances and easy charm, don't seem to have the nous to look beneath. Anyway, this devil attacked and killed a child.' Tears fill her eyes.

I hardly dare breathe. 'Who was she?'

'Mamie? A sweet girl, the daughter of the farmer, a little younger than me – in years; more in her head. They called it "simple" then – I expect there's a more politically correct term nowadays. But to him, she was barely human, just a defenceless little animal he could use and throw away. Hamid... well, Hamid tried to stop him, but he was too late, she was already dead. Mind you, if you mention *him* around here you'll get a different story. People are so ready to condemn according to their prejudices, especially if they don't travel. Blackie, they called him, and for my shame even I thought of him as the Dark Man. But he wasn't black at all, except his hair; just a really rather lovely chestnut brown. They hadn't ever seen a proper black man around these parts – though there were black American GIs posted further east...' She sighs. 'I was right there...' Olivia points to the centre of the rug. 'I thought I was going to die. That Nazi airman had his hands round my throat and I was beginning to lose consciousness, and that's when Hamid appeared. Like a genie out of the *Arabian Nights*. I would have gone the same way as Mamie if he hadn't come just at that moment. My guardian angel, that's what he was. It's why we named the parrot Gabriel – or Djibril as he is in Arabic. My darling Gabriel...' Her gaze goes distant and I can see her mind is wandering again.

'Cousin Olivia,' I say coaxingly. I have to know, can't hold back any longer. 'There was a landslide down in the tunnel and some bones were found. Pretty much a whole skeleton. The police took it away for forensic examination, but their initial report is that it's neither recent, nor ancient. Was it the Austrian airman?'

Her eyes go wide as if she is slowly waking up. 'Oh. Oh no. All these years I've kept that secret. All these years living in a house with a corpse down in the tunnel. Hardly daring to leave in case someone found it. His ghost walked, you know. It couldn't get past the sigils Hamid carved, but I'm sure it walked. That's why I needed you to brick up the cellar. So they'd never know.'

I take her hands in mine. 'Oh, Olivia. The things you've been through. I'm so sorry, I didn't know. But I don't think bricking up the cellar would have made any difference in the end. Secrets always find a way out, don't they?'

'It was self-defence. He'd have killed us all.' She pauses, looks pensive, weighing her words. But just as she opens her mouth again there is a knock at the door. We stare at one another.

'Let's pretend we're not in,' says Olivia.

It seems an attractive option but a moment later a face appears at the window. It is Rosie, who raps on the glass.

Olivia glares at her, then back at me. There's an odd smile on her face. 'Bad pennies always turn up, don't they?'

'You don't have to see her ever again if you don't want to,' I say, and I mean it. 'She's a wicked old woman and I won't have her upsetting you.'

'Oh, stop mooing and go and let her in. Time we had it all out, then I can rest and the ghosts can settle.'

Out in the hall the new phone sits on the console, all shining and smart: the landline went in at the weekend. I pick it up and quickly leave a message on Reda's mobile, in case I need back-up, but I needn't have worried: Rosie Sparrow is out there alone. She looks smaller than I remember. Is it because I know so much more about her? More than she knows I know? I am rather less afraid of her than I thought I would be, knowing the extent of her venality. Greed and hatred are such mean motivations: they diminish those who carry them, suck them dry from within. I open the door.

She brandishes a bunch of flowers. 'Brought her these.'

I wonder if you can poison flowers. I do not take them from her. Instead, I stare into the pale depths of her eyes, making myself as stern and unwelcoming as I am able. 'You'd better come in, then.' I usher her before me into the parlour.

Gabriel takes one look at Rosie, pushes the cage door open (has he fiddled the lock open?), leaps up onto the threshold and starts barking like a dog. I've never heard him do this before. I make a move to guide him back into the cage, but he evades me neatly and takes wing.

'I'm not coming in here while that devil's out of his cage!'

'You're free to leave.' Olivia waves a hand airily towards the door.

Keeping an eye on the devil – who has taken up his favourite lookout post on the bookcase – Rosie edges inside and thrusts the bouquet at Olivia. She is not, I notice, wearing gloves, so probably the flowers are not going to kill her.

'Peace offering.'

The old women face one another. How odd, I think, that time blurs the physical differences between us as we age. Looking at them now they're hard to tell apart in age: small and dense and packed with energy, though one has black eyes, the other pale. And of course Olivia has her own bad teeth, while Rosie has had hers expensively re-engineered.

'You know I can't stand chrysanthemums,' Olivia says uncharitably.

'They're dahlias.'

'Same thing.'

They glare at one another.

'You tried to kill me!'

'You tripped over your own feet.'

'You pushed me!'

'Did no such thing.'

I close the parlour door to make sure Gabriel does not escape. 'I'm really not sure you should be here,' I say to Rosie. 'After everything you've done.'

She juts her sharp little chin at me. 'I'm sure I got more right to be here than some little gold-digger from London, come down to pick over the old bird's bones.'

People do give themselves away by the things they accuse

others of. I adopt a conversational tone. 'Why have you been stealing from Olivia all these years?'

'You don't know the first thing about it!' Rosie barks.

'I talked to Olivia's bank manager. No wonder you've got a smart car and expensive teeth, and such a nice house.'

Her eyes spark pale fire at me. 'How dare you snoop on me!'

Olivia holds her hands up as if refereeing a match. 'Stop, both of you. Mary, sit down here where I can see you. Rebecca, sit over there.'

Mary? I wonder if Olivia's quite as recovered as I thought.

Rosie purses her lips. 'No one calls me that any more. I hate it. It's Rosie to everyone nowadays and I'll thank you to remember it.'

'I'm glad you've come. Because at last I can tell you what I've not had the courage to do all this time,' Olivia says to her. 'There really aren't any more secrets left that you can blackmail me with.'

'Blackmail? That's what you're telling people, is it?'

'What else could you possibly call three thousand pounds a month? For a bit of housekeeping?' I ask, feeling fiercely protective of my cousin.

Rosie glares at me. 'You know nothing. She's keeping a promise.' She jabs a finger at Olivia. 'A solemn vow.'

I stare at Rosie and at my cousin. In that instant they look spookily similar: the set of the jaw, the bone structure around the eye. There is something going here on that I don't quite understand.

'Just go home, Rosemary Sparrow,' Olivia says wearily. 'You've picked all the flesh off me for now. You and your good-for-nothing boys.'

'You leave my boys out of this.'

'They were using the cellar and tunnel for smuggling.' I offer the conjecture.

Olivia merely shrugs. 'Oh, I expect so.'

I sink back into the armchair, feeling as if I'm on dangerous ground. 'Were the Sparrows using the cellar with your knowledge?'

'We had an agreement of sorts.'

'But, smuggling?'

'We don't call it that down here,' Rosie says firmly. 'It's just a bit of this and that; just... trading. Been the way of the world for hundreds of years.'

'You really can't call drug smuggling a bit of this and that!' I object.

Olivia sits up a bit straighter. 'Drugs?'

Rosie purses her lips. 'No need to be shocked. Remember when we tried growing those plants up in the attic?'

'The marijuana?'

'That was a right to-do!'

'What about those electricity bills?'

They laugh. Olivia turns to me. 'We grew it on the cliff underneath the Roberts farm in the end. That worked much better, till the police helicopter spotted the plantation.'

The two old women are grinning slyly at one another now, a pair of geriatric criminal kingpins bound in a perverse conspiracy.

Whatever have I got caught up in? Drug-running, money-laundering, art-theft, attempted poisoning, and a Nazi buried in the tunnel. Panic rises in me. The police are coming tomorrow to 'have a word' with Olivia. She'll be a total liability. I can imagine her recounting to them her decades of misdeeds without an iota of shame and more than a touch of boastfulness. She won't be needing her stately en-suite room at this rate, she'll be banged up in a prison cell. In my mind, it cascades from there: newspapers, TV, tongue-in-cheek movies about elderly criminal masterminds putting one over on local law enforcement. The house that we have toiled over and all Olivia's beautiful paintings sequestered under the Proceeds of Crime Act...

Rosie turns beady eyes on me. 'Anyway, who says my boys are smuggling drugs?'

'There were packages in the cellar.'

'And you opened them, did you?'

I have to admit I did not. 'The police took away what they found.'

'And did they say it was drugs?'

'No...'

Rosie returns her gaze to Olivia. 'It isn't drugs.'

'Well, what is it, then?' I persist.

'If you must know, Miss Snoop, it's tobacco. They sell packets of it all over the place for a bit of pocket money. Nothing wrong with that.' She is defiant. 'People have done it for centuries down here. It's a time-honoured tradition.'

'It's still illegal, avoiding the import duty,' I say quietly. 'As is systematically poisoning Olivia.'

Rosie blinks, very fast. 'Poisoning?'

'I found it in the kitchen. Rat poison.'

Olivia sits up a bit straighter. Rosie shrugs. 'Bloody nuisance, those rats. They're everywhere.' She looks to Olivia. 'Anyway, you like the way I make your tea, don't you?'

'Did you put poison in Olivia's tea?' I ask her straight out.

'No.' Rosie folds her arms. 'Course not!'

Olivia leans forward. 'Poison?'

I explain about finding the tin in the cupboard with the tea things, the odd smell in the teacup, and then I come to a halt as a realization hits me. One of the cups decorated with forget-me-nots, the other with roses and *rosemary*. Mary, Rosie: Rosemary. So the cups wouldn't get mixed up; so the poisoner would not get poisoned.

'That smell was in the tea in the flask Rosie brought into the hospital for you. The doctors said your blood tests indicated liver damage.'

Rosie gazes at me stonily. 'Load of nonsense. How you going to prove any of that then, eh?'

'The tea was handed over to the laboratory for tests.'

Olivia is staring hard at her housekeeper now, her hands balled into fists. 'What have you done? You'd better tell me. Because I've had my suspicions.' She shoots me a look. 'I even left a letter with the solicitor. It says "in case of my death from unexplained causes" – though when you reach my age I doubt they count anything as unexplained – "please test my body for poison and then arrest Rosemary Sparrow". So, out with it, or else.'

Rosie's fingers make imprints on the skin of her forearms as she kneads the slack muscles. 'Well,' she mumbles at last, 'you're a right pain sometimes. It was a sort of punishment, to start with. You treated me like a servant, just because you got the house and the money and all, even though I should by rights have got half. It's not fair. It gets to a person after a while.'

'So you really did poison her?'

'It isn't really poisoning, though, is it?' she rallies. 'I mean, here she is. She isn't dead, is she? After all this time, she still isn't dead.' When she looks at me her eyes are mean and dried up, all the light gone out of them.

Olivia is appalled, understandably. 'You gave me rat poison?' she says faintly. 'In my tea?'

'Shepherd's pie, too. And your spag bol. Tomato sauce masked the taste better.'

'You told me the garlic was a tonic! I even looked it up in my herbal book, and there it was – good for the liver, and infection and the like. I remember we collected all the wild garlic round here during the war for the Herbal Medicine Committee—'

'It was me you sent out to pick all that stuff. To get me out of the house. So you could be with him!'

'Shut up. Shut up now.'

Rosie rubs her face, remembering. 'It was Jem gave me the idea. They used Rodine all over the farm to keep the rats down, had tons of the stuff, used to put it down in drainpipes they'd set up with grain to get the beggars used to going in to feed. He said it smelled like ramsons.' She shrugs and addresses me. 'I only used a tiny bit from time to time. Not enough to kill her. To teach her a lesson, when she was mean to me, which was often enough. Always thought yourself better than me, didn't you?' she shoots at Olivia, who folds her lips and says nothing. 'And, well, it became a habit when she was playing me up. Didn't do her much lasting harm, did it? It's probably gone off after all this time, anyway. She got the constitution of an ox! Haven't you, Livy? The constitution of an ox!'

'I knew I wasn't going mad,' Olivia says after a long moment of silence. 'Every time we fell out. Every time we had cross words, I would get ill. I suppose... deep down,

I knew what was going on, or I thought I deserved to be punished, after everything that happened. I suppose it's time to tell you the rest of it.'

26

Olivia

May 1945

'SOMEONE'S DAMAGED OUR GATE!' MARY ANNOUNCED dramatically. She stood in the middle of the kitchen with her hands on her hips, looking more than usually belligerent. The action made her skirt ride up and the material strain across the bodice. Her school uniform had become too tight for her, and had probably been that way for some time, Olivia realized. Details like this often escaped her, especially now that Mary was dressing herself. They couldn't afford to replace it: Olivia had traded their clothing rations with Mrs Clemo at the farm near the school, so at the very least it would need the seams letting out and the hem down. The idea of having to unpick and resew all this was unpalatable: of all the subjects at school Domestic Science had been Olivia's worst. How many times had Miss Appleyard made her re-sew the hem on that gingham apron? 'Ten stitches to the inch, Olivia. How many times do I have to tell you?

Honestly, this looks as if a gorilla did it...' The whole class had dissolved into giggles. Olivia had hated all of them, but Miss Appleyard most of all.

'What's happened to the gate?' she asked. She had been down to the cove to swim only that morning and it had seemed fine then.

'Someone's cut it all over with a knife!' Mary declared with possessive indignation. 'Crosses and triangles and things. It looks horrid.'

The child meant Hamid's protective carvings. Olivia almost laughed, but there was no point in baiting Mary: the two of them existed in a state of barely kept truce at the best of times. 'But those have been there for ages. If you came swimming with me, you'd have noticed.' And then her demon side won out. 'It would be good for you to get some exercise, you know – you're getting a bit plump.'

'Am not!' Mary folded her arms to hide her body.

Despite the rationing she had grown quite barrel-like, which made her stand out from the local children, who were quick and thin. It was probably down to Hamid's cooking: he managed to conjure deliciously rich food out of the scraps and tins they had in the house, the stocks he rendered down from carcass bones, the rabbits he trapped along the coast by night, from wild plants and herbs, from the potatoes and cauliflower and apples Olivia scrumped from the edges of the Roberts' fields. He would cook while Mary was at school and Olivia would stash his efforts in the pantry, or in a pan with a lid on, so that the child would later find her stirring a delicious stew flavoured with ramsons and mustard seed. Hamid had even set up beehives in their orchard and tended to the bees while Olivia and

Mary ate their supper in the kitchen: they had honey every day.

'I hate the sea,' Mary said fiercely. 'Besides, if I went swimming with you, you'd probably drown me. You'd love to get rid of me. You wish I'd vanish like my mother!'

This was so close to the truth that Olivia almost admitted it; she had learned to catch herself thinking uncharitable thoughts and bite back the words she longed to say. Not always, but sometimes. Hamid had chided her for her attitude to the child more than once. 'Can't you be a little gentler with her? She's got no parents, only you. Is it any wonder she's angry and bitter? There's so little love in her world, and you can see how she craves it.' He was right, he was always right. Even though he had never been in the same room as the two of them, he had ears like a bat, and the patience of a saint. He would make little biscuits for the child with the butter and flour Olivia bartered for in the village, the honey from their hives and the hazelnuts they scavenged out of the hedges. Mary scoffed them by the handful without any suspicion as to their origin.

'Back home,' Hamid would say wistfully, 'my mother made biscuits from almonds and butter that would melt in your mouth, shaped like gazelle horns and stars; pastries studded with fennel seeds and flavoured with orange blossom water. As a child I used to make them with her, shaping the stars and crescent moons because I had smaller fingers. How I wish I could do that for you and Mary.'

'Anyway,' said Mary now. 'It's not just me who's fat.' And with that sophisticated insult she fled upstairs.

By way of reprisal Olivia made her spam fritters for tea.

★

Later that night she lay in Hamid's arms in the back bedroom, which was as far away from Mary's room as it was possible to get on the upper floor. They kept it locked at all times. Olivia locked her own room too, partly to stop Mary trying the door and finding out she wasn't in her own bed, partly to prevent the child pinching hairclips, pencils and coins. There had been, a couple of months ago, a particularly unpleasant quarrel, after Olivia had caught Mary creeping out of her parents' room with a silk scarf she remembered her father buying her mother as a birthday gift. When she had challenged the child, a tussle had ensued. She had pulled the scarf out of Mary's fingers – but with it came her mother's pearl necklace, the three-stringed one she wore in her wedding photographs, and the string on the pearls had snapped, spilling the precious beads all over the floor and down the stairs. When Mary had refused to pick them up Olivia had slapped her hard – she had gone to school the next day with a welt on her cheek, despite cold compresses.

The next day she had set about Mary's room and unearthed a trove of magpied treasures from the bottom of her wardrobe: jewellery and perfume bottles, cigarette cases, coloured pencils, stockings, ribbons, a silver whistle, fishing flies hand-tied by her father, old photographs of people Olivia did not recognize, commemorative half-crowns, foreign stamps, boxes of matches and her favourite palette knife. She had taken them all downstairs and laid them out on the dining room table. They covered almost the entire surface. When Mary came home from school, Olivia had ushered her inside. 'I think I should call Sergeant Richards,' she said grimly, as the child squirmed in her grasp. There had been tears and apparent contrition. But that weekend some of Olivia's sketchbooks went missing. Mary did not come home till night had fallen. Olivia had heard a foot on the creaky stair and the door to her room open and close in a furtive manner. By then her fury had ebbed, but she took some satisfaction in knowing the child would probably have gone to bed hungry.

Since then they had lived in a state of imminent war, each wary of the other's worst impulses. Olivia knew Mary was snooping, trying to find some insurance against her threat to talk to Sergeant Richards; so they kept the spare room door locked at all times and had taken to making love while Mary was safely at school, and in the depths of the night with their hands over each other's mouths – Hamid's eyes shining dark crescents over her pale fingers – but still the bedsprings creaked and often they had to stop, falling away from one another to lie on their backs laughing silently in the dark, before completing each other's satisfaction with fingers and tongues.

'What will you do after the war?' Olivia whispered now into the night air. She had heard on the radio that the Allied forces were marching through Germany, besieging Berlin. It was hard to recall a time when life had been normal – she had been a child herself when war had broken out, and memories of the years before then consisted of fleeting images of beach picnics with her parents, lying in the sunny shallows at Porthcurnow, listening to the water lap and suck; her father driving fast through the narrow lanes with the top down in the car they'd had before the Flying 8, her mother clutching her silk headscarf; going to the pictures at the Savoy in Penzance on a Saturday morning to watch cartoons with her schoolfriends; getting an ice cream from Jelbert's on the way home. These memories had taken on the sepia tones of old photographs. They belonged to another world.

Hamid was quiet for a long time. Then he sighed. 'I will go home to Algeria.'

It was the answer Olivia dreaded. She knew it was what he would say, what he had to say – and do – but she had pushed the possibility to the back of her mind. The war was like an island in the flow of real time, and they had been happily marooned upon it.

'Couldn't you stay here? It'll be different when things return to normal.'

'They think I murdered that child.'

'But you didn't!'

'We can't prove my innocence, and then there's Mikael...'

They both thought about the body interred in the tunnel. 'It was self-defence,' Olivia said. 'Or rather, you saved me from him.'

'Who are they going to believe – a girl of sixteen and a runaway prisoner, or the farmer and all his workers? I'll have to go, Olivia. There's no choice.'

'I could come with you,' she whispered.

He laughed. 'And tend goats?'

'You worked in the city. We could be married and I would work in the city too. Perhaps Madame Duchamps would like an English companion?' She tried desperately to construct an alternative future for them, despite the jealousy of the Frenchwoman that gnawed at her heart.

'Let's not talk about this now.' Hamid turned to face her, cupped her cheek with a hand. 'Don't try to live in tomorrow, *chérie.*'

There were times when his philosophical nature infuriated her, times when it became too clear they came from different worlds. Olivia drew away, then rolled onto her side away from him. Her hot tears leaked into the cotton as she fought the urge to bawl into the darkness. When the worst of her misery was spent, she felt the need to bury her face in his chest and let the feel and smell of him obliterate the coming terror of losing him. But she could sense the tension in his body even at a distance, the way he held his body rigid communicating his unhappiness at her vented passion and his powerlessness to do anything about their impossible predicament.

That Tuesday afternoon Olivia was sitting in the dining room with the wireless on as she did her damnedest to patch a pair of socks when Winston Churchill's familiar voice boomed out. She did not pay attention as he reeled off a welter of foreign names of generals and air marshals representing high commands and expeditionary forces. It was only when he intoned, 'Hostilities will end officially at one minute past midnight tonight,' that comprehension began to dawn. The wooden mushroom she had been using to press out the heel she was darning slipped from her hands and skittered across the floor. The prime minister spoke on, announcing Germany's unconditional surrender and the Allies' victory in Europe. 'Finally,' he declared, 'almost the whole world was combined against the evil-doers who are now prostrate before us… The German war is at an end.'

Olivia stared at her hands. Then she flung down the sock and fled outside, barefoot. It was overcast and the grass was damp from a passing shower that still darkened the sky. She ran down through the orchard, to where Hamid was mending one of the beehives, her emotions battling for supremacy. A sort of rejoicing rose and swelled inside her – for they had won! – but at the same time heavy dread had gathered in her guts.

Hamid straightened up at the sound of her thundering footsteps, holding his tools as if to ward off attack. When he saw it was Olivia, his shoulders fell and he grinned. 'Why the hurry?' he called out, but as she came closer he took in her expression. 'What is it? What's the matter?'

'The war,' she cried. 'It's over. Germany has surrendered.'

He held her close, felt the sobs wracking her. 'But that's good, isn't it?' he said into the cloud of her hair. 'That's good, *chérie*.'

'I know!' she wailed, but still the tears poured out.

There would be cheering and celebrations all over Europe, except for here, she thought, where the two of them stood, a stillpoint in a vortex. It felt as if her world had fallen in.

She was going to lose him, and she couldn't bear it. Without a thought for sense or propriety, Olivia began to tear at his clothes, dragging his shirt tails out of his trousers, snatching at his belt. She kissed him so hard, covering them both in salt and mucus, that he laughed and held her away from him. 'You're a little wolf,' he chided her, 'a lioness – you're trying to eat me alive!' But he undid his trousers and kicked them off all the same. When they lay down in the long grass the bees buzzed lazily around them going from bluebell to wild hyacinth, from the apple blossom that garnished the orchard trees to the honeysuckle that twined through the brambles, back and forth, crossing and recrossing the air above their half-naked bodies as if weaving a protective spell with their busy wings.

It was here Mary found them an hour later, the children having been let out of school early to go home to celebrate the joyful news. She let out a piercing cry that woke the lovers from their doze; even the bees seemed to still.

As Olivia and Hamid broke their embrace, Mary shrieked, 'It's the blackie! The one who murdered Mamie! I'm telling Mr White!' and took to her heels.

Olivia shoved herself to her feet and went after her, but the child was faster, being shod, and propelled by terror. Down the steps Mary fled, and with the rattle and bang of the garden gate was off down the lane.

Hamid gained Olivia's side. 'I'll go after her.'

'No – someone will see you. She'll be heading down the hill to the barracks and the information post.' Though whether the sinister Mr White was still there she did not know – she had not seen him these past weeks. Would the men there believe a hysterical child? Did they know the rumours? She could not take the chance. She could catch Mary, she was sure of it. 'No, I'll go.'

Hamid caught her arm. 'Like that?'

She was, she realized, wearing only her unbuttoned shirt – and her bra, which was dangling loose across her chest. Her skirt and knickers lay scattered between the orchard trees, as if marking a crime scene. But the shirt was long: she started to do it up with fumbling fingers. 'Who cares? If she tells them and they come for you they'll kill you!'

'They'll have to catch me first! I can run fast and far if I have to.' He gestured towards the coast.

'There will be people out everywhere – there's nowhere you can hide.' Olivia forced her brain out of its rut of panic. 'Back to the house, quickly!'

She grabbed his hand and hauled him with her back up the steps. Ten minutes later she sat, dressed and breathless, in the front seat of the Flying 8 as Hamid turned the starting handle and the engine rumbled to life. He opened the passenger door to get in beside her but she shook her head. 'Lie down in the back and pull the blanket over you!'

She roared up through the lanes, taking the corners at a dangerously narrow angle, through the little settlements along the crest of the hills and down Chywoone Hill, meeting the coal lorry on the way up so that she had to slam on the brakes and steer hard onto a verge to avoid it. Pulling up by the old quay in Newlyn, she left Hamid with the instruction not to move, no matter what, grabbed her bag and ran out along the enormous old cobbles to where a line of fishing trawlers sat moored, awaiting the tide. She passed the first two boats, but at the third she paused, listening. The men aboard looked up at her.

'*Excusez-moi*,' she called down. '*Vous êtes belges?*'

Belgian trawlers had sat the war out in Newlyn, going out to fish alongside the local boats when the minesweeper had passed through. Olivia had seen the boats, and passed their crews in the street, sometimes exchanging a shy '*bonjour*' with the men, which made them grin from ear to ear. It was quickly established that they were indeed a Belgian crew, and that they were celebrating the declaration of Victory in Europe. They were beaming, delighted, and just a little drunk. Someone had broken out a bottle of spirits, which they were passing from one to another.

Olivia said she needed to discuss something. The captain came to the iron ladder and climbed up. A thin man with deep seams around his eyes and a large grey moustache, he took her hand and bowed his head – old-fashioned manners.

'Are you preparing to leave?' she asked in French.

'When the rest of my crew get out of the Swordfish,' he chuckled. 'I've sent Denis to roust them out.'

She opened the neck of the bag and angled it so that he could see inside. He took in the contents and his eyebrows shot up into the shade of his cap.

'To pay for passage,' she explained. 'It's all I have.'

'Why would you want to sail with us?'

'Not me. My friend. He is – ah – French.'

The man spat. 'We hate the French. *Collaborateurs!*'

'He speaks French,' Olivia said quickly. 'He comes from Algeria. From Oran. He got captured and they never realized he wasn't an enemy.'

The captain looked stern. 'Your people don't much like *les étrangers*.' Foreigners.

'I know. I hope you and your crew have been well treated while you've been here.'

'Magnificently, despite a few local difficulties.' He shrugged. 'And the food...! But why do you want so much for me to take him? War is over. He can go home any way he chooses.'

'His mother is dying. In...' she dredged for a Belgian city, 'in Antwerp.'

She could tell from his expression that he knew she was lying, but in the end he grinned and took the bag from her. He turned to his crew. 'Rémy, Michel, *ici!*'

He rattled off a series of instructions then turned back to her. 'They will come with you. People are much less likely to notice three men with a bottle of brandy than an Algerian on his own, *hein?*'

In the shelter of the trawler's cabin a little while later, Olivia hugged Hamid so hard that he laughed and said she was trying to break his ribs. 'I'll find you,' she sniffed. 'Wherever you are, I'll come to you. Write and tell me where you are.'

'I don't even know your address.'

All this time... but he had never needed to know. She told him and he repeated it over and over like a mantra. Then he took his prayer beads out of his pocket and slipped them over her hand. 'Keep them for me.'

They kissed once more, then the captain stepped back into the cabin. 'The crew are saying it's bad luck to have a woman on the boat,' he said, 'but I told them you're just a girl. Best not prove me wrong. Off you go!'

Olivia stood on the quay and watched the small vessel make its way out into the bay, feeling as if her heart was being pulled on a string which got tighter and tighter as the trawler sailed away. He was gone.

As she retraced her steps to the car the strains of a popular Vera Lynn song floated to her from the open window of one of the cottages overlooking the quay.

'*Some sunny day...*'

It was a melody designed to lift the spirits, to promote hope and gumption, but to Olivia it sounded tawdry and dishonest. She felt sure she would never see Hamid again.

27

October 1945

OLIVIA'S SUMMER PASSED IN HAZE OF GRIEF AND turpitude: she could hardly distinguish one day from the rest, was oblivious to the rejoicing around her at the end of the war, to the return of young men and women from their widespread deployments, to the removal of blackout blinds, barbed wire and troops. Huge world events barely grazed her consciousness: the resignation of Winston Churchill as prime minister when Labour won a surprise landslide victory in the general election; the bombing of Hiroshima and Nagasaki and the declaration of Victory in Japan. 'Twenty thousand tons of nuclear power in a bomb the size of a golf ball... This ends war as we know it', declared the front page of the *Daily Express* she found in the doctor's waiting room in Penzance, where she had presented herself one morning convinced she was dying of some mystery illness. She wasn't, but the sense of pressing doom followed her home.

She left Mary to walk to and from school on her own, rolling herself in the paisley quilt beneath which she and

Hamid had slept, and done many other things too. She kept the pillowcase on which his head had rested unwashed: she could still smell the spicy, male scent of him on it, though it seemed to fade a little with each passing day.

The house became grubby and unloved, which was much the way she felt, and so did Mary, whose springy ginger hair soon became as wild and matted as the coat of one of the feral cats that hunted in the orchard. One day she was sent home with a note from the school secretary which read: 'We know that things have been difficult, but we would ask you to please pay more attention to the cleanliness and neatness of your child and her clothing or we shall be forced to contact the authorities.'

Your child. Olivia closed her eyes in an excess of misery barely tempered by fury. Then she marched Mary down to the scullery and subjected her to an hour of soaping and scrubbing, punctuated with bites and scratches (by Mary) and slaps and vicious shaking (by Olivia). She broke a comb dragging it through the child's tangled hair and eventually resorted to lopping great hanks of it off with the kitchen scissors, which needed sharpening, when the knots defeated her.

'I hate you! I hate you, you fat cow!' Mary shrieked when at last she was set free.

She fled upstairs to her room, whence there issued a piercing wail a minute later as she caught sight of her ravaged head in the dressing table mirror. For the next week she refused point-blank to go to school, which was why when the telephone rang in the middle of Wednesday afternoon, it was Mary who answered it.

Olivia emerged from the parlour, where she had been

feeding the parrot, which was also looking rather the worse for wear. 'Who is it?'

Mary just thrust the receiver at her.

Olivia put it to her ear and listened to the hiss of ocean sounds. 'Hello,' she whispered in dread. The school, demanding where Mary was? The authorities, demanding to visit? Hamid, from wherever in the world he might be? Or a relative of his, reporting his death? She began to shake.

'Livy? Is that you, *chérie?*'

'Mummy!' The relief was so great, she had to sit on the floor before her knees gave way. 'Mummy, where are you?'

'Making my way home, darling. I'll be on the train from London on Saturday afternoon. Would you ask Jago to meet me at the station with the car?'

'Peace offering?'

Jago tucked the bar of Fry's Chocolate Cream into his top pocket and patted it with satisfaction. 'Peace offering.'

The purchase represented the last of her sweet rations for the month, but Olivia had decided it was worth it.

'No one will say anything, miss, I'll make sure of that. I already give Nipper a piece of my mind, and Jem knows better than to blab on thee.'

'It's not as if I've done anything wrong,' Olivia said defiantly.

He held her gaze for just a beat too long and Olivia felt something twist inside her – not shame, exactly, but some form of recognition and embarrassment.

The train was late. Rather than wait in awkward silence with Jago, Olivia waited at the barrier, watching as the engine huffed its way across the curving sweep of track skirting Mount's Bay. She remembered how she had seen her father off here, for the last time. How he had ruffled her hair and given her the Leica. It seemed to have taken place in another age, in a time before the tarnished present, when she had still been a child, and innocent. It occurred to her with a pang of guilt that she wished it were her father whose train she was here to meet, but that was a wicked thought and she tried, not entirely successfully, to push it away.

Minutes later, she picked her mother out in the crowd of arrivals, the feather in her hat bobbing as she strode down the platform, a porter at her side carrying her bags. Even at this distance Olivia could see that she had lost weight. Surreptitiously, she pulled the belt of her gabardine mac tighter till she could hardly breathe.

'Darling!'

Estelle Kitto enveloped her daughter in a cloud of perfume, then held her by the shoulders and regarded her critically. 'Gracious me, we really must get you to a hairstylist, you look as if you've been dragged through a hedge backwards.'

Olivia folded her arms like a buffer zone between them.

'And it's much too warm for that old mac!' Estelle laughed. She herself was immaculate in a tailored suit and high heels, looking as if she had stepped out of a photographic shoot for a magazine.

'It's the only thing I've got that fits me,' Olivia said mulishly. 'I've had to use all the clothes rations on Mary. She just keeps on growing.'

A cloud crossed Estelle Kitto's lovely face. 'Oh yes, Rosemary,' she said, and her expression became shuttered.

Jago secured the suitcases on the pull-out storage rack

on the back of the Flying 8 and off they went, Mrs Kitto chattering brightly all the way back, asking the farm manager for the news on all the locals – the incidents, deaths, scandals. Jago, in his usual taciturn way, gave her little to get her teeth into, leaving Olivia to break the news of the bombing of Penzance, the crash of the German plane, the death of Mamie Roberts and the escape of the POWs.

'Never did find that Nazi, nor that coloured fellow,' Jago finished.

Estelle caught her daughter's eye in the rear-view mirror. 'Good lord, such drama! I shall want to hear all about it when we get home.'

Olivia looked away.

They passed the cottages at Raginnis and Jago pulled the car up beside the sea gate, then with remarkable composure and a considerable show of strength, carried the two heavy cases up the steep steps, kicking aside the brambles and nettles that had colonized the garden following Olivia's summer of neglect.

All the way up the path Olivia tried to think of a good excuse for the presence of the parrot and came up empty. But just as they reached the front door it opened and there stood, pale against the gloom of the hallway, Mary – her white shift-dress and her shorn hair making her appear like the shade of some Victorian urchin.

At the sight of her Estelle became very still. Then she gestured for Jago to set the bags down in the hall and instructed him to secure the car in the garage and drop the key back through the letter box. When he was safely out of view and earshot, her shoulders dropped and she said sharply to the child, 'Why are you still here?'

Mary's pale eyes filled with alarm. 'I... I don't know.'

'Why hasn't your mother taken you away as soon as it was safe to do so, as we agreed?'

Mary wrapped her arms around her torso in an attempt at self-comfort and dropped her gaze to Mrs Kitto's elegant shoes. 'I don't know,' she repeated in a bare whisper.

Estelle was merciless. 'Where is your mother? Does she think she has some claim on me now that Tony's dead? She can think again!'

Olivia felt pieces of a puzzle click together in her head, making an unwelcome shape. But surely her father would never... not with the awful Winnie? She found herself looking at Mary anew, registering the sandy fairness of her hair, the distinctive pale blue of her eyes as Mary looked up in panic. How had she never seen the resemblance before?

'She went away,' the child choked out. 'She went away and left me.'

'Mrs Ogden said her mother was dying,' Olivia said quietly. 'Then she took the train upcountry and we never heard from her again.'

Estelle's scarlet mouth became a long, hard line. 'Well, the child can't stay here. I don't want anything to do with her.'

All these long months, Olivia had dreamed of the time she would be rid of the little sneak. But as her mother uttered these cruel words and she saw the child's chin rumple, something broke inside her. She took a deep breath. 'She has no one else in the world. Only us. Only here.'

Mrs Kitto turned away. 'I shall speak to the authorities.'

While her mother unpacked upstairs, Olivia put the kettle on and made tea. She still hadn't come up with a good excuse for the presence of the parrot and feared that in her current mood her mother was likely to banish him with Mary, but just as she was pouring out the second cup she heard a long whistle emanating from the parlour. Putting the teapot down, she fled up the hallway and peered nervously around the door-jamb. Estelle Kitto was staring into the cage, where Gabriel was lying winsomely sideways across his perch, all but batting his uppermost eyelid at her.

'How on earth did you come by this gorgeous creature?' she asked, without turning.

Relief made Olivia's knees sag. By the time she had recounted how she had saved the parrot from the village fishwives, who'd been threatening to pluck and eat him, her mother had the cage door open and Gabriel was sitting on her arm, clucking softly to himself like an oversized hen. 'Meshy moose key,' he muttered. 'Messy mush key.'

Estelle went very still. 'What did you say?' she asked the parrot, but he had closed his beak. She turned to her daughter. 'He's saying "no problem" in Arabic.' Mrs Kitto's brow wrinkled. 'How in the world has he picked up Arabic?'

An electric shock ran through Olivia's body, a sudden sharp joyous-painful memory of Hamid talking to the parrot in his strange foreign language, Gabriel making clicking noises with his tongue and occasionally repeating what he heard.

'I thought he was just saying nonsense words.'

'It's not even classical Arabic, either – that would be *maafi mushkil*. That pronunciation sounded more like *darija*...' her mother went on thoughtfully.

'Gosh,' Olivia said with forced brightness, trying to deflect the dangerous direction this conversation was taking.

'I didn't know you were such an expert on Arabic.' And then something dropped into place. 'Were you with Daddy in Algeria?' she asked suddenly. It seemed mad: Mummy had been working for the bank on Threadneedle Street, hadn't she? But suddenly she felt sure she had stumbled on another inconvenient truth. She recalled the phone calls, her mother's excuses for not visiting, the birthday gift of French luxuries, the crackles on the line, the sense of immense distance she had intuited on those rare occasions on which they had spoken.

Estelle shot her a narrow look. 'Don't be silly. Now go and take that coat off and make yourself a bit more presentable. I can see you've let the house go to rack and ruin while I've been away, but it's time to get everything back on track, and that includes dressing like a young lady again and not some shabby tomboy. I want to see you in a dress.'

'I haven't got anything that fits me,' Olivia repeated.

Estelle Kitto sighed. 'I'll take you into Simpson's in Penzance tomorrow. Go upstairs and do your best.'

Olivia rooted desperately through the chest and wardrobe and at last settled on a tweed skirt and an old shirt of Daddy's worn loose over the top of it. This, she topped off with a garish scarf tied at a jaunty angle which she hoped would distract her mother's eye from her other shortcomings, the least of which was the fact that her legs were as hairy as a caterpillar. But despite not being the most maternal of parents, Estelle was sharply observant.

'How in the world have you managed to put on so much weight during rationing, *chérie*?' She shook her head. 'That shirt looks terrible. At least tuck it in, here—'

There followed a short scuffle as Estelle attempted to

neaten her daughter's silhouette and Olivia did all she
could to resist her mother's strong hands at the already-
unsecured waistband of her skirt. When it became clear that
nothing was to be achieved without violence, they reached
an impasse. Olivia released her mother's wrists and stood
back. She was going to find out sooner or later: might as
well grasp the nettle now.

Estelle Kitto's gaze ranged over her daughter's body. 'My
God, Olivia, what have you done?'

'Isn't it obvious?'

The sound of the slap echoed off the wooden panelling.
Olivia did nothing to protect herself, just stood there, her
cheek reddening from the blow, breathing heavily.

Mary stared at the two women through the banister rails.
'I saw her naked with a man in the orchard.'

Estelle regarded her husband's child with cold eyes.

'He was trying to kill her, just like he killed Mamie,' Mary
went on in a rush. 'His skin was black, as black as the devil.'

28

Becky

'SHE WAS A PROPER LITTLE SNEAK,' OLIVIA SAYS WITH A sigh. 'Always spying and creeping around, bringing trouble down on me. I suppose she thought she'd ingratiate herself with Mother, but that woman was no fool.'

I stare from Olivia to Rosie – Rosemary – as we sit together in the parlour. Half-sisters, caught up in a web of lies and secrets like two species of fish dragged up out of the ocean in the same net.

'You brought trouble down on yourself!' Rosie says furiously. 'I thought he was trying to kill you, like he killed poor Mamie.'

'He didn't kill Mamie, and he wasn't trying to kill me, you goose!'

'I was only a child then,' Rosie huffs. 'I didn't know what was really going on. All I saw was this coloured chap lying on top of you. I couldn't imagine you wanted that. It was disgusting.' She slides a glance at me, then away. 'Dirty. Going with someone not your own kind.'

Olivia draws herself up. 'You ignorant old toad. Hamid

was a good man: the best I ever met, and the colour of his skin doesn't come into it.'

'It was a scandal,' Rosie mutters stubbornly. 'It was then and it always will be.'

'But she loved him, what's so scandalous about that?' I can't help myself.

'It doesn't matter any more,' Olivia says sadly. 'It's all so long ago.'

'Scandal never dies.' Rosie folds her hands sanctimoniously. 'I could have married better if it weren't for you. All those years of not even being able to show my face at church, people muttering about you in the village, children saying things at school.'

'You think you could have done better than poor Jem, do you? Who else would have taken on such a vicious baggage? I don't know how he's put up with you as long as he has.'

'At least I've not spent my life as a withered old spinster pining after a man as dark as the devil who left her in the family way!'

I ignore Rosie's nasty invective. 'Cousin Olivia, were you pregnant?'

She nods slowly. 'I found out just after Hamid left. All those times we slept together – I thought we were charmed, or that I couldn't conceive. By the time Mother came back there was no hiding it.

'"Who did this to you?" she demanded. "Was it a soldier? One of the farm boys?" I wouldn't tell her but of course Rosemary couldn't help but blab about Hamid, how I'd kept a murderer hidden in the house, and then somehow helped him to escape.' She turns to Rosie. 'It must have been embarrassing for you, dragging Sergeant Richards and

Mr White up to the house, but there being no sign of their suspect, eh? I expect they thought you were a proper little tittle-tattler.

'Anyway, Mother listened, of course, especially when Rosemary – dear Rosemary – showed her the drawings I'd done of Hamid, the sketchbooks she'd stolen. Your chance to show her which of us could be her best daughter, wasn't it? Look: Olivia's a harlot – I'm a good girl.' Her hands are balled into fists as she remembers. 'Mother took all the sketches and burned them, without a word.'

'When she found out I was pregnant I thought she was going to kill me: she had a wild look in her eye. She drafted in Mrs Tucker to come and take care of Rosemary and the house and drove me up to London in the Flying 8, with her foot down the whole way. Said we couldn't take the train in case anyone saw me. Then she left me up there with some people she knew and I stayed with them for six months or so, till my due date. But the baby was stillborn.'

Her dark eyes are wintry. 'After a while when I was recovered enough they put me on the train back to Penzance. By the time I got home Mother was already sick. She came back from the war with something wrong with her lungs; she'd caught some sort of flu and deteriorated day by day. It took months for her to die. That was when it all came out, when she was so weak. I was ruthless, made her answer my questions. It wasn't Winnie herself but her sister Imogen that my father had an affair with, but she died in childbirth and Winnie was left to bring the child up; I suppose that's why she was never really attached to her. Daddy arranged for the two of them to come to the safety of Cornwall after the bombing of Exeter, but Mummy never accepted it, so when Winnie arrived with Rosemary in tow it was just the excuse she needed to cut and run. I don't think she ever really wanted children – she certainly wasn't very maternal. It was Daddy she wanted, and excitement. So she volunteered for the SoE and got sent to Algiers to serve near him, but then he was sent to Sicily during the Allied invasion, and was lost in action there. After that she didn't care about anything any more. She went to France to work with the Resistance, became one of their boldest operatives, got decorated for it. She came back a different person, though. There was no love left in her at all, and I suppose that was why she treated us both so cruelly.

'When she died she left the house and everything in it to me and nothing at all to Rosemary. I tried to do right by her and Jem, but there's no such thing as happy families, is there?'

She gives me a small, sad smile. 'It was such a strange time. All sorts of things went on: society turned upside down. People went a little mad – with fear, with freedom, with defiance. Scratch the surface of any family history and you'll find a story that's been buried – babies born out of wedlock, affairs with visiting servicemen, bigamy and couples living together under an assumed name, illegal abortions and children adopted by the parents as their own. All sorts went on under cover of the war. It was a desperate time and people behaved as if they might die at any minute. But then they didn't and peace came and somehow society had to get back to being ordered and normal and all those untoward things got swept under the carpet and we weren't supposed to speak of them.

'I just wish...' Her face trembles. 'I just wish I'd seen my baby, just held him once. Or her. They never even told me what sex my child was. I couldn't even give it a name in my head. They just gave me a little bit of its hair, a strange, superstitious thing to do, but I kept it. I slipped it inside my locket. Just an old thing made out of Cornish pewter, not very valuable, not to anyone else, but it's disappeared, and now I have nothing.' She looks utterly stricken.

Rosie shuffles uncomfortably. She ducks her head and does something complicated with her scarf and jumper, then hands to Olivia a chunky oval pendant on a silver chain. 'I suppose you better have this back then,' she says gruffly. 'But there's nothing in it – it doesn't open.'

Olivia grabs the object and fiddles with the pendant. Some hidden mechanism operates with an audible click and it flips open. I crane over her hands. Inside is a lock of fine dark hair, tied with a tiny white satin bow, and behind that what appears to be a tiny photograph. Olivia tenderly removes the hair and brushes it against her cheek, her gaze inward and private. And now I can see that it is not a photo but a miniature portrait executed with loving attention to detail. Black hair, brown skin, brown eyes curved in mischievous half moons, a long straight nose, full lips, sharp facial bones. The portrait is so vital that it seems to beam benevolence out into the world. My heart seizes, then beats very fast.

The doorbell rings, shocking me to my feet, and the two old ladies stare at one another. I run to the window, and there is Reda, as if he has somehow been summoned by the opening of the locket. But even by the time I have explained who the visitor is and have let him in, my brain has done the mathematics.

Reda follows me into the parlour and his gaze sweeps the room, settles on Rosie, slides back to me. I give him a tiny shake of the head.

'I told my sister-in-law you were home,' he says to Olivia, 'and she made a gift for you!'

That same benevolence, that fierce love of life burning out of his eyes... but the set of his face is different, and the dates simply don't work. I am a romantic idiot, leaping to absurdly wrong conclusions.

Olivia, meanwhile, perks right up, eyeing the box. 'A gift?'

Reda winks at me. 'Becky and I will make a fresh pot of tea, and then you will see.'

I follow him out into the hallway, shutting the door behind me. Out in the kitchen while we boil a kettle and assemble a tea tray I bring him up to speed.

'A Nazi!' he whistles. 'What an amazing story. And an Algerian lover...' He grins at me and I feel my knees go a bit weak.

Then he says, 'Is it safe to leave Olivia and Rosie Sparrow together?'

'Honestly? I have no idea.'

But when we have made tea and piled up the tray and come back to the parlour door, there they are, heads bent together over the locket, and Gabriel is up on the bookcase, preening an outstretched wing contentedly, as if the company of two bickering old women is exactly what he likes best.

Reda puts the tray down on the table and the two old ladies stare at him, then at one another. There is something going on here, but I don't know quite what it is. Maybe it's just the pleasant spell cast by the entrance of a handsome man into a room of women – certainly, Rosie shows no sign of the disgust she had expressed at the idea of Hamid's darker skin.

I pour out cups of tea for everyone, then Reda whips away the cloth that he placed over the centrepiece, and reveals a plateful of exquisite pastries curved into crescent moons dusted with icing sugar. Each has a series of tiny marks pricked into it: little triangles and circles, lines and dots, just like the patterns on the sea gate.

Olivia picks one up and brings it close. 'Oh!' she exclaims. 'Thank you so much.'

'*Je vous en prie, madame.*' He places a courtly hand over his heart.

'*Shokran bezef!*' Olivia declares, and they beam at one another, delighted by this cosmopolitan exchange. She takes a tiny bite, sits back with her eyes closed. At last she asks faintly, 'Where did you say you got these?'

'My brother's wife, Amina, made them. She learned the recipe from our mother.'

'Hamid used to make biscuits like this, though we couldn't get hold of almonds during the war. We had to gather hazelnuts out of the hedges, roast and grind them: what a palaver! But I had ones just like this when I went to Morocco.'

'You have visited my country!' Reda sounds delighted: the two of them have mapped out a small, shared magical space.

She smiles, remembering. 'It was such a long time ago. Hamid sent me a letter, but it took such a long time to arrive. The day I received it I sent him a telegram and we arranged to meet in Casablanca. That trip was a marvel. He took me everywhere – to his sisters in Oujda, south into the mountains, way down into the desert. I rode a camel in the Sahara – can you imagine? We lay together under a canopy of stars, so many stars, and I wished that time would never end. But of course it was over far too soon and I was on a boat back to England. I cried all the way home.'

'Couldn't you have stayed?' I ask. 'Couldn't you have married him and stayed in North Africa, made a life together there?' I am disappointed that she came home: surely love would conquer everything?

'Hamid said it wasn't safe for me, especially in Algeria. There was unrest everywhere. The French authorities had cracked down, so there was a lot of ill feeling towards Europeans. It was before the war for independence officially broke out, but he knew it was coming. I tried to persuade him to come back to Cornwall with me, but he said he couldn't leave his family to fend for themselves.

'Then he sent me this.'

She digs in her handbag, brings out an envelope and takes from it a piece of folded paper marked with an official stamp in red ink and the letters 'ICRC' upon it.

29

Hamid

Arzew, Algeria, 1958

'IF YOU WRITE A LETTER I PROMISE WE WILL DO OUR VERY best to ensure it reaches the recipient.'

The visitor from the International Red Cross gazed at the prisoner before her, taking in his general thinness and fragility, the soiled bandages on his feet, the crooked set of his hands, the marks on his face and the scabs on his shaven scalp, and a tremor of pity ran through her.

'I'm sorry. It's all we can do. I wish we could do more for you...' She looked down, gathering herself, then lifted her chin and met his eyes. 'I'm afraid they will read whatever you write and if it is at all... problematic, I fear it will be censored or possibly even destroyed.' Her French was perfect, very precise.

The prisoner – Hamid Medjani – nodded once. 'I understand.'

She passed him the single sheet of paper, a pen, and ink. 'And they will be watching,' she indicated the guards lounging in the doorway, 'as they are listening now.'

THE SEA GATE

He gave her a lopsided smile, the scar across his face distorting briefly. Then he took the writing materials from her and with great concentration placed the fountain pen between right thumb and a forefinger that would not bend. It took him a little while to find a position that would work, then he bent his head over the desk and started slowly to form the words that crowded his mind.

How are you, my dearest Olivia? I am well, or at least I am better than I was. My right hand has healed sufficiently for me to write to you now, and this is a boon. I must write quickly, for I have only a short time, so forgive me if my letter is inadequate and expresses only a little of what my heart holds. God grant me the chance to write to you at greater length and under other circumstances one day.

He paused, touching the pen to his lips, readjusted his position on the uncomfortable chair and reapplied himself to his task.

As you will no doubt see from the provenance of this letter when, insha'allah, it reaches you, I am held in the prison at Arzew in my own country. I cannot tell you anything of how I came to be here, so I will not waste words on that. Just know that I live, and that while I live I think of you.

The days pass slowly here and I have a lot of time to think and to dream. And when I do, I dream of Cornwall – of my blue-grey country – in contrast to this, my red country – red for the soil, red for the sun, red for the blood that has been shed here for so long. I hope they will not censor that – all countries' histories are bloody, are they not?

I remember how you tried to teach me to swim in the cove beneath the house, how we sat in the sun on the steps below the sea gate, out of sight of the rest of the world, looking down on a gull sliding through the air, paired with its sand-borne shadow on the beach below us. Do you remember that little bit of magic that we shared? The bird existing in two different elements at once – in the air; on the land.

So am I now: I exist most of all in my head, in my dreams. I skim through the Cornish skies even though my earthly body is trapped here. I am with you, my love, in the wild blue expanses of my mind: they can never take that away from me.

A discreet cough interrupts his reverie. 'Monsieur Medjani? I am sorry, you must finish now.' She indicated the guards, who had now stepped into the room. 'They must take you back into the cells, and I must leave.'

Hamid grimaced. Writing quickly, he added, '*Je t'aimerai toujours…*'

I will love you for ever.

Then he blew on the paper, imbuing the drying ink with his prayers, folded it and handed it to the Red Cross woman.

'I greatly appreciate all you are trying to do for us,' he said. 'But I fear we are damned souls.'

He watched as her dark eyes swam and she blinked rapidly. 'God bless you,' she said, getting to her feet. Then

she turned away and walked rapidly out of the room
and the guards came to pick him up and carry him back
to hell.

30

Becky

REDA READS THE LETTER FIRST IN HIS PERFECT FRENCH, and I see that his hand – usually so sure and steady in all that he does – is shaking. He reaches the end and his voice catches. Then he translates it into English for us.

At the end of his recitation a solemn silence falls, broken only by Olivia blowing her nose loudly into a tissue.

'That was the last time I ever heard from him,' she says at last. 'Hamid was held by the French authorities in the prison camp at Arzew, outside Oran. The International Red Cross sent the letter to me after they had managed to force through an official visit, but after that I never heard from him again.' She sniffs and gazes into the flames of the fire. 'I think he must have died. But now I will never know.'

'Oh, Olivia.' What pain to have carried through all these decades. 'I'm so sorry,' I say. 'It's a very beautiful letter.'

Reda folds the piece of paper reverentially and returns it to Olivia, who pats and strokes it, then slips it back into her handbag.

'I know the rest of the story,' he says quietly.

Olivia becomes very still. 'How do you know? How can you?'

Reda looks away, his gaze distant. 'In our family Hamid is a hero.'

We all stare at him.

'In your family?' I ask, feeling my skin prickle.

He meets my eye, his expression somehow managing to be both defiant and sorrowful. 'I must admit now that I am not here purely by coincidence.' Then he announces to the room, 'Hamid Medjani was my great-uncle: my grandfather's brother.'

Olivia gives an audible gasp. Reda takes her hand and enfolds it in his. He rubs his thumb across her papery old skin as caressingly as she touched the letter.

'I am sorry, dear lady. I do not know whether you will want to hear the rest of the tale. It does not have a happy ending.'

'I must.' Her voice is raw with emotion. 'You must tell me.'

'You are sure?'

Olivia nods once. As she juts her chin you can see the ghostly profile of the girl she once was, fierce and capable, full of life.

Reda takes a deep breath, then begins. 'My grandfather was Omar Medjani, Hamid's second youngest brother. They both fought for the FLN – the Front de Libération Nationale – for the independence of Algeria. I don't know how much you understand of the politics of North Africa, but the French were not just colonialists in Algeria, but oppressive masters. They ruled with an iron fist. In our history there were many atrocities, many massacres. A lot of bad blood. The war for independence was brutal. Hamid returned from Europe after the Second World War hoping for peace and a way to reclaim his life, but what he found horrified him. His father and brother Nazim were killed by the French in retaliation for attacks on Europeans in Setif, in Oran. It did not matter that they had taken no part in the unrest: they were caught by a French patrol out in the hills with their herd and executed for being in the wrong place at the wrong time. Their bodies were hung in the local village square, for the flies. They would not even let the family give them a decent Islamic burial.

'And this was what Hamid went back to. He joined the Resistance and worked his way up through the organization in no time: he was brave and resourceful. He ran a guerrilla unit out of Oran, and they carried out many audacious raids, but eventually he was betrayed and captured and imprisoned – in the camp at Arzew, from where he wrote that letter.' Now he takes a deep breath. 'Perhaps it is not wise to dwell on the details of what happened next.'

'Tell me,' Olivia says fiercely. 'I want to know everything, no matter how harrowing. I spent years trying to trace him. I got in touch with the Red Cross and they tried to find him, but he had disappeared...'

Reda lets his breath out slowly: a man preparing to lift a heavy weight. 'My grandfather Omar and our cousins launched a daring raid on the prison camp. They got Hamid out! They carried him – he could not walk. They had broken his feet, just as before they had broken his hands... if that is too much detail, I am sorry. He was treated very badly by the French, and he was too weak. They laid him in the shade of a cedar tree on the top of a hill overlooking the sea, gazing out into the blue. According to my grandfather he kept saying a word over and over: *Olivia*. They thought he was speaking French, that he wanted olives, so they brought him olives. And then – this has gone down in family legend – he said, "I am going back to my little paradise, to Chynalls." And then he died. I am sad to say this, it breaks my heart to tell you.'

Tears are leaking out of Olivia's eyes, and when I raise my hand to my face my own cheek is wet.

'He had told Omar about his time in Cornwall. He called it the most beautiful place in the world. He said he had fallen in love there but he never spoke the young woman's name, for the good of her reputation, not until he died,' Reda continues. 'Just as in the letter, he speaks decorously of birds, of magic: never of anything explicit. Omar told the story to my father, and my father told it to me. My parents' generation, they did not travel – but for our generation, for my brother Mohamed and me, it's different. As soon as we made some money we went to France and worked till we got passports – ironic, no, the country that oppressed our ancestors? And then we came to look for Cornwall. We looked for a place called Chynalls, but no one knew a Chynalls – we found Chyenhal, and it was pretty enough, but we couldn't see the sea from there, and there was no sea gate down to a secret cove. But we loved the region: it was wild and beautiful. And Mo, he met Amina in Penzance and married her – imagine that: crossing continents to find the love of your life, a Moroccan girl raised in Cornwall! It really did seem we were brought here by fate.

'And then Becky called our number, out of the blue.'

He turns his gaze upon me but I cannot get the words past the lump in my throat. With her free hand Olivia is holding a tissue to her eyes; even Rosie looks overcome. 'Rebecca,' my cousin says quietly. 'Upstairs there's a cardboard box under the bed in the front bedroom. You'll find a photo album in there. Would you bring it to me?'

I cannot admit that I am already familiar with this box and its contents. Up I go, drag the box out, unearth the album and fetch it down, lay it in Olivia's lap. She flicks through it, sometimes smiling sadly, sometimes laughing to herself. She shows Rosie the photos of her and Jem. Rosie squints at them as if she can hardly believe her own image could have been captured and hidden away in the album for over half a century. 'Our wedding day,' she says at last. 'We were no more than children.'

Olivia is turning pages faster and faster now. Venice and Paris flit by; Rome and Florence. When she comes to the desert photos, she tarries. Reda, too fascinated to keep a polite distance, cranes his neck. When she turns another leaf he puts his hand on the page. 'Can I see?'

She angles the album towards him. The photo that has caught his attention is of a family group, all in native dress – kaftans and headwraps. There are four men, three women and several children, some babes in arms. They are all grinning widely, eyes narrowed against the sun: the photographer has been merciless in her quest for a sharp image. All except for the man on the end, who gives us only his profile, but I recognize him at once as the man in the miniature.

'When was this taken?' Reda asks.

Olivia thinks for a moment. 'That would have been in the summer of 1954. My goodness, it was hot. And I was wearing tweed!' She fiddles the photo off its adhesive hinges and turns it over. Written in the bottom right-hand corner in pencil is 'Oujda, Aug 1954'.

It could have been 1854, I think, the image is so timeless. 'That's just three months before the war broke out,' Reda says, scrutinizing the faces. 'There is Hamid,' he indicates the man with the striking profile, 'and next to him my grandfather, the tallest of them all. The woman beside him is my grandmother Habiba, and the baby in her arms is my father! And this…' he points to a solemn girl with watchful eyes standing in front of a small dark woman on the edge of the group, the woman's hands resting protectively – possessively? – on the child's shoulders. 'I believe this is your daughter, yours and Hamid's.'

Olivia gives a small cry. Then she shakes her head. 'No, no, you're mistaken. We did not have a child. At least, none that survived,' she adds bleakly.

But Reda is unperturbed. 'This is my great-aunt, Samira,' he says, tapping the image of the small dark woman. 'They say she was cursed by God, never able to have children. But then, a miracle! Two men appeared in the village one day, asking for the Medjani family. They brought with them a letter, and a baby. I have seen that letter – that, too, has entered our family legend. It was written in French, from a woman called Estelle Leveaux.'

Olivia utters a yelp. 'That was my mother's name, before she married my father.'

'It was the name she used, I am told, when she fought with the French Resistance towards the end of the war. The men who came were her colleagues – maquis fighters. Madame Leveaux had contacted them months later and arranged for them to take the child and a sum of money to the Medjani family. The letter said simply that the child was Hamid's and that she wished them to raise it in secret.'

Olivia pressed her hands together to stop them trembling. 'No,' she kept saying. 'No, no. This can't be right. The baby died. I was told that the baby died. Mummy wouldn't... surely, she would never...'

Rosie lets out a cackle. 'Well, fancy that, she lied to you all that time. Your mam was a hard woman, and cold as the grave!' she declares triumphantly. 'All these years. Well, well, well.'

Olivia ignores her. She grasps Reda's arm. 'Do you have the letter? Can I see it?'

'Sorry, no, but I know who does. Shall I finish the story?'

Olivia's eyes are full of tears but she nods and releases him.

'The elders of the family gathered to discuss the matter and it was decided that the baby should be given to Samira and her husband Kasem to raise. The money the Frenchmen brought was a significant sum, enough to build a house and buy some land as well as to provide for the child's future, so Samira and her sister Yasmin and their husbands moved across the border to the safety of Oujda. They never told Hamid; it was decided it was best that he did not know. Kasem was too proud to have anyone know that the girl was not his, and Samira was so happy to have a child at last. They called her "Ayah", which means "miracle" or "sign from God" in Arabic.

'Samira told us the story just before Mo and I set out on our journey. She was an old lady then, and she'd outlasted three husbands!'

'And what about Ayah?' I ask. 'Did she know about her true parentage?'

'Omar told her after Hamid's death. She was only twelve, but very grown up, and very clever. A bit too clever for her own good, it is said. She always had her head in a book, always making poems and songs. She was so proud to have a hero as her father – she made a song for him. It became quite well known, especially after Cheikha Rimitti adopted and recorded it. In my family we are very proud of this: Cheikha was a very famous Algerian singer and very, shall we say, progressive.' He winks at me.

Olivia has her eyes closed as she takes it all in. Tears continue to leak from under her papery eyelids. I take the tissue from her limp fingers and dab her cheeks dry.

When she opens her eyes again she looks at us with the forbidding black gaze of the girl in the portrait. 'How could she be so cruel?' she demands. She grabs the album and brings it close so that she can study the face of the solemn child. I had thought the sun struck the girl more full on than the other subjects in the photograph, but now I see her skin is a shade lighter than the rest of her family. And she has Olivia's chin – so pugnacious! – and a similarity around the eyes, too.

'Isn't it better that Ayah was adopted by Hamid's family, than farmed out to complete strangers in England?' I ask.

'I suppose so,' she says grudgingly, unable to tear her gaze away from the photo. I can see her weighing up all the years that were lost to her, long childless years, years without love, without hope. It seems immeasurably cruel.

'What happened to Ayah?' I ask Reda, rather dreading the answer.

He grins. 'She was the first person in our family to go to university. She has a degree in French, and she taught music and French at a school in Oujda for most of her life. She had two husbands, and five children. She has had a wonderful life: she still does. You could speak to her yourself, if you would like to.'

A stunned silence settles over the room, until Gabriel breaks it by flapping his wings and soaring overhead, like a great scarlet blessing – or a curse. At once, Rosie shoots to her feet and flaps her hands at him. 'Get away, you old devil! Put him in his cage!' she tells Reda, who quietly does exactly that.

'How... how would I do that?' Olivia asks when the commotion has finally settled. 'Speak to her?'

Reda takes out his phone and opens the Skype app. 'Shall we see if she's in?'

I can hardly breathe as the Skype tone burbles away and the phone crackles, then Reda is chatting in a tumble of guttural, staccato sounds which are punctuated by a lighter female voice. 'She's nervous,' Reda tells us, 'but she says OK. How about you, Olivia? Are you ready to meet your daughter?'

Olivia cannot speak, but she nods.

Reda taps an icon and an image starts to coalesce on the screen. He holds the phone out to Olivia and she takes it from him. Her hand is shaking so much that Reda smiles and takes the weight of the phone, holds it up so the two elderly women can see one another. For a long moment neither of them says a word. I can see Ayah only obliquely. Curiosity drives me out of my seat and around the back of the sofa to peer over Olivia's shoulder.

'*Bonsoir*,' says Ayah, and '*Bonsoir*,' Olivia echoes. '*Plaisir de faire votre connaissance*,' which makes Ayah trill with laughter and chide her for such formality, and after that they are off, gabbling away in French. I catch only the odd word here and there, enough to know that they are enjoying the encounter, so instead, I concentrate on the image of the woman on the screen.

Ayah has high cheekbones and lively eyes sunk under deeply arched brows. Fine lines wreath her mouth and fan out from the corners of her eyes and she speaks expressively, using her free hand to make expansive gestures. Every time she does the collection of little silver bangles clatters musically on her wrist; she wears a ring on every finger, and her nails are polished in a rich coral. She smiles often, her eyes becoming delighted, dark half-moons. She appears confident and engaging, and for the most part cheerful. It is only when Olivia is speaking and she leans forward to concentrate on the unfamiliar accent that you can make out her frown lines and the gentle sag of her neck muscles, which she has tried to camouflage with a cerise wool scarf that contrasts with her mass of black-and-silver hair, which springs unconfined in a great cascade to her shoulders in an explosion of curls and waves – not quite an Afro, but not entirely Western either.

I suppose, from the old photographs of her family in their traditional clothing, I was expecting a robe and head-scarf but instead she looks the quintessential third-age woman, still engaged in her community, in learning and life, charming and agile in conversation. And yet there is a recognizable resemblance. I cannot help but think how Olivia might have looked had she had a happier life and not exiled herself in this house, tied to her past and her sorrows, anchored to the body buried in the tunnel.

Towards the end of the call Reda chats to his cousin, asking after the relatives and responding to questions about his own side of the family. Then Ayah disappears from our view, returning a moment later with a square of paper, which she unfolds and holds out to the screen.

'"To the family of Hamid Medjani,"' Reda reads out, translating as he goes, '"please take this child: she is your blood responsibility. The money enclosed should suffice to raise and educate her. My daughter has no idea that the child survived: I expect you to maintain this confidence. Do not ever attempt to contact her, or me.

'"*Veuillez agréer, messieurs, l'assurance de ma parfaite considération.*

'"Estelle Leveaux."'

There is silence, then Olivia says, 'That was her maiden name. And I recognize my mother's handwriting. There is no mistaking it.'

She leans back and Reda turns the phone towards me and Rosie, who at once covers her face, saying, 'No, no, no, I don't speak foreign.' I just wave and smile and say that I am sorry but I don't speak French, and am slightly horrified when she responds, 'Oh, please don't concern yourself, I speak a little English.'

After that Reda introduces her to Gabriel, who dips his head and taps the bars of his cage, possibly in response to the jangling of her bracelets.

'Hellooo, Djibril,' she coos.

I wait for him to swear and appal her, but he just whistles and clicks, making the noises he makes for Reda.

At last goodbyes are said all round, the connection is cut, and we all look at Olivia. She is pink in the cheeks and appears full of suppressed energy, as if she has just received an injection of life or has witnessed a miracle, which I suppose she has.

She grabs Reda's hands and holds them in a tight grip. 'Thank you, thank you so much. What a marvel she is. I can't believe...' The thought trails away. Then she gathers herself. 'It must have cost you a fortune, a long call like that, all the way to Morocco.'

Reda laughs. 'It's magic, dear Olivia, and magic is free.'

The next morning, I set breakfast for two in the dining room and Olivia and I talk about inconsequential things – the richness of the egg I have poached for her and how her paternal Cornish grandmother regarded double-yolkers as a sign of good luck; my poor tea-making skills ('You must be patient and not squeeze the teabag, it makes it bitter'), how the creeper needs to be cut back around the window. Every so often, though, her gaze goes distant and a beatific smile suffuses her face. I know she is thinking about the previous day's revelations, remembering talking to Ayah, recalling that she has a daughter; that she and Hamid have a child who lives on in the world.

I reach across the table and take her hand. 'Happy?' I ask.

'Life can still surprise you, even at my age.' She pauses. 'So, tell me about Reda.'

I feel a twinge at the change of subject and make to get to my feet to clear away the breakfast things, but she won't let go. Her grip is remarkably strong for a woman who has suffered a recent stroke. 'Tell you what?' It feels very odd having the tables turned on me like this: it's Olivia who holds the secrets, not me.

Olivia folds her lips. 'If you don't want to tell me, I suppose it's your own business.'

'I'm just not sure what you want to know.'

'Oh, for goodness' sake, girl. Have you slept with him yet?'

My mouth falls open. 'What?' I shriek, and from the parlour Gabriel echoes 'What?' malignly.

'He's a very attractive fellow.'

I can feel my cheeks going pink. 'He is. And very kind, too. Kindness is underrated, don't you think?'

'Stop being evasive.'

My God, she is tenacious. 'No, I haven't slept with him yet.' I didn't mean to say 'yet' – it just seemed to slip out.

'Well, someone else will snatch him up if you don't.'

'I don't even know if he's single. He could be married with a dozen children for all I know.'

'Stupid goose. Don't you see the way he looks at you? I thought people were supposed to be getting more intelligent. But it appears not.'

'Stop now!' I am feeling rather cross. 'If I want to sleep with Reda it will be in my own good time – not because some bossy old lady is pushing me into it.'

'Well, I certainly wouldn't hang around if I were you.' Her eyes gleam with mischief.

Epilogue

One year later

'WE CAN WATCH THEM FROM HERE.'

'Only with binoculars!'

Olivia is proving to be just as exigent as Rosie always said she would be. My patience is tried often, but she's still a lot easier to live with than Eddie. Apart from his upcoming trial for handling stolen goods (for Cousin Olivia's paintings appear not to have been an isolated transgression), it turns out that Eddie has managed to get Lola the Brazilian waitress pregnant, and her father is demanding Eddie make an honest woman of her, which won't please him at all. This rather amuses me: he and I were engaged for the best part of ten years, but now he's well and truly caught. The idea of Eddie getting up in the night for feeds and nappy-changing entertains me – but perhaps he'll become a better man for taking on the responsibilities of fatherhood. After all, it appears that miracles really do happen.

James and Evie are filing for divorce. It seems that once Evie was elected to parliament she decided she could do better than my brother and within months had embarked on a clandestine affair with the home secretary, whose marriage had also broken down. They were all over the papers and the Internet for a while; I had James on the phone to me in tears, which was a strange turnaround. He came with me to my scan in London when I mustered the courage to give myself up to my consultant. As I passed through the magnetic hoop, with the contrast liquid burning through my veins, I thought of the protective carvings on the sea gate. When I sat with my brother outside her office, waiting to hear my fate, I held the string of *misbaha* beads in my hand, imbued with Olivia's kisses, and thought of the painting of the little boat ploughing a course through dark seas towards the line of light. It had seemed to me then to represent elemental forces over which we had no control; now I see it as a brave little vessel buoyed up by beliefs and hopes, crewed by comrades and lovers, propelled by courage in the face of apparently overwhelming odds. My knees felt so weak when I got up to go into the appointment that I thought I might collapse, but the consultant beamed at me. 'Your scan is absolutely clear,' she said. 'There is no sign whatever of what we thought we saw on the last scan. You are cancer free.'

Those may be two of the most beautiful words in the English language.

'Go away,' she told me, clasping my hands. 'Live your life, and be happy.'

That night, I regarded myself in the full-length mirror in my London hotel room and marvelled at how my scars have faded and thought about the pots Eddie would sometimes make, then deliberately and carefully break, before resetting them with molten gold (so that he could sell them for much more money). At the time I thought this practice inauthentic and pretentious, but I am starting to look at some things in life in a different way. *Kintsukuroi* is the name for this ancient Japanese art, which teaches that broken objects are not something to hide away but should be displayed with pride, for they are stronger and more beautiful for surviving the breakage. I think I, too, am stronger and more beautiful for surviving my travails.

The pale band on the finger on which I wore Eddie's ring is now almost indistinguishable from the surrounding skin: Cornish sun and sea and joy have reconfigured me. On the other hand I wear a ring of Berber silver decorated with little circles and triangles: 'The eye of the partridge, for beauty; the *nuqat* for safety and home,' as Reda said when he slipped it on my hand on his return from a visit home a few weeks back.

'It's not an engagement ring, is it?' I asked, half-alarmed, half-hopeful.

'It's whatever you wish it to be.'

'We could take a taxi down into the village and back,' I suggest now.

Olivia draws herself up. 'Nonsense! We'll take the car!'

I remind her gently that I no longer have a car. I can't afford to keep one. I am working part time at the college in Penzance teaching art and photography, and I tutor students privately here as well. Olivia has been teaching me photography. I am amazed at her skill and her memory, both undimmed by her advanced age. 'It's all about contrast and framing,' she tells me. 'With a camera you are drawing in light.' The old Leica still works beautifully: it was clearly made in a different time to our world of built-in obsolescence. My students mainly use digital cameras; I've had to learn a lot of new techniques, but I'm loving the experiments I share with my students and the portfolios we are compiling.

She tuts. 'No, *the* car. The Flying 8.'

I stare at her. 'I can't drive that!'

'Well I can!'

'But, Olivia, the path up to the garage…'

'Call that young man of yours,' she commands me.

'He's not really at my beck and call,' I admonish gently.

'Go on.' She is quite determined.

So I take the handset into the kitchen, out of earshot: she has ears like a bat. 'Oh my God, Reda, Olivia has hatched up a mad scheme.'

He chuckles when I tell him and says he'll drive the truck over, then we can all go down to the village in that when the 'old tank' won't start. We exchange a few more words and then I return to Olivia. 'He's coming.'

'Of course he is.' She folds her hands in her lap and smiles like a sphinx.

It takes a good half hour to make our way up to the garage through the woods. Olivia is insistent that she cover the ground 'under her own steam'. 'I'm not dead yet,' she keeps saying.

In one hand she carries her handbag, in the other her stick. Reda has her by the elbow: she refused to be carried. I run ahead and open the garage doors and there it is, the Flying 8, like a dragon slumbering in its cave. I run my hand over its shiny bonnet. It's a museum piece, and that's where it belongs.

I open the driver's door, and Olivia sits heavily sideways on the seat and stiffly swings her legs in. She waits till I am settled on the rear seat, while Reda waits by the entrance to close the garage doors, if by some miracle the old car still works. With a flourish, Olivia pulls the starter button towards her: an extraordinary mechanism. As I had expected, the engine gives no more than a genteel cough, then dies.

'Are you sure there's petrol in it?' I ask.

'Her,' Olivia corrects me firmly. 'And yes, of course I am. Unless someone's thieved it.' She pulls the cord again and the engine almost catches, then stutters into silence.

It's getting dark now. The fireworks will be starting soon.

'Shouldn't we just go in the truck?' I offer, but 'Have a little faith!' she fires back and pulls the cord a third time... and all of a sudden the engine roars to life, deafening in the confines of the garage, the fumes from the petrol almost overwhelming. Olivia puts the car in gear and nearly runs Reda over as she exits the garage.

He leaps into the passenger seat, grinning from ear to ear. 'This is amazing! You are amazing, Olivia!'

As we make our way down the steep hill into the village I can see his distorted reflection in the wing mirror, his whole head round with glee, his teeth and eyes shining, though I know he is ready at any moment to leap to Olivia's aid if she is unable to brake or turn the wheel quickly enough. Everyone we pass smiles and points at the lovely old classic car – it's not something you see every day. Parking it is, of course, a nightmare. In the end Olivia simply brings the

Flying 8 to a halt outside the chapel and turns the engine off. When I point out the yellow lines we are parked on she huffs. 'Always used to park here and I'm far too old to change my ways now.'

Hoping the traffic warden is happily engaged elsewhere this evening, we walk slowly down through the little winding streets to the harbour where a throng has gathered for the annual festival – people in anoraks and bobble hats, parkas and scarves, clutching drinks outside the pub, chattering gaily. I catch a glimpse of Rosie and Jem and their sons at the other end of the railing by the war memorial, Jem looking stooped and thin, Rosie a barrel in her long black coat, their sons in their perennial puffa jackets. They are accompanied by two middle-aged women with identical haircuts and a gaggle of teenagers – their wives and children, as I now know. Ezra and Saul got off with not much more than a slap on the wrist for their illegal cigarette operation. The inability to build a useful case against them was in large part down to Olivia, who became obstinately vague when questioned about their comings and goings, about the traces of marijuana in the cellar, and about the body in the tunnel, which remains a mystery to the authorities, though the coroner's office have deemed it 'an historic corpse' but not an antiquity. It appears even Rosie, who has also escaped without even a formal interview about the poisoning since Olivia refused to press charges, knew nothing about the body, down there in the dark all this time. However, since news of the discovery of the bones she has become very superstitious about even setting foot in the house, and is convinced that Gabriel is possessed by the spirit of the dead man – whoever he may be. Lots of stories have circulated about a thwarted German invasion force that tried to make landing under the cover of darkness and were fought off by the doughty locals. It amazes me that such recent events can become so hazily distorted in a relatively short space of time – it makes you question the whole idea of accepted history. I dare say further tests will put an end to the wilder of these tales, which seems rather a shame.

Rosie and her family are not getting any more money from Olivia now either, not just because her secrets are out, but because there really isn't much money left, and they are hardly living in penury. We sold two of the smaller paintings at auction and raised enough to clear her debts, but we're mainly subsisting on what little I make from my teaching and my own art.

'Wait until I'm dead before you sell any of the others,' Olivia instructed me. 'They'll be worth a lot more then, especially once you've written the book.'

Except I am not 'writing' the book: I do not have the requisite skills. But the young man at the auction house put me in touch with a local journalist called Lisa, and she and I are putting together a proposal about art world mysteries and frauds, focusing on the OK Painter and showcasing her art. I am doing the legwork and Lisa is doing the writing. I have found in her a lively new friend. I'd forgotten how much fun it is to have a shared creative project.

Reda and I position Olivia safely at the rail outside the pub and Reda slips inside and returns with three small glasses of whisky. 'To fortify us against the cold.'

'I thought—' I start, and he winks.

'I'm sure God won't mind at all.'

And then the fireworks start – a great fiesta of noise and

colour. We down our whiskies and Reda takes the glasses back into the pub. On his return he slips an arm around my waist, pulls me towards him and kisses me hard until a very different kind of fireworks burst inside me.

'Enough of that!' Olivia says, but I can hear the humour in her tone. Reda and I exchange a complicit smile and separate. We stand on either side of her and crane our necks as the fireworks burst into colour, leaving behind a tracery of smoke like fan vaulting against the cathedral of the night sky.

'It reminds me of the war,' Olivia says between blasts of rockets. 'It was the happiest time of my life.'

She squeezes my hand and I squeeze back. We look out into the dark harbour as another fusillade goes off and silver flowers bloom, then cascade like meteor showers.

'And the saddest,' she whispers into the night.

Acknowledgments

THE SEA GATE IS A BOOK ABOUT FAMILY SECRETS. I HAD
conceived of and started writing it before a number of our
own family skeletons tumbled out of the closet and changed
the stories I had been told all my life. So, thank you to my
unexpected half-brother, Jay, who made contact with me
out of the blue: that was quite a surprise. I'm quite sure that
what Olivia says towards the end of the book is true, and
that if you 'scratch the surface of any family history... you'll
find a story that's been buried'.

For wonderfully vivid of memories of Cornwall during
wartime I owe thanks to my mother, Brenda, and the old
boys in the village, especially Jack Guard, Alan Johns and
Arthur Brown. Not one of those four has survived to see
the book published and it makes me sad that their wisdom
and tales of mischief and the old ways have gone with them.

I must also thank my beloved husband Abdel Bakrim and
my dear friends Philippa McEwan and Sara Macdonald
for their support through the writing of the novel and the
reading of draft after draft; my agent Danny Baror, my
publisher Nic Cheetham and my editors Madeleine O'Shea
and Nita Pronovost; my cover designers, production, sales,

marketing and publicity teams. They say it takes a village to raise a child: well, it also takes a community to bring a book into the world. What would I do without you all?